PENGUIN ⓟ C

THE DISTRACTED PREACHER
AND OTHER TALES

THOMAS HARDY was born at Higher Bockhampton, near Dorchester, on 2 June 1840. He was educated locally at the village school and later in Dorchester. At sixteen he was articled to the Dorchester architect and church restorer John Hicks, although he continued his studies under the guidance of Horace Moule, a Cambridge graduate, whose later suicide affected Hardy and his writing deeply. In 1862 he went to London to pursue his architectural career and also began writing. He returned to Dorset in 1867 to become assistant to John Hicks, at the same time beginning his first novel, *The Poor Man and the Lady*, of which only fragments remain. In 1870 Hardy was sent to St Juliot in Cornwall and it was here that he met his first wife, Emma Gifford, whom he married in 1874; in the same year *Far from the Madding Crowd* was published and met with considerable success. In the previous three years he had published *Desperate Remedies* (1871), *Under the Greenwood Tree* (1872) and *A Pair of Blue Eyes* (1873). In 1878 Hardy moved back to London and in this year *The Return of the Native* appeared. His reputation as a writer grew and he became a well-known figure in London's literary circles. In 1885 he returned to Dorset to live at Max Gate and over the next three years he published *The Mayor of Casterbridge* (1886), which many regard as his greatest tragic novel, *The Woodlanders* (1887), and his first collection of short stories, *Wessex Tales* (1888). In 1891 *Tess of the D'Urbervilles* appeared and in 1895 his last novel, *Jude the Obscure*. During the latter part of his life Hardy devoted himself to poetry, publishing his first collection of verse, *Wessex Poems*, in 1898. He also worked on his autobiography, *The Early Life of Thomas Hardy* (published posthumously in 1928), at the same time burning his old letters, notebooks and private papers. Thomas Hardy died on 11 January 1928.

As well as her highly acclaimed novels and short stories, Susan Hill is the author of numerous radio plays, including a collected volume *The Cold Country and Other Plays*. She is a frequent broadcaster and regular contributor of literary journalism to various periodicals. In 1972 she was elected a Fellow of the Royal Society of Literature, and she is an Honorary Fellow of King's College, London. Susan Hill is married to the Shakespeare scholar Stanley Wells and has two daughters. They live in Gloucestershire.

The Distracted Preacher
and Other Tales

* *Thomas Hardy* *

EDITED WITH AN
INTRODUCTION AND NOTES BY
SUSAN HILL

PENGUIN BOOKS

PENGUIN BOOKS

Published by the Penguin Group
Penguin Books Ltd, 80 Strand, London WC2R 0RL, England
Penguin Putnam Inc., 375 Hudson Street, New York, New York 10014, USA
Penguin Books Australia Ltd, 250 Camberwell Road, Camberwell, Victoria 3124, Australia
Penguin Books Canada Ltd, 10 Alcorn Avenue, Toronto, Ontario, Canada M4V 3B2
Penguin Books India (P) Ltd, 11 Community Centre, Panchsheel Park, New Delhi – 110 017, India
Penguin Books (NZ) Ltd, Cnr Rosedale and Airborne Roads, Albany, Auckland, New Zealand
Penguin Books (South Africa) (Pty) Ltd, 24 Sturdee Avenue, Rosebank 2196, South Africa

Penguin Books Ltd, Registered Offices: 80 Strand, London WC2R 0RL, England

www.penguin.com

This selection first published 1979
028

Printed in England by Clays Ltd, St Ives plc
Set in Intertype Lectura

www.greenpenguin.co.uk

Penguin Books is committed to a sustainable
future for our business, our readers and our planet.
This book is made from Forest Stewardship
Council™ certified paper.

ALWAYS LEARNING **PEARSON**

CONTENTS

1839   Thomas Hardy, builder and mason of Higher Bockhampton near Dorchester, marries Jemima Hand, cook and servantmaid, at Melbury Osmund on 22 December.

1840   Their eldest son Thomas Hardy born at Higher Bockhampton, 2 June.

1848   He attends village school at Bockhampton built by the lady of the manor, Mrs Julia Martin of Kingston Maurward. His mother gives him Dryden's *Virgil*, Johnson's *Rasselas*. First visit to London about this time.

1849–56   Goes to school at Dorchester to learn Latin. Sees traditional harvest supper and dance in Kingston Maurward barn. Plays fiddle at weddings and dances; begins learning French and German; reads the novels of Harrison Ainsworth and Dumas père.

1856–62   He is articled to one of his father's employers, the architect and church-restorer John Hicks, whose office in Dorchester is next door to the school kept by the Rev. William Barnes, the Dorset poet and philologist. Witnesses the public execution of Martha Brown outside Dorchester County Gaol. Horace Moule, a university-educated classical scholar and eight years Hardy's senior, becomes his mentor. Studies Greek dramatists with Moule. Reads Darwin's *Origin of Species* (1859). Writes his first poem, *Domicilium*.

1862–7   Leaves Dorchester for London in the year of the Exhibition, 1862. Works as assistant architect to Arthur Blomfield. Attends operas and theatre, explores London, visits National Gallery almost daily, dances at Willis's Rooms, sees Cremorne and the Argyle. Reads Spencer, Huxley, J. S. Mill, Shelley, Browning, Scott and Swinburne. In 1865 publishes his first article, 'How I Built Myself a House' (*Chambers' Journal*). Buys Walker's *Rhyming Dictionary* and begins sending poems to periodicals (they are rejected).

1867–70   Returns to Higher Bockhampton to assist Hicks at Dorchester. Begins his first novel (now lost) *The Poor Man and the Lady.* May have had an understanding with his cousin Tryphena Sparks, the model for Fancy Day and Sue Bridehead. (She went to London to train as a teacher in 1870, married seven years later, and died in 1890.) Completes *The Poor Man* in 1868; it is accepted by Chapman and Hall, but their reader, George Meredith, advises Hardy not to publish. Hicks dies, and Hardy moves to Weymouth to work for his successor, Crickmay. Begins writing *Desperate Remedies.* In 1870 Crickmay sends Hardy to St Juliot, Cornwall, to make plans for the restoration of the church. Here he meets his future wife, Emma Lavinia Gifford, the rector's sister-in-law.

1870–85   Publishes *Desperate Remedies* in 1871, followed by *Under the Greenwood Tree,* 1872, and *A Pair of Blue Eyes,* 1873. Leslie Stephen serializes *Far from the Madding Crowd* in *The Cornhill Magazine.* Horace Moule commits suicide at Cambridge. Publication and success of *Far from the Madding Crowd* in 1874. Hardy marries Emma Lavinia Gifford at St Peter's Church, Paddington, and encouraged by her abandons architecture for novel-writing. They take a short Continental honeymoon and after brief residences at Surbiton, Swanage and Yeovil, settle at Sturminster Newton in 1876. In this year *The Hand of Ethelberta* is published. 1878 sees publication of *The Return of the Native* and the end of Hardy's 'Sturminster Newton idyll'. They remove to Upper Tooting. Hardy joins Savile Club and becomes a well-known literary figure in London, attending parties and 'crushes'. In 1880 publishes *The Trumpet-Major,* falls seriously ill and is bedridden for six months while writing *A Laodicean.* In 1881 Hardy publishes *A Laodicean,* and takes a house at Wimborne Minster. Visits Paris in 1882 after publication of *Two on a Tower.* Moves to Dorchester in 1883 to supervise the building of his house at Max Gate, taking occupation in 1885.

1885–97   The next three years see the publication of *The Mayor of Casterbridge,* 1886, *The Woodlanders,* 1887, and his first collection of short stories, *Wessex Tales,* 1888. In the spring of 1887 the Hardys tour Italy, visiting Genoa, Pisa, Florence, Rome, Venice and Milan, returning via London, where Hardy meets Browning and Arnold. From now on they usually visit London in the spring, and sometimes the Continent or Scotland. *A Group of Noble Dames* and *Tess of the D'Urbervilles* are published in 1891; and in the following year Hardy's father dies. In 1893 the Hardys visit Dublin at the invitation of Mrs Henniker (authoress, a daughter of Richard Monckton Milnes). In 1894 publishes *Life's Little Ironies*. About this time strain manifests itself in Hardy's home life, especially during the writing of *Jude the Obscure* (published 1896). Hardy resolves to write no more novels, though he publishes *The Well-Beloved* (written ten years earlier) in 1897.

1898–1912   In 1898 Hardy publishes his first collection of verse, *Wessex Poems*, and in 1902 *Poems of the Past and Present*. In this year he begins *The Dynasts*, of which the first part appears in 1904, the year of his mother's death. Two subsequent parts are published in 1906 and 1908, in which year he also brings out a selection of William Barnes's poems. In 1909 he publishes *Time's Laughing-Stocks*, and in the following year is awarded the Order of Merit and the freedom of Dorchester. He makes a final revision of his novels in 1912, and in November his wife suddenly dies.

1913–28   In March 1913 Hardy makes a pilgrimage to St Juliot and his wife's birthplace at Plymouth. He marries in February 1914 Florence Emily Dugdale, whom he had met through Mrs Henniker in 1904 and who had acted as his secretary and general assistant since 1912. In 1913 receives honorary degree of Litt. D. from Cambridge University (in 1920 Oxford University was to follow suit) and publishes *A Changed Man and Other Tales*. In 1914 publishes *Satires of Circumstance* (including 'Poems 1912–13'). In 1915 his sister Mary dies. *Moments of Vision* published 1917; *Late Lyrics and Earlier*, 1922; and in 1923 a verse play, *The Famous Tragedy of the Queen of Cornwall*. *Human Shows*, the last collection of poems to appear in his lifetime, is published in 1925. During these years he works at his autobiography, *The Early Life of Thomas Hardy*, supposedly written by Florence Emily Hardy (published posthumously in 1928), at the same time burning his old letters, notebooks and private papers. Dies 11 January 1928, and his ashes are laid in Poets' Corner of Westminster Abbey at the same time that his heart is buried in the grave of his first wife at Stinsford, next to the tombs of his parents. This year sees the publication of his posthumous collection of poems, *Winter Words*.

INTRODUCTION

1. *Thomas Hardy as a Short Story Writer*

IT was to poetry that Thomas Hardy finally and completely committed himself as a creative artist; it is as a novelist that he is best and most widely known and celebrated – he is at least as popular today among ordinary readers as during his own lifetime. Both Hardy the poet and Hardy the novelist have received a great deal of scholarly attention and acclaim, and, in addition, the life and personality of Hardy the man have aroused fascinated interest.

By contrast, his short stories have fared poorly, receiving relatively scant and dismissive treatment at the hands of many commentators, and being nowadays too little read, partly as a result of this critical neglect, partly because the short story itself has rather fallen out of favour. Yet they form a significant and decent-sized portion of his work – there are forty-nine stories in all, four full volumes in the Wessex edition, out of which I have chosen eleven (arranged in chronological order of first publication) which are among the best and the most representative; the most grudging assessment should allow that well over half of the total are very good as stories, and of considerable interest for the reflective light they throw on the rest of Hardy's prose fiction. Some are masterpieces, and even the failures partake of his total imaginative vision, and fail in such a characteristically Hardyan way that they make a contribution to our understanding of his art and technique.

Above all, though, they are eminently readable and delightfully accessible; they do not intimidate. Those aspects of Hardy's writing which most often irritate or repel – the syntactical mannerisms and convolutions, the archaisms and insensitively placed abstract or learned references – are largely absent from the stories.

The prose style is direct and lucid, relaxed, yet simultaneously maintaining a tension which both holds the reader and carries the narrative forward, and which allows for as much revelation as the form itself will hold, and some development of character. There is descriptive writing, scene-painting of an evocative and occasionally breathtaking kind (as in the picture of the army camp on the Downs at early morning, in *The Melancholy Hussar*). Telling details are selected and set in like jewels, but because he had not the space in which to spread and indulge himself, Hardy responds by making a virtue of economy, restraint and simplicity.

Because the stories were not produced out of a spontaneous bubbling-up of inspiration to which he could not choose but attend, but always in response to a direct request from the editors of magazines and for money, they have been branded as pot-boilers in more than the most obvious sense and seen as suffering from all the worst effects of hasty conception and cursory production. In some cases this is true. But much that is best, straightforward and simple about the stories and, more important still, most suitable to the form itself, seems to me to arise just because Hardy did not worry anxiously over them. The more seriously he took his fiction the more he was inclined to fret, and this fretting affected his style. The worst obscurities and complexities which sometimes tangle the surface of his prose are not so much a result of his grappling with complex intellectual, philosophical and moral issues, and failing to express them in fictional terms – though he often was so grappling and sometimes he failed – as of a touching but misguided desire to impress, to appear sophisticated in learning.

But in his short stories he is dedicated simply to the business of telling a tale well and being done; and though there are historical and classical allusions and a sprinkling of recondite words and phrases – and these are by no means always merely redundant decorations – there are few stylistic obstructions to the reader's immersion in, and thorough appreciation of, the narrative.

Nevertheless, it would be doing Hardy a disservice if an attempt to right the balance and to win a wider and more admiring public for his short stories spilled over into an uncritical and blanket enthusiasm. I have said that some of them are failures; others are seriously limited or flawed and, paradoxically, just as his more relaxed and brisk approach to the writing of stories tended to bring out some of the best and keep at bay some of the worst aspects of his art, so it gave rise to the greatest faults, of attitude and of construction.

Coincidence often reaches out a long arm in Hardy's fiction. Lives are altered in their courses, fates are determined and plots resolved by chance, bad luck or, as some see it, the machinations of a malevolent fate. So it is in life, and the extent to which Hardy loads the dice has been exaggerated. It is the prerogative, even the purpose, of the artist to emphasize and underline particular aspects of the raw material which he takes from nature; this is one of the means by which he transforms that material and imbues it with his own creative vision and personality, before shaping it into his own pattern. As Hardy himself put it: 'Art is a changing of the actual proportions and order of things, so as to bring out more forcibly . . . that feature in them which appeals most strongly to the idiosyncrasy of the artist.' *

In his best novels and stories he does this and still maintains a balance. Some of the events, both life-shaping and incidental, come about because certain characters behave in certain ways – what they do, or refrain from doing, or cause to happen to them, is a direct result of the kind of people they are; other events are imposed on them from without, by chance – or the author himself – and we are asked to accept, to suspend disbelief in and be convinced by, the whole work of fiction and its outcome. It may be more difficult to achieve this balance in the short story, which has a number of inbuilt pitfalls, but it is perfectly possible, as Hardy demonstrates in some of the best of them.

But he can also be cursory in the extreme, imposing a plot like a heavy corset which stifles any potential life underneath. A deadline, insufficient commitment to, and thought about, a particular story, low imaginative intensity and lack of sustained care, all of these contribute to the cavalier attitude which can

* *The Life of Thomas Hardy* by Florence Emily Hardy.

produce wooden, two-dimensional characters, manipulated by the author and at the mercy of chance events, being pushed towards the thud of an artificial conclusion.

There may be little excuse for this and Hardy must have been aware that, to say the least, he was not giving of his best on these occasions. But to do him justice, it is possible that his creative mind was elsewhere, for he was producing most of the short stories over the same period of years as many major novels, including *The Mayor of Casterbridge*, *The Woodlanders*, *Tess of the d'Urbervilles* and *Jude the Obscure.*

Because they have not always seemed satisfactory as examples of the short story, various efforts have been made to reclassify them, as 'ballads' or 'tales'. Certainly there are some typical elements of the ballad in them – the frequent use of a narrator and discursive unfolding of dramatic, even bizarre events in a homely setting; and Hardy himself chose the title 'Wessex Tales' for the first published collection, though any distinctions made between 'tale' and 'story' are unconvincing beyond a certain elementary point. But the change of nomenclature can be helpful if it serves as a reminder of the period at which they were written – the late nineteenth century – and the fact that that was well before the development of the modern short story as we know it in the work of Katharine Mansfield, say, or D. H. Lawrence and Hemingway, or (though he was in fact Hardy's contemporary) Henry James. Otherwise we shall expect of Hardy what he was not intending or equipped to give.

He has suffered considerably from the myths which have arisen as a result of repeated exaggerations and distortions of his text, and one of the commonest fallacies is that he was quintessentially a countryman who wrote almost exclusively of country matters and, moreover, that the country characters who feature predominantly in his books are the unlettered, unskilled, agricultural working class. He wrote of them, of course, but only occasionally, just as he was concerned for only part of the time with events in a remotely rural setting. Hardy was a man of social and intellectual aspirations and achievements, who worked and lived in London and continued to spend five months of every year there after he had made his permanent home in Dorset. Many of his short stories are set in the *towns* of Wessex and are about the professional middle classes, teachers, lawyers, clergy, businessmen, and their families. Often they concern the rise of such people, like Hardy himself, from humbler and more deeply rural origins, their ambitions for education, wealth and social status and the tensions to which such ambitions give rise, between past and present, old and new friends and loyalties, beliefs and values, habits and manners.

Even in the more exclusively country tales, unskilled labourers are in the minority, and the background; the characters are farmers, often comfortably set-up, landowners and employers, or else the tradespeople, shopkeepers and craftsmen of the market towns.

One complete group is separate from the rest: the county aristocracy. Hardy writes of the skeletons in their cupboards – illegitimacy, murder, insanity, incest – in the rather unsuccessful collection, *A Group of Noble Dames*. These people are neither rising nor falling, but have long been firmly settled at the top of the ladder, and Hardy also sets them, for the most part, in the eighteenth century, so that the whole effect is of distance and isolation from the general stream of life and their static situation leads to a deadness in the stories.

The fact that Hardy is very good indeed at portraying women, that he understood them intuitively and reveals most convincingly their inner natures and psychological subtleties as well as their outward appearance and behaviour, has been so emphasized that his male characters are sometimes seen, by contrast, as weak and two-dimensional, existing in the shadow of the women in whom the writer was really interested.

If we look at some of his fiction, we may see how the impression arose. If we look at the whole of it, the balance is at once restored. The short stories contribute to that balance, for they are dominated here by women, here by men, of a variety of kinds, though with certain psychological types recurring. A number of the women – Ella Marchmill in *An Imaginative Woman*, Lizzy in *The Distracted Preacher*, Edith Harnham in

On the Western Circuit − are restless, lively and bored, educated and intelligent enough to yearn to break out of the confines of limited rural society and its repetitious activities, or prosaic, claustrophobic marriage. It is a familiar figure in Hardy and typically, it is a personality which provokes behaviour leading to misfortune and disaster. There are also single country girls who suffer at the hands of the clever and sophisticated, often a townee and usually male, and when he is concerned with men, Hardy frequently examines their ambitions or insensitivity or hypocrisy in a full and steady light. But he can portray the plain, good man beautifully − Ned Hipcroft in *The Fiddler of the Reels* − as well as the rogue, the solid citizen, the eccentric, the bully and the fool.

But whether the focus of the author's attention is a man or a woman in any particular story, the relationship between them is the theme of almost all. Hardy was preoccupied with affairs of the heart, with love requited or frustrated, fulfilled or doomed, with the meetings, partings, deceptions and self-deceptions of lovers − the whole business of courtship and romance, and the disillusion and distress, or mere tedium, of any subsequent matrimony. A few of the couples are ordinary enough but in the short stories, as in the novels, we are brought up time and again against an even more specific and idiosyncratic aspect of sexual affairs. John Bayley puts it succinctly: 'Hardy's favourite theme is an incongruous love situation in a peculiar setting.' *

Such a theme features in all but one (*The Grave by the Handpost*) of the stories collected here, and in a good proportion of the rest. Hardy worried at it throughout his fiction-writing career, setting up couple after oddly-assorted couple, studying the perverseness of human nature in romantic and sexual matters from various angles and pursuing its outcome to many bitter conclusions. There are discrepancies of social class between the lovers (*The Son's Veto*), age (*A Mere Interlude*), temperament and character (*The Distracted Preacher*), intelligence and education (*On the Western Circuit*) and nationality (*The Melancholy Hussar*).

* *An Essay on Hardy* (Cambridge University Press, 1978).

But it is noteworthy that although individual scenes may provide an element of the 'peculiar setting', in general the backgrounds are rather less extraordinary than in several of the novels. Hardy's fascination with the unusual, the bizarre, grotesque and macabre, is certainly in evidence in these stories: Baptista Trewthen lies in bed in a hotel room, between the living body of her present husband and the dead one of his predecessor (*A Mere Interlude*); Gertrude Lodge visits the county gaol after a public execution in order to touch the corpse of the hanged man with her withered arm; Barbara of the House of Grebe is horrified out of her love for her former husband by being obliged by her sadistic new one to contemplate his mutilated statue.

This aspect of the writer and its place in his work as a whole can also be over-stressed. It is not only that Hardy was by no means unusual or obsessive among imaginative writers, and, indeed, other artists, in his taste for the odd and the gruesome, particularly when set in juxtaposition with more mundane matters – rather the contrary. Much more importantly, a realization both of his inclination towards the weird, and of the carefully controlled and very limited part it actually plays in his fiction, serves to underline his self-control and artistic sensitivity and restraint. His skill in inserting a grotesque or morbid incident or detail at exactly the right point, so as to achieve maximum effect, is immense. It is on the few occasions when he piles up horrors or peculiarities gratuitously that he is an unsatisfactory, because unbalanced, writer. For, on the whole, Thomas Hardy is an infinitely more balanced artist than he has been made to appear.

However, it is not the occasional bizarre touches which alienate some readers but what is felt to be the improbability of his stories in general, particularly those with the most strikingly unusual characters and eventful plots. Certainly Hardy did not believe that it was the job of a fiction-writer simply to serve up a slice of mundane, everyday life, but the extravagance of his plots is often more apparent than real, and for the most part the action lies well within the bounds of both psychological and practical credibility. In a note of 1893 he makes it penetratingly clear that he was acutely conscious of the essential and delicate nature of these problems:

A story must be exceptional enough to justify its telling. We tale-tellers are all Ancient Mariners, and none of us is warranted in stopping Wedding Guests (in other words, the hurrying public) unless he has something more unusual to relate than the ordinary experience of every average man and woman.

The whole secret of fiction and the drama – in the constructional part – lies in the adjustment of things unusual to things eternal and universal. The writer who knows exactly how exceptional and how non-exceptional his events should be made, possesses the key to the art.*

That quotation, and especially the second paragraph of it, seems to me to sum up the aims and achievements of Hardy's fiction and to indicate the very reason for its existence. And once again it is when, for whatever reason, he fails to get the balance right between what he calls 'things unusual' and 'things eternal and universal', the exceptional and the ordinary, that it is hard to suspend disbelief in the result.

Nevertheless, we should not go to Hardy at all if we do not want to be told a rare tale, to be amazed, disturbed and intrigued, and it is his insistence upon the necessity of a writer having something extraordinary to relate that reveals how firmly rooted he is in a past tradition – the tradition of, among others, the balladist, the storyteller sitting with a group of listeners around a fire.

When this aspect of him is to the fore, and when the stories are thoroughly country stories, often containing some of the traditional, oral superstitions and folk-lore of the Wessex people, Hardy is unmistakably a writer belonging to his own or an earlier century.

The explanation of his ability to arrest and retain the reader's attention lies partly in the nature of the stories he chooses to tell, but just as much in his way of telling them, the sheer narrative skill. That is not an easy quality to analyse; it depends upon an innate sense of length and pace, which in turn are related to prose style and its rhythms, and the careful propor-

* *The Life of Thomas Hardy* by Florence Emily Hardy.

tions of and balance between description, dialogue and the straightforward recounting of events and actions, together with a knowledge of exactly what to put in and what to leave out, what to state and what to imply.

The opening of a story serves one of the most crucial functions of all. Upon its power and effectiveness, the hold over the reader's attention and the success of the complete narrative structure depend.

The novelist may begin in any one of a number of possible ways, approach his story from a variety of different angles and – even though some will be more suitable than others – still achieve essentially the same result, produce the same novel in the end, no matter which he chooses. It is not simply that he has more time and space because the novel is longer, but that the novel is an essentially different literary form from the short story; it has more dimensions and can successfully contain more irregularities and discrepancies within itself. A good novel can survive and overcome a weak, diffuse or misdirected opening; a short story almost never can.

With very few exceptions the openings of Hardy's short stories are masterly and absolutely suited to the rest of what follows. His most typical way of beginning (and it is true of the novels also) is to set a scene, and if we examine carefully how he does so we understand at once one of the reasons why his books and stories have been so successful when adapted to the cinema or television screen. For he uses, as it were, the camera's eye, first standing well back and sweeping broadly over an extensive landscape, before zooming in to pick out and scrutinize a smaller detail – one cottage, or hut, a solitary traveller on the road that traverses a barrow. The method is the same when he moves from a general view of a street or a group of people, to fix his attention on one house, one individual.

Some abstract conclusions have been drawn from the way Hardy often sets the small figures of men and women and creatures against a vast landscape; it has been seen as the overriding image of a whole philosophy about the insignificance and minuteness of human beings and the huge aloofness and impersonality of nature. Such an implication is certainly contained in these scenes and our general impression of their meaning is a valid one, but it is a mistake to see Hardy's intentions as always or exclusively metaphorical. He is often simply a watcher, a depicter and describer, with the eye of a camera or of a landscape painter; he is selecting and giving artistic emphasis to and putting a frame around what he sees, to create a remarkable and arresting visual image which will lead us into a fascinating human story. In a part of the country where the downs are high and exposed to the elements and the sky, and there are few trees to break the continuous eyeline for miles, a human being, on foot or on horseback, or a single dwelling, does inevitably appear tiny and dominated by nature.

When he is beginning a novel, Hardy expands his passage of descriptive scene-setting, wandering in at a discursive pace towards the point at which characters about whom the plot is to centre are observed, then introduced. He cannot use this relaxed method of opening a short story, yet very little seems to be lost, so good is he at painting his scene in a few swift, economical strokes, being sparing yet also exact and telling in his use of detail, and leaving a satisfying amount to the imagination of the individual reader.

Of the other principal types of opening used by Hardy, one, in which a narrator takes the pipe out of his mouth or sets down his glass, clears his throat and introduces the tale, belongs firmly to the old-fashioned, ballad-style tradition; the other seems to bring Hardy forward in time to take his place in style and spirit among twentieth-century short story writers. The method is direct, even abrupt. Instead of being led slowly, and from a distance, towards setting and characters, we are put straight down in their midst at a point when events are already under way.

When William Marchmill had finished his inquiries for lodgings at the well-known watering-place of Solentsea in Upper Wessex, he returned to the hotel to find his wife.

(*An Imaginative Woman*)

Instead of the focus narrowing gradually from a wide general view down to smaller and more particular details, it fixes straight away on such a one.

To the eyes of a man viewing it from behind, the nut-brown hair was a wonder and a mystery. Under the black beaver hat surmounted by its tuft of black feathers, the long locks, braided and twisted and coiled like the rushes of a basket, composed a rare, if somewhat barbaric, example of ingenious art.

(The Son's Veto)

In both these instances, and in others, the style of opening seems to suit the setting – in town, not country – and the more educated and sophisticated personalities of the protagonists.

I have said that most of Hardy's short stories, and all of his novels, are principally about love affairs. They have another common element – a character, of whatever kind, who plays a particular role upon which the story pivots. The role is that of the intruder, the person coming, in one sense or another, from outside the secure circle which is at the heart of the story, to disrupt and disturb, threatening and breaking up the established order of things, and it is often inextricably bound up with the love relationship – the very thing, indeed, that makes it an incongruous one. In *The Distracted Preacher* the intruder is Stockdale, the minister, arriving among the closely-knit villagers, all of whom are involved in the smuggling, and in any case an outsider and destined to remain so by the very fact of his being a clergyman. Just as Matthäus Tina is automatically one because he is a foreigner, though in *The Melancholy Hussar* it is the whole regiment who are intruders into the quiet, circumscribed life of the neighbourhood. In *On the Western Circuit* the lawyer Raye breezes in from London and from the professional classes, into the small-town lives of Edith Harnham and the simple maid, Anna, to cause emotional (and in Anna's case, physical) disruption. Seduction is sometimes the form the intrusion takes. Wat Ollamoor, the demonic fiddler of the reels invades the village and the hearts and bodies of its girls, causing moral breakdown and widespread misery.

But the stranger from without is not necessarily male. Gertrude, in *The Withered Arm*, coming to this part of the country for the first time as Lodge's bride, is the outsider, ignorant of the situation that formerly existed between her husband and Rhoda Brook and of the present *status quo*, as well as of local superstitions and customs. And in *An Imaginative Woman* the stranger, the poet Robert Trewe who invades Ella Marchmill's heart and provokes the hysterical behaviour which leads to marital tragedy, is not even aware of his role.

The device is useful because it establishes a clear and satisfying narrative pattern, and yet it is at the same time capable of endless permutations and enables incident to be dependent upon and emerge from the characters and their relationships. Hardy's use of the intruder figure is regular and interesting, but it would be misleading to draw too many conclusions about his artistic psychology from its prominence in his work, for it is one of the basic themes of literature and forms an element in ballads, tales and short stories, both well before and after Hardy's time. In this, as in so many other aspects of his fiction, he is rooted firmly in the past English tradition.

Yet however true this may be, the real reason we read and admire Hardy is because he is *Hardy*, with a literary persona, a creative intelligence and an imaginative vision uniquely and unmistakably his own; and, when all questions of prose style, subject matter, location, character-type and personal philosophy have been taken into account, he possesses that extra quality which is, in the last resort, indefinable, as such things always are. The short stories add to, enrich and expand our knowledge and appreciation of him because they are so clearly and inseparably part of his work, and because they are permeated by that atmosphere, narrative power and vivid and deep sense of place and its intimate relation to character which are the essentials of Hardy's genius.

2. *The Selected Stories*

THE DISTRACTED PREACHER
(from *Wessex Tales*)

This early, long story is one of Hardy's most flawless, a perfect comedy with some noticeably Shakespearean touches. It is light-hearted but, like his novel *Under the Greenwood Tree*, in the same mood of comic-pastoral, has a vein of sadness and seriousness underlying the often uproarious surface, which is reminiscent of *Twelfth Night*; there is the basic disparity of temperament and life-style between the ill-matched lovers, Stockdale and Lizzy, the serious risk to their security, and to their very lives, run by the smuggling villagers, and indeed, the whole moral issue involved.

Though he lost his religious faith early in adult life, Hardy remained a churchgoer, devoted to the ceremonies, music and literature, the whole ambience, of the Established Church. But he could be a bitter denouncer of the clergy. His portrait of the young Nonconformist minister here is, by contrast, decidedly tender – the man is silly but honest and decent and genuinely stricken by the role he is manoeuvred into by Lizzy. It is impossible to dismiss him as priggish or stuffy, for there is something endearing about his grave efforts to disapprove of what Lizzy does and give her wise counsel, even while falling in love with her. If he has a touch of pomposity, Hardy deals with it gently, unlike the way he ruthlessly shows up Latimer, the chief customs officer, a balloon of self-importance and conceit who is pricked lightly once or twice before being punctured altogether in the ambush scene – which contains more Shakespearean echoes. Latimer has something of Falstaff and even of Malvolio about him, but the closest parallel is with Dogberry in *Much Ado About Nothing*.

The original ending of the story is not successful, as Hardy knew, but we must accept the reason he gives for it in his note to the 1912 edition. The preferred conclusion may well have proved psychologically more likely and artistically more satisfying, but it is difficult to gauge its complete rightness when Hardy only adds it in its cursory form instead of rewriting the last pages of the story entirely.

A MERE INTERLUDE
(from *A Changed Man and Other Tales*)

At a first reading, this story may seem to rely heavily upon chance and coincidence, with some purely arbitrary twists of plot imposed by the author from without. But in studying it, and particularly the characters of its protagonists, more closely, we can see that many of the incidents happen as they do precisely because of the kind of people they are. Baptista manages her life by fits and starts, one moment taking some measure of control and making a bold, impulsive decision, but for the rest simply drifting, acquiescing to other people or following the general tide of events, out of lethargy and the inability to think of a better alternative. It is notable how, in a short space, Hardy indicates at least part of the reason why she is like this; her mother is deaf, loquacious and opinionated, and Baptista has long given up trying to make her own voice and desires heard and has gone along with her, for the sake of peace and quiet and to spare herself effort. And so she gives in to the breezy, over-confident Charles, a character cleverly conveyed, for the most part through dialogue. He is not altogether likeable but we can see his attraction for Baptista. He is assertive, plausible and impetuous and also something of a moral coward.

There is one external force that plays an essential part in the plot – the weather. If it had not been foggy, the boat would have sailed and Baptista would never have met Charles. If it had not been so hot, he would never have gone for the fatal sea bathe, and the resort would not have become so crowded with visitors that the landlady is persuaded to let the room next to that one housing the dead body, because Baptista and her new husband cannot get another. It is all quite likely, and the natural elements often play just such an active role in Hardy's plots.

The ending is charming and most felicitous. What really happens is that Baptista begins to grow up, to profit from her previous folly and lack of character and the misfortunes they have led her into. In spite of the disparity in age and personality, affection is beginning to develop between her and Heddegan, partly based upon a knowledge and acceptance of their earlier, mutual deceitfulness. There is a reconciliation and so a possibility of future maturity and happiness; it is a comedy in the deepest sense.

THE WITHERED ARM
(from *Wessex Tales*)

Rooted in Wessex and in the early superstitions and legends of the area which Hardy heard about from his mother and grandmother and which fascinated him all his life, this is one of the best known and most gripping of his stories. It has typical elements of the macabre and grotesque and he builds up these details with deadly effect in scene after scene. When Gertrude Lodge arrives alone on the outskirts of Casterbridge she looks first at the general view across the countryside towards the distant roofs of the town, and then her eye is gradually drawn towards the men moving about on the skyline and, finally, to the gallows they are erecting. Fascination and horror mount within her and within the reader when she is taken into the prison and brought close up to the body of the hanged man; when she touches the corpse's neck the tension of the scene reaches a climax – for there is a strong sexual element in these incidents.

It is one of the most visual of the stories, a series of tableaux or peepshows of the kind enjoyed by Hardy from boyhood at travelling fairs and circuses, and, in its calmer descriptive passages, like landscape paintings.

It is also a remarkable portrait of a woman, Rhoda Brook, driven by jealousy and righteous indignation at her treatment by Lodge which has brought her to poverty, social disgrace and isolation, and a moving account of her growing relationship with Gertrude, whom she hates yet comes to like, recognizing her youthful goodness and innocence, and that she, too, is a victim. The release of these pent-up emotions in the incubus dream, and Gertrude's subsequent affliction, are psychologically most telling.

A TRAGEDY OF TWO AMBITIONS
(from *Life's Little Ironies*)

There is something Dickensian in the viciousness and irony of this attack of Hardy's upon a certain kind of time-serving clergyman, through his depiction of the Halborough brothers, and especially the elder, Joshua. He has no mercy on them and they carry the seeds of their own misery and destruction within them in what is properly called a tragedy, in the classical sense of an irreconcilable conflict and the Chaucerian sense of a 'falling from high estate'.

The brothers have little interest in or true commitment to the Christian religion and see the Church purely in terms of their own future worldly advancement. This is, of course, an indictment not only of them but of the institution itself, which allowed itself to be so misused in Hardy's day and earlier.

Even as boys they are single-minded, blinkered and cold, refusing to diverge, for half an hour of play, from the narrow path of study, conceived as a means to material profit.

They are snobbish, intent upon hauling their young sister up the social ladder with them, partly for fear that she might otherwise impede them by proving a disgrace, and deeply ashamed of their origins. It is scarcely surprising that they should resent and be embarrassed by their father, though Hardy enlists our sympathy for him in his splendidly incongruous, rumbustious appearance in the Cathedral Close with the gypsy woman on his arm, and we relish his over-familiar accosting of the Dean, and Joshua's horror. But he is a feckless drinker who dissipated his wife's hard-scrimped money and so ruined his sons' chances of education, an insensitive and boorish man. All he has is heart, warmth, carelessness and a zest for life – in total contrast to the mean-spirited young priests.

Like so many characters in Hardy, they cause a mighty event to take place (their father's death) not by what they do but by what they fail to do. They have been extremely provoked by him and many murders have been committed with less excuse. But it is the calculated suppression of feeling, the ability to stand by and listen to the old man calling out as he drowns and do nothing to save him, which is so utterly chilling and which puts them quite beyond any indulgent understanding. This is the very opposite of a killing committed in the passion of the moment.

It is a dark, intensely moral parable with innumerable biblical overtones and everything in it works towards the central point, including the fact that, for once, the female characters, though interestingly and roundly conveyed, remain in the background.

THE MELANCHOLY HUSSAR
(from *Wessex Tales*)

Among the most prominent virtues of the short stories is the force with which characters – even those who only make a fleeting appearance and do not occupy the centre of the action – claim our interest and sympathy during a brief acquaintance. But it must be said that they are not often really moving. *The Melancholy Hussar* is a notable exception. It is a deeply felt tale and the beautiful simplicity with which it is told helps greatly towards engaging our emotions, which are stirred partly by the doomed love relationship itself and by Phyllis Grove's lonely, unhappy situation with her lugubrious father, and partly because the whole is lent poignancy by being framed in the past and recollected and retold to the narrator, before Phyllis's death as a very old woman.

Hardy was particularly good at conveying the sense of freshness and optimism and the fatal rashness of youth, and the contrast between its impulsive innocence and the sourness and suspicion of those who have lived longer without gaining more than years.

BARBARA OF THE HOUSE OF GREBE
(from *A Group of Noble Dames*)

In response to a commission for a short novel, Hardy produced instead ten stories about the aristocratic families of Wessex called *A Group of Noble Dames*, linked together within an arbitrary framework reminiscent of Boccaccio's *Decameron*; various narrators tell the tales, four before and six after dinner one evening. Hardy claimed that they were true, but although he relied partly on Hutchins's *History and Antiquities of the County of Dorset*, he also invented and falsified a good deal. F. B. Pinion says, 'The collection may therefore be regarded as a curious amalgam of history, tradition, scandal and fiction.' *

They seem to me to be almost entirely failures, written with little commitment, the plots groaning and over-laden with far-fetched events, with wooden, two-dimensional characters and little entertainment value. The one fine exception is *Barbara of the House of Grebe* – though this, too, has received much adverse criticism, and it cannot in any sense be called a likeable or sympathetic piece. T. S. Eliot, in *After Strange Gods* (Faber, 1934), said that it portrayed 'a world of pure evil' and certainly the smell of the sulphur seems to rise from its pages.

It is like some lurid, brightly lit tableau, set within a hard-edged black frame, Gothic in its trappings, melodramatic, grue-some, cruel – and, in those terms, utterly successful. What makes it seem horrible and not at all – as such tales often become – risible, is a certain restraint Hardy exercises; there are enough unpleasant events but not one too many. It is quite different, in its heartlessness and coldness as well as its Gothic style, from anything else he wrote, but in spite of ourselves, we

* New Wessex Edition of the Stories of Thomas Hardy, ed. F. B. Pinion (Macmillan, 1977).

are affected by it and forced to admire the skill with which it is done.

ON THE WESTERN CIRCUIT
(from *Life's Little Ironies*)

Hardy's pessimism about the married state, which is generally the outcome of any romance, is nowhere more apparent than in this bleak little story, so typical of him in certain moods. His view of it is implied in the descriptions of the discontented, bored Edith Harnham's life with her rich wine-merchant husband, though the fault seems to be largely hers; she accepted him because she was getting older and no better match presented itself, though she does not love or like him and he is irritated by her. Nevertheless, Hardy states it all matter-of-factly, without directly blaming her – that is just the way things are, in marriage, that is how young women are encouraged to be.

Poor, illiterate, well-intentioned Anna, so anxious to marry the young lawyer who has seduced her, is also likely to lead a miserable life in the future with a husband whom she has deceived and who despises her, and to whom she will be a social embarrassment and emotional burden. It is her fault, too, but some of the blame is his for taking advantage of her innocence and willingness. Both will pay.

But Hardy does much more than imply – he states roundly his view of the love–courtship–marriage pattern.

... they gazed at each other with smiles, and with that unmistakable expression which means so little at the moment, yet so often leads up to passion, heartache, union, disunion, devotion, overpopulation, drudgery, content, resignation, despair.

In this, and in its tone, its contrast between innocence and sophistication, town and country, and the particular way in which its lovers are ill-matched, this story has strong links with two others, *The Son's Veto* and *An Imaginative Woman*, from the aptly entitled collection *Life's Little Ironies*.

THE SON'S VETO
(from *Life's Little Ironies*)

Like other stories in the collection *Life's Little Ironies*, this has, as one of its themes, marriage between people of different social class and educational attainment and the miserable consequences of it. Sophy is out of place in the dreary city to which her older, clergyman husband is obliged to take her from her native village, since the news of their marriage would cause a scandal there. And he, too, is made unwell and unhappy by it. Hardy expresses the whole situation in one poignant image:

> Mr Twycott had never rallied, and now lay in a well-packed cemetery to the south of the great city, where, if all the dead it contained had stood erect and alive, not one would have known him or recognized his name.

The indictment of the Twycotts' son is as strong as that of the two Halborough brothers, also ambitious clergymen, in *A Tragedy of Two Ambitions*. He, like them, is ashamed of his mother (and, unlike them, with no just cause) merely because she speaks in a country way, knows no one of social importance, and wants to marry a rural tradesman. The boy, Randolph, is bitterly described as seen at her funeral – 'from the mourning-coach a young smooth-shaven priest in a high waistcoat looked black as a cloud at the shopkeeper standing there' – and, for some reason, it is the adjective 'smooth-shaven' which is the most derogatory.

The story is moving in its sense of a lost past and happiness, and of the memories of those whose roots are in the country – one of Hardy's strongest themes, and the nostalgia is strengthened by the scene in which the vegetable carts, swaying with fresh country produce, lumber through the silent dawn streets of the city, watched with pleasure by the lonely invalid Sophy from her window.

Above all, the story (which Hardy thought his best) is about distance and separation – between city and country, Sophy and her husband, Sophy and her son, her lover and her son, and, finally, between her lover and herself – and its end is their separation by death.

THE FIDDLER OF THE REELS
(from *Life's Little Ironies*)

Almost alone among Hardy's stories, this has been singled out time and again for critical attention and universal praise, often being held up as the only example of a story of real merit that he wrote. Its central character has great power and memorability and the narrative line of the story is gripping. Wat Ollamoor is repellent – swarthy, greasy, 'weird and wizardly', a mad, diabolic, siren-figure – disliked by men and yet fatally attractive to women, and Hardy goes out of his way, in his physical descriptions, to stress how perverse and apparently magically induced their passion is. Ollamoor is the embodiment of evil, he has power and revels in it, its effect amuses him. He is contrasted in every way with the sturdy, self-sufficient, honest artisan, Ned Hipcroft, a reliable though scarcely a romantic figure. Car'line turns to him when her real needs are too strong to ignore, but she will dance again to the fiddler's tune the moment he reappears – it is a familiar situation in Hardy, the rivalry of the good man and the attractive villain.

Every detail of the story, and all of its images, add to the metaphorical effect of the whole, and though the Great Exhibition is brought in a little uneasily (the story was written for the Exhibition number of *Scribner's Magazine*, published in May 1893 to mark the Chicago World Fair) it does not really jar.

Yet I believe the story has been over-praised, and for the very obviousness of its virtues. It is rather *too* well made, rather over-neat, and it somehow lacks the subtleties and depths of others which are much better and quite unjustly neglected. Like Wat Ollamoor, its slickness is seductive but ultimately somewhat shallow.

AN IMAGINATIVE WOMAN
(from *Life's Little Ironies*)

Ella Marchmill is a stupid woman, and Hardy's portrait of her is a clever, knowing and entirely credible one, of someone with too many fancies and vague ambitions but no talent, and too much time on her hands. She is self-indulgent, spoilt and discontented, uninterested in, though occasionally sentimental about, her children, out of sympathy with a husband who is prosaic and a philistine, but wishes her no ill and is generous and affectionate in a limited way. Their marriage, like all such matches in Hardy, is doomed from the beginning, being between two hopelessly dissimilar characters and embarked upon, like that of Edith Harnham in *On the Western Circuit*, in thoughtless desperation from 'the necessity of getting life-leased at all costs'.

In the London society in which he moved for some months of every year, Hardy may well have met young women with similar poetic inclinations and fluttering temperaments, who attached themselves to a famous artistic personality and blew up their scanty impressions by 'day-dreams and night-sighs' into all-consuming passions.

Robert Trewe is a representative figure, deliberately kept hovering just out of sight on the edge of the story, never making a real entry into it as he always, in person, fails to enter Ella's own life.

The story has an urbane and totally contemporary air, without any reference to rural life or society or to the past, and it seems to bring Hardy forward in time – its setting is Victorian, but it might well be the 1920s.

THE GRAVE BY THE HANDPOST
(from *A Changed Man and Other Tales*)

There is little to say about this neat but slightly superficial story, except that in some way it seems to bring Hardy's wheel of fiction full circle – and it is a wheel which has turned out of the light into darkness. It was one of the last three stories he wrote and it takes him back to Wessex, to a group of characters about whom he wrote in his early novel, *Under the Greenwood Tree*, the singers and players of the parish church choir. Hardy knew of them from boyhood, from the stories of his father who played the fiddle at Puddletown church. But these are changed men. There is a darkness, a bitterness, an air of bleak chill and morbidity about this story which is in strong contrast to the light-heartedness and humour of the novel. This may ostensibly be a Christmas tale, but it features a betrayal, two suicides and a stake being driven through a dead body. The choir still plays old familiar tunes and speaks with burred West Country accents, but its involvement and even relish in the melancholy incidents is depressing.

The tale seems to throw a shadow over the Wessex world, and to mock and give the lie to our memory of it as a place of gaiety, sweetness and light, of rural innocence and charm. Our memories play us false.

HARDY'S Wessex is so familiar that it is hard to realize how odd it is that a novelist should have tied himself by so many strings to a particular tract of territory. Many novelists have set their scenes in real places, or have written with some features of a familiar landscape always before them. But Hardy has done something different. Almost every step taken by his characters is taken along real roads or over real heaths; the towns and villages, the hills, even many of the houses are identifiable. It is as if Hardy's imagination could not work unless with solid ground under its feet, with solid objects to be seen around it. Many of the characters, there is little doubt, contain more or less of one real person, more or less of another, with elements drawn purely from imagination or from the accumulated layers of experience, which comes to much the same thing. But with the topography, Hardy was rarely satisfied with anything less than a one-to-one correspondence between the fictional and the real.

While the detail of Hardy's topographical nomenclature may become tedious, the fact that the landscape is identifiable does give the novels a special quality, as of a day-dream, with half-real figures moving over a real world. One might say – if it can be said with respect – that it is this which leaves the novels with a touch of the magazine-story still, in which the ingenuous reader may lose himself – or herself – in vicarious adventures. And part of the immense popularity of Hardy certainly derives from the interest of the places written about, and particularly the more picturesque.

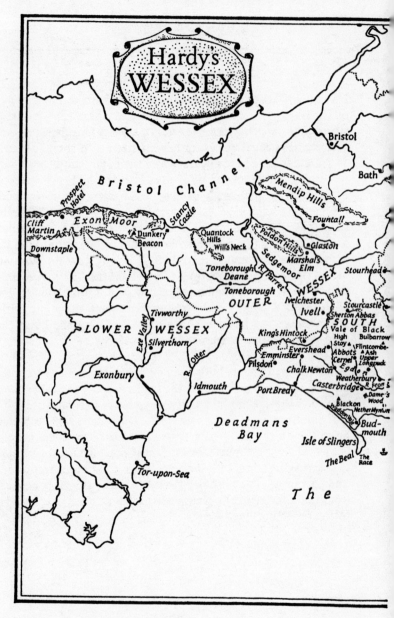

Hardy's WESSEX

Bristol

Bath

Bristol Channel

Prospect Hotel

Mendip Hills

Fountall

Cliff Martin

Exon Moor

Stancy Castle

Dunkery Beacon

Quantock Hills

Will's Neck

Poldon Hills

Glaston

Downstaple

Toneborough Deane

Marshal's Elm

Sedgemoor

R. Parret

Stourhead

WESSEX

Toneborough

OUTER

Ivelchester

Ivell

Stourcastle

Sherton Abbas

SOUTH

Vale of Black

Tivworthy

Exe Valley

LOWER WESSEX

King's Hintock

High Stoy

Bulbarrow

Flintcombe-Ash

Silverthorn

R. Otter

Emminster

Evershead

Abbots Cernel

Upper Longpuck

Exonbury

Pilsdon

Chalk Newton

Weatherbury

R. From

Idmouth

Port Bredy

Casterbridge

Dame's Wood

Blackon

Nether Mynton

Deadmans Bay

Bud-mouth

Isle of Slingers

Tor-upon-Sea

The Beal

The Race

The

36

R. Thames
Lumsdon
Christminster

NORTH

The Brown House
Alfredston
Cresscombe
Marygreen

WESSEX

MID

Marlbury Downs

Gaymead
Aldbrickham

Castle Royal

Kennetbridge

Batton Castle

WESSEX

Inkpen Beacon

The Great Plain

Stoke Barehills
Quartershot

Weydon Priors

Icenway House

Stonehenge

UPPER

WESSEX

Melchester

Wintoncester

Fernel Hall
Deansleigh Park

Leddenton
Shaston
Wingreen
The Slopes
The Chase
Trantridge Cross
Chaseborough
Lornton Inn

Southampton

WESSEX

Shottsford Forum
Badbury Ring
Middleton Abbey
Welland
Yewsholt
Warborne

The Great
Bramshurst
Forest

Kingsbere
Heath
Talbothays
Chene Manor
Havenpool

Anglebury

Portsmouth
Solentsea

Wellbridge
Corvesgate
Sandbourne
Knollsea

Lulwind Cove
Lightship

The Island

Channel

N

0   10   20   30 miles

Fictitious names: Exonbury
Real names: Portsmouth

H. A. Shelley

37

HARDY'S NAME	REAL NAME
Abbot's-Cernel	Cerne Abbas
Abbotsea	Abbotsbury
Aldbrickham	Reading
Alfredston	Wantage
Anglebury	Wareham
Badbury Rings	A hill near Wimborne Minster
Budmouth	Weymouth
Bulbarrow	A hill near Sturminster Newton
Casterbridge	Dorchester
Chalk Newton	Maiden Newton
Chaseborough	Cranborne
Christminster	Oxford
Cresscombe	Letcombe Basset
Damer's Wood	Came Wood near Dorchester
Dogbury	A hill near High Stoy
Durnover	Fordington
Egdon Heath	A composite of the heaths between Bournemouth and Dorchester
Emminster	Beaminster
Evershead	Evershot
Exonbury	Exeter
Fensworth	Letcombe Regis
Flintcombe-Ash	Nettlecombe-Tout
Greenhill	Woodbury Hill near Bere Regis
Hope Cove	Church Hope
Kennetbridge	Newbury
Kingsbere and *King's Bere*	Bere Regis
Leddenton	Gillingham
Longpuddle	Piddlehinton (also called by Hardy *Upper Longpuddle*)
Lulwind Cove	Lulworth Cove
Lumsdon	Cumnor
Marlott	Marnhull
Marygreen	Fawley

Melchester	Salisbury
Mellstock	Stinsford and Lower and Higher Bockhampton
Middleton Abbey	Milton Abbas
Nether-Moynton	Owermoigne
Norcombe Hill	A hill near Toller Down
Nuttlebury	Hazelbury Bryan
Oxwell Hall	Poxwell
Port Bredy	Bridport
Pos'ham	Portisham
Quartershot	Aldershot
Rainbarrow	Rainbarrows, a mound north of the Dorchester-Wareham road
Ridgeway	A road between Dorchester and Weymouth
Roy Town	Troy Town
St Aldhelm's Head	St Alban's Head
Sandbourne	Bournemouth
Shaston	Shaftesbury
Sherton	Sherborne
Shottesford and *Shottsford Forum*	Blandford
Stoke-Barehills	Basingstoke
Stourcastle	Sturminster Newton
Upper Longpuddle	Piddlehinton
Weatherbury	Puddletown
Wellbridge	Wool
Wintonchester	Winchester
Yalbury Wood	Yellowham Wood

HOW HIS COLD WAS CURED

I

SOMETHING delayed the arrival of the Wesleyan minister, and a young man came temporarily in his stead. It was on the thirteenth of January 183– that Mr Stockdale, the young man in question, made his humble entry into the village, unknown, and almost unseen. But when those of the inhabitants who styled themselves of his connection became acquainted with him, they were rather pleased with the substitute than otherwise, though he had scarcely as yet acquired ballast of character sufficient to steady the consciences of the hundred-and-forty Methodists of pure blood who, at this time, lived in Nether-Moynton, and to give in addition supplementary support to the mixed race which went to church in the morning and chapel in the evening, or when there was a tea – as many as a hundred-and-ten people more, all told, and including the parish-clerk in the winter-time, when it was too dark for the vicar to observe who passed up the street at seven o'clock – which, to be just to him, he was never anxious to do.

It was owing to this overlapping of creeds that the celebrated population-puzzle arose among the denser gentry of the district around Nether-Moynton: how could it be that a parish containing fifteen score of strong full-grown Episcopalians,[1] and nearly thirteen score of well-matured Dissenters,[2] numbered barely two-and-twenty score adults in all?

The young man being personally interesting, those with whom he came in contact were content to waive for a while the graver question of his sufficiency. It is said that at this time of his life his eyes were affectionate, though without a ray of levity; that his hair was curly, and his figure tall; that he was, in short, a very lovable youth, who won upon his female hearers

as soon as they saw and heard him, and caused them to say,
'Why didn't we know of this before he came, that we might
have gi'ed him a warmer welcome!'

The fact was that, knowing him to be only provisionally
selected, and expecting nothing remarkable in his person or
doctrine, they and the rest of his flock in Nether-Moynton had
felt almost as indifferent about his advent as if they had been
the soundest church-going parishioners in the country, and he
their true and appointed parson. Thus when Stockdale set foot
in the place nobody had secured a lodging for him, and though
his journey had given him a bad cold in the head he was forced
to attend to that business himself. On inquiry he learnt that
the only possible accommodation in the village would be
found at the house of one Mrs Lizzy Newberry, at the upper
end of the street.

It was a youth who gave this information, and Stockdale
asked him who Mrs Newberry might be.

The boy said that she was a widow-woman, who had got no
husband, because he was dead. Mr Newberry, he added, had
been a well-to-do man enough, as the saying was, and a farmer;
but he had gone off in a decline. As regarded Mrs Newberry's
serious side, Stockdale gathered that she was one of the trimmers[3] who went to church and chapel both.

'I'll go there,' said Stockdale, feeling that, in the absence
of purely sectarian lodgings, he could do no better.

'She's a little particular, and wont hae gover'ment folks,[4] or
curates, or the pa'son's friends, or such like,' said the lad
dubiously.

'Ah, that may be a promising sign: I'll call. Or no; just you
go up and ask first if she can find room for me. I have to see
one or two persons on another matter. You will find me down at
the carrier's.'

In a quarter of an hour the lad came back, and said that Mrs
Newberry would have no objection to accommodate him,
whereupon Stockdale called at the house. It stood within a
garden-hedge, and seemed to be roomy and comfortable. He
saw an elderly woman, with whom he made arrangements to
come the same night, since there was no inn in the place, and

he wished to house himself as soon as possible; the village being a local centre from which he was to radiate at once to the different small chapels in the neighbourhood. He forthwith sent his luggage to Mrs Newberry's from the carrier's, where he had taken shelter, and in the evening walked up to his temporary home.

As he now lived there, Stockdale felt it unnecessary to knock at the door; and entering quietly he had the pleasure of hearing footsteps scudding away like mice into the back quarters. He advanced to the parlour, as the front room was called, though its stone floor was scarcely disguised by the carpet, which only overlaid the trodden areas, leaving sandy deserts under the furniture. But the room looked snug and cheerful. The firelight shone out brightly, trembling on the bulging mouldings of the table-legs, playing with brass knobs and handles, and lurking in great strength on the under surface of the chimney-piece. A deep arm-chair, covered with horsehair, and studded with a countless throng of brass nails, was pulled up on one side of the fireplace. The tea-things were on the table, the teapot cover was open, and a little handbell had been laid at that precise point towards which a person seated in the great chair might be expected instinctively to stretch his hand.

Stockdale sat down, not objecting to his experience of the room thus far, and began his residence by tinkling the bell. A little girl crept in at the summons, and made tea for him. Her name, she said, was Marther Sarer, and she lived out there, nodding towards the road and village generally. Before Stockdale had got far with his meal a tap sounded on the door behind him, and on his telling the inquirer to come in, a rustle of garments caused him to turn his head. He saw before him a fine and extremely well-made young woman, with dark hair, a wide, sensible, beautiful forehead, eyes that warmed him before he knew it, and a mouth that was in itself a picture to all appreciative souls.

'Can I get you anything else for tea?' she said, coming forward a step or two, an expression of liveliness on her features, and her hand waving the door by its edge.

'Nothing, thank you,' said Stockdale, thinking less of what

he replied than of what might be her relation to the household.

'You are quite sure?' said the young woman, apparently aware that he had not considered his answer.

He conscientiously examined the tea-things, and found them all there. 'Quite sure, Miss Newberry,' he said.

'It is Mrs Newberry,' she said. 'Lizzy Newberry. I used to be Lizzy Simpkins.'

'O, I beg your pardon, Mrs Newberry.' And before he had occasion to say more she left the room.

Stockdale remained in some doubt till Martha Sarah came to clear the table. 'Whose house is this, my little woman?' said he.

'Mrs Lizzy Newberry's, sir.'

'Then Mrs Newberry is not the old lady I saw this afternoon?'

'No. That's Mrs Newberry's mother. It was Mrs Newberry who comed in to you just by now, because she wanted to see if you was good-looking.'

Later in the evening, when Stockdale was about to begin supper, she came again. 'I have come myself, Mr Stockdale,' she said. The minister stood up in acknowledgment of the honour. 'I am afraid little Marther might not make you understand. What will you have for supper? — there's cold rabbit, and there's a ham uncut.'

Stockdale said he could get on nicely with those viands, and supper was laid. He had no more than cut a slice when tap-tap came to the door again. The minister had already learnt that this particular rhythm in taps denoted the fingers of his enkindling landlady, and the doomed young fellow buried his first mouthful under a look of receptive blandness.

'We have a chicken in the house, Mr Stockdale — I quite forgot to mention it just now. Perhaps you would like Marther Sarer to bring it up?'

Stockdale had advanced far enough in the art of being a young man to say that he did not want the chicken, unless she brought it up herself; but when it was uttered he blushed at the daring gallantry of the speech, perhaps a shade too strong for a serious man and a minister. In three minutes the chicken appeared, but, to his great surprise, only in the hands of Martha Sarah. Stockdale was disappointed, which perhaps it was intended that he should be.

He had finished supper, and was not in the least anticipating Mrs Newberry again that night, when she tapped and entered as before. Stockdale's gratified look told that she had lost nothing by not appearing when expected. It happened that the cold in the head from which the young man suffered had increased with the approach of night, and before she had spoken he was seized with a violent fit of sneezing which he could not anyhow repress.

Mrs Newberry looked full of pity. 'Your cold is very bad to-night, Mr Stockdale.'

Stockdale replied that it was rather troublesome.

'And I've a good mind —' she added archly, looking at the cheerless glass of water on the table, which the abstemious minister was going to drink.

'Yes, Mrs Newberry?'

'I've a good mind that you should have something more likely to cure it than that cold stuff.'

'Well,' said Stockdale, looking down at the glass, 'as there is no inn here, and nothing better to be got in the village, of course it will do.'

To this she replied, 'There is something better, not far off, though not in the house. I really think you must try it, or you may be ill. Yes, Mr Stockdale, you shall.' She held up her finger, seeing that he was about to speak. 'Don't ask what it is; wait, and you shall see.'

Lizzy went away, and Stockdale waited in a pleasant mood. Presently she returned with her bonnet and cloak on, saying, 'I am so sorry, but you must help me to get it. Mother has gone to bed. Will you wrap yourself up, and come this way, and please bring that cup with you?'

Stockdale, a lonely young fellow, who had for weeks felt a great craving for somebody on whom to throw away superfluous interest, and even tenderness, was not sorry to join her; and followed his guide through the back door, across the garden, to the bottom, where the boundary was a wall. This wall was low, and beyond it Stockdale discerned in the night shades several grey headstones, and the outlines of the church roof and tower.

'It is easy to get up this way,' she said, stepping upon a bank which abutted on the wall; then putting her foot on the top of the stonework, and descending by a spring inside, where the ground was much higher, as is the manner of graveyards to be. Stockdale did the same, and followed her in the dusk across the irregular ground till they came to the tower door, which, when they had entered, she softly closed behind them.

'You can keep a secret?' she said, in a musical voice.

'Like an iron chest!' said he fervently.

Then from under her cloak she produced a small lighted lantern, which the minister had not noticed that she carried at all. The light showed them to be close to the singing-gallery stairs,[5] under which lay a heap of lumber of all sorts, but consisting mostly of decayed framework, pews, panels, and pieces of flooring, that from time to time had been removed from their original fixings in the body of the edifice and replaced by new.

'Perhaps you will drag some of those boards aside?' she said, holding the lantern over her head to light him better. 'Or will you take the lantern while I move them?'

'I can manage it,' said the young man, and acting as she ordered, he uncovered, to his surprise, a row of little barrels bound with wood hoops, each barrel being about as large as the nave[6] of a heavy waggon-wheel. When they were laid open Lizzy fixed her eyes on him, as if she wondered what he would say.

'You know what they are?' she asked, finding that he did not speak.

'Yes, barrels,' said Stockdale simply. He was an inland man, the son of highly respectable parents, and brought up with a single eye to the ministry; and the sight suggested nothing beyond the fact that such articles were there.

'You are quite right, they are barrels,' she said, in an emphatic tone of candour that was not without a touch of irony.

Stockdale looked at her with an eye of sudden misgiving. 'Not smugglers' liquor?' he said.

'Yes,' said she. 'They are tubs of spirit that have accidentally floated over in the dark from France.'

In Nether-Moynton and its vicinity at this date people always smiled at the sort of sin called in the outside world illicit trading; and these little kegs of gin and brandy were as well known to the inhabitants as turnips. So that Stockdale's innocent ignorance, and his look of alarm when he guessed the sinister mystery, seemed to strike Lizzy first as ludicrous, and then as very awkward for the good impression that she wished to produce upon him.

'Smuggling is carried on here by some of the people,' she said in a gentle, apologetic voice. 'It has been their practice for generations, and they think it no harm. Now, will you roll out one of the tubs?'

'What to do with it?' said the minister.

'To draw a little from it to cure your cold,' she answered. 'It is so 'nation[7] strong that it drives away that sort of thing in a jiffy. O, it is all right about our taking it. I may have what I like; the owner of the tubs says so. I ought to have had some in the house, and then I shouldn't ha' been put to this trouble; but I drink none myself, and so I often forget to keep it indoors.'

'You are allowed to help yourself, I suppose, that you may not inform where their hiding-place is?'

'Well, no; not that particularly; but I may take any if I want it. So help yourself.'

'I will, to oblige you, since you have a right to it,' murmured the minister; and though he was not quite satisfied with his part in the performance, he rolled one of the 'tubs' out from the corner into the middle of the tower floor. 'How do you wish me to get it out – with a gimlet, I suppose?'

'No, I'll show you,' said his interesting companion; and she held up with her other hand a shoemaker's awl and a hammer. 'You must never do these things with a gimlet, because the wood-dust gets in; and when the buyers pour out the brandy that would tell them that the tub had been broached. An awl makes no dust, and the hole nearly closes up again. Now tap one of the hoops forward.'

Stockdale took the hammer and did so.

'Now make the hole in the part that was covered by the hoop.'

He made the hole as directed. 'It won't run out,' he said.

'O yes it will,' said she. 'Take the tub between your knees, and squeeze the heads; and I'll hold the cup.'

Stockdale obeyed; and the pressure taking effect upon the tub, which seemed to be thin, the spirit spirted out in a stream. When the cup was full he ceased pressing, and the flow immediately stopped. 'Now we must fill up the keg with water,' said Lizzy, 'or it will cluck like forty hens when it is handled, and show that 'tis not full.'

'But they tell you you may take it?'

'Yes, the *smugglers*; but the *buyers* must not know that the smugglers have been kind to me at their expense.'

'I see,' said Stockdale doubtfully. 'I much question the honesty of this proceeding.'

By her direction he held the tub with the hole upwards, and while he went through the process of alternately pressing and ceasing to press, she produced a bottle of water, from which she took mouthfuls, conveying each to the keg by putting her pretty lips to the hole, where it was sucked in at each recovery of the cask from pressure. When it was again full he plugged the hole, knocked the hoop down to its place, and buried the tub in the lumber as before.

'Aren't the smugglers afraid that you will tell?' he asked, as they recrossed the churchyard.

'O no; they are not afraid of that. I couldn't do such a thing.'

'They have put you into a very awkward corner,' said Stockdale emphatically. 'You must, of course, as an honest person, sometimes feel that it is your duty to inform – really you must.'

'Well, I have never particularly felt it as a duty; and, besides, my first husband –' She stopped, and there was some confusion in her voice. Stockdale was so honest and unsophisticated that he did not at once discern why she paused: but at last he did perceive that the words were a slip, and that no woman would have uttered 'first husband' by accident unless she had thought

47

pretty frequently of a second. He felt for her confusion, and allowed her time to recover and proceed. 'My husband,' she said, in a self-corrected tone, 'used to know of their doings, and so did my father, and kept the secret. I cannot inform, in fact, against anybody.'

'I see the hardness of it,' he continued, like a man who looked far into the moral of things. 'And it is very cruel that you should be tossed and tantalized between your memories and your conscience. I do hope, Mrs Newberry, that you will soon see your way out of this unpleasant position.'

'Well, I don't just now,' she murmured.

By this time they had passed over the wall and entered the house, where she brought him a glass and hot water, and left him to his own reflections. He looked after her vanishing form, asking himself whether he, as a respectable man, and a minister, and a shining light, even though as yet only of the half-penny-candle sort, were quite justified in doing this thing. A sneeze settled the question; and he found that when the fiery liquor was lowered by the addition of twice or thrice the quantity of water, it was one of the prettiest cures for a cold in the head that he had ever known, particularly at this chilly time of the year.

Stockdale sat in the deep chair about twenty minutes sipping and meditating, till he at length took warmer views of things, and longed for the morrow, when he would see Mrs Newberry again. He then felt that, though chronologically at a short distance, it would in an emotional sense be very long before to-morrow came, and walked restlessly round the room. His eye was attracted by a framed and glazed sampler in which a running ornament of fir-trees and peacocks surrounded the following pretty bit of sentiment:

> Rose-leaves smell when roses thrive,
> Here's my work while I'm alive;
> Rose-leaves smell when shrunk and shed,
> Here's my work when I am dead.

Lizzy Simpkins.   Fear God.   Honour the King.
Aged 11 years.

' 'Tis hers,' he said to himself. 'Heavens, how I like that name!'

Before he had done thinking that no other name from Abigail to Zenobia would have suited his young landlady so well, tap-tap came again upon the door; and the minister started as her face appeared yet another time, looking so disinterested that the most ingenious would have refrained from asserting that she had come to affect his feelings by her seductive eyes.

'Would you like a fire in your room, Mr Stockdale, on account of your cold?'

The minister, being a little pricked in the conscience for countenancing her in watering the spirits, saw here a way to self-chastisement. 'No, I thank you,' he said firmly; 'it is not necessary. I have never been used to one in my life, and it would be giving way to luxury too far.'

'Then I won't insist,' she said, and disconcerted him by vanishing instantly.

Wondering if she was vexed by his refusal, he wished that he had chosen to have a fire, even though it should have scorched him out of bed and endangered his self-discipline for a dozen days. However, he consoled himself with what was in truth a rare consolation for a budding lover, that he was under the same roof with Lizzy; her guest, in fact, to take a poetical view of the term lodger; and that he would certainly see her on the morrow.

The morrow came, and Stockdale rose early, his cold quite gone. He had never in his life so longed for the breakfast hour as he did that day, and punctually at eight o'clock, after a short walk to reconnoitre the premises, he re-entered the door of his dwelling. Breakfast passed, and Martha Sarah attended, but nobody came voluntarily as on the night before to inquire if there were other wants which he had not mentioned, and which she would attempt to gratify. He was disappointed, and went out, hoping to see her at dinner. Dinner time came; he sat down to the meal, finished it, lingered on for a whole hour, although two new teachers were at that moment waiting at the chapel-door to speak to him by appointment. It was useless to wait longer, and he slowly went his way down the lane, cheered by the thought that, after all, he would see her in the evening, and perhaps engage again in the delightful tub-broaching in the neighbouring church tower, which proceeding he resolved to render more moral by steadfastly insisting that no water should be introduced to fill up, though the tub should cluck like all the hens in Christendom. But nothing could disguise the fact that it was a queer business; and his countenance fell when he thought how much more his mind was interested in that matter than in his serious duties.

However, compunction vanished with the decline of day. Night came, and his tea and supper; but no Lizzy Newberry, and no sweet temptations. At last the minister could bear it no longer, and said to his quaint little attendant, 'Where is Mrs Newberry to-day?' judiciously handing a penny as he spoke.

'She's busy,' said Martha.

'Anything serious happened?' he asked, handing another penny, and revealing yet additional pennies in the background.

'O no – nothing at all!' said she, with breathless confidence. 'Nothing ever happens to her. She's only biding upstairs in bed because 'tis her way sometimes.'

Being a young man of some honour he would not question further, and assuming that Lizzy must have a bad headache, or other slight ailment, in spite of what the girl had said, he went to bed dissatisfied, not even setting eyes on old Mrs Simpkins. 'I said last night that I should see her to-morrow,' he reflected; 'but that was not to be!'

Next day he had better fortune, or worse, meeting her at the foot of the stairs in the morning, and being favoured by a visit or two from her during the day – once for the purpose of making kindly inquiries about his comfort, as on the first evening, and at another time to place a bunch of winter-violets on his table, with a promise to renew them when they drooped. On these occasions there was something in her smile which showed how conscious she was of the effect she produced, though it must be said that it was rather a humorous than a designing consciousness, and savoured more of pride than of vanity.

As for Stockdale, he clearly perceived that he possessed unlimited capacity for backsliding, and wished that tutelary saints[8] were not denied to Dissenters. He set a watch upon his tongue and eyes for the space of one hour and a half, after which he found it was useless to struggle further, and gave himself up to the situation. 'The other minister will be here in a month,' he said to himself when sitting over the fire. 'Then I shall be off, and she will distract my mind no more! ... And then, shall I go on living by myself for ever? No; when my two years of probation are finished, I shall have a furnished house to live in, with a varnished door and a brass knocker; and I'll march straight back to her, and ask her flat, as soon as the last plate is on the dresser!'

Thus a titillating fortnight was passed by young Stockdale, during which time things proceeded much as such matters have done ever since the beginning of history. He saw the object of attachment several times one day, did not see her at all the next, met her when he least expected to do so, missed her when hints and signs as to where she should be at a given hour almost amounted to an appointment. This mild coquetry was perhaps fair enough under the circumstances of their being so closely lodged, and Stockdale put up with it as philosophically as he was able. Being in her own house she could, after vexing him or disappointing him of her presence, easily win him back by suddenly surrounding him with those little attentions which her position as his landlady put it in her power to bestow. When he had waited indoors half the day to see her, and on finding that she would not be seen, had gone off in a huff to the dreariest and dampest walk he could discover, she would restore equilibrium in the evening with 'Mr Stockdale, I have fancied you must feel draught o' nights from your bedroom window, and so I have been putting up thicker curtains this afternoon while you were out'; or, 'I noticed that you sneezed twice again this morning, Mr Stockdale. Depend upon it that cold is hanging about you yet; I am sure it is – I have thought of it continually; and you must let me make a posset[9] for you.'

Sometimes in coming home he found his sitting-room re-arranged, chairs placed where the table had stood, and the table ornamented with the few fresh flowers and leaves that could be obtained at this season, so as to add a novelty to the room. At times she would be standing on a chair outside the house, trying to nail up a branch of the monthly rose which the winter wind had blown down; and of course he stepped forward to assist her, when their hands got mixed in passing the shreds and nails. Thus they became friends again after a disagreement. She would utter on these occasions some pretty and deprecatory remark on the necessity of her troubling him anew; and he would straightway say that he would do a hundred times as much for her if she should so require.

HOW HE SAW TWO OTHER MEN

II

Matters being in this advancing state, Stockdale was rather surprised one cloudy evening, while sitting in his room, at hearing her speak in low tones of expostulation to some one at the door. It was nearly dark, but the shutters were not yet closed, nor the candles lighted; and Stockdale was tempted to stretch his head towards the window. He saw outside the door a young man in clothes of a whitish colour, and upon reflection judged their wearer to be the well-built and rather handsome miller who lived below. The miller's voice was alternately low and firm, and sometimes it reached the level of positive entreaty; but what the words were Stockdale could in no way hear.

Before the colloquy had ended, the minister's attention was attracted by a second incident. Opposite Lizzy's home grew a clump of laurels, forming a thick and permanent shade. One of the laurel boughs now quivered against the light background of sky, and in a moment the head of a man peered out, and remained still. He seemed to be also much interested in the conversation at the door, and was plainly lingering there to watch and listen. Had Stockdale stood in any other relation to Lizzy than that of a lover, he might have gone out and investigated the meaning of this: but being as yet but an unprivileged ally, he did nothing more than stand up and show himself against the firelight, whereupon the listener disappeared, and Lizzy and the miller spoke in lower tones.

Stockdale was made so uneasy by the circumstance, that as soon as the miller was gone, he said, 'Mrs Newberry, are you aware that you were watched just now, and your conversation heard?'

'When?' she said.

'When you were talking to that miller. A man was looking from the laurel-tree as jealously as if he could have eaten you.'

She showed more concern than the trifling event seemed to demand, and he added, 'Perhaps you were talking of things you did not wish to be overheard?'

'I was talking only on business,' she said.

'Lizzy, be frank!' said the young man. 'If it was only on business, why should anybody wish to listen to you?'

She looked curiously at him. 'What else do you think it could be, then?'

'Well – the only talk between a young woman and man that is likely to amuse an eavesdropper.'

'Ah yes,' she said, smiling in spite of her preoccupation. 'Well, my cousin Owlett has spoken to me about matrimony, every now and then, that's true; but he was not speaking of it then. I wish he had been speaking of it, with all my heart. It would have been much less serious for me.'

'O Mrs Newberry!'

'It would. Not that I should ha' chimed in with him, of course. I wish it for other reasons. I am glad, Mr Stockdale, that you have told me of that listener. It is a timely warning, and I must see my cousin again.'

'But don't go away till I have spoken,' said the minister. 'I'll out with it at once, and make no more ado. Let it be Yes or No between us, Lizzy; please do!' And he held out his hand, in which she freely allowed her own to rest, but without speaking.

'You mean Yes by that?' he asked, after waiting a while.

'You may be my sweetheart, if you will.'

'Why not say at once you will wait for me until I have a house and can come back to marry you.'

'Because I am thinking – thinking of something else,' she said with embarrassment. 'It all comes upon me at once, and I must settle one thing at a time.'

'At any rate, dear Lizzy, you can assure me that the miller shall not be allowed to speak to you except on business? You have never directly encouraged him?'

She parried the question by saying, 'You see, he and his party have been in the habit of leaving things on my premises sometimes, and as I have not denied him, it makes him rather forward.'

'Things – what things?'

'Tubs – they are called Things here.'

'But why don't you deny him, my dear Lizzy?'

'I cannot well.'

'You are too timid. It is unfair of him to impose so upon you, and get your good name into danger by his smuggling tricks. Promise me that the next time he wants to leave his tubs here you will let me roll them into the street?'

She shook her head. 'I would not venture to offend the neighbours so much as that,' said she, 'or do anything that would be so likely to put poor Owlett into the hands of the Customs-men.'

Stockdale sighed, and said that he thought hers a mistaken generosity when it extended to assisting those who cheated the king of his dues. 'At any rate, you will let me make him keep his distance as your lover, and tell him flatly that you are not for him?'

'Please not, at present,' she said. 'I don't wish to offend my old neighbours. It is not only Mr Owlett who is concerned.'

'This is too bad,' said Stockdale impatiently.

'On my honour, I won't encourage him as my lover,' Lizzy answered earnestly. 'A reasonable man will be satisfied with that.'

'Well, so I am,' said Stockdale, his countenance clearing.

THE MYSTERIOUS GREATCOAT

III

Stockdale now began to notice more particularly a feature in the life of his fair landlady, which he had casually observed but scarcely ever thought of before. It was that she was markedly irregular in her hours of rising. For a week or two she would be tolerably punctual, reaching the ground-floor within a few minutes of half-past seven. Then suddenly she would not be visible till twelve at noon, perhaps for three or four days in succession; and twice he had certain proof that she did not leave her room till half-past three in the afternoon. The second time that this extreme lateness came under his notice was on a day when he had particularly wished to consult with her about his future movements; and he concluded, as he always had done, that she had a cold, headache, or other ailment, unless she had kept herself invisible to avoid meeting and talking to him, which he could hardly believe. The former supposition was disproved, however, by her innocently saying, some days later, when they were speaking on a question of health, that she had never had a moment's heaviness, headache, or illness of any kind since the previous January twelvemonth.

'I am glad to hear it,' said he. 'I thought quite otherwise.'

'What, do I look sickly?' she asked, turning up her face to show the impossibility of his gazing on it and holding such a belief for a moment.

'Not at all; I merely thought so from your being sometimes obliged to keep your room through the best part of the day.'

'O, as for that – it means nothing,' she murmured, with a look which some might have called cold, and which was the worst look that he liked to see upon her. 'It is pure sleepiness, Mr Stockdale.'

'Never!'

'It is, I tell you. When I stay in my room till half-past three in the afternoon, you may always be sure that I slept soundly till three, or I shouldn't have stayed there.'

'It is dreadful,' said Stockdale, thinking of the disastrous effects of such indulgence upon the household of a minister, should it become a habit of everyday occurrence.

'But then,' she said, divining his good and prescient thoughts, 'it only happens when I stay awake all night. I don't go to sleep till five or six in the morning sometimes.'

'Ah, that's another matter,' said Stockdale. 'Sleeplessness to such an alarming extent is real illness. Have you spoken to a doctor?'

'O no – there is no need for doing that – it is all natural to me.' And she went away without further remark.

Stockdale might have waited a long time to know the real cause of her sleeplessness, had it not happened that one dark night he was sitting in his bedroom jotting down notes for a sermon, which occupied him perfunctorily for a considerable time after the other members of the household had retired. He did not get to bed till one o'clock. Before he had fallen asleep he heard a knocking at the front door, first rather timidly performed, and then louder. Nobody answered it, and the person knocked again. As the house still remained undisturbed, Stockdale got out of bed, went to his window, which overlooked the door, and opening it, asked who was there.

A young woman's voice replied that Susan Wallis was there, and that she had come to ask if Mrs Newberry could give her some mustard to make a plaster with, as her father was taken very ill on the chest.

The minister, having neither bell nor servant, was compelled to act in person. 'I will call Mrs Newberry,' he said. Partly dressing himself, he went along the passage and tapped at Lizzy's door. She did not answer, and, thinking of her erratic habits in the matter of sleep, he thumped the door persistently, when he discovered, by its moving ajar under his knocking, that it had only been gently pushed to. As there was now a sufficient entry for the voice, he knocked no longer, but said in firm tones, 'Mrs Newberry, you are wanted.'

The room was quite silent; not a breathing, not a rustle, came from any part of it. Stockdale now sent a positive shout through the open space of the door: 'Mrs Newberry!' – still no answer, or movement of any kind within. Then he heard sounds from the opposite room, that of Lizzy's mother, as if she had been aroused by his uproar though Lizzy had not, and was dressing herself hastily. Stockdale softly closed the younger woman's door and went on to the other, which was opened by Mrs Simpkins before he could reach it. She was in her ordinary clothes, and had a light in her hand.

'What's the person calling about?' she said in alarm.

Stockdale told the girl's errand, adding seriously, 'I cannot wake Mrs Newberry.'

'It is no matter,' said her mother. 'I can let the girl have what she wants as well as my daughter.' And she came out of the room and went downstairs.

Stockdale retired towards his own apartment, saying, however, to Mrs Simpkins from the landing, as if on second thoughts, 'I suppose there is nothing the matter with Mrs Newberry, that I could not wake her?'

'O no,' said the old lady hastily. 'Nothing at all.'

Still the minister was not satisfied. 'Will you go in and see?' he said. 'I should be much more at ease.'

Mrs Simpkins returned up the staircase, went to her daughter's room, and came out again almost instantly. 'There is nothing at all the matter with Lizzy,' she said; and descended again to attend to the applicant, who, having seen the light, had remained quiet during this interval.

Stockdale went into his room and lay down as before. He heard Lizzy's mother open the front door, admit the girl, and then the murmured discourse of both as they went to the store-cupboard for the medicament required. The girl departed, the door was fastened, Mrs Simpkins came upstairs, and the house was again in silence. Still the minister did not fall asleep. He could not get rid of a singular suspicion, which was all the more harassing in being, if true, the most unaccountable thing within his experience. That Lizzy Newberry was in her bed-room when he made such a clamour at the door he could not possibly convince himself, notwithstanding that he had heard her come upstairs at the usual time, go into her chamber, and shut herself up in the usual way. Yet all reason was so much against her being elsewhere, that he was constrained to go back again to the unlikely theory of a heavy sleep, though he had heard neither breath nor movement during a shouting and knocking loud enough to rouse the Seven Sleepers.[10]

Before coming to any positive conclusion he fell asleep himself, and did not awake till day. He saw nothing of Mrs Newberry in the morning, before he went out to meet the rising sun, as he liked to do when the weather was fine; but as this was by no means unusual, he took no notice of it. At breakfast-time he knew that she was not far off by hearing her in the kitchen, and though he saw nothing of her person, that back apartment being rigorously closed against his eyes, she seemed to be talking, ordering, and bustling about among the pots and skimmers[11] in so ordinary a manner, that there was no reason for his wasting more time in fruitless surmise.

The minister suffered from these distractions, and his extemporized sermons were not improved thereby. Already he often said Romans for Corinthians in the pulpit, and gave out hymns in strange cramped metres, that hitherto had always been skipped, because the congregation could not raise a tune to fit them. He fully resolved that as soon as his few weeks of stay approached their end he would cut the matter short, and commit himself by proposing a definite engagement, repenting at leisure if necessary.

With this end in view, he suggested to her on the evening after her mysterious sleep that they should take a walk together just before dark, the latter part of the proposition being introduced that they might return home unseen. She consented to go; and away they went over a stile, to a shrouded footpath suited for the occasion. But, in spite of attempts on both sides, they were unable to infuse much spirit into the ramble. She looked rather paler than usual, and sometimes turned her head away.

'Lizzy,' said Stockdale reproachfully, when they had walked in silence a long distance.

'Yes,' said she.

'You yawned – much my company is to you!' He put it in that way, but he was really wondering whether her yawn could possibly have more to do with physical weariness from the night before than mental weariness of that present moment. Lizzy apologized, and owned that she was rather tired, which gave him an opening for a direct question on the point; but his modesty would not allow him to put it to her; and he uncomfortably resolved to wait.

The month of February passed with alternations of mud and frost, rain and sleet, east winds and north-westerly gales. The hollow places in the ploughed fields showed themselves as pools of water, which had settled there from the higher levels, and had not yet found time to soak away. The birds began to get lively, and a single thrush came just before sunset each evening, and sang hopefully on the large elm-tree which stood nearest to Mrs Newberry's house. Cold blasts and brittle earth had given place to an oozing dampness more unpleasant in itself than frost; but it suggested coming spring, and its unpleasantness was of a bearable kind.

Stockdale had been going to bring about a practical understanding with Lizzy at least half a dozen times; but, what with the mystery of her apparent absence on the night of the neighbour's call, and her curious way of lying in bed at unaccountable times, he felt a check within him whenever he wanted to speak out. Thus they still lived on as indefinitely affianced lovers, each of whom hardly acknowledged the other's claim to the name of chosen one. Stockdale persuaded himself that his hesitation was owing to the postponement of the ordained minister's arrival, and the consequent delay in his own departure, which did away with all necessity for haste in his courtship; but perhaps it was only that his discretion was reasserting itself, and telling him that he had better get clearer ideas of Lizzy before arranging for the grand contract of his life with her. She, on her part, always seemed ready to be urged further on that question than he had hitherto attempted to go; but she was none the less independent, and to a degree which would have kept from flagging the passion of a far more mutable man.

On the evening of the first of March he went casually into his bedroom about dusk, and noticed lying on a chair a greatcoat, hat, and breeches. Having no recollection of leaving any clothes of his own in that spot, he went and examined them as well as he could in the twilight, and found that they did not belong to him. He paused for a moment to consider how they might have got there. He was the only man living in the house; and yet these were not his garments, unless he had made a mistake. No, they were not his. He called up Martha Sarah.

'How did these things come in my room?' he said, flinging the objectionable articles to the floor.

Martha said that Mrs Newberry had given them to her to brush, and that she had brought them up there thinking they must be Mr Stockdale's, as there was no other gentleman a-lodging there.

'Of course you did,' said Stockdale. 'Now take them down to your mis'ess, and say they are some clothes I have found here and know nothing about.'

As the door was left open he heard the conversation downstairs. 'How stupid!' said Mrs Newberry, in a tone of confusion. 'Why, Marther Sarer, I did not tell you to take 'em to Mr Stockdale's room?'

'I thought they must be his as they was so muddy,' said Martha humbly.

'You should have left 'em on the clothes-horse,' said the young mistress severely; and she came upstairs with the garments on her arm, quickly passed Stockdale's room, and threw them forcibly into a closet at the end of a passage. With this the incident ended, and the house was silent again.

There would have been nothing remarkable in finding such clothes in a widow's house had they been clean; or moth-eaten, or creased, or mouldy from long lying by; but that they should be splashed with recent mud bothered Stockdale a good deal. When a young pastor is in the aspen stage of attachment, and open to agitation at the merest trifles, a really substantial incongruity of this complexion is a disturbing thing. However, nothing further occurred at that time; but he became watchful, and given to conjecture, and was unable to forget the circumstance.

One morning, on looking from his window, he saw Mrs Newberry herself brushing the tails of a long drab greatcoat, which, if he mistook not, was the very same garment as the one that had adorned the chair of his room. It was densely splashed up to the hollow of the back with neighbouring Nether-Moynton mud, to judge by its colour, the spots being distinctly visible to him in the sunlight. The previous day or two having been wet, the inference was irresistible that the wearer had quite recently been walking some considerable distance about the lanes and fields. Stockdale opened the window and looked out, and Mrs Newberry turned her head. Her face became slowly red; she never had looked prettier, or more incomprehensible. He waved his hand affectionately, and said good-morning; she answered with embarrassment, having ceased her occupation on the instant that she saw him, and rolled up the coat half-cleaned.

Stockdale shut the window. Some simple explanation of her proceeding was doubtless within the bounds of possibility; but he himself could not think of one; and he wished that she had placed the matter beyond conjecture by voluntarily saying something about it there and then.

But, though Lizzy had not offered an explanation at the moment, the subject was brought forward by her at the next time of their meeting. She was chatting to him concerning some other event, and remarked that it happened about the time when she was dusting some old clothes that had belonged to her poor husband.

'You keep them clean out of respect to his memory?' said Stockdale tentatively.

'I air and dust them sometimes,' she said, with the most charming innocence in the world.

'Do dead men come out of their graves and walk in mud?' murmured the minister, in a cold sweat at the deception that she was practising.

'What did you say?' asked Lizzy.

'Nothing, nothing,' said he mournfully. 'Mere words – a phrase that will do for my sermon next Sunday.' It was too plain that Lizzy was unaware that he had seen fresh pedestrian splashes upon the skirts of the tell-tale overcoat, and that she imagined him to believe it had come direct from some chest or drawer.

The aspect of the case was now considerably darker. Stockdale was so much depressed by it that he did not challenge her explanation, or threaten to go off as a missionary to benighted islanders, or reproach her in any way whatever. He simply parted from her when she had done talking, and lived on in perplexity, till by degrees his natural manner became sad and constrained.

AT THE TIME OF THE NEW MOON

IV

The following Thursday was changeable, damp, and gloomy; and the night threatened to be windy and unpleasant. Stockdale had gone away to Knollsea in the morning, to be present at some commemoration service there, and on his return he was met by the attractive Lizzy in the passage. Whether influenced by the tide of cheerfulness which had attended him that day, or by the drive through the open air, or whether from a natural disposition to let bygones alone, he allowed himself to be fascinated into forgetfulness of the greatcoat incident, and upon the whole passed a pleasant evening; not so much in her society as within sound of her voice, as she sat talking in the back parlour to her mother, till the latter went to bed. Shortly after this Mrs Newberry retired, and then Stockdale prepared to go upstairs himself. But before he left the room he remained standing by the dying embers awhile, thinking long of one thing and another; and was only aroused by the flickering of his candle in the socket as it suddenly declined and went out. Knowing that there were a tinder-box, matches, and another candle in his bedroom, he felt his way upstairs without a light. On reaching his chamber he laid his hand on every possible ledge and corner for the tinder-box,[12] but for a long time in vain. Discovering it at length, Stockdale produced a spark, and was kindling the brimstone, when he fancied that he heard a movement in the passage. He blew harder at the lint, the match flared up, and looking by aid of the blue light through the door, which had been standing open all this time, he was surprised to see a male figure vanishing round the top of the staircase with the evident intention of escaping unobserved. The personage wore the clothes which Lizzy had been brushing, and something in the outline and gait suggested to the minister that the wearer was Lizzy herself.

But he was not sure of this; and, greatly excited, Stockdale determined to investigate the mystery, and to adopt his own way for doing it. He blew out the match without lighting the candle, went into the passage, and proceeded on tiptoe towards Lizzy's room. A faint grey square of light in the direction of the chamber-window as he approached told him that the door was open, and at once suggested that the occupant was gone. He turned and brought down his fist upon the handrail of the staircase: 'It was she; in her late husband's coat and hat!'

Somewhat relieved to find that there was no intruder in the case, yet none the less surprised, the minister crept down the stairs, softly put on his boots, overcoat, and hat, and tried the front door. It was fastened as usual: he went to the back door, found this unlocked, and emerged into the garden. The night was mild and moonless, and rain had lately been falling, though for the present it had ceased. There was a sudden dropping from the trees and bushes every now and then, as each passing wind shook their boughs. Among these sounds Stockdale heard the faint fall of feet upon the road outside, and he guessed from the step that it was Lizzy's. He followed the sound, and, helped by the circumstance of the wind blowing from the direction in which the pedestrian moved, he got nearly close to her, and kept there, without risk of being overheard. While he thus followed her up the street or lane, as it might indifferently be called, there being more hedge than houses on either side, a figure came forward to her from one of the cottage doors. Lizzy stopped; the minister stepped upon the grass and stopped also.

'Is that Mrs Newberry?' said the man who had come out, whose voice Stockdale recognized as that of one of the most devout members of his congregation.

'It is,' said Lizzy.

'I be quite ready – I've been here this quarter-hour.'

'Ah, John,' said she, 'I have bad news; there is danger to-night for our venture.'

'And d'ye tell o't! I dreamed there might be.'

'Yes,' she said hurriedly; 'and you must go at once round to where the chaps are waiting, and tell them they will not be wanted till to-morrow night at the same time. I go to burn the lugger off.'[13]

'I will,' he said; and instantly went off through a gate, Lizzy continuing her way.

On she tripped at a quickening pace till the lane turned into the turnpike-road, which she crossed, and got into the track for Ringsworth. Here she ascended the hill without the least hesitation, passed the lonely hamlet of Holworth, and went down the vale on the other side. Stockdale had never taken any extensive walks in this direction, but he was aware that if she persisted in her course much longer she would draw near to the coast, which was here between two and three miles distant from Nether-Moynton; and as it had been about a quarter-past eleven o'clock when they set out, her intention seemed to be to reach the shore about midnight.

Lizzy soon ascended a small mound, which Stockdale at the same time adroitly skirted on the left; and a dull monotonous roar burst upon his ear. The hillock was about fifty yards from the top of the cliffs, and by day it apparently commanded a full view of the bay. There was light enough in the sky to show her disguised figure against it when she reached the top, where she paused, and afterwards sat down. Stockdale, not wishing on any account to alarm her at this moment, yet desirous of being near her, sank upon his hands and knees, crept a little higher up, and there stayed still.

The wind was chilly, the ground damp, and his position one in which he did not care to remain long. However, before he had decided to leave it, the young man heard voices behind him. What they signified he did not know; but, fearing that Lizzy was in danger, he was about to run forward and warn her that she might be seen, when she crept to the shelter of a little bush which maintained a precarious existence in that exposed spot; and her form was absorbed in its dark and stunted outline as if she had become part of it. She had evidently heard the men as well as he. They passed near him, talking in loud and careless tones, which could be heard above the uninterrupted washings of the sea, and which suggested that they were not engaged in any business at their own risk. This proved to be the fact: some of their words floated across to him, and caused him to forget at once the coldness of his situation.

'What's the vessel?'

'A lugger, about fifty tons.'

'From Cherbourg, I suppose?'

'Yes, 'a b'lieve.'

'But it don't all belong to Owlett?'

'O no. He's only got a share. There's another or two in it – a farmer and such like, but the names I don't know.'

The voices died away, and the heads and shoulders of the men diminished towards the cliff, and dropped out of sight.

'My darling has been tempted to buy a share by that unbeliever Owlett,' groaned the minister, his honest affection for Lizzy having quickened to its intensest point during these moments of risk to her person and name. 'That's why she's here,' he said to himself. 'O, it will be the ruin of her!'

His perturbation was interrupted by the sudden bursting out of a bright and increasing light from the spot where Lizzy was in hiding. A few seconds later, and before it had reached the height of a blaze, he heard her rush past him down the hollow like a stone from a sling, in the direction of home. The light now flared high and wide, and showed its position clearly. She had kindled a bough of furze and stuck it into the bush under which she had been crouching; the wind fanned the flame, which crackled fiercely, and threatened to consume the bush as well as the bough. Stockdale paused just long enough to notice thus much, and then followed rapidly the route taken by the young woman. His intention was to overtake her, and reveal himself as a friend; but run as he would he could see nothing of her. Thus he flew across the open country about Holworth, twisting his legs and ankles in unexpected fissures and descents, till, on coming to the gate between the downs and the road, he was forced to pause to get breath. There was no audible movement either in front or behind him, and he now concluded that she had not outrun him, but that, hearing him at her heels, and believing him one of the excise party, she had hidden herself somewhere on the way, and let him pass by.

He went on at a more leisurely pace towards the village. On reaching the house he found his surmise to be correct, for the gate was on the latch, and the door unfastened, just as he had left them. Stockdale closed the door behind him, and waited silently in the passage. In about ten minutes he heard the same light footstep that he had heard in going out; it paused at the gate, which opened and shut softly, and then the door-latch was lifted, and Lizzy came in.

Stockdale went forward and said at once, 'Lizzy, don't be frightened. I have been waiting up for you.'

She started, though she had recognized the voice. 'It is Mr Stockdale, isn't it?' she said.

'Yes,' he answered, becoming angry now that she was safe indoors, and not alarmed. 'And a nice game I've found you out in to-night. You are in man's clothes, and I am ashamed of you!'

Lizzy could hardly find a voice to answer this unexpected reproach.

'I am only partly in man's clothes,' she faltered, shrinking back to the wall. 'It is only his greatcoat and hat and breeches that I've got on, which is no harm, as he was my own husband; and I do it only because a cloak blows about so, and you can't use your arms. I have got my own dress under just the same — it is only tucked in! Will you go away upstairs and let me pass? I didn't want you to see me at such a time as this!'

'But I have a right to see you! How do you think there can be anything between us now?' Lizzy was silent. 'You are a smuggler,' he continued sadly.

'I have only a share in the run,' she said.

'That makes no difference. Whatever did you engage in such a trade as that for, and keep it such a secret from me all this time?'

'I don't do it always. I only do it in winter-time when 'tis new moon.'

'Well, I suppose that's because it can't be done anywhen else. . . You have regularly upset me, Lizzy.'

'I am sorry for that,' Lizzy meekly replied.

'Well now,' said he more tenderly, 'no harm is done as yet. Won't you for the sake of me give up this blamable and danger-ous practice altogether?'

'I must do my best to save this run,' said she, getting rather husky in the throat. 'I don't want to give you up – you know that; but I don't want to lose my venture. I don't know what to do now! Why I have kept it so secret from you is that I was afraid you would be angry if you knew.'

'I should think so! I suppose if I had married you without finding this out you'd have gone on with it just the same?'

'I don't know. I did not think so far ahead. I only went to-night to burn the folks off, because we found that the preventive-men[14] knew where the tubs were to be landed.'

'It is a pretty mess to be in altogether, is this,' said the dis-tracted young minister. 'Well, what will you do now?'

Lizzy slowly murmured the particulars of their plan, the chief of which were that they meant to try their luck at some other point of the shore the next night; that three landing-places were always agreed upon before the run was attempted, with the understanding that, if the vessel was 'burnt off' from the first point, which was Ringsworth, as it had been by her to-night, the crew should attempt to make the second, which was Lulwind Cove, on the second night; and if there, too, danger threatened, they should on the third night try the third place, which was behind a headland further west.

'Suppose the officers hinder them landing there too?' he said, his attention to this interesting programme displacing for a moment his concern at her share in it.

'Then we shan't try anywhere else all this dark – that's what we call the time between moon and moon – and perhaps they'll string the tubs to a stray-line, and sink 'em a little-ways from shore, and take the bearings; and then when they have a chance they'll go to creep for 'em.'

'What's that?'

'O, they'll go out in a boat and drag a creeper – that's a grapnel – along the bottom till it catch hold of the stray-line.' [15]

The minister stood thinking; and there was no sound within doors but the tick of the clock on the stairs, and the quick breathing of Lizzy, partly from her walk and partly from agitation, as she stood close to the wall, not in such complete darkness but that he could discern against its whitewashed surface the greatcoat, breeches, and broad hat which covered her.

'Lizzy, all this is very wrong,' he said. 'Don't you remember the lesson of the tribute-money? [16] "Render unto Caesar the things that are Caesar's." Surely you have heard that read times enough in your growing up?'

'He's dead,' she pouted.

'But the spirit of the text is in force just the same.'

'My father did it, and so did my grandfather, and almost everybody in Nether-Moynton lives by it, and life would be so dull if it wasn't for that, that I should not care to live at all.'

'I am nothing to live for, of course,' he replied bitterly. 'You would not think it worth while to give up this wild business and live for me alone?'

'I have never looked at it like that.'

'And you won't promise and wait till I am ready?'

'I cannot give you my word to-night.' And, looking thoughtfully down, she gradually moved and moved away, going into the adjoining room, and closing the door between them. She remained there in the dark till he was tired of waiting, and had gone up to his own chamber.

Poor Stockdale was dreadfully depressed all the next day by the discoveries of the night before. Lizzy was unmistakably a fascinating young woman, but as a minister's wife she was hardly to be contemplated. 'If I had only stuck to father's little grocery business, instead of going in for the ministry, she would have suited me beautifully!' he said sadly, until he remembered that in that case he would never have come from his distant home to Nether-Moynton, and never have known her.

The estrangement between them was not complete, but it was sufficient to keep them out of each other's company. Once during the day he met her in the garden-path, and said, turning a reproachful eye upon her, 'Do you promise, Lizzy?' But she did not reply. The evening drew on, and he knew well enough that Lizzy would repeat her excursion at night – her half offended manner had shown that she had not the slightest intention of altering her plans at present. He did not wish to repeat his own share of the adventure; but, act as he would, his uneasiness on her account increased with the decline of day. Supposing that an accident should befall her, he would never forgive himself for not being there to help, much as he disliked the idea of seeming to countenance such unlawful escapades.

HOW THEY WENT TO LULWIND COVE

V

As he had expected, she left the house at the same hour at night, this time passing his door without stealth, as if she knew very well that he would be watching, and were resolved to brave his displeasure. He was quite ready, opened the door quickly, and reached the back door almost as soon as she.

'Then you will go, Lizzy?' he said as he stood on the step beside her, who now again appeared as a little man with a face altogether unsuited to his clothes.

'I must,' she said, repressed by his stern manner.

'Then I shall go too,' said he.

'And I am sure you will enjoy it!' she exclaimed in more buoyant tones. 'Everybody does who tries it.'

'God forbid that I should!' he said. 'But I must look after you.'

They opened the wicket and went up the road abreast of

each other, but at some distance apart, scarcely a word passing between them. The evening was rather less favourable to smuggling enterprise than the last had been, the wind being lower, and the sky somewhat clear towards the north.

'It is rather lighter,' said Stockdale.

' 'Tis, unfortunately,' said she. 'But it is only from those few stars over there. The moon was new to-day at four o'clock, and I expected clouds. I hope we shall be able to do it this dark, for when we have to sink 'em for long it makes the stuff taste bleachy,[17] and folks don't like it so well.'

Her course was different from that of the preceding night, branching off to the left over Lord's Barrow as soon as they had got out of the lane and crossed the highway. By the time they reached Shaldon Down, Stockdale, who had been in perplexed thought as to what he should say to her, decided that he would not attempt expostulation now, while she was excited by the adventure, but wait till it was over, and endeavour to keep her from such practices in future. It occurred to him once or twice, as they rambled on that should they be surprised by the Preventive-guard, his situation would be more awkward than hers, for it would be difficult to prove his true motive in coming to the spot; but the risk was a slight consideration beside his wish to be with her.

They now arrived at a ravine which lay on the outskirts of Shaldon, a village two miles on their way towards the point of the shore they sought. Lizzy broke the silence this time: 'I have to wait here to meet the carriers. I don't know if they have come yet. As I told you, we go to Lulwind Cove to-night, and it is two miles further than Ringsworth.'

It turned out that the men had already come; for while she spoke two or three dozen heads broke the line of the slope, and a company of them at once descended from the bushes where they had been lying in wait. These carriers were men whom Lizzy and other proprietors regularly employed to bring the tubs from the boat to a hiding-place inland. They were all young fellows of Nether-Moynton, Shaldon, and the neighbourhood, quiet and inoffensive persons, even though some held heavy sticks, who simply engaged to carry the cargo for Lizzy and her cousin Owlett, as they would have engaged in any other labour for which they were fairly well paid.

At a word from her they closed in together. 'You had better take it now,' she said to them; and handed to each a packet. It contained six shillings, their remuneration for the night's undertaking, which was paid beforehand without reference to success or failure; but, besides this, they had the privilege of selling as agents when the run was successfully made. As soon as it was done, she said to them, 'The place is the old one, Dagger's Grave, near Lulwind Cove'; the men till that moment not having been told whither they were bound, for obvious reasons. 'Mr Owlett will meet you there,' added Lizzy. 'I shall follow behind, to see that we are not watched.'

The carriers went on, and Stockdale and Mrs Newberry followed at a distance of a stone's throw. 'What do these men do by day?' he said.

'Twelve or fourteen of them are labouring men. Some are brickmakers, some carpenters, some shoemakers, some thatchers. They are all known to me very well. Nine of 'em are of your own congregation.'

'I can't help that,' said Stockdale.

'O, I know you can't. I only told you. The others are more church-inclined, because they supply the pa'son with all the spirits he requires, and they don't wish to show unfriendliness to a customer.'

'How do you choose 'em?' said Stockdale.

'We choose 'em for their closeness, and because they are strong and surefooted, and able to carry a heavy load a long way without being tired.'

Stockdale sighed as she enumerated each particular, for it proved how far involved in the business a woman must be who was so well acquainted with its conditions and needs. And yet he felt more tenderly towards her at this moment than he had felt all the foregoing day. Perhaps it was that her experienced manner and bold indifference stirred his admiration in spite of himself.

'Take my arm, Lizzy,' he murmured.

'I don't want it,' she said. 'Besides, we may never be to each other again what we once have been.'

'That depends upon you,' said he, and they went on again as before.

The hired carriers paced along over Shaldon Down with as little hesitation as if it had been day, avoiding the cart-way, and leaving the village of East Shaldon on the left, so as to reach the crest of the hill at a lonely trackless place not far from the ancient earthwork[18] called Round Pound. A quarter-hour more of brisk walking brought them within sound of the sea, to the place called Dagger's Grave, not many hundred yards from Lulwind Cove. Here they paused, and Lizzy and Stockdale came up with them, when they went on together to the verge of the cliff. One of the men now produced an iron bar, which he drove firmly into the soil a yard from the edge, and attached to it a rope that he had uncoiled from his body. They all began to descend, partly stepping, partly sliding down the incline, as the rope slipped through their hands.

'You will not go to the bottom, Lizzy?' said Stockdale anxiously.

'No. I stay here to watch,' she said. 'Mr Owlett is down there.'

The men remained quite silent when they reached the shore; and the next thing audible to the two at the top was the dip of heavy oars, and the dashing of waves against a boat's bow. In a moment the keel gently touched the shingle, and Stockdale heard the footsteps of the thirty-six carriers running forwards over the pebbles towards the point of landing.

There was a sousing in the water as of a brood of ducks plunging in, showing that the men had not been particular about keeping their legs, or even their waists, dry from the brine: but it was impossible to see what they were doing, and in a few minutes the shingle was trampled again. The iron bar sustaining the rope, on which Stockdale's hand rested, began to swerve a little, and the carriers one by one appeared climbing up the sloping cliff, dripping audibly as they came, and sustaining themselves by the guide-rope. Each man on reaching the top was seen to be carrying a pair of tubs, one on his back and one on his chest, the two being slung together by cords passing round the chine hoops,[19] and resting on the carrier's shoulders. Some of the stronger men carried three by putting an extra one on the top behind, but the customary load was a pair, these being quite weighty enough to give their bearer the sensation of having chest and backbone in contact after a walk of four or five miles.

'Where is Mr Owlett?' said Lizzy to one of them.

'He will not come up this way,' said the carrier. 'He's to bide on shore till we be safe off.' Then, without waiting for the rest, the foremost men plunged across the down; and, when the last had ascended, Lizzy pulled up the rope, wound it round her arm, wriggled the bar from the sod, and turned to follow the carriers.

'You are very anxious about Owlett's safety,' said the minister.

'Was there ever such a man!' said Lizzy. 'Why, isn't he my cousin?'

'Yes. Well, it is a bad night's work,' said Stockdale heavily. 'But I'll carry the bar and rope for you.'

'Thank God, the tubs have got so far all right,' said she.

Stockdale shook his head, and, taking the bar, walked by her side towards the downs; and the moan of the sea was heard no more.

'Is this what you meant the other day when you spoke of having business with Owlett?' the young man asked.

'This is it,' she replied. 'I never see him on any other matter.'

'A partnership of that kind with a young man is very odd.'

'It was begun by my father and his, who were brother-laws.'

Her companion could not blind himself to the fact that where tastes and pursuits were so akin as Lizzy's and Owlett's, and where risks were shared, as with them, in every undertaking, there would be a peculiar appropriateness in her answering Owlett's standing question on matrimony in the affirmative. This did not soothe Stockdale, its tendency being rather to stimulate in him an effort to make the pair as inappropriate as possible, and win her away from this nocturnal crew to correctness of conduct and a minister's parlour in some far-removed inland county.

They had been walking near enough to the file of carriers for Stockdale to perceive that, when they got into the road to the village, they split up into two companies of unequal size, each of which made off in a direction of its own. One company, the smaller of the two, went towards the church, and by the time that Lizzy and Stockdale reached their own house these men had scaled the churchyard wall, and were proceeding noiselessly over the grass within.

'I see that Mr Owlett has arranged for one batch to be put in the church again,' observed Lizzy. 'Do you remember my taking you there the first night you came?'

'Yes, of course,' said Stockdale. 'No wonder you had permission to broach the tubs – they were his, I suppose?'

'No, they were not – they were mine; I had permission from myself. The day after that they went several miles inland in a waggon-load of manure, and sold very well.'

At this moment the group of men who had made off to the left some time before began leaping one by one from the hedge opposite Lizzy's house, and the first man, who had no tubs upon his shoulders, came forward.

'Mrs Newberry, isn't it?' he said hastily.

'Yes, Jim,' said she. 'What's the matter?'

'I find that we can't put any in Badger's Clump to-night, Lizzy,' said Owlett. 'The place is watched. We must sling the apple-tree in the orchet if there's time. We can't put any more under the church lumber than I have sent on there, and my mixen [20] hev already more in en than is safe.'

'Very well,' she said. 'Be quick about it – that's all. What can I do?'

'Nothing at all, please. Ah, it is the minister! – you two that can't do anything had better get indoors and not be zeed.'

While Owlett thus conversed, in a tone so full of contraband anxiety and so free from lover's jealousy, the men who followed him had been descending one by one from the hedge; and it unfortunately happened that when the hindmost took his leap, the cord slipped which sustained his tubs: the result

was that both the kegs fell into the road, one of them being
stove in by the blow.

' 'Od drown it all!' said Owlett, rushing back.

'It is worth a good deal, I suppose?' said Stockdale.

'O no – about two guineas and half to us now,' said Lizzy
excitedly. 'It isn't that – it is the smell! It is so blazing strong
before it has been lowered by water, that it smells dreadfully
when spilt in the road like that! I do hope Latimer won't pass
by till it is gone off.'

Owlett and one or two others picked up the burst tub and
began to scrape and trample over the spot, to disperse the
liquor as much as possible; and then they all entered the gate
of Owlett's orchard, which adjoined Lizzy's garden on the right.
Stockdale did not care to follow them, for several on recognizing him had looked wonderingly at his presence, though they
said nothing. Lizzy left his side and went to the bottom of the
garden, looking over the hedge into the orchard, where the men
could be dimly seen bustling about, and apparently hiding the
tubs. All was done noiselessly, and without a light; and when
it was over they dispersed in different directions, those who
had taken their cargoes to the church having already gone off
to their homes.

Lizzy returned to the garden-gate, over which Stockdale was
still abstractedly leaning. 'It is all finished: I am going indoors
now,' she said gently. 'I will leave the door ajar for you.'

'O no – you needn't,' said Stockdale; 'I am coming too.'

But before either of them had moved, the faint clatter of
horses' hoofs broke upon the ear, and it seemed to come from
the point where the track across the down joined the hard road.

'They are just too late!' cried Lizzy exultingly.

'Who?' said Stockdale.

'Latimer, the riding-officer,[21] and some assistant of his. We
had better go indoors.'

They entered the house, and Lizzy bolted the door. 'Please
don't get a light, Mr Stockdale,' she said.

'Of course I will not,' said he.

'I thought you might be on the side of the king,' said Lizzy,
with faintest sarcasm.

'I am,' said Stockdale. 'But, Lizzy Newberry, I love you, and you know it perfectly well; and you ought to know, if you do not, what I have suffered in my conscience on your account these last few days!'

'I guess very well,' she said hurriedly. 'Yet I don't see why. Ah, you are better than I!'

The trotting of the horses seemed to have again died away, and the pair of listeners touched each other's fingers in the cold 'Good-night' of those whom something seriously divided. They were on the landing, but before they had taken three steps apart, the tramp of the horsemen suddenly revived, almost close to the house. Lizzy turned to the staircase window, opened the casement about an inch, and put her face close to the aperture. 'Yes, one of 'em is Latimer,' she whispered. 'He always rides a white horse. One would think it was the last colour for a man in that line.'

Stockdale looked, and saw the white shape of the animal as it passed by; but before the riders had gone another ten yards Latimer reined in his horse, and said something to his companion which neither Stockdale nor Lizzy could hear. Its drift was, however, soon made evident, for the other man stopped also; and sharply turning the horses' heads they cautiously retraced their steps. When they were again opposite Mrs Newberry's garden, Latimer dismounted, and the man on the dark horse did the same.

Lizzy and Stockdale, intently listening and observing the proceedings, naturally put their heads as close as possible to the slit formed by the slightly opened casement; and thus it occurred that at last their cheeks came positively into contact. They went on listening, as if they did not know of the singular incident which had happened to their faces, and the pressure of each to each rather increased than lessened with the lapse of time.

They could hear the Customs-men sniffing the air like hounds as they paced slowly along. When they reached the spot where the tub had burst, both stopped on the instant.

'Ay, ay, 'tis quite strong here,' said the second officer. 'Shall we knock at the door?'

'Well, no,' said Latimer. 'Maybe this is only a trick to put us off the scent. They wouldn't kick up this stink anywhere near their hiding-place. I have known such things before.'

'Anyhow, the things, or some of 'em, must have been brought this way,' said the other.

'Yes,' said Latimer musingly. 'Unless 'tis all done to tole [22] us the wrong way. I have a mind that we go home for to-night without saying a word, and come the first thing in the morning with more hands. I know they have storages about here, but we can do nothing by this owl's light. We will look round the parish and see if everybody is in bed, John; and if all is quiet, we will do as I say.'

They went on, and the two inside the window could hear them passing leisurely through the whole village, the street of which curved round at the bottom and entered the turnpike road at another junction. This way the officers followed, and the amble of their horses died quite away.

'What will you do?' said Stockdale, withdrawing from his position.

She knew that he alluded to the coming search by the officers, to divert her attention from their own tender incident by the casement, which he wished to be passed over as a thing rather dreamt of than done. 'O, nothing,' she replied, with as much coolness as she could command under her disappointment at his manner. 'We often have such storms as this. You would not be frightened if you knew what fools they are. Fancy riding o' horseback through the place; of course they will hear and see nobody while they make that noise; but they are always afraid to get off, in case some of our fellows should burst out upon 'em, and tie them up to the gate-post, as they have done before now. Good-night, Mr Stockdale.'

She closed the window and went to her room, where a tear fell from her eyes; and that not because of the alertness of the riding-officers.

THE GREAT SEARCH AT NETHER-MOYNTON

VI

Stockdale was so excited by the events of the evening, and the dilemma that he was placed in between conscience and love, that he did not sleep, or even doze, but remained as broadly awake as at noonday. As soon as the grey light began to touch ever so faintly the whiter objects in his bedroom he arose, dressed himself, and went downstairs into the road.

The village was already astir. Several of the carriers had heard the well-known canter of Latimer's horse while they were undressing in the dark that night, and had already communicated with each other and Owlett on the subject. The only doubt seemed to be about the safety of those tubs which had been left under the church gallery-stairs, and after a short discussion at the corner of the mill, it was agreed that these should be removed before it got lighter, and hidden in the middle of a double hedge bordering the adjoining field. However, before anything could be carried into effect, the footsteps of many men were heard coming down the lane from the highway.

'Damn it, here they be,' said Owlett, who, having already drawn the hatch[23] and started his mill for the day, stood stolidly at the mill-door covered with flour, as if the interest of his whole soul was bound up in the shaking walls around him.

The two or three with whom he had been talking dispersed to their usual work, and when the Customs-officers, and the formidable body of men they had hired, reached the village cross, between the mill and Mrs Newberry's house, the village wore the natural aspect of a place beginning its morning labours.

'Now,' said Latimer to his associates, who numbered thirteen men in all, 'what I know is that the things are somewhere in this here place. We have got the day before us, and 'tis hard if we can't light upon 'em and get 'em to Budmouth Customhouse before night. First we will try the fuel-houses, and then we'll work our way into the chimmers,[24] and then to the ricks and stables, and so creep round. You have nothing but your noses to guide ye, mind, so use 'em to-day if you never did in your lives before.'

Then the search began. Owlett, during the early part, watched from his mill-window, Lizzy from the door of her house, with the greatest self-possession. A farmer down below, who also had a share in the run, rode about with one eye on his fields and the other on Latimer and his myrmidons,[25] prepared to put them off the scent if he should be asked a question. Stockdale, who was no smuggler at all, felt more anxiety than the worst of them, and went about his studies with a heavy heart, coming frequently to the door to ask Lizzy some question or other on the consequences to her of the tubs being found.

'The consequences,' she said quietly, 'are simply that I shall lose 'em. As I have none in the house or garden, they can't touch me personally.'

'But you have some in the orchard?'

'Mr Owlett rents that of me, and he lends it to others. So it will be hard to say who put any tubs there if they should be found.'

There was never such a tremendous sniffing known as that which took place in Nether-Moynton parish and its vicinity this day. All was done methodically, and mostly on hands and knees. At different hours of the day they had different plans. From daybreak to breakfast-time the officers used their sense of smell in a direct and straightforward manner only, pausing nowhere but at such places as the tubs might be supposed to be secreted in at that very moment, pending their removal on the following night. Among the places tested and examined were:

Hollow trees	Cupboards	Culverts
Potato-graves[26]	Clock-cases	Hedgerows
Fuel-houses	Chimney-flues	Faggot-ricks[27]
Bedrooms	Rainwater-butts	Haystacks
Apple-lofts	Pigsties	Coppers and ovens.

After breakfast they recommenced with renewed vigour, taking a new line; that is to say, directing their attention to clothes that might be supposed to have come in contact with the tubs in their removal from the shore, such garments being usually tainted with the spirit, owing to its oozing between the staves. They now sniffed at

Smock-frocks	Smiths' and shoemakers' aprons
Old shirts and waistcoats	Knee-naps [28] and hedging-gloves
Coats and hats	Tarpaulins
Breeches and leggings	Market-cloaks
Women's shawls and gowns	Scarecrows.

And as soon as the mid-day meal was over, they pushed their search into places where the spirits might have been thrown away in alarm:

Horse-ponds	Mixens	Sinks in yards
Stable-drains	Wet ditches	Road-scrapings, and
Cinder-heaps	Cesspools	Back-door gutters.

But still these indefatigable Custom-house men discovered nothing more than the original tell-tale smell in the road opposite Lizzy's house, which even yet had not passed off.

'I'll tell ye what it is, men,' said Latimer, about three o'clock in the afternoon, 'we must begin over again. Find them tubs I will.'

The men, who had been hired for the day, looked at their hands and knees, muddy with creeping on all fours so frequently, and rubbed their noses, as if they had almost had enough of it; for the quantity of bad air which had passed into each one's nostril had rendered it nearly as insensible as a flue. However, after a moment's hesitation, they prepared to start anew, except three, whose power of smell had quite succumbed under the excessive wear and tear of the day.

By this time not a male villager was to be seen in the parish. Owlett was not at his mill, the farmers were not in their fields, the parson was not in his garden, the smith had left his forge, and the wheelwright's shop was silent.

'Where the divil are the folk gone?' said Latimer, waking up to the fact of their absence, and looking round. 'I'll have 'em up for this! Why don't they come and help us? There's not a man about the place but the Methodist parson, and he's an old woman. I demand assistance in the king's name!'

'We must find the jineral²⁹ public afore we can demand that,' said his lieutenant.

'Well, well, we shall do better without 'em,' said Latimer, who changed his moods at a moment's notice. 'But there's great cause of suspicion in this silence and this keeping out of sight, and I'll bear it in mind. Now we will go across to Owlett's orchard and see what we can find there.'

Stockdale, who heard this discussion from the garden-gate, over which he had been leaning, was rather alarmed, and thought it a mistake of the villagers to keep so completely out of the way. He himself, like the Preventives, had been wondering for the last half-hour what could have become of them. Some labourers were of necessity engaged in distant fields, but the master-workmen should have been at home; though one and all, after just showing themselves at their shops, had apparently gone off for the day. He went in to Lizzy, who sat at a back window sewing, and said, 'Lizzy, where are the men?'

Lizzy laughed. 'Where they mostly are when they're run so hard as this.' She cast her eyes to heaven. 'Up there,' she said.

Stockdale looked up. 'What – on the top of the church tower?' he asked, seeing the direction of her glance.

'Yes.'

'Well, I expect they will soon have to come down,' said he gravely. 'I have been listening to the officers, and they are going to search the orchard over again, and then every nook in the church.'

Lizzy looked alarmed for the first time. 'Will you go and tell our folk?' she said. 'They ought to be let know.' Seeing his conscience struggling within him like a boiling pot, she added, 'No, never mind, I'll go myself.'

She went out, descended the garden, and climbed over the churchyard wall at the same time that the preventive-men were ascending the road to the orchard. Stockdale could do no less than follow her. By the time that she reached the tower entrance he was at her side, and they entered together.

Nether-Moynton church tower was, as in many villages, without a turret, and the only way to the top was by going up to the singers' gallery, and thence ascending by a ladder to a square trap-door in the floor of the bell-loft, above which a permanent ladder was fixed, passing through the bells to a hole in the roof. When Lizzy and Stockdale reached the gallery and looked up, nothing but the trap-door and the five holes for the bell-ropes appeared. The ladder was gone.

'There's no getting up,' said Stockdale.

'O yes, there is,' said she. 'There's an eye looking at us at this moment through a knot-hole in that trap-door.'

And as she spoke the trap opened, and the dark line of the ladder was seen descending against the white-washed wall. When it touched the bottom Lizzy dragged it to its place, and said, 'If you'll go up, I'll follow.'

The young man ascended and presently found himself among consecrated bells[30] for the first time in his life, nonconformity having been in the Stockdale blood for some generations. He eyed them uneasily, and looked round for Lizzy. Owlett stood here, holding the top of the ladder.

'What, be you really one of us?' said the miller.

'It seems so,' said Stockdale sadly.

'He's not,' said Lizzy, who overheard. 'He's neither for nor against us. He'll do us no harm.'

She stepped up beside them, and then they went on to the next stage, which, when they had clambered over the dusty bell-carriages, was of easy ascent, leading towards the hole through which the pale sky appeared, and into the open air. Owlett remained behind for a moment, to pull up the lower ladder.

'Keep down your heads,' said a voice, as soon as they set foot on the flat.

Stockdale here beheld all the missing parishioners, lying on their stomachs on the tower roof, except a few who, elevated on their hands and knees, were peeping through the embrasures of the parapet. Stockdale did the same, and saw the village lying like a map below him, over which moved the figures of the Customs-men, each foreshortened to a crablike object, the crown of his hat forming a circular disc in the centre of him. Some of the men had turned their heads when the young preacher's figure arose among them.

'What, Mr Stockdale?' said Matt Grey, in a tone of surprise.

'I'd as lief[31] that it hadn't been,' said Jim Clarke. 'If the pa'son should see him a trespassing here in his tower, 'twould be none the better for we, seeing how 'a do hate chapel-members. He'd never buy a tub of us again, and he's as good a customer as we have got this side o' Warm'll.'

'Where is the pa'son?' said Lizzy.

'In his house, to be sure, that he mid[32] see nothing of what's going on – where all good folks ought to be, and this young man likewise.'

'Well, he has brought some news,' said Lizzy. 'They are going to search the orchard and church; can we do anything if they should find?'

'Yes,' said her cousin Owlett. 'That's what we've been talking o', and we have settled our line. Well, be dazed!'[33]

The exclamation was caused by his perceiving that some of the searchers, having got into the orchard, and begun stooping and creeping hither and thither, were pausing in the middle, where a tree smaller than the rest was growing. They drew closer, and bent lower than ever upon the ground.

'O, my tubs!' said Lizzy faintly, as she peered through the parapet at them.

'They have got 'em, 'a b'lieve,' said Owlett.

The interest in the movements of the officers was so keen that not a single eye was looking in any other direction; but at that moment a shout from the church beneath them attracted the attention of the smugglers, as it did also of the party in the orchard, who sprang to their feet and went towards the church-yard wall. At the same time those of the Government men who had entered the church unperceived by the smugglers cried aloud, 'Here be some of 'em at last.'

The smugglers remained in a blank silence, uncertain whether 'some of 'em' meant tubs or men; but again peeping cautiously over the edge of the tower they learnt that tubs were the things descried; and soon these fated articles were brought one by one into the middle of the churchyard from their hiding-place under the gallery-stairs.

'They are going to put 'em on Hinton's vault till they find the rest!' said Lizzy hopelessly. The Customs-men had, in fact, begun to pile up the tubs on a large stone slab which was fixed there; and when all were brought out from the tower, two or three of the men were left standing by them, the rest of the party again proceeding to the orchard.

The interest of the smugglers in the next manoeuvres of their enemies became painfully intense. Only about thirty tubs had been secreted in the lumber of the tower, but seventy were hidden in the orchard, making up all that they had brought ashore as yet, the remainder of the cargo having been tied to a sinker and dropped overboard for another night's operations. The Preventives, having re-entered the orchard, acted as if they were positive that here lay hidden the rest of the tubs, which they were determined to find before nightfall. They spread themselves out round the fields, and advancing on all fours as before, went anew round every apple-tree in the enclosure. The young tree in the middle again led them to pause, and at length the whole company gathered there in a way which signified that a second chain of reasoning had led to the same results as the first.

When they had examined the sod hereabouts for some minutes, one of the men rose, ran to a disused part of the church where tools were kept, and returned with the sexton's pickaxe and shovel, with which they set to work.

'Are they really buried there?' said the minister, for the grass was so green and uninjured that it was difficult to believe it had been disturbed. The smugglers were too interested to reply, and presently they saw, to their chagrin, the officers stand several on each side of the tree; and, stooping and applying their hands to the soil, they bodily lifted the tree and the turf around it. The apple-tree now showed itself to be growing in a shallow box, with handles for lifting at each of the four sides. Under the site of the tree a square hole was revealed, and an officer went and looked down.

'It is all up now,' said Owlett quietly. 'And now all of ye get down before they notice we are here; and be ready for our next move. I had better bide here till dark, or they may take me on suspicion, as 'tis on my ground. I'll be with ye as soon as day-light begins to pink in.'

'And I?' said Lizzy.

'You please look to the linch-pins and screws; then go in-doors and know nothing at all. The chaps will do the rest.'

The ladder was replaced, and all but Owlett descended, the men passing off one by one at the back of the church, and vanishing on their respective errands. Lizzy walked boldly along the street, followed closely by the minister.

'You are going indoors, Mrs Newberry?' he said.

She knew from the words 'Mrs Newberry' that the division between them had widened yet another degree.

'I am not going home,' she said. 'I have a little thing to do before I go in. Martha Sarah will get your tea.'

'O, I don't mean on that account,' said Stockdale. 'What *can* you have to do further in this unhallowed affair?'

'Only a little,' she said.

'What is that? I'll go with you.'

'No, I shall go by myself. Will you please go indoors? I shall be there in less than an hour.'

'You are not going to run any danger, Lizzy?' said the young man, his tenderness reasserting itself.

'None whatever – worth mentioning,' answered she, and went down towards the Cross.

Stockdale entered the garden gate, and stood behind it look-ing on. The Preventive-men were still busy in the orchard, and at last he was tempted to enter and watch their proceedings. When he came closer he found that the secret cellar, of whose existence he had been totally unaware, was formed by timbers placed across from side to side about a foot under the ground, and grassed over.

The officers looked up at Stockdale's fair and downy coun-tenance, and evidently thinking him above suspicion, went on with their work again. As soon as all the tubs were taken out they began tearing up the turf, pulling out the timbers, and breaking in the sides, till the cellar was wholly dismantled and shapeless, the apple-tree lying with its roots high to the air. But the hole which had in its time held so much contraband merchandise was never completely filled up, either then or afterwards, a depression in the greensward marking the spot to this day.

THE WALK TO WARM'ELL CROSS AND AFTERWARDS

VII

As the goods had all to be carried to Budmouth that night, the next object of the Custom-house officers was to find horses and carts for the journey, and they went about the village for that purpose. Latimer strode hither and thither with a lump of chalk in his hand, marking broad-arrows so vigorously on every vehicle and set of harness that he came across, that it seemed as if he would chalk broad-arrows on the very hedges and roads. The owner of every conveyance so marked was bound to give it up for Government purposes. Stockdale, who had had enough of the scene, turned indoors thoughtful and depressed. Lizzy was already there, having come in at the back, though she had not yet taken off her bonnet. She looked tired, and her mood was not much brighter than his own. They had but little to say to each other; and the minister went away and attempted to read; but at this he could not succeed, and he shook the little bell for tea.

Lizzy herself brought in the tray, the girl having run off into the village during the afternoon, too full of excitement at the proceedings to remember her state of life. However, almost before the sad lovers had said anything to each other, Martha came in in a steaming state.

'O, there's such a stoor,[34] Mrs Newberry and Mr Stockdale! The king's officers can't get the carts ready nohow at all! They pulled Thomas Artnell's, and William Rogers's, and Stephen Sprake's carts into the road, and off came the wheels, and down fell the carts; and they found there was no linch-pins in the arms; and then they tried Samuel Shane's waggon, and found that the screws were gone from he, and at last they looked at the dairyman's cart, and he's got none neither! They have gone now to the blacksmith's to get some made, but he's nowhere to be found!'

Stockdale looked at Lizzy, who blushed very slightly, and went out of the room, followed by Martha Sarah. But before they had got through the passage there was a rap at the front door, and Stockdale recognized Latimer's voice addressing Mrs Newberry, who had turned back.

'For God's sake, Mrs Newberry, have you seen Hardman the blacksmith up this way? If we could get hold of him, we'd e'en a'most drag him by the hair of his head to his anvil, where he ought to be.'

'He's an idle man, Mr Latimer,' said Lizzy archly. 'What do you want him for?'

'Why, there isn't a horse in the place that has got more than three shoes on, and some have only two. The waggon-wheels be without strakes,[35] and there's no linch-pins to the carts. What with that, and the bother about every set of harness being out of order, we shan't be off before nightfall – upon my soul we shan't. 'Tis a rough lot, Mrs Newberry, that you've got about you here; but they'll play at this game once too often, mark my words they will! There's not a man in the parish that don't deserve to be whipped.'

It happened that Hardman was at that moment a little further up the lane, smoking his pipe behind a holly-bush. When Latimer had done speaking he went on in this direction, and Hardman, hearing the riding-officer's steps, found curiosity too strong for prudence. He peeped out from the bush at the very moment that Latimer's glance was on it. There was nothing left for him to do but to come forward with unconcern.

'I've been looking for you for the last hour!' said Latimer with a glare in his eye.

'Sorry to hear that,' said Hardman. 'I've been out for a stroll, to look for more hid tubs, to deliver 'em up to Gover'ment.'

'O yes, Hardman, we know it,' said Latimer, with withering sarcasm. 'We know that you'll deliver 'em up to Gover'ment. We know that all the parish is helping us, and have been all day! Now you please walk along with me down to your shop, and kindly let me hire ye in the king's name.'

They went down the lane together; and presently there resounded from the smithy the ring of a hammer not very briskly swung. However, the carts and horses were got into some sort of travelling condition, but it was not until after the clock had struck six, when the muddy roads were glistening under the horizontal light of the fading day. The smuggled tubs were soon packed into the vehicles, and Latimer, with three of his assistants, drove slowly out of the village in the direction of the port of Budmouth, some considerable number of miles distant, the other men of the Preventive-guard being left to watch for the remainder of the cargo, which they knew to have been sunk somewhere between Ringsworth and Lulwind Cove, and to unearth Owlett, the only person clearly implicated by the discovery of the cave.

Women and children stood at the doors as the carts, each chalked with the Government pitchfork, passed in the increasing twilight; and as they stood they looked at the confiscated property with a melancholy expression that told only too plainly the relation which they bore to the trade.

'Well, Lizzy,' said Stockdale, when the crackle of the wheels had nearly died away. 'This is a fit finish to your adventure. I am truly thankful that you have got off without suspicion, and the loss only of the liquor. Will you sit down and let me talk to you?'

'By and by,' she said. 'But I must go out now.'

'Not to that horrid shore again?' he said blankly.

'No, not there. I am only going to see the end of this day's business.'

He did not answer to this, and she moved towards the door slowly, as if waiting for him to say something more.

'You don't offer to come with me,' she added at last. 'I suppose that's because you hate me after all this!'

'Can you say it, Lizzy, when you know I only want to save you from such practices? Come with you! – of course I will, if it is only to take care of you. But why will you go out again?'

'Because I cannot rest indoors. Something is happening, and I must know what. Now, come!' And they went into the dusk together.

When they reached the turnpike-road she turned to the right, and he soon perceived that they were following the direction of the Preventive-men and their load. He had given her his arm, and every now and then she suddenly pulled it back, to signify that he was to halt a moment and listen. They had walked rather quickly along the first quarter of a mile, and on the second or third time of standing still she said, 'I hear them ahead – don't you?'

'Yes,' he said; 'I hear the wheels. But what of that?'

'I only want to know if they get clear away from the neighbourhood.'

'Ah,' said he, a light breaking upon him. 'Something desperate is to be attempted! – and now I remember there was not a man about the village when we left.'

'Hark!' she murmured. The noise of the cartwheels had stopped, and given place to another sort of sound.

' 'Tis a scuffle!' said Stockdale. 'There'll be murder! Lizzy, let go my arm; I am going on. On my conscience, I must not stay here and do nothing!'

'There'll be no murder, and not even a broken head,' she said. 'Our men are thirty to four of them: no harm will be done at all.'

'Then there *is* an attack!' exclaimed Stockdale; 'and you knew it was to be. Why should you side with men who break the laws like this?'

'Why should you side with men who take from country traders what they have honestly bought wi' their own money in France?' said she firmly.

'They are not honestly bought,' said he.

'They are,' she contradicted. 'I and Mr Owlett and the others paid thirty shillings for every one of the tubs before they were put on board at Cherbourg, and if a king who is nothing to us sends his people to steal our property, we have a right to steal it back again.'

Stockdale did not stop to argue the matter, but went quickly in the direction of the noise, Lizzy keeping at his side. 'Don't you interfere, will you, dear Richard?' she said anxiously, as they drew near. 'Don't let us go any closer; 'tis at Warm'ell

Cross where they are seizing 'em. You can do no good, and you may meet with a hard blow!'

'Let us see first what is going on,' he said. But before they had got much further the noise of the cartwheels began again; and Stockdale soon found that they were coming towards him. In another minute the three carts came up, and Stockdale and Lizzy stood in the ditch to let them pass.

Instead of being conducted by four men, as had happened when they went out of the village, the horses and carts were now accompanied by a body of from twenty to thirty, all of whom, as Stockdale perceived to his astonishment, had blackened faces. Among them walked six or eight huge female figures, whom, from their wide strides, Stockdale guessed to be men in disguise. As soon as the party discerned Lizzy and her companion four or five fell back, and when the carts had passed, came close to the pair.

'There is no walking up this way for the present,' said one of the gaunt women, who wore curls a foot long, dangling down the sides of her face, in the fashion of the time. Stockdale recognized this lady's voice as Owlett's.

'Why not?' said Stockdale. 'This is the public highway.'

'Now look here, youngster,' said Owlett. 'O, 'tis the Methodist parson! – what, and Mrs Newberry! Well, you'd better not go up that way, Lizzy. They've all run off, and folks have got their own again.'

The miller then hastened on and joined his comrades. Stockdale and Lizzy also turned back. 'I wish all this hadn't been forced upon us,' she said regretfully. 'But if those Coast-men had got off with the tubs, half the people in the parish would have been in want for the next month or two.'

Stockdale was not paying much attention to her words, and he said, 'I don't think I can go back like this. Those four poor Preventives may be murdered for all I know.'

'Murdered!' said Lizzy impatiently. 'We don't do murder here.'

'Well, I shall go as far as Warm'ell Cross to see,' said Stockdale decisively; and, without wishing her safe home or anything else, the minister turned back. Lizzy stood looking at him till his form was absorbed in the shades; and then, with sadness, she went in the direction of Nether-Moynton.

The road was lonely, and after nightfall at this time of the year there was often not a passer for hours. Stockdale pursued his way without hearing a sound beyond that of his own footsteps; and in due time he passed beneath the trees of the plantation which surrounded the Warm'ell Cross-road. Before he had reached the point of intersection he heard voices from the thicket.

'Hoi-hoi-hoi! Help, help!'

The voices were not at all feeble or despairing, but they were unmistakably anxious. Stockdale had no weapon, and before plunging into the pitchy darkness of the plantation he pulled a stake from the hedge, to use in case of need. When he got among the trees he shouted – 'What's the matter – where are you?'

'Here,' answered the voices; and, pushing through the brambles in that direction, he came near the objects of his search.

'Why don't you come forward?' said Stockdale.

'We be tied to the trees!'

'Who are you?'

'Poor Will Latimer the Customs-officer!' said one plaintively. 'Just come and cut these cords, there's a good man. We were afraid nobody would pass by to-night.'

Stockdale soon loosened them, upon which they stretched their limbs and stood at their ease.

'The rascals!' said Latimer, getting now into a rage, though he had seemed quite meek when Stockdale first came up. ' 'Tis the same set of fellows. I know they were Moynton chaps to a man.'

'But we can't swear to 'em,' said another. 'Not one of 'em spoke.'

'What are you going to do?' said Stockdale.

'I'd fain[36] go back to Moynton, and have at 'em again!' said Latimer.

'So would we!' said his comrades.

'Fight till we die!' said Latimer.

'We will, we will!' said his men.

'But,' said Latimer, more frigidly, as they came out of the plantation, 'we don't *know* that these chaps with black faces were Moynton men? And proof is a hard thing.'

'So it is,' said the rest.

'And therefore we won't do nothing at all,' said Latimer, with complete dispassionateness. 'For my part, I'd sooner be them than we. The clitches [37] of my arms are burning like fire from the cords those two strapping women tied round 'em. My opinion is, now I have had time to think o't, that you may serve your Gover'ment at too high a price. For these two nights and days I have not had an hour's rest; and, please God, here's for home-along.'

The other officers agreed heartily to this course; and, thanking Stockdale for his timely assistance, they parted from him at the Cross, taking themselves the western road, and Stockdale going back to Nether-Moynton.

During that walk the minister was lost in reverie of the most painful kind. As soon as he got into the house, and before entering his own rooms, he advanced to the door of the little back parlour in which Lizzy usually sat with her mother. He found her there alone. Stockdale went forward, and, like a man in a dream, looked down upon the table that stood between him and the young woman, who had her bonnet and cloak still on. As he did not speak, she looked up from her chair at him, with misgiving in her eye.

'Where are they gone?' he then said listlessly.

'Who? – I don't know. I have seen nothing of them since. I came straight in here.'

'If your men can manage to get off with those tubs, it will be a great profit to you, I suppose?'

'A share will be mine, a share my cousin Owlett's, a share to each of the two farmers, and a share divided amongst the men who helped us.'

'And you still think,' he went on slowly, 'that you will not give this business up?'

Lizzy rose, and put her hand upon his shoulder. 'Don't ask

that,' she whispered. 'You don't know what you are asking. I must tell you, though I meant not to do it. What I make by that trade is all I have to keep my mother and myself with.'

He was astonished. 'I did not dream of such a thing,' he said. 'I would rather have scraped the roads, had I been you. What is money compared with a clear conscience?'

'My conscience is clear. I know my mother, but the king I have never seen. His dues are nothing to me. But it is a great deal to me that my mother and I should live.'

'Marry me, and promise to give it up. I will keep your mother.'

'It is good of you,' she said, moved a little. 'Let me think of it by myself. I would rather not answer now.'

She reserved her answer till the next day, and came into his room with a solemn face. 'I cannot do what you wished!' she said passionately. 'It is too much to ask. My whole life ha' been passed in this way.' Her words and manner showed that before entering she had been struggling with herself in private, and that the contention had been strong.

Stockdale turned pale, but he spoke quietly. 'Then, Lizzy, we must part. I cannot go against my principles in this matter, and I cannot make my profession a mockery. You know how I love you, and what I would do for you; but this one thing I cannot do.'

'But why should you belong to that profession?' she burst out. 'I have got this large house; why can't you marry me, and live here with us, and not be a Methodist preacher any more? I assure you, Richard, it is no harm, and I wish you could only see it as I do! We only carry it on in winter: in summer it is never done at all. It stirs up one's dull life at this time o' the year, and gives excitement, which I have got so used to now that I should hardly know how to do 'ithout it. At nights, when the wind blows, instead of being dull and stupid, and not noticing whether it do blow or not, your mind is afield, even if you are not afield yourself; and you are wondering how the chaps are getting on; and you walk up and down the room, and look out o' window, and then you go out yourself, and know your way about as well by night as by day, and have hairbreadth escapes from old Latimer and his fellows, who are too stupid ever to really frighten us, and only make us a bit nimble.'

'He frightened you a little last night, anyhow: and I would advise you to drop it before it is worse.'

She shook her head. 'No, I must go on as I have begun. I was born to it. It is in my blood, and I can't be cured. O, Richard, you cannot think what a hard thing you have asked, and how sharp you try me when you put me between this and my love for 'ee!'

Stockdale was leaning with his elbow on the mantelpiece, his hands over his eyes. 'We ought never to have met, Lizzy,' he said. 'It was an ill day for us! I little thought there was anything so hopeless and impossible in our engagement as this. Well, it is too late now to regret consequences in this way. I have had the happiness of seeing you and knowing you at least.'

'You dissent from Church, and I dissent from State,' she said. 'And I don't see why we are not well matched.'

He smiled sadly, while Lizzy remained looking down, her eyes beginning to overflow.

That was an unhappy evening for both of them, and the days that followed were unhappy days. Both she and he went mechanically about their employments, and his depression was marked in the village by more than one of his denomination with whom he came in contact. But Lizzy, who passed her days indoors, was unsuspected of being the cause: for it was generally understood that a quiet engagement to marry existed between her and her cousin Owlett, and had existed for some time.

Thus uncertainly the week passed on; till one morning Stockdale said to her: 'I have had a letter, Lizzy. I must call you that till I am gone.'

'Gone?' said she blankly.

'Yes,' he said. 'I am going from this place. I felt it would be better for us both that I should not stay after what has happened. In fact, I couldn't stay here, and look on you from day to day, without becoming weak and faltering in my course. I have just heard of an arrangement by which the other minister can arrive here in about a week; and let me go elsewhere.'

That he had all this time continued so firmly fixed in his resolution came upon her as a grievous surprise. 'You never loved me!' she said bitterly.

'I might say the same,' he returned; 'but I will not. Grant me one favour. Come and hear my last sermon on the day before I go.'

Lizzy, who was a church-goer on Sunday mornings, frequently attended Stockdale's chapel in the evening with the rest of the double-minded; and she promised.

It became known that Stockdale was going to leave, and a good many people outside his own sect were sorry to hear it. The intervening days flew rapidly away, and on the evening of the Sunday which preceded the morning of his departure Lizzy sat in the chapel to hear him for the last time. The little building was full to overflowing, and he took up the subject which all had expected, that of the contraband trade so extensively practised among them. His hearers, in laying his words to their own hearts, did not perceive that they were more particularly directed against Lizzy, till the sermon waxed warm, and Stockdale nearly broke down with emotion. In truth his own earnestness, and her sad eyes looking up at him, were too much for the young man's equanimity. He hardly knew how he ended. He saw Lizzy, as through a mist, turn and go away with the rest of the congregation; and shortly afterwards followed her home.

She invited him to supper, and they sat down alone, her mother having, as was usual with her on Sunday nights, gone to bed early.

'We will part friends, won't we?' said Lizzy, with forced gaiety, and never alluding to the sermon: a reticence which rather disappointed him.

'We will,' he said, with a forced smile on his part; and they sat down.

It was the first meal that they had ever shared together in their lives, and probably the last that they would so share.

When it was over, and the indifferent conversation could no longer be continued, he arose and took her hand. 'Lizzy,' he said, 'do you say we must part – do you?'

'You do,' she said solemnly. 'I can say no more.'

'Nor I,' said he. 'If that is your answer, good-bye!'

Stockdale bent over her and kissed her, and she involuntarily returned his kiss. 'I shall go early,' he said hurriedly. 'I shall not see you again.'

And he did leave early. He fancied, when stepping forth into the grey morning light, to mount the van which was to carry him away, that he saw a face between the parted curtains of Lizzy's window, but the light was faint, and the panes glistened with wet; so he could not be sure. Stockdale mounted the vehicle, and was gone; and on the following Sunday the new minister preached in the chapel of the Moynton Wesleyans.

One day, two years after the parting, Stockdale, now settled in a midland town, came into Nether-Moynton by carrier in the original way. Jogging along in the van that afternoon he had put questions to the driver, and the answers that he received interested the minister deeply. The result of them was that he went without the least hesitation to the door of his former lodging. It was about six o'clock in the evening, and the same time of year as when he had left; now, too, the ground was damp and glistening, the west was bright, and Lizzy's snowdrops were raising their heads in the border under the wall.

Lizzy must have caught sight of him from the window, for by the time that he reached the door she was there holding it open: and then, as if she had not sufficiently considered her act of coming out, she drew herself back, saying with some constraint, 'Mr Stockdale!'

'You knew it was,' said Stockdale, taking her hand. 'I wrote to say I should call.'

'Yes, but you did not say when,' she answered.

'I did not. I was not quite sure when my business would lead me to these parts.'

'You only came because business brought you near?'

'Well, that is the fact; but I have often thought I should like to come on purpose to see you... But what's all this that has happened? I told you how it would be, Lizzy, and you would not listen to me.'

'I would not,' she said sadly. 'But I had been brought up to that life; and it was second nature to me. However, it is all over now. The officers have blood-money[38] for taking a man dead or alive, and the trade is going to nothing. We were hunted down like rats.'

'Owlett is quite gone, I hear.'

'Yes. He is in America. We had a dreadful struggle that last time, when they tried to take him. It is a perfect miracle that he lived through it; and it is a wonder that I was not killed. I was shot in the hand. It was not by aim; the shot was really meant for my cousin; but I was behind, looking on as usual, and the bullet came to me. It bled terribly, but I got home without fainting; and it healed after a time. You know how he suffered?'

'No,' said Stockdale. 'I only heard that he just escaped with his life.'

'He was shot in the back; but a rib turned the ball. He was badly hurt. We would not let him be took. The men carried him all night across the meads to Kingsbere, and hid him in a barn, dressing his wound as well as they could, till he was so far recovered as to be able to get about. Then he was caught, and tried with the others at the assizes; but they all got off. He had given up his mill for some time; and at last he went to Bristol, and took a passage to America, where he's settled.'

'What do you think of smuggling now?' said the minister gravely.

'I own that we were wrong,' said she. 'But I have suffered for it. I am very poor now, and my mother has been dead these twelve months... But won't you come in, Mr Stockdale?'

Stockdale went in; and it is to be supposed that they came to an understanding; for a fortnight later there was a sale of Lizzy's furniture, and after that a wedding at a chapel in a neighbouring town.

He took her away from her old haunts to the home that he had made for himself in his native county, where she studied her duties as a minister's wife with praiseworthy assiduity. It is said that in after years she wrote an excellent tract called *Render unto Caesar; or, The Repentant Villagers,* in which her own experience was anonymously used as the introductory story. Stockdale got it printed, after making some corrections, and putting in a few powerful sentences of his own; and many hundreds of copies were distributed by the couple in the course of their married life.

AUTHOR'S NOTE. The ending of this story with the marriage of Lizzy and the minister was almost *de rigueur* in an English magazine at the time of writing. But at this late date, thirty years after, it may not be amiss to give the ending that would have been preferred to the writer to the convention used above. Moreover it corresponds more closely with the true incidents of which the tale is a vague and flickering shadow. Lizzy did not, in fact, marry the minister, but – much to her credit in the author's opinion – stuck to Jim the smuggler, and emigrated with him after their marriage, an expatrial step rather forced upon him by his adventurous antecedents. They both died in Wisconsin between 1850 and 1860. (May 1912)

I

THE traveller in school-books, who vouched in dryest tones for the fidelity to fact of the following narrative, used to add a ring of truth to it by opening with a nicety of criticism on the heroine's personality. People were wrong, he declared, when they surmised that Baptista Trewthen was a young woman with scarcely emotions or character. There was nothing in her to love, and nothing to hate – so ran the general opinion. That she showed few positive qualities was true. The colours and tones which changing events paint on the faces of active womankind were looked for in vain upon hers. But still waters run deep; and no crisis had come in the years of her early maidenhood to demonstrate what lay hidden within her, like metal in a mine.

She was the daughter of a small farmer in St Maria's, one of the Isles of Lyonesse beyond Off-Wessex, who had spent a large sum, as there understood, on her education, by sending her to the mainland for two years. At nineteen she was entered at the Training College for Teachers, and at twenty-one nominated to a school in the country, near Tor-upon-Sea, whither she proceeded after the Christmas examination and holidays.

The months passed by from winter to spring and summer, and Baptista applied herself to her new duties as best she could, till an uneventful year had elapsed. Then an air of abstraction pervaded her bearing as she walked to and fro, twice a day, and she showed the traits of a person who had something on her mind. A widow, by name Mrs Wace, in whose house Baptista Trewthen had been provided with a sitting-room and bedroom till the schoolhouse should be built, noticed this change in her youthful tenant's manner, and at last ventured to press her with a few questions.

'It has nothing to do with the place, nor with you,' said Miss Trewthen.

'Then it is the salary?'

'No, nor the salary.'

'Then it is something you have heard from home, my dear.'

Baptista was silent for a few moments. 'It is Mr Heddegan,' she murmured. 'Him they used to call David Heddegan before he got his money.'

'And who is the Mr Heddegan they used to call David?'

'An old bachelor at Giant's Town, St Maria's, with no relations whatever, who lives about a stone's throw from father's. When I was a child he used to take me on his knee and say he'd marry me some day. Now I am a woman the jest has turned earnest, and he is anxious to do it. And father and mother says I can't do better than have him.'

'He's well off?'

'Yes – he's the richest man we know – as a friend and neighbour.'

'How much older did you say he was than yourself?'

'I didn't say. Twenty years at least.'

'And an unpleasant man in the bargain perhaps?'

'No – he's not unpleasant.'

'Well, child, all I can say is that I'd resist any such engagement if it's not palatable to 'ee. You are comfortable here, in my little house, I hope. All the parish like 'ee: and I've never been so cheerful, since my poor husband left me to wear his wings, as I've been with 'ee as my lodger.'

The schoolmistress assured her landlady that she could return the sentiment. 'But here comes my perplexity,' she said. 'I don't like keeping school. Ah, you are surprised – you didn't suspect it. That's because I've concealed my feeling. Well, I simply hate school. I don't care for children – they are unpleasant, troublesome little things, whom nothing would delight so much as to hear that you had fallen down dead. Yet I would even put up with them if it was not for the inspector. For three months before his visit I didn't sleep soundly. And the Committee of Council[1] are always changing the Code,[2] so that you don't know what to teach, and what to leave untaught. I think father and mother are right. They say I shall never excel as a schoolmistress if I dislike the work so, and that therefore I ought to get settled by marrying Mr Heddegan. Between us two, I like him better than school; but I don't like him quite so much as to wish to marry him.'

These conversations, once begun, were continued from day to day; till at length the young girl's elderly friend and land-lady threw in her opinion on the side of Miss Trewthen's parents. All things considered, she declared, the uncertainty of the school, the labour, Baptista's natural dislike for teaching, it would be as well to take what fate offered, and make the best of matters by wedding her father's old neighbour and pros-perous friend.

The Easter holidays came round, and Baptista went to spend them as usual in her native isle, going by train into Off-Wessex and crossing by packet[3] from Pen-zephyr. When she returned in the middle of April her face wore a more settled aspect.

'Well?' said the expectant Mrs Wace.

'I have agreed to have him as my husband,' said Baptista, in an off-hand way. 'Heaven knows if it will be for the best or not. But I have agreed to do it, and so the matter is settled.'

Mrs Wace commended her; but Baptista did not care to dwell on the subject; so that allusion to it was very infrequent be-tween them. Nevertheless, among other things, she repeated to the widow from time to time in monosyllabic remarks that the wedding was really impending; that it was arranged for the summer, and that she had given notice of leaving the school at the August holidays. Later on she announced more specific-ally that her marriage was to take place immediately after her return home at the beginning of the month aforesaid.

She now corresponded regularly with Mr Heddegan. Her letters from him were seen, at least on the outside, and in part within, by Mrs Wace. Had she read more of their interiors than the occasional sentences shown her by Baptista she would have perceived that the scratchy, rusty handwriting of Miss Trew-then's betrothed conveyed little more matter than details of their future housekeeping, and his preparations for the same, with innumerable 'my dears' sprinkled in disconnectedly, to show the depth of his affection without the inconveniences of syntax.

II

It was the end of July – dry, too dry, even for the season, the delicate green herbs and vegetables that grew in this favoured end of the kingdom tasting rather of the watering-pot than of the pure fresh moisture from the skies. Baptista's boxes were packed, and one Saturday morning she departed by a waggonette to the station, and thence by train to Pen-zephyr, from which port she was, as usual, to cross the water immediately to her home, and become Mr Heddegan's wife on the Wednesday of the week following.

She might have returned a week sooner. But though the wedding day had loomed so near, and the banns were out, she delayed her departure till this last moment, saying it was not necessary for her to be at home long beforehand. As Mr Heddegan was older than herself, she said, she was to be married in her ordinary summer bonnet and grey silk frock, and there were no preparations to make that had not been amply made by her parents and intended husband.

In due time, after a hot and tedious journey, she reached Pen-zephyr. She here obtained some refreshment, and then went towards the pier, where she learnt to her surprise that the little steamboat plying between the town and the islands had left at eleven o'clock; the usual hour of departure in the afternoon having been forestalled in consequence of the fogs which had for a few days prevailed towards evening, making twilight navigation dangerous.

This being Saturday, there was now no other boat till Tuesday, and it became obvious that here she would have to remain for the three days, unless her friends should think fit to rig out one of the island sailing-boats and come to fetch her – a not very likely contingency, the sea distance being nearly forty miles.

Baptista, however, had been detained in Pen-zephyr on more

than one occasion before, either on account of bad weather or some such reason as the present, and she was therefore not in any personal alarm. But, as she was to be married on the following Wednesday, the delay was certainly inconvenient to a more than ordinary degree, since it would leave less than a day's interval between her arrival and the wedding ceremony.

Apart from this awkwardness she did not much mind the accident. It was indeed curious to see how little she minded. Perhaps it would not be too much to say that, although she was going to do the critical deed of her life quite willingly, she experienced an indefinable relief at the postponement of her meeting with Heddegan. But her manner after making discovery of the hindrance was quiet and subdued, even to passivity itself; as was instanced by her having, at the moment of receiving information that the steamer had sailed, replied 'Oh,' so coolly to the porter with her luggage, that he was almost disappointed at her lack of disappointment.

The question now was, should she return again to Mrs Wace, in the village of Lower Wessex, or wait in the town at which she had arrived. She would have preferred to go back, but the distance was too great; moreover, having left the place for good, and somewhat dramatically, to become a bride, a return, even for so short a space, would have been a trifle humiliating.

Leaving, then, her boxes at the station, her next anxiety was to secure a respectable, or rather genteel, lodging in the popular seaside resort confronting her. To this end she looked about the town, in which, though she had passed through it half-a-dozen times, she was practically a stranger.

Baptista found a room to suit her over a fruiterer's shop; where she made herself at home, and set herself in order after her journey. An early cup of tea having revived her spirits she walked out to reconnoitre.

Being a schoolmistress she avoided looking at the schools, and having a sort of trade connection with books, she avoided looking at the booksellers; but wearying of the other shops she inspected the churches; not that for her own part she cared much about ecclesiastical edifices; but tourists looked at them, and so would she – a proceeding for which no one would have

credited her with any great originality, such, for instance, as
that she subsequently showed herself to possess. The churches
soon oppressed her. She tried the Museum, but came out because it seemed lonely and tedious.

Yet the town and the walks in this land of strawberries, these
headquarters of early English flowers and fruit, were then, as
always, attractive. From the more picturesque streets she went
to the town gardens, and the Pier, and the Harbour, and looked
at the men at work there, loading and unloading as in the time
of the Phoenicians.[4]

'Not Baptista? Yes, Baptista it is!'

The words were uttered behind her. Turning round she gave
a start, and became confused, even agitated, for a moment.
Then she said in her usual undemonstrative manner, 'O – is it
really you, Charles?'

Without speaking again at once, and with a half-smile, the
new-comer glanced her over. There was much criticism, and
some resentment – even temper – in his eye.

'I am going home,' continued she. 'But I have missed the
boat.'

He scarcely seemed to take in the meaning of this explanation, in the intensity of his critical survey. 'Teaching still? What
a fine schoolmistress you make, Baptista, I warrant!' he said
with a slight flavour of sarcasm, which was not lost upon her.

'I know I am nothing to brag of,' she replied. 'That's why I
have given up.'

'O – given up? You astonish me.'

'I hate the profession.'

'Perhaps that's because I am in it.'

'O no, it isn't. But I am going to enter on another life altogether. I am going to be married next week to Mr David Heddegan.'

The young man – fortified as he was by a natural cynical
pride and passionateness – winced at this unexpected reply,
notwithstanding.

'Who is Mr David Heddegan?' he asked, as indifferently as
lay in his power.

She informed him the bearer of the name was a general merchant of Giant's Town, St Maria's Island – her father's nearest neighbour and oldest friend.

'Then we shan't see anything more of you on the mainland?' inquired the schoolmaster.

'O, I don't know about that,' said Miss Trewthen.

'Here endeth the career of the belle of the boarding-school your father was foolish enough to send you to. A "general merchant's" wife in the Lyonesse Isles. Will you sell pounds of soap and pennyworths of tin tacks, or whole bars of saponaceous matter,⁵ and great tenpenny nails?'

'He's not in such a small way as that!' she almost pleaded. 'He owns ships, though they are rather little ones!'

'O, well, it is much the same. Come, let us walk on; it is tedious to stand still. I thought you would be a failure in education,' he continued, when she obeyed him and strolled ahead. 'You never showed power that way. You remind me much of some of those women who think they are sure to be great actresses if they go on the stage, because they have a pretty face, and forget that what we require is acting. But you found your mistake, didn't you?'

'Don't taunt me, Charles.' It was noticeable that the young schoolmaster's tone caused her no anger or retaliatory passion; far otherwise: there was a tear in her eye. 'How is it you are at Pen-zephyr?' she inquired.

'I don't taunt you. I speak the truth, purely in a friendly way, as I should to any one I wished well. Though for that matter I might have some excuse even for taunting you. Such a terrible hurry as you've been in. I hate a woman who is in such a hurry.'

'How do you mean that?'

'Why – to be somebody's wife or other – anything's wife rather than nobody's. You couldn't wait for me, O, no. Well, thank God, I'm cured of all that!'

'How merciless you are!' she said bitterly. 'Wait for you? What does that mean, Charley? You never showed – anything to wait for – anything special towards me.'

'O come, Baptista dear; come!'

'What I mean is, nothing definite,' she expostulated. 'I suppose you liked me a little; but it seemed to me to be only a pastime on your part, and that you never meant to make an honourable engagement of it.'

'There, that's just it! You girls expect a man to mean business at the first look. No man when he first becomes interested in a woman has any definite scheme of engagement to marry her in his mind, unless he is meaning a vulgar mercenary marriage. However, I *did* at last mean an honourable engagement, as you call it, come to that.'

'But you never said so, and an indefinite courtship soon injures a woman's position and credit, sooner than you think.'

'Baptista, I solemnly declare that in six months I should have asked you to marry me.'

She walked along in silence, looking on the ground, and appearing very uncomfortable. Presently he said, 'Would you have waited for me if you had known?' To this she whispered in a sorrowful whisper, 'Yes!'

They went still farther in silence – passing along one of the beautiful walks on the outskirts of the town, yet not observant of scene or situation. Her shoulder and his were close together, and he clasped his fingers round the small of her arm – quite lightly, and without any attempt at impetus; yet the act seemed to say, 'Now I hold you, and my will must be yours.'

Recurring to a previous question of hers he said, 'I have merely run down here for a day or two from school near Trufal, before going off to the north for the rest of my holiday. I have seen my relations at Redrutin quite lately, so I am not going there this time. How little I thought of meeting you! How very different the circumstances would have been if, instead of parting again as we must in half-an-hour or so, possibly for ever, you had been now just going off with me, as my wife, on our honeymoon trip. Ha – ha – well – so humorous is life!'

She stopped suddenly. 'I must go back now – this is altogether too painful, Charley! It is not at all a kind mood you are in to-day.'

'I don't want to pain you – you know I do not,' he said more gently. 'Only it just exasperates me – this you are going to do. I wish you would not.'

'What?'

'Marry him. There, now I have showed you my true sentiments.'

'I must do it now,' said she.

'Why?' he asked, dropping the off-hand masterful tone he
had hitherto spoken in, and becoming earnest; still holding her
arm, however, as if she were his chattel to be taken up or put
down at will. 'It is never too late to break off a marriage that's
distasteful to you. Now I'll say one thing; and it is truth: I
wish you would marry me instead of him, even now, at the last
moment, though you have served me so badly.'

'O, it is not possible to think of that!' she answered hastily,
shaking her head. 'When I get home all will be prepared – it is
ready even now – the things for the party, the furniture, Mr
Heddegan's new suit, and everything. I should require the
courage of a tropical lion to go home there and say I wouldn't
carry out my promise!'

'Then go, in Heaven's name! But there would be no necessity
for you to go home and face them in that way. If we were to
marry, it would have to be at once, instantly; or not at all. I
should think your affection not worth the having unless you
agreed to come back with me to Trufal this evening, where we
could be married by licence on Monday morning. And then no
Mr David Heddegan or anybody else could get you away from
me.'

'I must go home by the Tuesday boat,' she faltered. 'What
would they think if I did not come?'

'You could go home by that boat just the same. All the difference would be that I should go with you. You could leave me
on the quay, where I'd have a smoke, while you went and saw
your father and mother privately; you could then tell them
what you had done, and that I was waiting not far off; that I
was a schoolmaster in a fairly good position, and a young man
you had known when you were at the Training College. Then I
would come boldly forward; and they would see that it could
not be altered, and so you wouldn't suffer a lifelong misery by
being the wife of a wretched old gaffer you don't like at all.
Now, honestly; you do like me best, don't you, Baptista?'

'Yes.'

'Then we will do as I say.'

She did not pronounce a clear affirmative. But that she consented to the novel proposition at some moment or other of that walk was apparent by what occurred a little later.

III

An enterprise of such pith required, indeed, less talking than consideration. The first thing they did in carrying it out was to return to the railway station, where Baptista took from her luggage a small trunk of immediate necessaries which she would in any case have required after missing the boat. That same afternoon they travelled up the line to Trufal.

Charles Stow (as his name was), despite his disdainful indifference to things, was very careful of appearances, and made the journey independently of her though in the same train. He told her where she could get board and lodgings in the city; and with merely a distant nod to her of a provisional kind, went off to his own quarters, and to see about the licence.

On Sunday she saw him in the morning across the nave of the pro-cathedral. In the afternoon they walked together in the fields, where he told her that the licence would be ready next day, and would be available the day after, when the ceremony could be performed as early after eight o'clock as they should choose.

His courtship, thus renewed after an interval of two years, was as impetuous, violent even, as it was short. The next day came and passed, and the final arrangements were made. Their agreement was to get the ceremony over as soon as they possibly could the next morning, so as to go on to Pen-zephyr at once, and reach that place in time for the boat's departure the same day. It was in obedience to Baptista's earnest request that Stow consented thus to make the whole journey to Lyonesse by land and water at one heat, and not break it at Pen-zephyr; she seemed to be oppressed with a dread of lingering anywhere, this great first act of disobedience to her parents once accomplished, with the weight on her mind that her home had to be convulsed by the disclosure of it. To face her difficulties over the water immediately she had created them was, however, a course more desired by Baptista than by her lover; though for once he gave way.

The next morning was bright and warm as those which had preceded it. By six o'clock it seemed nearly noon, as is often the case in that part of England in the summer season. By nine they were husband and wife. They packed up and departed by the earliest train after the service; and on the way discussed at length what she should say on meeting her parents, Charley dictating the turn of each phrase. In her anxiety they had travelled so early that when they reached Pen-zephyr they found there were nearly two hours on their hands before the steamer's time of sailing.

Baptista was extremely reluctant to be seen promenading the streets of the watering-place with her husband till, as above stated, the household at Giant's Town should know the unexpected course of events from her own lips; and it was just possible, if not likely, that some Lyonessian might be prowling about there, or even have come across the sea to look for her. To meet any one to whom she was known, and to have to reply to awkward questions about the strange young man at her side before her well-framed announcement had been delivered at proper time and place, was a thing she could not contemplate with equanimity. So, instead of looking at the shops and harbour, they went along the coast a little way.

The heat of the morning was by this time intense. They clambered up on some cliffs, and while sitting there, looking around at St Michael's Mount and other objects, Charles said to her that he thought he would run down to the beach at their feet, and take just one plunge into the sea.

Baptista did not much like the idea of being left alone; it was gloomy, she said. But he assured her he would not be gone more than a quarter of an hour at the outside, and she passively assented.

Down he went, disappeared, appeared again, and looked back. Then he again proceeded, and vanished, till, as a small waxen object, she saw him emerge from the nook that had screened him, cross the white fringe of foam, and walk into the undulating mass of blue. Once in the water he seemed less inclined to hurry than before; he remained a long time; and, unable either to appreciate his skill or criticize his want of it at that distance, she withdrew her eyes from the spot, and gazed at the still outline of St Michael's – now beautifully toned in grey.

Her anxiety for the hour of departure, and to cope at once with the approaching incidents that she would have to manipulate as best she could, sent her into a reverie. It was now Tuesday; she would reach home in the evening – a very late time they would say; but, as the delay was a pure accident, they would deem her marriage to Mr Heddegan to-morrow still practicable. Then Charles would have to be produced from the background. It was a terrible undertaking to think of, and she almost regretted her temerity in wedding so hastily that morning. The rage of her father would be so crushing; the reproaches of her mother so bitter; and perhaps Charles would answer hotly, and perhaps cause estrangement till death. There had obviously been no alarm about her at St Maria's, or somebody would have sailed across to inquire for her. She had, in a letter written at the beginning of the week, spoken of the hour at which she intended to leave her country schoolhouse; and from this her friends had probably perceived that by such timing she would run a risk of losing the Saturday boat. She had missed it, and as a consequence sat here on the shore as Mrs Charles Stow.

This brought her to the present, and she turned from the outline of St Michael's Mount to look about for her husband's form. He was, as far as she could discover, no longer in the sea. Then he was dressing. By moving a few steps she could see where his clothes lay. But Charles was not beside them.

Baptista looked back again at the water in bewilderment, as if her senses were the victim of some sleight of hand. Not a speck or spot resembling a man's head or face showed anywhere. By this time she was alarmed, and her alarm intensified when she perceived a little beyond the scene of her husband's bathing a small area of water, the quality of whose surface

differed from that of the surrounding expanse as the coarse vegetation of some foul patch in a mead differs from the fine green
of the remainder. Elsewhere it looked flexuous,[6] here it looked
vermiculated[7] and lumpy, and her marine experiences suggested to her in a moment that two currents met and caused a
turmoil at this place.

She descended as hastily as her trembling limbs would
allow. The way down was terribly long, and before reaching
the heap of clothes it occurred to her that, after all, it would
be best to run first for help. Hastening along in a lateral direction she proceeded inland till she met a man, and soon afterwards two others. To them she exclaimed, 'I think a gentleman
who was bathing is in some danger. I cannot see him as I could.
Will you please run and help him, at once, if you will be so
kind?'

She did not think of turning to show them the exact spot,
indicating it vaguely by the direction of her hand, and still
going on her way with the idea of gaining more assistance.
When she deemed, in her faintness, that she had carried the
alarm far enough, she faced about and dragged herself back
again. Before reaching the now dreaded spot she met one of the
men.

'We can see nothing at all, Miss,' he declared.

Having gained the beach, she found the tide in, and no sign
of Charley's clothes. The other men whom she had besought
to come had disappeared, it must have been in some other
direction, for she had not met them going away. They, finding
nothing, had probably thought her alarm a mere conjecture,
and given up the quest.

Baptista sank down upon the stones near at hand. Where
Charley had undressed was now sea. There could not be the
least doubt that he was drowned, and his body sucked under by
the current; while his clothes, lying within high-water mark,
had probably been carried away by the rising tide.

She remained in a stupor for some minutes, till a strange
sensation succeeded the aforesaid perceptions, mystifying her
intelligence, and leaving her physically almost inert. With his
personal disappearance, the last three days of her life with him

seemed to be swallowed up, also his image, in her mind's eye, waned curiously, receded far away, grew stranger and stranger, less and less real. Their meeting and marriage had been so sudden, unpremeditated, adventurous, that she could hardly believe that she had played her part in such a reckless drama. Of all the few hours of her life with Charles, the portion that most insisted in coming back to memory was their fortuitous encounter on the previous Saturday, and those bitter reprimands with which he had begun the attack, as it might be called, which had piqued her to an unexpected consummation.

A sort of cruelty, an imperiousness, even in his warmth, had characterized Charles Stow. As a lover he had ever been a bit of a tyrant; and it might pretty truly have been said that he had stung her into marriage with him at last. Still more alien from her life did these reflections operate to make him; and then they would be chased away by an interval of passionate weeping and mad regret. Finally, there returned upon the confused mind of the young wife the recollection that she was on her way homeward, and that the packet would sail in three-quarters of an hour.

Except the parasol in her hand, all she possessed was at the station awaiting her onward journey.

She looked in that direction; and, entering one of those undemonstrative phases so common with her, walked quietly on.

At first she made straight for the railway; but suddenly turning she went to a shop and wrote an anonymous line announcing his death by drowning to the only person she had ever heard Charles mention as a relative. Posting this stealthily, and with a fearful look around her, she seemed to acquire a terror of the late events, pursuing her way to the station as if followed by a spectre.

When she got to the office she asked for the luggage that she had left there on the Saturday as well as the trunk left on the morning just lapsed. All were put in the boat, and she herself followed. Quickly as these things had been done, the whole proceeding, nevertheless, had been almost automatic on Baptista's part, ere she had come to any definite conclusion on her course.

Just before the bell rang she heard a conversation on the pier, which removed the last shade of doubt from her mind, if any had existed, that she was Charles Stow's widow. The sentences were but fragmentary, but she could easily piece them out.

'A man drowned – swam out too far – was a stranger to the place – people in boat – saw him go down – couldn't get there in time.'

The news was little more definite than this as yet: though it may as well be stated once for all that the statement was true. Charley, with the over-confidence of his nature, had ventured out too far for his strength, and succumbed in the absence of assistance, his lifeless body being at that moment suspended in the transparent mid-depths of the bay. His clothes, however, had merely been gently lifted by the rising tide, and floated into a nook hard by, where they lay out of sight of the passers-by till a day or two after.

IV

In ten minutes they were steaming out of the harbour for their voyage of four or five hours, at whose ending she would have to tell her strange story.

As Pen-zephyr and all its environing scenes disappeared behind Mousehole and St Clement's Isle, Baptista's ephemeral, meteor-like husband impressed her yet more as a fantasy. She was still in such a trance-like state that she had been an hour on the little packet-boat before she became aware of the agitating fact that Mr Heddegan was on board with her. Involuntarily she slipped from her left hand the symbol of her wifehood.

'Hee-hee! Well, the truth is, I wouldn't interrupt 'ee. "I reckon she don't see me, or won't see me," I said, "and what's the hurry? She'll see enough o' me soon!" I hope ye be well, mee deer?'

He was a hale, well-conditioned man of about five and fifty, of the complexion common to those whose lives are passed on the bluffs and beaches of an ocean isle. He extended the four quarters of his face in a genial smile, and his hand for a grasp of the same magnitude. She gave her own in surprised docility, and he continued:

'I couldn't help coming across to meet 'ee. What an unfortunate thing you missing the boat and not coming Saturday! They meant to have warned 'ee that the time was changed, but forgot it at the last moment. The truth is that I should have informed 'ee myself, but I was that busy finishing up a job last week, so as to have this week free, that I trusted to your father for attending to these little things. However, so plain and quiet as it is all to be, it really do not matter so much as it might otherwise have done, and I hope ye haven't been greatly put out. Now, if you'd sooner that I should not be seen talking to 'ee – if 'ee feel shy at all before strangers – just say. I'll leave 'ee to yourself till we get home.'

'Thank you much. I am indeed a little tired, Mr Heddegan.'

He nodded urbane acquiescence, strolled away immediately, and minutely inspected the surface of the funnel, till some female passengers of Giant's Town tittered at what they must have thought a rebuff – for the approaching wedding was known to many on St Maria's Island, though to nobody elsewhere. Baptista coloured at their satire, and called him back, and forced herself to commune with him in at least a mechanically friendly manner.

The opening event had been thus different from her expectation, and she had adumbrated no act to meet it. Taken aback she passively allowed circumstances to pilot her along; and so the voyage was made.

It was near dusk when they touched the pier of Giant's Town, where several friends and neighbours stood awaiting them. Her father had a lantern in his hand. Her mother, too, was there, reproachfully glad that the delay had at last ended so simply. Mrs Trewthen and her daughter went together along the Giant's Walk, or promenade, to the house, rather in advance of her husband and Mr Heddegan, who talked in loud tones which reached the women over their shoulders.

Some would have called Mrs Trewthen a good mother; but

though well meaning she was maladroit, and her intentions missed their mark. This might have been partly attributable to the slight deafness from which she suffered. Now, as usual, the chief utterances came from her lips.

'Ah, yes, I'm so glad, my child, that you've got over safe. It is all ready, and everything so well arranged, that nothing but misfortune could hinder you settling as, with God's grace, becomes 'ee. Close to your mother's door a'most, 'twill be a great blessing, I'm sure; and I was very glad to find from your letters that you'd held your word sacred. That's right – make your word your bond always. Mrs Wace seems to be a sensible woman. I hope the Lord will do for her as he's doing for you no long time hence. And how did 'ee get over the terrible journey from Tor-upon-Sea to Pen-zephyr? Once you'd done with the railway, of course, you seemed quite at home. Well, Baptista, conduct yourself seemly, and all will be well.'

Thus admonished, Baptista entered the house, her father and Mr Heddegan immediately at her back. Her mother had been so didactic that she had felt herself absolutely unable to broach the subjects in the centre of her mind.

The familiar room, with the dark ceiling, the well-spread table, the old chairs, had never before spoken so eloquently of the times ere she knew or had heard of Charley Stow. She went upstairs to take off her things, her mother remaining below to complete the disposition of the supper, and attend to the preparation of to-morrow's meal, altogether composing such an array of pies, from pies of fish to pies of turnips, as was never heard of outside the Western Duchy.[8] Baptista, once alone, sat down and did nothing; and was called before she had taken off her bonnet.

'I'm coming,' she cried, jumping up, and speedily disapparelling herself, brushed her hair with a few touches and went down.

Two or three of Mr Heddegan's and her father's friends had dropped in, and expressed their sympathy for the delay she had been subjected to. The meal was a most merry one except to Baptista. She had desired privacy, and there was none; and to break the news was already a greater difficulty than it had been at first. Everything around her, animate and inanimate, great and small, insisted that she had come home to be married; and she could not get a chance to say nay.

One or two people sang songs, as overtures to the melody of the morrow, till at length bedtime came, and they all withdrew, her mother having retired a little earlier. When Baptista found herself again alone in her bedroom the case stood as before: she had come home with much to say, and she had said nothing.

It was now growing clear even to herself that Charles being dead, she had not determination sufficient within her to break tidings which, had he been alive, would have imperatively announced themselves. And thus with the stroke of midnight came the turning of the scale; her story should remain untold. It was not that upon the whole she thought it best not to attempt to tell it; but that she could not undertake so explosive a matter. To stop the wedding now would cause a convulsion in Giant's Town little short of volcanic. Weakened, tired, and terrified as she had been by the day's adventures, she could not make herself the author of such a catastrophe. But how refuse Heddegan without telling? It really seemed to her as if her marriage with Mr Heddegan were about to take place as if nothing had intervened.

Morning came. The events of the previous days were cut off from her present existence by scene and sentiment more completely than ever. Charles Stow had grown to be a special being of whom, owing to his character, she entertained rather fearful than loving memory. Baptista could hear when she awoke that her parents were already moving about downstairs. But she did not rise till her mother's rather rough voice resounded up the staircase as it had done on the preceding evening.

'Baptista! Come, time to be stirring! The man will be here, by Heaven's blessing, in three-quarters of an hour. He has looked in already for a minute or two – and says he's going to the church to see if things be well forward.'

Baptista arose, looked out of the window, and took the easy course. When she emerged from the regions above she was arrayed in her new silk frock and best stockings, wearing a linen jacket over the former for breakfasting, and her common slippers over the latter, not to spoil the new ones on the rough precincts of the dwelling.

It is unnecessary to dwell at any great length on this part of the morning's proceedings. She revealed nothing; and married Heddegan, as she had given her word to do, on that appointed August day.

v

Mr Heddegan forgave the coldness of his bride's manner during and after the wedding ceremony, full well aware that there had been considerable reluctance on her part to acquiesce in this neighbourly arrangement, and, as a philosopher of long standing, holding that whatever Baptista's attitude now, the conditions would probably be much the same six months hence as those which ruled among other married couples.

An absolutely unexpected shock was given to Baptista's listless mind about an hour after the wedding service. They had nearly finished the mid-day dinner when the now husband said to her father, 'We think of starting about two. And the breeze being so fair we shall bring up inside Pen-zephyr new pier about six at least.'

'What – are we going to Pen-zephyr?' said Baptista. 'I don't know anything of it.'

'Didn't you tell her?' asked her father of Heddegan.

It transpired that, owing to the delay in her arrival, this proposal too, among other things, had in the hurry not been mentioned to her, except some time ago as a general suggestion that they would go somewhere. Heddegan had imagined that any trip would be pleasant, and one to the mainland the pleasantest of all.

She looked so distressed at the announcement that her husband willingly offered to give it up, though he had not had a holiday off the island for a whole year. Then she pondered on the inconvenience of staying at Giant's Town, where all the inhabitants were bonded by the circumstances of their situation, into a sort of family party, which permitted and encouraged on such occasions as these oral criticism that was apt to disturb the equanimity of newly married girls, and would especially worry Baptista in her strange situation. Hence, unexpectedly, she agreed not to disorganize her husband's plans for the wedding jaunt, and it was settled that, as originally intended, they should proceed in a neighbour's sailing boat to the metropolis of the district.

In this way they arrived at Pen-zephyr without difficulty or mishap. Bidding adieu to Jenkin and his man, who had sailed them over, they strolled arm in arm off the pier, Baptista silent, cold, and obedient. Heddegan had arranged to take her as far as Plymouth before their return, but to go no further than where they had landed that day. Their first business was to find an inn; and in this they had unexpected difficulty, since for some reason or other – possibly the fine weather – many of the nearest at hand were full of tourists and commercial travellers. He led her on till he reached a tavern which, though comparatively unpretending, stood in as attractive a spot as any in the town; and this, somewhat to their surprise after their previous experience, they found apparently empty. The considerate old man, thinking that Baptista was educated to artistic notions, though he himself was deficient in them, had decided that it was most desirable to have, on such an occasion as the present, an apartment with 'a good view' (the expression being one he had often heard in use among tourists); and he therefore asked for a favourite room on the first floor, from which a bow-window protruded, for the express purpose of affording such an outlook.

The landlady, after some hesitation, said she was sorry that particular apartment was engaged; the next one, however, or any other in the house, was unoccupied.

'The gentleman who has the best one will give it up to-morrow, and then you can change into it,' she added, as Mr Heddegan hesitated about taking the adjoining and less commanding one.

'We shall be gone to-morrow, and shan't want it,' he said.

Wishing not to lose customers, the landlady earnestly continued that since he was bent on having the best room, perhaps the other gentleman would not object to move at once into the one they despised, since, though nothing could be seen from the window, the room was equally large.

'Well, if he doesn't care for a view,' said Mr Heddegan, with the air of a highly artistic man who did.

'O no – I am sure he doesn't,' she said. 'I can promise that you shall have the room you want. If you would not object to go for a walk for half an hour, I could have it ready, and your things in it, and a nice tea laid in the bow-window by the time you come back?'

This proposal was deemed satisfactory by the fussy old tradesman, and they went out. Baptista nervously conducted him in an opposite direction to her walk of the former day in other company, showing on her wan face, had he observed it, how much she was beginning to regret her sacrificial step for mending matters that morning.

She took advantage of a moment when her husband's back was turned to inquire casually in a shop if anything had been heard of the gentleman who was sucked down in the eddy while bathing.

The shopman said, 'Yes, his body has been washed ashore,' and had just handed Baptista a newspaper on which she discerned the heading, 'A Schoolmaster drowned while bathing,' when her husband turned to join her. She might have pursued the subject without raising suspicion; but it was more than flesh and blood could do, and completing a small purchase almost ran out of the shop.

'What is your terrible hurry, mee deer?' said Heddegan, hastening after.

'I don't know – I don't want to stay in shops,' she gasped.

'And we won't,' he said. 'They are suffocating this weather. Let's go back and have some tay!'[9]

They found the much desired apartment awaiting their entry. It was a sort of combination bed and sitting-room, and the table was prettily spread with high tea in the bow-window, a bunch of flowers in the midst, and a best-parlour chair on each side. Here they shared the meal by the ruddy light of the vanishing sun. But though the view had been engaged, regardless of expense, exclusively for Baptista's pleasure, she did not direct any keen attention out of the window. Her gaze as often fell on the floor and walls of the room as elsewhere, and on the table as much as on either, beholding nothing at all.

But there was a change. Opposite her seat was the door, upon which her eyes presently became riveted like those of a little bird upon a snake. For, on a peg at the back of the door, there hung a hat; such a hat – surely, from its peculiar make, the actual hat – that had been worn by Charles. Conviction grew to certainty when she saw a railway ticket sticking up from the band. Charles had put the ticket there – she had noticed the act.

Her teeth almost chattered; she murmured something incoherent. Her husband jumped up and said, 'You are not well! What is it? What shall I get 'ee?'

'Smelling salts!' she said, quickly and desperately; 'at that chemist's shop you were in just now.'

He jumped up like the anxious old man that he was, caught up his own hat from a back table, and without observing the other hastened out and downstairs.

Left alone she gazed and gazed at the back of the door, then spasmodically rang the bell. An honest-looking country maidservant appeared in response.

'A hat!' murmured Baptista, pointing with her finger. 'It does not belong to us.'

'O yes, I'll take it away,' said the young woman with some hurry. 'It belongs to the other gentleman.'

She spoke with a certain awkwardness, and took the hat out of the room. Baptista had recovered her outward composure. 'The other gentleman?' she said. 'Where is the other gentleman?'

'He's in the next room, ma'am. He removed out of this to oblige 'ee.'

'How can you say so? I should hear him if he were there,' said Baptista, sufficiently recovered to argue down an apparent untruth.

'He's there,' said the girl, hardily.

'Then it is strange that he makes no noise,' said Mrs Heddegan, convicting the girl of falsity by a look.

'He makes no noise; but it is not strange,' said the servant.

All at once a dread took possession of the bride's heart, like a cold hand laid thereon; for it flashed upon her that there was a possibility of reconciling the girl's statement with her own knowledge of facts.

'Why does he make no noise?' she weakly said.

The waiting-maid was silent, and looked at her questioner. 'If I tell you, ma'am, you won't tell missis?' she whispered.

Baptista promised.

'Because he's a-lying dead!' said the girl. 'He's the schoolmaster that was drownded yesterday.'

'O!' said the bride, covering her eyes. 'Then he was in this room till just now?'

'Yes,' said the maid, thinking the young lady's agitation natural enough. 'And I told missis that I thought she oughtn't to have done it, because I don't hold it right to keep visitors so much in the dark where death's concerned; but she said the gentleman didn't die of anything infectious; she was a poor, honest, innkeeper's wife, she says, who had to get her living by making hay while the sun sheened. And owing to the drownded gentleman being brought here, she said, it kept so many people away that we were empty, though all the other houses were full. So when your good man set his mind upon the room, and she would have lost good paying folk if he'd not had it, it wasn't to be supposed, she said, that she'd let anything stand in the way. Ye won't say that I've told ye, please m'm? All the linen has been changed, and as the inquest won't be till tomorrow, after you are gone, she thought you wouldn't know a word of it, being strangers here.'

The returning footsteps of her husband broke off further narration. Baptista waved her hand, for she could not speak. The waiting-maid quickly withdrew, and Mr Heddegan entered with the smelling salts and other nostrums.[10]

'Any better?' he questioned.

'I don't like the hotel,' she exclaimed, almost simultaneously. 'I can't bear it — it doesn't suit me!'

'Is that all that's the matter?' he returned pettishly (this being the first time of his showing such a mood). 'Upon my heart and life such trifling is trying to any man's temper, Baptista! Sending me about from here to yond, and then when I come back saying 'ee don't like the place that I have sunk so much money and words to get for 'ee. 'Od dang it all, 'tis enough to – But I won't say any more at present, mee deer, though it is just too much to expect to turn out of the house now. We shan't get another quiet place at this time of the evening – every other inn in the town is bustling with rackety folk of one sort and t'other, while here 'tis as quiet as the grave – the country, I would say. So bide still, d'ye hear, and tomorrow we shall be out of the town altogether – as early as you like.'

The obstinacy of age had, in short, overmastered its complaisance, and the young woman said no more. The simple course of telling him that in the adjoining room lay a corpse which had lately occupied their own might, it would have seemed, have been an effectual one without further disclosure, but to allude to *that* subject, however it was disguised, was more than Heddegan's young wife had strength for. Horror broke her down. In the contingency one thing only presented itself to her paralyzed regard – that here she was doomed to abide, in a hideous contiguity to the dead husband and the living, and her conjecture did, in fact, bear itself out. That night she lay between the two men she had married – Heddegan on the one hand, and on the other through the partition against which the bed stood, Charles Stow.

VI

Kindly time had withdrawn the foregoing event three days from the present of Baptista Heddegan. It was ten o'clock in the morning; she had been ill, not in an ordinary or definite sense, but in a state of cold stupefaction, from which it was difficult to arouse her so much as to say a few sentences. When questioned she had replied that she was pretty well.

Their trip, as such, had been something of a failure. They had gone on as far as Falmouth, but here he had given way to her entreaties to return home. This they could not very well do without repassing through Pen-zephyr, at which place they had now again arrived.

In the train she had seen a weekly local paper, and read there a paragraph detailing the inquest on Charles. It was added that the funeral was to take place at his native town of Redrutin on Friday.

After reading this she had shown no reluctance to enter the fatal neighbourhood of the tragedy, only stipulating that they should take their rest at a different lodging from the first; and now comparatively braced up and calm – indeed a cooler creature altogether than when last in the town, she said to David that she wanted to walk out for a while, as they had plenty of time on their hands.

'To a shop as usual, I suppose, mee deer?'

'Partly for shopping,' she said. 'And it will be best for you, dear, to stay in after trotting about so much, and have a good rest while I am gone.'

He assented; and Baptista sallied forth. As she had stated, her first visit was made to a shop, a draper's. Without the exercise of much choice she purchased a black bonnet and veil, also a black stuff gown; a black mantle she already wore. These articles were made up into a parcel which, in spite of the saleswoman's offers, her customer said she would take with her. Bearing it on her arm she turned to the railway, and at the station got a ticket for Redrutin.

Thus it appeared that, on her recovery from the paralyzed mood of the former day, while she had resolved not to blast utterly the happiness of her present husband by revealing the history of the departed one, she had also determined to indulge a certain odd, inconsequent, feminine sentiment of decency, to the small extent to which it could do no harm to any person. At Redrutin she emerged from the railway carriage in the black attire purchased at the shop, having during the transit made the change in the empty compartment she had chosen. The other clothes were now in the bandbox[11] and parcel. Leaving these at the cloak-room she proceeded onward, and after a wary survey reached the side of a hill whence a view of the burial ground could be obtained.

It was now a little before two o'clock. While Baptista waited a funeral procession ascended the road. Baptista hastened across, and by the time the procession entered the cemetery gates she had unobtrusively joined it.

In addition to the schoolmaster's own relatives (not a few), the paragraph in the newspapers of his death by drowning had drawn together many neighbours, acquaintances, and on-lookers. Among them she passed unnoticed, and with a quiet step pursued the winding path to the chapel, and afterwards thence to the grave. When all was over, and the relatives and idlers had withdrawn, she stepped to the edge of the chasm. From beneath her mantle she drew a little bunch of forget-me-nots, and dropped them in upon the coffin. In a few minutes she also turned and went away from the cemetery. By five o'clock she was again in Pen-zephyr.

'You have been a mortal long time!' said her husband, crossly. 'I allowed you an hour at most, mee deer.'

'It occupied me longer,' said she.

'Well – I reckon it is wasting words to complain. Hang it, ye look so tired and wisht[12] that I can't find heart to say what I would!'

'I am – weary and wisht, David; I am. We can get home to-morrow for certain, I hope?'

'We can. And please God we will!' said Mr Heddegan heartily, as if he too were weary of his brief honeymoon. 'I must be into business again on Monday morning at latest.'

They left by the next morning steamer, and in the afternoon took up their residence in their own house at Giant's Town.

The hour that she reached the island it was as if a material weight had been removed from Baptista's shoulders. Her husband attributed the change to the influence of the local breezes after the hot-house atmosphere of the mainland. However that might be, settled here, a few doors from her mother's dwelling, she recovered in no very long time much of her cus-tomary bearing, which was never very demonstrative. She accepted her position calmly, and faintly smiled when her neighbours learned to call her Mrs Heddegan, and said she seemed likely to become the leader of fashion in Giant's Town.

Her husband was a man who had made considerably more money by trade than her father had done: and perhaps the greater profusion of surroundings at her command than she had heretofore been mistress of, was not without an effect upon her. One week, two weeks, three weeks passed; and, being pre-eminently a young woman who allowed things to drift, she did nothing whatever either to disclose or conceal traces of her first marriage; or to learn if there existed possibilities – which there undoubtedly did – by which that hasty contract might become revealed to those about her at any unexpected moment.

While yet within the first month of her marriage, and on an evening just before sunset, Baptista was standing within her garden adjoining the house, when she saw passing along the road a personage clad in a greasy black coat and battered tall hat, which, common enough in the slums of a city, had an odd appearance in St Maria's. The tramp, as he seemed to be, marked her at once – bonnetless and unwrapped as she was her features were plainly recognizable – and with an air of friendly surprise came and leant over the wall.

'What! don't you know me?' said he.

She had some dim recollection of his face, but said that she was not acquainted with him.

'Why, your witness to be sure, ma'am. Don't you mind the man that was mending the church-window when you and your intended husband walked up to be made one; and the clerk called me down from the ladder, and I came and did my part by writing my name and occupation?'

Baptista glanced quickly around; her husband was out of ear-shot. That would have been of less importance but for the fact that the wedding witnessed by this personage had not been the wedding with Mr Heddegan, but the one on the day previous.

'I've had a misfortune since then, that's pulled me under,' continued her friend. 'But don't let me damp yer wedded joy by naming the particulars. Yes, I've seen changes since; though 'tis but a short time ago – let me see, only a month next week, I think; for 'twere the first or second day in August.'

'Yes – that's when it was,' said another man, a sailor, who had come up with a pipe in his mouth, and felt it necessary to join in (Baptista having receded to escape further speech). 'For that was the first time I set foot in Giant's Town; and her husband took her to him the same day.'

A dialogue then proceeded between the two men outside the wall, which Baptista could not help hearing.

'Ay, I signed the book that made her one flesh,' repeated the decayed glazier. 'Where's her good-man?'

'About the premises somewhere; but you don't see 'em together much,' replied the sailor in an undertone. 'You see, he's older than she.'

'Older? I should never have thought it from my own observation,' said the glazier. 'He was a remarkably handsome man.'

'Handsome? Well, there he is – we can see for ourselves.'

David Heddegan had, indeed, just shown himself at the upper end of the garden; and the glazier, looking in bewilderment from the husband to the wife, saw the latter turn pale.

Now that decayed glazier was a far-seeing and cunning man – too far-seeing and cunning to allow himself to thrive by simple and straightforward means – and he held his peace, till he could read more plainly the meaning of this riddle, merely adding carelessly, 'Well – marriage do alter a man, 'tis true. I should never ha' knowed him!'

He then stared oddly at the disconcerted Baptista, and moving on to where he could again address her, asked her to do him a good turn, since he once had done the same for her. Understanding that he meant money, she handed him some, at which he thanked her, and instantly went away.

VII

She had escaped exposure on this occasion; but the incident had been an awkward one, and should have suggested to Baptista that sooner or later the secret must leak out. As it was, she suspected that at any rate she had not heard the last of the glazier.

In a day or two, when her husband had gone to the old town on the other side of the island, there came a gentle tap at the door, and the worthy witness of her first marriage made his appearance a second time.

'It took me hours to get to the bottom of the mystery — hours!' he said with a gaze of deep confederacy which offended her pride very deeply. 'But thanks to a good intellect I've done it. Now, ma'am, I'm not a man to tell tales, even when a tale would be so good as this. But I'm going back to the mainland again, and a little assistance would be as rain on thirsty ground.'

'I helped you two days ago,' began Baptista.

'Yes — but what was that, my good lady? Not enough to pay my passage to Pen-zephyr. I came over on your account, for I thought there was a mystery somewhere. Now I must go back on my own. Mind this — 'twould be very awkward for you if your old man were to know. He's a queer temper, though he may be fond.'

She knew as well as her visitor how awkward it would be; and the hush-money she paid was heavy that day. She had, however, the satisfaction of watching the man to the steamer, and seeing him diminish out of sight. But Baptista perceived that the system into which she had been led of purchasing silence thus was one fatal to her peace of mind, particularly if it had to be continued.

Hearing no more from the glazier she hoped the difficulty was past. But another week only had gone by, when, as she was pacing the Giant's Walk (the name given to the promenade), she met the same personage in the company of a fat woman carrying a bundle.

'This is the lady, my dear,' he said to his companion. 'This, ma'am, is my wife. We've come to settle in the town for a time, if so be we can find room.'

'That you won't do,' said she. 'Nobody can live here who is not privileged.'[13]

'I am privileged,' said the glazier, 'by my trade.'

Baptista went on, but in the afternoon she received a visit from the man's wife. This honest woman began to depict, in forcible colours, the necessity for keeping up the concealment.

'I will intercede with my husband, ma'am,' she said. 'He's a true man if rightly managed; and I'll beg him to consider your position. 'Tis a very nice house you've got here,' she added, glancing round, 'and well worth a little sacrifice to keep it.'

The unlucky Baptista staved off the danger on this third occasion as she had done on the previous two. But she formed a resolve that, if the attack were once more to be repeated she would face a revelation – worse though that must now be than before she had attempted to purchase silence by bribes. Her tormentors, never believing her capable of acting upon such an intention, came again; but she shut the door in their faces. They retreated, muttering something; but she went to the back of the house, where David Heddegan was.

She looked at him, unconscious of all. The case was serious; she knew that well; and all the more serious in that she liked him better now than she had done at first. Yet, as she herself began to see, the secret was one that was sure to disclose itself. Her name and Charles's stood indelibly written in the registers; and though a month only had passed as yet it was a wonder that his clandestine union with her had not already been discovered by his friends. Thus spurring herself to the inevitable, she spoke to Heddegan.

'David, come indoors. I have something to tell you.'

He hardly regarded her at first. She had discerned that during the last week or two he had seemed preoccupied, as if some private business harassed him. She repeated her request. He replied with a sigh, 'Yes, certainly, mee deer.'

When they had reached the sitting-room and shut the door she repeated, faintly, 'David, I have something to tell you – a sort of tragedy I have concealed. You will hate me for having so far deceived you; but perhaps my telling you voluntarily will make you think a little better of me than you would do otherwise.'

'Tragedy?' he said, awakening to interest. 'Much you can know about tragedies, mee deer, that have been in the world so short a time!'

She saw that he suspected nothing, and it made her task the harder. But on she went steadily. 'It is about something that happened before we were married,' she said.

'Indeed!'

'Not a very long time before – a short time. And it is about a lover,' she faltered.

'I don't much mind that,' he said mildly. 'In truth, I was in hopes 'twas more.'

'In hopes!'

'Well, yes.'

This screwed her up to the necessary effort. 'I met my old sweetheart. He scorned me, chid me, dared me, and I went and married him. We were coming straight here to tell you all what we had done; but he was drowned; and I thought I would say nothing about him: and I married you, David, for the sake of peace and quietness. I've tried to keep it from you, but have found I cannot. There – that's the substance of it, and you can never, never forgive me, I am sure!'

She spoke desperately. But the old man, instead of turning black or blue, or slaying her in his indignation, jumped up from his chair, and began to caper around the room in quite an ecstatic emotion.

'O, happy thing! How well it falls out!' he exclaimed, snapping his fingers over his head. 'Ha-ha – the knot is cut – I see a way out of my trouble – ha-ha!'

She looked at him without uttering a sound, till, as he still continued smiling joyfully, she said, 'O – what do you mean? Is it done to torment me?'

'No – no! O, mee deer, your story helps me out of the most heart-aching quandary a poor man ever found himself in! You see, it is this – I've got a tragedy, too; and unless you had had one to tell, I could never have seen my way to tell mine!'

'What is yours – what is it?' she asked, with altogether a new view of things.

'Well – it is a bouncer; mine is a bouncer!' said he, looking on the ground and wiping his eyes.

'Not worse than mine?'

'Well – that depends upon how you look at it. Yours had to do with the past alone; and I don't mind it. You see, we've been married a month, and it don't jar upon me as it would if we'd only been married a day or two. Now mine refers to past, present, and future; so that –'

'Past, present, and future!' she murmured. 'It never occurred to me that *you* had a tragedy too.'

'But I have!' he said, shaking his head. 'In fact, four.'

'Then tell 'em!' cried the young woman.

'I will – I will. But be considerate, I beg 'ee, mee deer. Well – I wasn't a bachelor when I married 'ee, any more than you were a spinster. Just as you was a widow-woman, I was a widow-man.'

'Ah!' said she, with some surprise. 'But is that all? – then we are nicely balanced,' she added, relieved.

'No – it is not all. There's the point. I am not only a widower.'

'O, David!'

'I am a widower with four tragedies – that is to say, four strapping girls – the eldest taller than you. Don't 'ee look so struck – dumb-like! It fell out in this way. I knew the poor woman, their mother, in Pen-zephyr for some years; and – to cut a long story short – I privately married her at last, just before she died. I kept the matter secret, but it is getting known among the people here by degrees. I've long felt for the children – that it is my duty to have them here, and do something for them. I have not had courage to break it to 'ee, but I've seen lately that it would soon come to your ears, and that hev worried me.'

'Are they educated?' said the ex-schoolmistress.

'No. I am sorry to say they have been much neglected; in truth, they can hardly read. And so I thought that by marrying a young schoolmistress I should get some one in the house who could teach 'em, and bring 'em into genteel condition, all for nothing. You see, they are growed up too tall to be sent to school.'

'O, mercy!' she almost moaned. 'Four great girls to teach the rudiments to, and have always in the house with me spelling over their books; and I hate teaching, it kills me. I am bitterly punished – I am, I am!'

'You'll get used to 'em, mee deer, and the balance of secrets – mine against yours – will comfort your heart with a sense of justice. I could send for 'em this week very well – and I will! In faith, I could send this very day. Baptista, you have relieved me of all my difficulty!'

Thus the interview ended, so far as this matter was concerned. Baptista was too stupefied to say more, and when she went away to her room she wept from very mortification at Mr Heddegan's duplicity. Education, the one thing she abhorred; the shame of it to delude a young wife so!

The next meal came round. As they sat, Baptista would not suffer her eyes to turn towards him. He did not attempt to intrude upon her reserve, but every now and then looked under the table and chuckled with satisfaction at the aspect of affairs. 'How very well matched we be!' he said, comfortably.

Next day, when the steamer came in, Baptista saw her husband rush down to meet it; and soon after there appeared at her door four tall, hipless, shoulderless girls, dwindling in height and size from the eldest to the youngest, like a row of Pan pipes;[14] at the head of them standing Heddegan. He smiled pleasantly through the grey fringe of his whiskers and beard, and turning to the girls said, 'Now come forrard, and shake hands properly with your stepmother.'

Thus she made their acquaintance, and he went out, leaving them together. On examination the poor girls turned out to be not only plain-looking, which she could have forgiven, but to have such a lamentably meagre intellectual equipment as to be hopelessly inadequate as companions. Even the eldest, almost her own age, could only read with difficulty words of two syllables; and taste in dress was beyond their comprehension. In the long vista of future years she saw nothing but dreary drudgery at her detested old trade without prospect of reward.

She went about quite despairing during the next few days — an unpromising, unfortunate mood for a woman who had not been married six weeks. From her parents she concealed everything. They had been amongst the few acquaintances of Heddegan who knew nothing of his secret, and were indignant enough when they saw such a ready-made household foisted upon their only child. But she would not support them in their remonstrances.

'No, you don't yet know all,' she said.

Thus Baptista had sense enough to see the retributive fairness of this issue. For some time, whenever conversation arose between her and Heddegan, which was not often, she always said, 'I am miserable, and you know it. Yet I don't wish things to be otherwise.'

But one day when he asked, 'How do you like 'em now?' her answer was unexpected. 'Much better than I did,' she said, quietly. 'I may like them very much some day.'

This was the beginning of a serener season for the chastened spirit of Baptista Heddegan. She had, in truth, discovered, underneath the crust of uncouthness and meagre articulation which was due to their Troglodytean[15] existence, that her unwelcomed daughters had natures that were unselfish almost to sublimity. The harsh discipline accorded to their young lives before their mother's wrong had been righted, had operated less to crush them than to lift them above all personal ambition. They considered the world and its contents in a purely objective way, and their own lot seemed only to affect them as that of certain human beings among the rest, whose troubles they knew rather than suffered.

This was such an entirely new way of regarding life to a woman of Baptista's nature, that her attention, from being first arrested by it, became deeply interested. By imperceptible pulses her heart expanded in sympathy with theirs. The sentences of her tragi-comedy, her life, confused till now, became clearer daily. That in humanity, as exemplified by these girls, there was nothing to dislike, but infinitely much to pity, she learnt with the lapse of each week in their company. She grew to like the girls of unpromising exterior, and from liking she got to love them; till they formed an unexpected point of junction between her own and her husband's interests, generating a sterling friendship at least, between a pair in whose existence there had threatened to be neither friendship nor love.

A LORN MILKMAID

I

It was an eighty-cow dairy, and the troop of milkers, regular and supernumerary, were all at work; for, though the time of year was as yet but early April, the feed lay entirely in water-meadows, and the cows were 'in full pail'.[1] The hour was about six in the evening, and three-fourths of the large, red, rectangular animals having been finished off, there was opportunity for a little conversation.

'He do bring home his bride to-morrow, I hear. They've come as far as Anglebury to-day.'

The voice seemed to proceed from the belly of the cow called Cherry, but the speaker was a milking-woman, whose face was buried in the flank of that motionless beast.

'Hav' anybody seen her?' said another.

There was a negative response from the first. 'Though they say she's a rosy-cheeked, tisty-tosty[2] little body enough,' she added; and as the milkmaid spoke she turned her face so that she could glance past her cow's tail to the other side of the barton,[3] where a thin, fading woman of thirty milked somewhat apart from the rest.

'Years younger than he, they say,' continued the second, with also a glance of reflectiveness in the same direction.

'How old do you call him, then?'

'Thirty or so.'

'More like forty,' broke in an old milkman near, in a long white pinafore or 'wropper', and with the brim of his hat tied down, so that he looked like a woman. ' 'A was born before our Great Weir was builded, and I hadn't man's wages when I laved[4] water there.'

The discussion waxed so warm that the purr of the milk

streams became jerky, till a voice from another cow's belly cried with authority, 'Now then, what the Turk[5] do it matter to us about Farmer Lodge's age, or Farmer Lodge's new mis'ess? I shall have to pay him nine pound a year for the rent of every one of these milchers,[6] whatever his age or hers. Get on with your work, or 'twill be dark afore we have done. The evening is pinking in[7] a'ready.' This speaker was the dairyman himself, by whom the milkmaids and men were employed.

Nothing more was said publicly about Farmer Lodge's wedding, but the first woman murmured under her cow to her next neighbour, ' 'Tis hard for *she*,' signifying the thin worn milkmaid aforesaid.

'O no,' said the second. 'He ha'n't spoke to Rhoda Brook for years.'

When the milking was done they washed their pails and hung them on a many-forked stand made as usual of the peeled limb of an oak-tree, set upright in the earth, and resembling a colossal antlered horn. The majority then dispersed in various directions homeward. The thin woman who had not spoken was joined by a boy of twelve or thereabout, and the twain went away up the field also.

Their course lay apart from that of the others, to a lonely spot high above the water-meads, and not far from the border of Egdon Heath, whose dark countenance was visible in the distance as they drew nigh to their home.

'They've just been saying down in barton that your father brings his young wife home from Anglebury to-morrow,' the woman observed. 'I shall want to send you for a few things to market, and you'll be pretty sure to meet 'em.'

'Yes, mother,' said the boy. 'Is father married then?'

'Yes ... You can give her a look, and tell me what she's like, if you do see her.'

'Yes, mother.'

'If she's dark or fair, and if she's tall – as tall as I. And if she seems like a woman who has ever worked for a living, or one that has been always well off, and has never done anything, and shows marks of the lady on her, as I expect she do.'

'Yes.'

They crept up the hill in the twilight and entered the cottage. It was built of mud-walls, the surface of which had been washed by many rains into channels and depressions that left none of the original flat face visible; while here and there in the thatch above a rafter showed like a bone protruding through the skin.

She was kneeling down in the chimney-corner, before two pieces of turf laid together with the heather inwards, blowing at the red-hot ashes with her breath till the turves flamed. The radiance lit her pale cheek, and made her dark eyes, that had once been handsome, seem handsome anew. 'Yes,' she resumed, 'see if she is dark or fair, and if you can, notice if her hands be white; if not, see if they look as though she had ever done housework, or are milker's hands like mine.'

The boy again promised, inattentively this time, his mother not observing that he was cutting a notch with his pocket-knife in the beech-backed chair.

THE YOUNG WIFE

II

The road from Anglebury to Holmstoke is in general level; but there is one place where a sharp ascent breaks its monotony. Farmers homeward-bound from the former market-town, who trot all the rest of the way, walk their horses up this short incline.

The next evening while the sun was yet bright a handsome new gig,[8] with a lemon-coloured body and red wheels, was spinning westward along the level highway at the heels of a powerful mare. The driver was a yeoman in the prime of life, cleanly shaven like an actor, his face being toned to that bluish-vermilion hue which so often graces a thriving farmer's features when returning home after successful dealings in the town. Beside him sat a woman, many years his junior – almost, indeed, a girl. Her face too was fresh in colour, but it was of a totally different quality – soft and evanescent, like the light under a heap of rose-petals.

Few people travelled this way, for it was not a main road; and the long white riband of gravel that stretched before them was empty, save of one small scarce-moving speck, which presently resolved itself into the figure of a boy, who was creeping on at a snail's pace, and continually looking behind him – the heavy bundle he carried being some excuse for, if not the reason of, his dilatoriness. When the bouncing gig-party slowed at the bottom of the incline above mentioned, the pedestrian was only a few yards in front. Supporting the large bundle by putting one hand on his hip, he turned and looked straight at the farmer's wife as though he would read her through and through, pacing along abreast of the horse.

The low sun was full in her face, rendering every feature, shade, and contour distinct, from the curve of her little nostril to the colour of her eyes. The farmer, though he seemed annoyed at the boy's persistent presence, did not order him to get out of the way; and thus the lad preceded them, his hard gaze never leaving her, till they reached the top of the ascent, when the farmer trotted on with relief in his lineaments – having taken no outward notice of the boy whatever.

'How that poor lad stared at me!' said the young wife.

'Yes, dear; I saw that he did.'

'He is one of the village, I suppose?'

'One of the neighbourhood. I think he lives with his mother a mile or two off.'

'He knows who we are, no doubt?'

'O yes. You must expect to be stared at just at first, my pretty Gertrude.'

'I do, – though I think the poor boy may have looked at us in the hope we might relieve him of his heavy load, rather than from curiosity.'

'O no,' said her husband off-handedly. 'These country lads will carry a hundredweight once they get it on their backs; besides his pack had more size than weight in it. Now, then, another mile and I shall be able to show you our house in the distance – if it is not too dark before we get there.' The wheels spun round, and particles flew from their periphery as before, till a white house of ample dimensions revealed itself, with farm-buildings and ricks at the back.

Meanwhile the boy had quickened his pace, and turning up a by-lane some mile and half short of the white farmstead, ascended towards the leaner pastures, and so on to the cottage of his mother.

She had reached home after her day's milking at the out-lying dairy, and was washing cabbage at the doorway in the declining light. 'Hold up the net a moment,' she said, without preface, as the boy came up.

He flung down his bundle, held the edge of the cabbage-net, and as she filled its meshes with the dripping leaves she went on, 'Well, did you see her?'

'Yes; quite plain.'

'Is she ladylike?'

'Yes; and more. A lady complete.'

'Is she young?'

'Well, she's growed up, and her ways be quite a woman's.'

'Of course. What colour is her hair and face?'

'Her hair is lightish, and her face as comely as a live doll's.'

'Her eyes, then, are not dark like mine?'

'No – of a bluish turn, and her mouth is very nice and red; and when she smiles, her teeth show white.'

'Is she tall?' said the woman sharply.

'I couldn't see. She was sitting down.'

'Then do you go to Holmstoke church to-morrow morning: she's sure to be there. Go early and notice her walking in, and come home and tell me if she's taller than I.'

'Very well, mother. But why don't you go and see for your-self?'

'I go to see her! I wouldn't look up at her if she were to pass my window this instant. She was with Mr Lodge, of course. What did he say or do?'

'Just the same as usual.'

'Took no notice of you?'

'None.'

Next day the mother put a clean shirt on the boy, and started him off for Holmstoke church. He reached the ancient little pile when the door was just being opened, and he was the first to enter. Taking his seat by the font, he watched all the parishioners file in. The well-to-do Farmer Lodge came nearly last; and his young wife, who accompanied him, walked up the aisle with the shyness natural to a modest woman who had appeared thus for the first time. As all other eyes were fixed upon her, the youth's stare was not noticed now.

When he reached home his mother said, 'Well?' before he had entered the room.

'She is not tall. She is rather short,' he replied.

'Ah!' said his mother, with satisfaction.

'But she's very pretty – very. In fact, she's lovely.' The youthful freshness of the yeoman's wife had evidently made an impression even on the somewhat hard nature of the boy.

'That's all I want to hear,' said his mother quickly. 'Now, spread the table-cloth. The hare you wired[9] is very tender; but mind that nobody catches you. – You've never told me what sort of hands she had.'

'I have never seen 'em. She never took off her gloves.'

'What did she wear this morning?'

'A white bonnet and a silver-coloured gownd.[10] It whewed and whistled so loud when it rubbed against the pews that the lady coloured up more than ever for very shame at the noise, and pulled it in to keep it from touching; but when she pushed into her seat, it whewed more than ever. Mr Lodge, he seemed pleased, and his waistcoat stuck out, and his great golden seals hung like a lord's; but she seemed to wish her noisy gownd anywhere but on her.'

'Not she! However, that will do now.'

These descriptions of the newly-married couple were continued from time to time by the boy at his mother's request, after any chance encounter he had had with them. But Rhoda Brook, though she might easily have seen young Mrs Lodge for herself by walking a couple of miles, would never attempt an excursion towards the quarter where the farmhouse lay. Neither did she, at the daily milking in the dairyman's yard on Lodge's outlying second farm, ever speak on the subject of the recent marriage. The dairyman, who rented the cows of Lodge, and knew perfectly the tall milkmaid's history, with manly kindliness always kept the gossip in the cow-barton from annoying Rhoda. But the atmosphere thereabout was full of the subject during the first days of Mrs Lodge's arrival; and from her boy's description and the casual words of the other milkers, Rhoda Brook could raise a mental image of the unconscious Mrs Lodge that was realistic as a photograph.

A VISION

III

One night, two or three weeks after the bridal return, when the boy was gone to bed, Rhoda sat a long time over the turf ashes that she had raked out in front of her to extinguish them. She contemplated so intently the new wife, as presented to her in her mind's eye over the embers, that she forgot the lapse of time. At last, wearied with her day's work, she too retired.

But the figure which had occupied her so much during this and the previous days was not to be banished at night. For the first time Gertrude Lodge visited the supplanted woman in her dreams. Rhoda Brook dreamed – since her assertion that she really saw, before falling asleep, was not to be believed – that the young wife, in the pale silk dress and white bonnet, but with features shockingly distorted, and wrinkled as by age, was sitting upon her chest as she lay. The pressure of Mrs Lodge's person grew heavier; the blue eyes peered cruelly into her face; and then the figure thrust forward its left hand mockingly, so as to make the wedding-ring it wore glitter in Rhoda's eyes. Maddened mentally, and nearly suffocated by pressure, the sleeper struggled; the incubus,[11] still regarding her, withdrew to the foot of the bed, only, however, to come forward by degrees, resume her seat, and flash her left hand as before.

Gasping for breath, Rhoda, in a last desperate effort, swung out her right hand, seized the confronting spectre by its obtrusive left arm, and whirled it backward to the floor, starting up herself as she did so with a low cry.

'O, merciful heaven!' she cried, sitting on the edge of the bed in a cold sweat; 'that was not a dream – she was here!'

She could feel her antagonist's arm within her grasp even now – the very flesh and bone of it, as it seemed. She looked on the floor whither she had whirled the spectre, but there was nothing to be seen.

Rhoda Brook slept no more that night, and when she went milking at the next dawn they noticed how pale and haggard she looked. The milk that she drew quivered into the pail; her hand had not calmed even yet, and still retained the feel of the arm. She came home to breakfast as wearily as if it had been supper-time.

'What was that noise in your chimmer,[12] mother, last night?' said her son. 'You fell off the bed, surely?'

'Did you hear anything fall? At what time?'

'Just when the clock struck two.'

She could not explain, and when the meal was done went silently about her household work, the boy assisting her, for he hated going afield on the farms, and she indulged his reluctance. Between eleven and twelve the garden-gate clicked, and she lifted her eyes to the window. At the bottom of the garden, within the gate, stood the woman of her vision. Rhoda seemed transfixed.

'Ah, she said she would come!' exclaimed the boy, also observing her.

'Said so – when? How does she know us?'

'I have seen and spoken to her. I talked to her yesterday.'

'I told you,' said the mother, flushing indignantly, 'never to speak to anybody in that house, or go near the place.'

'I did not speak to her till she spoke to me. And I did not go near the place. I met her in the road.'

'What did you tell her?'

'Nothing. She said, "Are you the poor boy who had to bring the heavy load from market?" And she looked at my boots, and said they would not keep my feet dry if it came on wet, because they were so cracked. I told her I lived with my mother, and we had enough to do to keep ourselves, and that's how it was; and she said then, "I'll come and bring you some better boots, and see your mother." She gives away things to other folks in the meads [13] besides us.'

Mrs Lodge was by this time close to the door – not in her silk, as Rhoda had dreamt of in the bedchamber, but in a morning hat, and gown of common light material, which became her better than silk. On her arm she carried a basket.

The impression remaining from the night's experience was still strong. Brook had almost expected to see the wrinkles, the scorn, and the cruelty on her visitor's face. She would have escaped an interview, had escape been possible. There was, however, no backdoor to the cottage, and in an instant the boy had lifted the latch to Mrs Lodge's gentle knock.

'I see I have come to the right house,' said she, glancing at the lad, and smiling. 'But I was not sure till you opened the door.'

The figure and action were those of the phantom; but her voice was so indescribably sweet, her glance so winning, her smile so tender, so unlike that of Rhoda's midnight visitant, that the latter could hardly believe the evidence of her senses. She was truly glad that she had not hidden away in sheer aversion, as she had been inclined to do. In her basket Mrs Lodge brought the pair of boots that she had promised to the boy, and other useful articles.

At these proofs of a kindly feeling towards her and hers Rhoda's heart reproached her bitterly. This innocent young thing should have her blessing and not her curse. When she left them a light seemed gone from the dwelling. Two days later she came again to know if the boots fitted; and less than a fortnight after that paid Rhoda another call. On this occasion the boy was absent.

'I walk a good deal,' said Mrs Lodge, 'and your house is the nearest outside our own parish. I hope you are well. You don't look quite well.'

Rhoda said she was well enough; and, indeed, though the paler of the two, there was more of the strength that endures in her well-defined features and large frame than in the softcheeked young woman before her. The conversation became quite confidential as regarded their powers and weaknesses; and when Mrs Lodge was leaving, Rhoda said, 'I hope you will find this air agree with you, ma'am, and not suffer from the damp of the water meads.'

The younger one replied that there was not much doubt of it, her general health being usually good. 'Though, now you remind me,' she added, 'I have one little ailment which puzzles me. It is nothing serious, but I cannot make it out.'

She uncovered her left hand and arm; and their outline confronted Rhoda's gaze as the exact original of the limb she had beheld and seized in her dream. Upon the pink round surface of the arm were faint marks of an unhealthy colour, as if produced by a rough grasp. Rhoda's eyes became riveted on the discolorations; she fancied that she discerned in them the shape of her own four fingers.

'How did it happen?' she said mechanically.

'I cannot tell,' replied Mrs Lodge, shaking her head. 'One night when I was sound asleep, dreaming I was away in some strange place, a pain suddenly shot into my arm there, and was so keen as to awaken me. I must have struck it in the daytime, I suppose, though I don't remember doing so.' She added, laughing, 'I tell my dear husband that it looks just as if he had flown into a rage and struck me there. O, I daresay it will soon disappear.'

'Ha, ha! Yes . . . On what night did it come?'

Mrs Lodge considered, and said it would be a fortnight ago on the morrow. 'When I awoke I could not remember where I was,' she added, 'till the clock striking two reminded me.'

She had named the night and the hour of Rhoda's spectral encounter, and Brook felt like a guilty thing. The artless disclosure startled her; she did not reason on the freaks of coincidence; and all the scenery of that ghastly night returned with double vividness to her mind.

'O, can it be,' she said to herself, when her visitor had departed, 'that I exercise a malignant power over people against my own will?' She knew that she had been slily called a witch since her fall; but never having understood why that particular stigma had been attached to her, it had passed disregarded. Could this be the explanation, and had such things as this ever happened before?

A SUGGESTION

IV

The summer drew on, and Rhoda Brook almost dreaded to meet Mrs Lodge again, notwithstanding that her feeling for the young wife amounted well-nigh to affection. Something in her own individuality seemed to convict Rhoda of crime. Yet a fatality[14] sometimes would direct the steps of the latter to the outskirts of Holmstoke whenever she left her house for any other purpose than her daily work; and hence it happened that their next encounter was out of doors. Rhoda could not avoid the subject which had so mystified her, and after the first few words she stammered, 'I hope your — arm is well again, ma'am?' She had perceived with consternation that Gertrude Lodge carried her left arm stiffly.

'No; it is not quite well. Indeed it is no better at all; it is rather worse. It pains me dreadfully sometimes.'

'Perhaps you had better go to a doctor, ma'am.'

She replied that she had already seen a doctor. Her husband had insisted upon her going to one. But the surgeon had not seemed to understand the afflicted limb at all; he had told her to bathe it in hot water, and she had bathed it, but the treatment had done no good.

'Will you let me see it?' said the milkwoman.

Mrs Lodge pushed up her sleeve and disclosed the place, which was a few inches above the wrist. As soon as Rhoda Brook saw it, she could hardly preserve her composure. There was nothing of the nature of a wound, but the arm at that point had a shrivelled look, and the outline of the four fingers appeared more distinct than at the former time. Moreover, she fancied that they were imprinted in precisely the relative position of her clutch upon the arm in the trance; the first finger towards Gertrude's wrist, and the fourth towards her elbow.

What the impress resembled seemed to have struck Gertrude herself since their last meeting. 'It looks almost like finger-marks,' she said; adding with a faint laugh, 'my husband says it is as if some witch, or the devil himself, had taken hold of me there, and blasted the flesh.'

Rhoda shivered. 'That's fancy,' she said hurriedly. 'I wouldn't mind it, if I were you.'

'I shouldn't so much mind it,' said the younger, with hesitation, 'if – if I hadn't a notion that it makes my husband – dislike me – no, love me less. Men think so much of personal appearance.'

'Some do – he for one.'

'Yes; and he was very proud of mine, at first.'

'Keep your arm covered from his sight.'

'Ah – he knows the disfigurement is there!' She tried to hide the tears that filled her eyes.

'Well, ma'am, I earnestly hope it will go away soon.'

And so the milkwoman's mind was chained anew to the subject by a horrid sort of spell as she returned home. The sense of having been guilty of an act of malignity increased, affect as she might to ridicule her superstition. In her secret heart Rhoda did not altogether object to a slight diminution of her successor's beauty, by whatever means it had come about; but she did not wish to inflict upon her physical pain. For though this pretty young woman had rendered impossible any reparation which Lodge might have made Rhoda for his past conduct, everything like resentment at the unconscious usurpation had quite passed away from the elder's mind.

If the sweet and kindly Gertrude Lodge only knew of the dream-scene in the bed-chamber, what would she think? Not to inform her of it seemed treachery in the presence of her friendliness; but tell she could not of her own accord – neither could she devise a remedy.

She mused upon the matter the greater part of the night; and the next day, after the morning milking, set out to obtain another glimpse of Gertrude Lodge if she could, being held to her by a gruesome fascination. By watching the house from a distance the milkmaid was presently able to discern the farmer's wife in a ride she was taking alone – probably to join her husband in some distant field. Mrs Lodge perceived her, and cantered in her direction.

'Good morning, Rhoda!' Gertrude said, when she had come up. 'I was going to call.'

Rhoda noticed that Mrs Lodge held the reins with some difficulty.

'I hope – the bad arm,' said Rhoda.

'They tell me there is possibly one way by which I might be able to find out the cause, and so perhaps the cure, of it,' replied the other anxiously. 'It is by going to some clever man over in Egdon Heath. They did not know if he was still alive – and I cannot remember his name at this moment; but they said that you knew more of his movements than anybody else hereabout, and could tell me if he were still to be consulted. Dear me – what was his name? But you know.'

'Not Conjuror [15] Trendle?' said her thin companion, turning pale.

'Trendle – yes. Is he alive?'

'I believe so,' said Rhoda, with reluctance.

'Why do you call him conjuror?'

'Well – they say – they used to say he was a – he had powers other folks have not.'

'O, how could my people be so superstitious as to recommend a man of that sort! I thought they meant some medical man. I shall think no more of him.'

Rhoda looked relieved, and Mrs Lodge rode on. The milkwoman had inwardly seen, from the moment she heard of her having been mentioned as a reference for this man, that there must exist a sarcastic feeling among the work-folk that a sorceress would know the whereabouts of the exorcist. They suspected her, then. A short time ago this would have given no concern to a woman of her common-sense. But she had a haunting reason to be superstitious now; and she had been seized with sudden dread that this Conjuror Trendle might name her as the malignant influence which was blasting the fair person of Gertrude, and so lead her friend to hate her for ever, and to treat her as some fiend in human shape.

But all was not over. Two days after, a shadow intruded into the window-pattern thrown on Rhoda Brook's floor by the afternoon sun. The woman opened the door at once, almost breathlessly.

'Are you alone?' said Gertrude. She seemed to be no less harassed and anxious than Brook herself.

'Yes,' said Rhoda.

'The place on my arm seems worse, and troubles me!' the young farmer's wife went on. 'It is so mysterious! I do hope it will not be an incurable wound. I have again been thinking of what they said about Conjuror Trendle. I don't really believe in such men, but I should not mind just visiting him, from curiosity – though on no account must my husband know. Is it far to where he lives?'

'Yes – five miles,' said Rhoda backwardly. 'In the heart of Egdon.'

'Well, I should have to walk. Could not you go with me to show me the way – say to-morrow afternoon?'

'O, not I; that is –,' the milkwoman murmured, with a start of dismay. Again the dread seized her that something to do with her fierce act in the dream might be revealed, and her character in the eyes of the most useful friend she had ever had be ruined irretrievably.

Mrs Lodge urged, and Rhoda finally assented, though with much misgiving. Sad as the journey would be to her, she could not conscientiously stand in the way of a possible remedy for her patron's strange affliction. It was agreed that, to escape suspicion of their mystic intent, they should meet at the edge of the heath at the corner of a plantation which was visible from the spot where they now stood.

CONJUROR TRENDLE

V

By the next afternoon Rhoda would have done anything to escape this inquiry. But she had promised to go. Moreover, there was a horrid fascination at times in becoming instrumental in throwing such possible light on her own character as would reveal her to be something greater in the occult world than she had ever herself suspected.

She started just before the time of day mentioned between them, and half-an-hour's brisk walking brought her to the south-eastern extension of the Egdon tract of country, where the fir plantation was. A slight figure, cloaked and veiled, was already there. Rhoda recognized, almost with a shudder, that Mrs Lodge bore her left arm in a sling.

They hardly spoke to each other, and immediately set out on their climb into the interior of this solemn country, which stood high above the rich alluvial soil they had left half-an-hour before. It was a long walk; thick clouds made the atmosphere dark, though it was as yet only early afternoon; and the wind howled dismally over the slopes of the heath – not improbably the same heath which had witnessed the agony of the Wessex King Ina,[16] presented to after-ages as Lear. Gertrude Lodge talked most, Rhoda replying with monosyllabic preoccupation. She had a strange dislike to walking on the side of her companion where hung the afflicted arm, moving round to the other when inadvertently near it. Much heather had been brushed by their feet when they descended upon a cart-track, beside which stood the house of the man they sought.

He did not profess his remedial practices openly, or care anything about their continuance, his direct interests being those of a dealer in furze,[17] turf, 'sharp sand',[18] and other local products. Indeed, he affected not to believe largely in his own powers, and when warts that had been shown him for cure miraculously disappeared – which it must be owned they infallibly did – he would say lightly, 'O, I only drink a glass of grog upon 'em at your expense – perhaps it's all chance,' and immediately turn the subject.

He was at home when they arrived, having in fact seen them descending into his valley. He was a grey-bearded man, with a reddish face, and he looked singularly at Rhoda the first moment he beheld her. Mrs Lodge told him her errand; and then with words of self-disparagement he examined her arm.

'Medicine can't cure it,' he said promptly. ' 'Tis the work of an enemy.'

Rhoda shrank into herself, and drew back.

'An enemy? What enemy?' asked Mrs Lodge.

He shook his head. 'That's best known to yourself,' he said. 'If you like, I can show the person to you, though I shall not myself know who it is. I can do no more; and don't wish to do that.'

She pressed him; on which he told Rhoda to wait outside where she stood, and took Mrs Lodge into the room. It opened immediately from the door; and, as the latter remained ajar, Rhoda Brook could see the proceedings without taking part in them. He brought a tumbler from the dresser, nearly filled it with water, and fetching an egg, prepared it in some private way; after which he broke it on the edge of the glass, so that the white went in and the yolk remained. As it was getting gloomy, he took the glass and its contents to the window, and told Gertrude to watch the mixture closely. They leant over the table together, and the milkwoman could see the opaline hue of the egg-fluid changing form as it sank in the water, but she was not near enough to define the shape that it assumed.[19]

'Do you catch the likeness of any face or figure as you look?' demanded the conjuror of the young woman.

She murmured a reply, in tones so low as to be inaudible to Rhoda, and continued to gaze intently into the glass. Rhoda turned, and walked a few steps away.

When Mrs Lodge came out, and her face was met by the light, it appeared exceedingly pale – as pale as Rhoda's – against the sad dun shades of the upland's garniture.[20] Trendle shut the door behind her, and they at once started homeward together. But Rhoda perceived that her companion had quite changed.

'Did he charge much?' she asked tentatively.

'O no – nothing. He would not take a farthing,' said Gertrude.

'And what did you see?' inquired Rhoda.

'Nothing I – care to speak of.' The constraint in her manner was remarkable; her face was so rigid as to wear an oldened aspect, faintly suggestive of the face in Rhoda's bed-chamber.

'Was it you who first proposed coming here?' Mrs Lodge suddenly inquired, after a long pause. 'How very odd, if you did!'

'No. But I am not sorry we have come, all things considered,' she replied. For the first time a sense of triumph possessed her, and she did not altogether deplore that the young thing at her side should learn that their lives had been antagonized by other influences than their own.

The subject was no more alluded to during the long and dreary walk home. But in some way or other a story was whispered about the many-dairied lowland that winter that Mrs Lodge's gradual loss of the use of her left arm was owing to her being 'overlooked'[21] by Rhoda Brook. The latter kept her own counsel about the incubus, but her face grew sadder and thinner; and in the spring she and her boy disappeared from the neighbourhood of Holmstoke.

A SECOND ATTEMPT

VI

Half a dozen years passed away, and Mr and Mrs Lodge's married experience sank into prosiness, and worse. The farmer was usually gloomy and silent: the woman whom he had wooed for her grace and beauty was contorted and disfigured in the left limb; moreover, she had brought him no child, which rendered it likely that he would be the last of a family who had occupied that valley for some two hundred years. He thought of Rhoda Brook and her son; and feared this might be a judgement from heaven upon him.

The once blithe-hearted and enlightened Gertrude was changing into an irritable, superstitious woman, whose whole time was given to experimenting upon her ailment with every quack remedy she came across. She was honestly attached to her husband, and was ever secretly hoping against hope to win back his heart again by regaining some at least of her personal beauty. Hence it arose that her closet was lined with bottles, packets, and ointment-pots of every description – nay, bunches of mystic herbs, charms, and books of necromancy, which in her schoolgirl time she would have ridiculed as folly.

'Damned if you won't poison yourself with these apothecary messes and witch mixtures some time or other,' said her husband, when his eye chanced to fall upon the multitudinous array.

She did not reply, but turned her sad, soft glance upon him in such heart-swollen reproach that he looked sorry for his words, and added, 'I only meant it for your good, you know, Gertrude.'

'I'll clear out the whole lot, and destroy them,' said she huskily, 'and try such remedies no more!'

'You want somebody to cheer you,' he observed. 'I once thought of adopting a boy; but he is too old now. And he is gone away I don't know where.'

She guessed to whom he alluded; for Rhoda Brook's story had in the course of years become known to her; though not a word had ever passed between her husband and herself on the subject. Neither had she ever spoken to him of her visit to Conjuror Trendle, and of what was revealed to her, or she thought was revealed to her, by that solitary heathman.

She was now five-and-twenty; but she seemed older. 'Six years of marriage, and only a few months of love,' she sometimes whispered to herself. And then she thought of the apparent cause, and said, with a tragic glance at her withering limb, 'If I could only again be as I was when he first saw me!'

She obediently destroyed her nostrums and charms; but there remained a hankering wish to try something else – some other sort of cure altogether. She had never revisited Trendle since she had been conducted to the house of the solitary by Rhoda against her will; but it now suddenly occurred to Gertrude that she would, in a last desperate effort at deliverance from this seeming curse, again seek out the man, if he yet lived. He was entitled to a certain credence, for the indistinct form he had raised in the glass had undoubtedly resembled the only woman in the world who – as she now knew, though not then – could have a reason for bearing her ill-will. The visit should be paid.

This time she went alone, though she nearly got lost on the heath, and roamed a considerable distance out of her way. Trendle's house was reached at last, however: he was not indoors, and instead of waiting at the cottage, she went to where his bent figure was pointed out to her at work a long way off. Trendle remembered her, and laying down the handful of furze-roots which he was gathering and throwing into a heap, he offered to accompany her in her homeward direction, as the distance was considerable and the days were short. So they walked together, his head bowed nearly to the earth, and his form of a colour with it.

'You can send away warts and other excrescences, I know,' she said; 'why can't you send away this?' And the arm was uncovered.

'You think too much of my powers!' said Trendle; 'and I am old and weak now, too. No, no; it is too much for me to attempt in my own person. What have ye tried?'

She named to him some of the hundred medicaments and counterspells which she had adopted from time to time. He shook his head.

'Some were good enough,' he said approvingly; 'but not many of them for such as this. This is of the nature of a blight, not of the nature of a wound; and if you ever do throw it off, it will be all at once.'

'If I only could!'

'There is only one chance of doing it known to me. It has never failed in kindred afflictions, – that I can declare. But it is hard to carry out, and especially for a woman.'

'Tell me!' said she.

'You must touch with the limb the neck of a man who's been hanged.'

She started a little at the image he had raised.

'Before he's cold – just after he's cut down,' continued the conjuror impassively.

'How can that do good?'

'It will turn the blood and change the constitution. But, as I say, to do it is hard. You must go to the jail when there's a hanging, and wait for him when he's brought off the gallows. Lots have done it, though perhaps not such pretty women as you. I used to send dozens for skin complaints. But that was in former times. The last I sent was in '13 – near twelve years ago.'

He had no more to tell her; and, when he had put her into a straight track homeward, turned and left her, refusing all money as at first.

A RIDE

VII

The communication sank deep into Gertrude's mind. Her nature was rather a timid one; and probably of all remedies that the white wizard[22] could have suggested there was not one which would have filled her with so much aversion as this, not to speak of the immense obstacles in the way of its adoption.

Casterbridge, the county-town, was a dozen or fifteen miles off; and though in those days, when men were executed for horse-stealing, arson, and burglary, an assize seldom passed without a hanging, it was not likely that she could get access to the body of the criminal unaided. And the fear of her husband's anger made her reluctant to breathe a word of Trendle's suggestion to him or to anybody about him.

She did nothing for months, and patiently bore her disfigurement as before. But her woman's nature, craving for renewed love, through the medium of renewed beauty (she was but twenty-five), was ever stimulating her to try what, at any rate, could hardly do her any harm. 'What came by a spell will go by a spell surely,' she would say. Whenever her imagination pictured the act she shrank in terror from the possibility of it: then the words of the conjuror, 'It will turn your blood', were seen to be capable of a scientific no less than a ghastly interpretation; the mastering desire returned, and urged her on again.

There was at this time but one county paper, and that her husband only occasionally borrowed. But old-fashioned days had old-fashioned means, and news was extensively conveyed by word of mouth from market to market, or from fair to fair, so that, whenever such an event as an execution was about to take place, few within a radius of twenty miles were ignorant of the coming sight; and, so far as Holmstoke was concerned, some enthusiasts had been known to walk all the way to Casterbridge and back in one day, solely to witness the spectacle. The next assizes were in March; and when Gertrude Lodge heard that they had been held, she inquired stealthily at the inn as to the result, as soon as she could find opportunity.

She was, however, too late. The time at which the sentences were to be carried out had arrived, and to make the journey and obtain admission at such short notice required at least her husband's assistance. She dared not tell him, for she had found by delicate experiment that these smouldering village beliefs made him furious if mentioned, partly because he half entertained them himself. It was therefore necessary to wait for another opportunity.

Her determination received a fillip from learning that two epileptic children had attended from this very village of Holmstoke many years before with beneficial results, though the experiment had been strongly condemned by the neighbouring clergy. April, May, June, passed; and it is no overstatement to say that by the end of the last-named month Gertrude wellnigh longed for the death of a fellow-creature. Instead of her formal prayers each night, her unconscious prayer was, 'O Lord, hang some guilty or innocent person soon!'

This time she made earlier inquiries, and was altogether more systematic in her proceedings. Moreover, the season was summer, between the haymaking and the harvest, and in the leisure thus afforded him her husband had been holiday-taking away from home.

The assizes were in July, and she went to the inn as before. There was to be one execution – only one – for arson.

Her greatest problem was not how to get to Casterbridge, but what means she should adopt for obtaining admission to the jail. Though access for such purposes had formerly never been denied, the custom had fallen into desuetude; and in contemplating her possible difficulties, she was again almost driven to fall back upon her husband. But, on sounding him about the assizes, he was so uncommunicative, so more than usually cold, that she did not proceed, and decided that whatever she did she would do alone.

Fortune, obdurate hitherto, showed her unexpected favour. On the Thursday before the Saturday fixed for the execution, Lodge remarked to her that he was going away from home for another day or two on business at a fair, and that he was sorry he could not take her with him.

She exhibited on this occasion so much readiness to stay at home that he looked at her in surprise. Time had been when she would have shown deep disappointment at the loss of such a jaunt. However, he lapsed into his usual taciturnity, and on the day named left Holmstoke.

It was now her turn. She at first had thought of driving, but on reflection held that driving would not do, since it would necessitate her keeping to the turnpike-road,[23] and so increase by tenfold the risk of her ghastly errand being found out. She decided to ride, and avoid the beaten track, notwithstanding that in her husband's stables there was no animal just at present which by any stretch of imagination could be considered a lady's mount, in spite of his promise before marriage to always keep a mare for her. He had, however, many cart-horses, fine ones of their kind; and among the rest was a serviceable creature, an equine Amazon, with a back as broad as a sofa, on which Gertrude had occasionally taken an airing when unwell. This horse she chose.

On Friday afternoon one of the men brought it round. She was dressed, and before going down looked at her shrivelled arm. 'Ah!' she said to it, 'if it had not been for you this terrible ordeal would have been saved me!'

When strapping up the bundle in which she carried a few articles of clothing, she took occasion to say to the servant, 'I take these in case I should not get back to-night from the person I am going to visit. Don't be alarmed if I am not in by ten, and close up the house as usual. I shall be at home to-morrow for certain.' She meant then to tell her husband privately: the deed accomplished was not like the deed projected. He would almost certainly forgive her.

And then the pretty palpitating Gertrude Lodge went from her husband's homestead; but though her goal was Casterbridge she did not take the direct route thither through Stickleford. Her cunning course at first was in precisely the opposite direction. As soon as she was out of sight, however, she turned to the left, by a road which led into Egdon, and on entering the heath wheeled round, and set out in the true course, due westerly. A more private way down the county could not be imagined; and as to direction, she had merely to keep her horse's head to a point a little to the right of the sun. She knew that she would light upon a furze-cutter or cottager of some sort from time to time, from whom she might correct her bearing.

Though the date was comparatively recent, Egdon was much less fragmentary in character than now. The attempts — successful and otherwise — at cultivation on the lower slopes, which intrude and break up the original heath into small detached heaths, had not been carried far; Enclosure Acts[24] had not taken effect, and the banks and fences which now exclude the cattle of those villagers who formerly enjoyed rights of commonage thereon, and the carts of those who had turbary privileges[25] which kept them in firing all the year round, were not erected. Gertrude, therefore, rode along with no other obstacles than the prickly furze-bushes, the mats of heather, the white water-courses, and the natural steeps and declivities of the ground.

Her horse was sure, if heavy-footed and slow, and though a draught animal, was easy-paced; had it been otherwise, she was not a woman who could have ventured to ride over such a bit of country with a half-dead arm. It was therefore nearly eight o'clock when she drew rein to breathe her bearer on the last outlying high point of heath-land towards Casterbridge, previous to leaving Egdon for the cultivated valleys.

She halted before a pool called Rushy-pond, flanked by the ends of two hedges; a railing ran through the centre of the pond, dividing it in half. Over the railing she saw the low green country; over the green trees the roofs of the town; over the roofs a white flat façade, denoting the entrance to the county jail. On the roof of this front specks were moving about; they seemed to be workmen erecting something. Her flesh crept. She descended slowly, and was soon amid corn-fields and pastures. In another half-hour, when it was almost dusk, Gertrude reached the White Hart, the first inn of the town on that side.

Little surprise was excited by her arrival; farmers' wives rode on horseback then more than they do now; though, for that matter, Mrs Lodge was not imagined to be a wife at all; the innkeeper supposed her some harum-skarum young woman who had come to attend 'hang-fair' next day. Neither her husband nor herself ever dealt in Casterbridge market, so that she was unknown. While dismounting she beheld a crowd of boys standing at the door of a harness-maker's shop just above the inn, looking inside it with deep interest.

'What is going on there?' she asked of the ostler.

'Making the rope for to-morrow.'

She throbbed responsively, and contracted her arm.

' 'Tis sold by the inch afterwards,' the man continued. 'I could get you a bit, miss, for nothing, if you'd like?'

She hastily repudiated any such wish, all the more from a curious creeping feeling that the condemned wretch's destiny was becoming interwoven with her own; and having engaged a room for the night, sat down to think.

Up to this time she had formed but the vaguest notions about her means of obtaining access to the prison. The words of the cunning-man [26] returned to her mind. He had implied that she should use her beauty, impaired though it was, as a pass-key. In her inexperience she knew little about jail functionaries; she had heard of a high-sheriff and an under-sheriff, but dimly only. She knew, however, that there must be a hangman, and to the hangman she determined to apply.

A WATER-SIDE HERMIT

VIII

At this date, and for several years after, there was a hangman to almost every jail. Gertrude found, on inquiry, that the Casterbridge official dwelt in a lonely cottage by a deep slow river flowing under the cliff on which the prison buildings were situate – the stream being the self-same one, though she did not know it, which watered the Stickleford and Holmstoke meads lower down in its course.

Having changed her dress, and before she had eaten or drunk – for she could not take her ease till she had ascertained some particulars – Gertrude pursued her way by a path along the water-side to the cottage indicated. Passing thus the outskirts of the jail, she discerned on the level roof over the gateway three rectangular lines against the sky, where the specks had been moving in her distant view; she recognized what the erection was, and passed quickly on. Another hundred yards brought her to the executioner's house, which a boy pointed out. It stood close to the same stream, and was hard by a weir, the waters of which emitted a steady roar.

While she stood hesitating the door opened, and an old man came forth shading a candle with one hand. Locking the door on the outside, he turned to a flight of wooden steps fixed against the end of the cottage, and began to ascend them, this being evidently the staircase to his bedroom. Gertrude hastened forward, but by the time she reached the foot of the ladder he was at the top. She called to him loudly enough to be heard above the roar of the weir; he looked down and said, 'What d'ye want here?'

'To speak to you a minute.'

The candle-light, such as it was, fell upon her imploring, pale, upturned face, and Davies (as the hangman was called) backed down the ladder. 'I was just going to bed,' he said; ' "Early to bed and early to rise," but I don't mind stopping a minute for such a one as you. Come into house.' He reopened the door, and preceded her to the room within.

The implements of his daily work, which was that of a jobbing gardener, stood in a corner, and seeing probably that she looked rural, he said, 'If you want me to undertake country work I can't come, for I never leave Casterbridge for gentle nor simple[27] – not I. My real calling is officer of justice,' he added formally.

'Yes, yes! That's it. To-morrow!'

'Ah! I thought so. Well, what's the matter about that? 'Tis no use to come here about the knot – folks do come continually, but I tell 'em one knot is as merciful as another if ye keep it under the ear. Is the unfortunate man a relation; or, I should say, perhaps' (looking at her dress) 'a person who's been in your employ?'

'No. What time is the execution?'

'The same as usual – twelve o'clock, or as soon after as the London mail-coach gets in. We always wait for that, in case of a reprieve.'

'O – a reprieve – I hope not!' she said involuntarily.

'Well, – hee, hee! – as a matter of business, so do I! But still, if ever a young fellow deserved to be let off, this one does; only just turned eighteen, and only present by chance when the rick was fired. Howsomever, there's not much risk of it, as they are obliged to make an example of him, there having been so much destruction of property that way lately.'

'I mean,' she explained, 'that I want to touch him for a

charm, a cure of an affliction, by the advice of a man who has proved the virtue of the remedy.'

'O yes, miss! Now I understand. I've had such people come in past years. But it didn't strike me that you looked of a sort to require blood-turning. What's the complaint? The wrong kind for this, I'll be bound.'

'My arm.' She reluctantly showed the withered skin.

'Ah! – 'tis all a-scram!'[28] said the hangman, examining it.

'Yes,' said she.

'Well,' he continued, with interest, 'that *is* the class o' subject, I'm bound to admit! I like the look of the wownd; it is truly as suitable for the cure as any I ever saw. 'Twas a knowing-man that sent 'ee, whoever he was.'

'You can contrive for me all that's necessary?' she said breathlessly.

'You should really have gone to the governor of the jail, and your doctor with 'ee, and given your name and address – that's how it used to be done, if I recollect. Still, perhaps, I can manage it for a trifling fee.'

'O, thank you! I would rather do it this way, as I should like it kept private.'

'Lover not to know, eh?'

'No – husband.'

'Aha! Very well. I'll get 'ee a touch of the corpse.'

'Where is it now?' she said, shuddering.

'It? – *he*, you mean; he's living yet. Just inside that little small winder up there in the glum.'[29] He signified the jail on the cliff above.

She thought of her husband and her friends. 'Yes, of course,' she said; 'and how am I to proceed?'

He took her to the door. 'Now, do you be waiting at the little wicket in the wall, that you'll find up there in the lane, not later than one o'clock. I will open it from the inside, as I shan't come home to dinner till he's cut down. Good-night. Be punctual; and if you don't want anybody to know 'ee, wear a veil. Ah – once I had such a daughter as you!'

She went away, and climbed the path above, to assure herself that she would be able to find the wicket next day. Its outline was soon visible to her – a narrow opening in the outer wall of the prison precincts. The steep was so great that, having reached the wicket, she stopped a moment to breathe; and, looking back upon the water-side cot,[30] saw the hangman again ascending his outdoor staircase. He entered the loft or chamber to which it led, and in a few minutes extinguished his light.

The town clock struck ten, and she returned to the White Hart as she had come.

A RENCOUNTER

IX

It was one o'clock on Saturday. Gertrude Lodge, having been admitted to the jail as above described, was sitting in a waiting-room within the second gate, which stood under a classic archway of ashlar,[31] then comparatively modern, and bearing the inscription, 'COVNTY JAIL: 1793'. This had been the façade she saw from the heath the day before. Near at hand was a passage to the roof on which the gallows stood.

The town was thronged, and the market suspended; but Gertrude had seen scarcely a soul. Having kept her room till the hour of the appointment, she had proceeded to the spot by a way which avoided the open space below the cliff where the spectators had gathered; but she could, even now, hear the multitudinous babble of their voices, out of which rose at intervals the hoarse croak of a single voice uttering the words, 'Last dying speech and confession!' There had been no reprieve, and the execution was over; but the crowd still waited to see the body taken down.

Soon the persistent woman heard a trampling overhead, then a hand beckoned to her, and, following directions, she went out and crossed the inner paved court beyond the gatehouse, her knees trembling so that she could scarcely walk. One of her arms was out of its sleeve, and only covered by her shawl.

On the spot at which she had now arrived were two trestles,

and before she could think of their purpose she heard heavy feet descending stairs somewhere at her back. Turn her head she would not, or could not, and, rigid in this position, she was conscious of a rough coffin passing her shoulder, borne by four men. It was open, and in it lay the body of a young man, wearing the smockfrock of a rustic, and fustian[32] breeches. The corpse had been thrown into the coffin so hastily that the skirt of the smockfrock was hanging over. The burden was temporarily deposited on the trestles.

By this time the young woman's state was such that a grey mist seemed to float before her eyes, on account of which, and the veil she wore, she could scarcely discern anything: it was as though she had nearly died, but was held up by a sort of galvanism.[33]

'Now!' said a voice close at hand, and she was just conscious that the word had been addressed to her.

By a last strenuous effort she advanced, at the same time hearing persons approaching behind her. She bared her poor curst arm; and Davies, uncovering the face of the corpse, took Gertrude's hand, and held it so that her arm lay across the dead man's neck, upon a line the colour of an unripe blackberry, which surrounded it.

Gertrude shrieked: 'the turn o' the blood', predicted by the conjuror, had taken place. But at that moment a second shriek rent the air of the enclosure: it was not Gertrude's, and its effect upon her was to make her start round.

Immediately behind her stood Rhoda Brook, her face drawn, and her eyes red with weeping. Behind Rhoda stood Gertrude's own husband; his countenance lined, his eyes dim, but without a tear.

'D—n you! what are you doing here?' he said hoarsely.

'Hussy – to come between us and our child now!' cried Rhoda. 'This is the meaning of what Satan showed me in the vision! You are like her at last!' And clutching the bare arm of the younger woman, she pulled her unresistingly back against the wall. Immediately Brook had loosened her hold the fragile young Gertrude slid down against the feet of her husband. When he lifted her up she was unconscious.

The mere sight of the twain had been enough to suggest to her that the dead young man was Rhoda's son. At that time the relatives of an executed convict had the privilege of claiming the body for burial, if they chose to do so; and it was for this purpose that Lodge was awaiting the inquest with Rhoda. He had been summoned by her as soon as the young man was taken in the crime, and at different times since; and he had attended in court during the trial. This was the 'holiday' he had been indulging in of late. The two wretched parents had wished to avoid exposure; and hence had come themselves for the body, a waggon and sheet for its conveyance and covering being in waiting outside.

Gertrude's case was so serious that it was deemed advisable to call to her the surgeon who was at hand. She was taken out of the jail into the town; but she never reached home alive. Her delicate vitality, sapped perhaps by the paralysed arm, collapsed under the double shock that followed the severe strain, physical and mental, to which she had subjected herself during the previous twenty-four hours. Her blood had been 'turned' indeed – too far. Her death took place in the town three days after.

Her husband was never seen in Casterbridge again; once only in the old market-place at Anglebury, which he had so much frequented, and very seldom in public anywhere. Burdened at first with moodiness and remorse, he eventually changed for the better, and appeared as a chastened and thoughtful man. Soon after attending the funeral of his poor young wife he took steps towards giving up the farms in Holmstoke and the adjoining parish, and, having sold every head of his stock, he went away to Port-Bredy, at the other end of the county, living there in solitary lodgings till his death two years later of a painless decline. It was then found that he had bequeathed the whole of his not inconsiderable property to a reformatory for boys, subject to the payment of a small annuity to Rhoda Brook, if she could be found to claim it.

For some time she could not be found; but eventually she reappeared in her old parish, – absolutely refusing, however, to have anything to do with the provision made for her. Her monotonous milking at the dairy was resumed, and followed for many long years, till her form became bent, and her once abundant dark hair white and worn away at the forehead – perhaps by long pressure against the cows. Here, sometimes, those who knew her experiences would stand and observe her, and wonder what sombre thoughts were beating inside that impassive, wrinkled brow, to the rhythm of the alternating milk-streams.

I

THE shouts of the village-boys came in at the window, accompanied by broken laughter from loungers at the inn-door; but the brothers Halborough worked on.

They were sitting in a bedroom of the master-millwright's house, engaged in the untutored reading of Greek and Latin. It was no tale of Homeric blows and knocks,[1] Argonautic voyaging,[2] or Theban family woe[3] that inflamed their imaginations and spurred them onward. They were plodding away at the Greek Testament, immersed in a chapter of the idiomatic and difficult Epistle to the Hebrews.

The Dog-day[4] sun in its decline reached the low ceiling with slanting sides, and the shadows of the great goat's-willow swayed and interchanged upon the walls like a spectral army manoeuvring. The open casement which admitted the remoter sounds now brought the voice of some one close at hand. It was their sister, a pretty girl of fourteen, who stood in the court below.

'I can see the tops of your heads! What's the use of staying up there? I like you not to go out with the street-boys; but do come and play with me!'

They treated her as an inadequate interlocutor, and put her off with some slight word. She went away disappointed. Presently there was a dull noise of heavy footsteps at the side of the house, and one of the brothers sat up. 'I fancy I hear him coming,' he murmured, his eyes on the window.

A man in the light drab clothes of an old-fashioned country tradesman approached from round the corner, reeling as he came. The elder son flushed with anger, rose from his books, and descended the stairs. The younger sat on, till, after the lapse of a few minutes, his brother re-entered the room.

'Did Rosa see him?'

'No.'

'Nor anybody?'

'No.'

'What have you done with him?'

'He's in the straw-shed. I got him in with some trouble, and he has fallen asleep. I thought this would be the explanation of his absence! No stones dressed for Miller Kench, the great wheel of the saw-mills waiting for new float-boards,[5] even the poor folk not able to get their waggons wheeled.'

'What *is* the use of poring over this!' said the younger, shutting up Donnegan's *Lexicon*[6] with a slap. 'O if we had only been able to keep mother's nine hundred pounds, what we could have done!'

'How well she had estimated the sum necessary! Four hundred and fifty each, she thought. And I have no doubt that we could have done it on that, with care.'

This loss of the nine hundred pounds was the sharp thorn of their crown. It was a sum which their mother had amassed with great exertion and self-denial, by adding to a chance legacy such other small amounts as she could lay hands on from time to time; and she had intended with the hoard to indulge the dear wish of her heart – that of sending her sons, Joshua and Cornelius, to one of the Universities, having been informed that from four hundred to four hundred and fifty each might carry them through their terms with such great economy as she knew she could trust them to practise. But she had died a year or two before this time, worn out by too keen a strain towards these ends; and the money, coming unreservedly into the hands of their father, had been nearly dissipated. With its exhaustion went all opportunity and hope of a university degree for the sons.

'It drives me mad when I think of it,' said Joshua, the elder. 'And here we work and work in our own bungling way, and the utmost we can hope for is a term of years as national school-masters,[7] and possible admission to a Theological college, and ordination as despised licentiates.'[8]

The anger of the elder was reflected as simple sadness in the face of the other. 'We can preach the Gospel as well without a hood[9] on our surplices as with one,' he said with feeble consolation.

'Preach the Gospel – true,' said Joshua with a slight pursing of mouth. 'But we can't rise!'

'Let us make the best of it, and grind on.'

The other was silent, and they drearily bent over their books again.

The cause of all this gloom, the millwright Halborough, now snoring in the shed, had been a thriving master-machinist, notwithstanding his free and careless disposition, till a taste for a more than adequate quantity of strong liquor took hold of him; since when his habits had interfered with his business sadly. Already millers went elsewhere for their gear, and only one set of hands was now kept going, though there were formerly two. Already he found a difficulty in meeting his men at the week's end, and though they had been reduced in number there was barely enough work to do for those who remained.

The sun dropped lower and vanished, the shouts of the village children ceased to resound, darkness cloaked the students' bedroom, and all the scene outwardly breathed peace. None knew of the fevered youthful ambitions that throbbed in two breasts within the quiet creeper-covered walls of the millwright's house.

In a few months the brothers left the village of their birth to enter themselves as students in a training college for schoolmasters; first having placed their young sister Rosa under as efficient a tuition at a fashionable watering-place as the means at their disposal could command.

II

A man in semi-clerical dress was walking along the road which led from the railway-station into a provincial town. As he walked he read persistently, only looking up once now and then to see that he was keeping on the foot-track and to avoid other passengers. At those moments, whoever had known the former students at the millwright's would have perceived that one of them, Joshua Halborough, was the peripatetic reader here.

What had been simple force in the youth's face was energized judgement in the man's. His character was gradually writing itself out in his countenance. That he was watching his own career with deeper and deeper interest, that he continually 'heard his days before him', and cared to hear little else, might have been hazarded from what was seen there. His ambitions were, in truth, passionate, yet controlled; so that the germs of many more plans than ever blossomed to maturity had place in him; and forward visions were kept purposely in twilight, to avoid distraction.

Events so far had been encouraging. Shortly after assuming the mastership of his first school he had obtained an introduction to the Bishop of a diocese far from his native county, who had looked upon him as a promising young man and taken him in hand. He was now in the second year of his residence at the theological college of the cathedral-town, and would soon be presented for ordination.

He entered the town, turned into a back street, and then into a yard, keeping his book before him till he set foot under the arch of the latter place. Round the arch was written 'National School', and the stonework of the jambs was worn away as nothing but boys and the waves of ocean will wear it. He was soon amid the sing-song accents of the scholars.

His brother Cornelius, who was the schoolmaster here, laid down the pointer with which he was directing attention to the Capes of Europe, and came forward.

'That's his brother Jos!' whispered one of the sixth-standard boys. 'He's going to be a pa'son. He's now at college.'

'Corney is going to be one too, when he's saved enough money,' said another.

After greeting his brother, whom he had not seen for several months, the junior began to explain his system of teaching geography.

But Halborough the elder took no interest in the subject. 'How about your own studies?' he asked. 'Did you get the books I sent?'

Cornelius had received them, and he related what he was doing.

'Mind you work in the morning. What time do you get up?'

The younger replied: 'Half-past five.'

'Half-past four is not a minute too soon this time of the year. There is no time like the morning for construing.[10] I don't know why, but when I feel even too dreary to read a novel I can translate – there is something mechanical about it I suppose. Now, Cornelius, you are rather behindhand, and have some heavy reading before you if you mean to get out of this next Christmas.'

'I am afraid I have.'

'We must soon sound the Bishop. I am sure you will get a title[11] without difficulty when he has heard all. The sub-dean, the principal of my college, says that the best plan will be for you to come there when his lordship is present at an examination, and he'll get you a personal interview with him. Mind you make a good impression upon him. I found in my case that that was everything, and doctrine almost nothing. You'll do for a deacon, Corney, if not for a priest.'

The younger remained thoughtful. 'Have you heard from Rosa lately?' he asked; 'I had a letter this morning.'

'Yes. The little minx writes rather too often. She is home-sick – though Brussels must be an attractive place enough. But she must make the most of her time over there. I thought a year would be enough for her, after that high-class school at Sandbourne, but I have decided to give her two, and make a good job of it, expensive as the establishment is.'

Their two rather harsh faces had softened directly they began to speak of their sister, whom they loved more ambitiously than they loved themselves.

'But where is the money to come from, Joshua?'

'I have already got it.' He looked round, and finding that some boys were near withdrew a few steps. 'I have borrowed it at five per cent from the farmer who used to occupy the farm next our field. You remember him.'

'But about paying him?'

'I shall pay him by degrees out of my stipend. No, Cornelius, it was no use to do the thing by halves. She promises to be a most attractive, not to say beautiful, girl. I have seen that for years; and if her face is not her fortune, her face and her brains together will be, if I observe and contrive aright. That she should be, every inch of her, an accomplished and refined woman, was indispensable for the fulfilment of her destiny, and for moving onwards and upwards with us; and she'll do it, you will see. I'd half starve myself rather than take her away from that school now.'

They looked round the school they were in. To Cornelius it was natural and familiar enough, but to Joshua, with his limited human sympathies, who had just dropped in from a superior sort of place, the sight jarred unpleasantly, as being that of something he had left behind. 'I shall be glad when you are out of this,' he said, 'and in your pulpit, and well through your first sermon.'

'You may as well say inducted into my fat living, while you are about it.'

'Ah, well – don't think lightly of the Church. There's a fine work for any man of energy in the Church, as you'll find,' he said fervidly. 'Torrents of infidelity to be stemmed, new views of old subjects to be expounded, truths in spirit to be substituted for truths in the letter . . .' He lapsed into reverie with the vision of his career, persuading himself that it was ardour for Christianity which spurred him on, and not pride of place. He had shouldered a body of doctrine, and was prepared to defend it tooth and nail, solely for the honour and glory that warriors win.

'If the Church is elastic, and stretches to the shape of the time, she'll last, I suppose,' said Cornelius. 'If not –. Only think, I bought a copy of Paley's *Evidences*,[12] best edition, broad margins, excellent preservation, at a bookstall the other day for – ninepence; and I thought that at this rate Christianity must be in rather a bad way.'

'No, no!' said the other almost angrily. 'It only shows that such defences are no longer necessary. Men's eyes can see the truth without extraneous assistance. Besides, we are in for Christianity, and must stick to her whether or no. I am just now going right through Pusey's *Library of the Fathers*.'[13]

'You'll be a bishop, Joshua, before you have done!'

'Ah!' said the other bitterly, shaking his head. 'Perhaps I might have been – I might have been! But where is my D.D. or LL.D.; and how be a bishop without that kind of appendage? Archbishop Tillotson[14] was the son of a Sowerby clothier, but he was sent to Clare College. To hail Oxford or Cambridge as *alma mater*[15] is not for me – for us! My God! when I think of what we should have been – what fair promise has been blighted by that cursed, worthless –'

'Hush, hush! ... But I feel it, too, as much as you. I have seen it more forcibly lately. You would have obtained your degree long before this time – possibly fellowship – and I should have been on my way to mine.'

'Don't talk of it,' said the other. 'We must do the best we can.'

They looked out of the window sadly, through the dusty panes, so high up that only the sky was visible. By degrees the haunting trouble loomed again, and Cornelius broke the silence with a whisper: 'He has called on me!'

The living pulses died on Joshua's face, which grew arid as a clinker. 'When was that?' he asked quickly.

'Last week.'

'How did he get here – so many miles?'

'Came by railway. He came to ask for money.'

'Ah!'

'He says he will call on you.'

Joshua replied resignedly. The theme of their conversation spoilt his buoyancy for that afternoon. He returned in the evening, Cornelius accompanying him to the station; but he did not read in the train which took him back to the Fountall Theological College, as he had done on the way out. That ineradicable trouble still remained as a squalid spot in the expanse of his life. He sat with the other students in the cathedral choir next day; and the recollection of the trouble obscured the purple splendour thrown by the panes upon the floor.

It was afternoon. All was as still in the Close as a cathedral-green can be between the Sunday services, and the incessant cawing of the rooks was the only sound. Joshua Halborough had finished his ascetic lunch, and had gone into the library, where he stood for a few moments looking out of the large window facing the green. He saw walking slowly across it a man in a fustian coat and a battered white hat with a much-ruffled nap, having upon his arm a tall gipsy-woman wearing long brass earrings. The man was staring quizzically at the west front of the cathedral, and Halborough recognized in him the form and features of his father. Who the woman was he knew not. Almost as soon as Joshua became conscious of these things, the sub-dean, who was also the principal of the college, and of whom the young man stood in more awe than of the Bishop himself, emerged from the gate and entered a path across the Close. The pair met the dignitary, and to Joshua's horror his father turned and addressed the sub-dean.

What passed between them he could not tell. But as he stood in a cold sweat he saw his father place his hand familiarly on the sub-dean's shoulder; the shrinking response of the latter, and his quick withdrawal, told his feeling. The woman seemed to say nothing, but when the sub-dean had passed by they came on towards the college gate.

Halborough flew along the corridor and out at a side door, so as to intercept them before they could reach the front entrance, for which they were making. He caught them behind a clump of laurel.

'By Jerry, here's the very chap! Well, you're a fine fellow, Jos, never to send your father as much as a twist o' baccy on such an occasion, and to leave him to travel all these miles to find 'ee out!'

'First, who is this?' said Joshua Halborough with pale dignity, waving his hand towards the buxom woman with the great earrings.

'Dammy, the mis'ess! Your step-mother! Didn't you know I'd married? She helped me home from market one night, and we came to terms, and struck the bargain. Didn't we, Selinar?'

'Oi, by the great Lord an' we did!' simpered the lady.

'Well, what sort of a place is this you are living in?' asked the millwright. 'A kind of house-of-correction,[16] apparently?'

Joshua listened abstractedly, his features set to resignation. Sick at heart he was going to ask them if they were in want of any necessary, any meal, when his father cut him short by saying, 'Why, we've called to ask ye to come round and take pot-luck with us at the Cock-and-Bottle, where we've put up for the day, on our way to see mis'ess's friends at Binegar Fair, where they'll be lying under canvas for a night or two. As for the victuals at the Cock I can't testify to 'em at all; but for the drink, they've the rarest drop of Old Tom that I've tasted for many a year.'

'Thanks; but I am a teetotaller; and I have lunched,' said Joshua, who could fully believe his father's testimony to the gin, from the odour of his breath. 'You see we have to observe regular habits here; and I couldn't be seen at the Cock-and-Bottle just now.'

'O dammy, then don't come, your reverence. Perhaps you won't mind standing treat for those who can be seen there?'

'Not a penny,' said the younger firmly. 'You've had enough already.'

'Thank you for nothing. By the bye, who was that spindle-legged, shoe-buckled parson feller we met by now? He seemed to think we should poison him!'

Joshua remarked coldly that it was the principal of his college, guardedly inquiring, 'Did you tell him whom you were come to see?'

His father did not reply. He and his strapping gipsy wife – if she were his wife – stayed no longer, and disappeared in the direction of the High Street. Joshua Halborough went back to the library. Determined as was his nature, he wept hot tears upon the books, and was immeasurably more wretched that afternoon than the unwelcome millwright. In the evening he sat down and wrote a letter to his brother, in which, after stating what had happened, and expatiating upon this new disgrace in the gipsy wife, he propounded to plan for raising money sufficient to induce the couple to emigrate to Canada. 'It is our only chance,' he said. 'The case as it stands is maddening. For a successful painter, sculptor, musician, author, who takes society by storm, it is no drawback, it is sometimes even a romantic recommendation, to hail from outcasts and profligates. But for a clergyman of the Church of England! Cornelius, it is fatal! To succeed in the Church, people must believe in you, first of all, as a gentleman, secondly as a man of means, thirdly as a scholar, fourthly as a preacher, fifthly, perhaps, as a Christian, — but always first as a gentleman, with all their heart and soul and strength. I would have faced the fact of being a small machinist's son, and have taken my chance, if he'd been in any sense respectable and decent. The essence of Christianity is humility, and by the help of God I would have brazened it out. But this terrible vagabondage and disreputable connection! If he does not accept my terms and leave the country, it will extinguish us and kill me. For how can we live, and relinquish our high aim, and bring down our dear sister Rosa to the level of a gipsy's step-daughter?'

III

There was excitement in the parish of Narrobourne one day. The congregation had just come out from morning service, and the whole conversation was of the new curate, Mr Halborough, who had officiated for the first time, in the absence of the rector.

Never before had the feeling of the villagers approached a level which could be called excitement on such a matter as this. The droning which had been the rule in that quiet old place for a century seemed ended at last. They repeated the text to each other as a refrain: 'O Lord, be thou my helper!' [17] Not within living memory till to-day had the subject of the sermon formed the topic of conversation from the church door to the churchyard gate, to the exclusion of personal remarks on those who had been present, and on the week's news in general.

The thrilling periods of the preacher hung about their minds all that day. The parish being steeped in indifferentism, it happened that when the youths and maidens, middle-aged and old people, who had attended church that morning, recurred as by a fascination to what Halborough had said, they did so more or less indirectly, and even with the subterfuge of a light laugh that was not real, so great was their shyness under the novelty of their sensations.

What was more curious than that these unconventional villagers should have been excited by a preacher of a new school after forty years of familiarity with the old hand who had had charge of their souls, was the effect of Halborough's address upon the occupants of the manor-house pew, including the owner of the estate. These thought they knew how to discount the mere sensational sermon, how to minimize flash oratory to its bare proportions; but they had yielded like the rest of the assembly to the charm of the newcomer.

Mr Fellmer, the landowner, was a young widower, whose mother, still in the prime of life, had returned to her old position in the family mansion since the death of her son's wife in the year after her marriage, at the birth of a fragile little girl. From the date of his loss to the present time, Fellmer had led an inactive existence in the seclusion of the parish; a lack of motive seemed to leave him listless. He had gladly reinstated his mother in the gloomy house, and his main occupation now lay in stewarding his estate, which was not large. Mrs Fellmer, who had sat beside him under Halborough this morning, was a cheerful, straightforward woman, who did her marketing and her alms-giving in person, was fond of old-fashioned flowers, and walked about the village on very wet days visiting the parishioners. These, the only two great ones of Narrobourne, were impressed by Joshua's eloquence as much as the cottagers.

Halborough had been briefly introduced to them on his arrival some days before, and, their interest being kindled, they waited a few moments till he came out of the vestry, to walk down the churchyard-path with him. Mrs Fellmer spoke warmly of the sermon, of the good fortune of the parish in his advent, and hoped he had found comfortable quarters.

Halborough, faintly flushing, said that he had obtained very fair lodgings in the roomy house of a farmer, whom he named.

She feared he would find it very lonely, especially in the evenings, and hoped they would see a good deal of him. When would he dine with them? Could he not come that day – it must be so dull for him the first Sunday evening in country lodgings?

Halborough replied that it would give him much pleasure, but that he feared he must decline. 'I am not altogether alone,' he said. 'My sister, who has just returned from Brussels, and who felt, as you do, that I should be rather dismal by myself, has accompanied me hither to stay a few days till she has put my rooms in order and set me going. She was too fatigued to come to church, and is waiting for me now at the farm.'

'O, but bring your sister – that will be still better! I shall be delighted to know her. How I wish I had been aware! Do tell her, please, that we had no idea of her presence.'

Halborough assured Mrs Fellmer that he would certainly bear the message; but as to her coming he was not so sure. The real truth was, however, that the matter would be decided by him, Rosa having an almost filial respect for his wishes. But he was uncertain as to the state of her wardrobe, and had determined that she should not enter the manor-house at a disadvantage that evening, when there would probably be plenty of opportunities in the future of her doing so becomingly.

He walked to the farm in long strides. This, then, was the outcome of his first morning's work as curate here. Things had gone fairly well with him. He had been ordained; he was in a comfortable parish, where he would exercise almost sole supervision, the rector being infirm. He had made a deep impression at starting, and the absence of a hood seemed to have done him no harm. Moreover, by considerable persuasion and payment, his father and the dark woman had been shipped off to Canada, where they were not likely to interfere greatly with his interests.

Rosa came out to meet him. 'Ah! you should have gone to church like a good girl,' he said.

'Yes – I wished I had afterwards. But I do so hate church as a rule that even your preaching was underestimated in my mind. It was too bad of me!'

The girl who spoke thus playfully was fair, tall, and sylph-like, in a muslin dress, and with just the coquettish *désinvolture*[18] which an English girl brings home from abroad, and loses again after a few months of native life. Joshua was the reverse of playful; the world was too important a concern for him to indulge in light moods. He told her in decided, practical phraseology of the invitation.

'Now, Rosa, we must go – that's settled – if you've a dress that can be made fit to wear all on the hop like this. You didn't, of course, think of bringing an evening dress to such an out-of-the-way place?'

But Rosa had come from the wrong city to be caught napping in those matters. 'Yes, I did,' said she. 'One never knows what may turn up.'

'Well done! Then off we go at seven.'

The evening drew on, and at dusk they started on foot, Rosa pulling up the edge of her skirt under her cloak out of the way of the dews, so that it formed a great wind-bag all round her, and carrying her satin shoes under her arm. Joshua would not let her wait till she got indoors before changing them, as she proposed, but insisted on her performing that operation under a tree, so that they might enter as if they had not walked. He was nervously formal about such trifles, while Rosa took the whole proceeding – walk, dressing, dinner, and all – as a pastime. To Joshua it was a serious step in life.

A more unexpected kind of person for a curate's sister was never presented at a dinner. The surprise of Mrs Fellmer was unconcealed. She had looked forward to a Dorcas, or Martha, or Rhoda[19] at the outside, and a shade of misgiving crossed her face. It was possible that, had the young lady accompanied her brother to church, there would have been no dining at Narrobourne House that day.

Not so with the young widower, her son. He resembled a

sleeper who had awaked in a summer noon expecting to find it only dawn. He could scarcely help stretching his arms and yawning in their faces, so strong was his sense of being suddenly aroused to an unforeseen thing. When they had sat down to table he at first talked to Rosa somewhat with the air of a ruler in the land; but the woman lurking in the acquaintance soon brought him to his level, and the girl from Brussels saw him looking at her mouth, her hands, her contour, as if he could not quite comprehend how they got created: then he dropped into the more satisfactory stage which discerns no particulars.

He talked but little; she said much. The homeliness of the Fellmers, to her view, though they were regarded with such awe down here, quite disembarrassed her. The squire had become so unpractised, had dropped so far into the shade during the last year or so of his life, that he had almost forgotten what the world contained till this evening reminded him. His mother, after her first moments of doubt, appeared to think that he must be left to his own guidance, and gave her attention to Joshua.

With all his foresight and doggedness of aim, the result of that dinner exceeded Halborough's expectations. In weaving his ambitions he had viewed his sister Rosa as a slight, bright thing to be helped into notice by his abilities; but it now began to dawn upon him that the physical gifts of nature to her might do more for them both than nature's intellectual gifts to himself. While he was patiently boring the tunnel Rosa seemed about to fly over the mountain.

He wrote the next day to his brother, now occupying his own old rooms in the theological college, telling him exultingly of the unanticipated *début* of Rosa at the manor-house. The next post brought him a reply of congratulation, dashed with the counteracting intelligence that his father did not like Canada – that his gipsy wife had deserted him, which made him feel so dreary that he thought of returning home.

In his recent satisfaction at his own successes Joshua Halborough had well-nigh forgotten his chronic trouble – latterly screened by distance. But it now returned upon him; he saw more in this brief announcement than his brother seemed to see. It was the cloud no bigger than a man's hand.[20]

IV

The following December, a day or two before Christmas, Mrs Fellmer and her son were walking up and down the broad gravel path which bordered the east front of the house. Till within the last half-hour the morning had been a drizzling one, and they had just emerged for a short turn before luncheon.

'You see, dear mother,' the son was saying, 'it is the peculiarity of my position which makes her appear to me in such a desirable light. When you consider how I have been crippled at starting, how my life has been maimed; that I feel anything like publicity distasteful, that I have no political ambition, and that my chief aim and hope lie in the education of the little thing Annie has left me, you must see how desirable a wife like Miss Halborough would be, to prevent my becoming a mere vegetable.'

'If you adore her, I suppose you must have her!' replied his mother with dry indirectness. 'But you'll find that she will not be content to live on here as you do, giving her whole mind to a young child.'

'That's just where we differ. Her very disqualification, that of being a nobody, as you call it, is her recommendation in my eyes. Her lack of influential connections limits her ambition. From what I know of her, a life in this place is all that she would wish for. She would never care to go outside the park-gates if it were necessary to stay within.'

'Being in love with her, Albert, and meaning to marry her, you invent your practical reasons to make the case respectable. Well, do as you will; I have no authority over you, so why should you consult me? You mean to propose on this very occasion, no doubt. Don't you, now?'

'By no means. I am merely revolving the idea in my mind. If

on further acquaintance she turns out to be as good as she has hitherto seemed – well, I shall see. Admit, now, that you like her.'

'I readily admit it. She is very captivating at first sight. But as a stepmother to your child! You seem mighty anxious, Albert, to get rid of me!'

'Not at all. And I am not so reckless as you think. I don't make up my mind in a hurry. But the thought having occurred to me, I mention it to you at once, mother. If you dislike it, say so.'

'I don't say anything. I will try to make the best of it if you are determined. When does she come?'

'To-morrow.'

All this time there were great preparations in train at the curate's, who was now a householder. Rosa, whose two or three weeks' stay on two occasions earlier in the year had so affected the squire, was coming again, and at the same time her younger brother Cornelius, to make up a family party. Rosa, who journeyed from the Midlands, could not arrive till late in the evening, but Cornelius was to get there in the afternoon, Joshua going out to meet him in his walk across the fields from the railway.

Everything being ready in Joshua's modest abode he started on his way, his heart buoyant and thankful, if ever it was in his life. He was of such good report himself that his brother's path into holy orders promised to be unexpectedly easy; and he longed to compare experiences with him, even though there was on hand a more exciting matter still. From his youth he had held that, in old-fashioned country places, the Church conferred social prestige up to a certain point at a cheaper price than any other profession or pursuit; and events seemed to be proving him right.

He had walked about half an hour when he saw Cornelius coming along the path; and in a few minutes the two brothers met. The experiences of Cornelius had been less immediately interesting than those of Joshua, but his personal position was satisfactory, and there was nothing to account for the singularly subdued manner that he exhibited, which at first Joshua set down to the fatigue of over-study; and he proceeded to the subject of Rosa's arrival in the evening, and the probable consequences of this her third visit. 'Before next Easter she'll be his wife, my boy,' said Joshua with grave exultation.

Cornelius shook his head. 'She comes too late!' he returned.

'What do you mean?'

'Look here.' He produced the Fountall paper, and placed his finger on a paragraph, which Joshua read. It appeared under the report of Petty Sessions, and was a commonplace case of disorderly conduct, in which a man was sent to prison for seven days for breaking windows in that town.

'Well?' said Joshua.

'It happened during an evening that I was in the street; and the offender is our father.'

'Not – how – I sent him more money on his promising to stay in Canada?'

'He is home, safe enough.' Cornelius in the same gloomy tone gave the remainder of his information. He had witnessed the scene, unobserved of his father, and had heard him say that he was on his way to see his daughter, who was going to marry a rich gentleman. The only good fortune attending the untoward incident was that the millwright's name had been printed as Joshua Alborough.

'Beaten! We are to be beaten on the eve of our expected victory!' said the elder brother. 'How did he guess that Rosa was likely to marry? Good Heaven! Cornelius, you seem doomed to bring bad news always, do you not!'

'I do,' said Cornelius. 'Poor Rosa!'

It was almost in tears, so great was their heart-sickness and shame, that the brothers walked the remainder of the way to Joshua's dwelling. In the evening they set out to meet Rosa, bringing her to the village in a fly; and when she had come into the house, and was sitting down with them, they almost forgot their secret anxiety in contemplating her, who knew nothing about it.

Next day the Fellmers came, and the two or three days after that were a lively time. That the squire was yielding to his impulses – making up his mind – there could be no doubt. On

Sunday Cornelius read the service, and Joshua preached. Mrs Fellmer was quite maternal towards Rosa, and it appeared that she had decided to welcome the inevitable with a good grace. The pretty girl was to spend yet another afternoon with the elder lady, superintending some parish treat at the house in observance of Christmas, and afterwards to stay on to dinner, her brothers to fetch her in the evening. They were also invited to dine, but they could not accept owing to an engagement.

The engagement was of a sombre sort. They were going to meet their father, who would that day be released from Fountall Gaol, and try to persuade him to keep away from Narrobourne. Every exertion was to be made to get him back to Canada, to his old home in the Midlands – anywhere, so that he would not impinge disastrously upon their courses, and blast their sister's prospects of the auspicious marriage which was just then hanging in the balance.

As soon as Rosa had been fetched away by her friends at the manor-house her brothers started on their expedition, without waiting for dinner or tea. Cornelius, to whom the mill-wright always addressed his letters when he wrote any, drew from his pocket and re-read as he walked the curt note which had led to this journey being undertaken; it was despatched by their father the night before, immediately upon his liberation, and stated that he was setting out for Narrobourne at the moment of writing; that having no money he would be obliged to walk all the way; that he calculated on passing through the intervening town of Ivell about six on the following day, where he should sup at the Castle Inn, and where he hoped they would meet him with a carriage-and-pair, or some other such conveyance, that he might not disgrace them by arriving like a tramp.

'That sounds as if he gave a thought to our position,' said Cornelius.

Joshua knew the satire that lurked in the paternal words, and said nothing. Silence prevailed during the greater part of their journey. The lamps were lighted in Ivell when they entered the streets, and Cornelius, who was quite unknown in this neighbourhood, and who, moreover, was not in clerical attire, decided that he should be the one to call at the Castle Inn. Here, in answer to his inquiry under the darkness of the archway, they told him that such a man as he had described left the house about a quarter of an hour earlier, after making a meal in the kitchen-settle. He was rather the worse for liquor.

'Then,' said Joshua, when Cornelius joined him outside with this intelligence, 'we must have met and passed him! And now that I think of it, we did meet some one who was unsteady in his gait, under the trees on the other side of Hendford Hill, where it was too dark to see him.'

They rapidly retraced their steps; but for a long stretch of the way home could discern nobody. When, however, they had gone about three-quarters of the distance, they became conscious of an irregular footfall in front of them, and could see a whitish figure in the gloom. They followed dubiously. The figure met another wayfarer – the single one that had been encountered upon this lonely road – and they distinctly heard him ask the way to Narrobourne. The stranger replied – what was quite true – that the nearest way was by turning in at the stile by the next bridge, and following the footpath which branched thence across the meadows.

When the brothers reached the stile they also entered the path, but did not overtake the subject of their worry till they had crossed two or three meads, and the lights from Narrobourne manor-house were visible before them through the trees. Their father was no longer walking; he was seated against the wet bank of an adjoining hedge. Observing their forms he shouted, 'I'm going to Narrobourne; who may you be?'

They went up to him, and revealed themselves, reminding him of the plan which he had himself proposed in his note, that they should meet him at Ivell.

'By Jerry, I'd forgot it!' he said. 'Well, what do you want me to do?' His tone was distinctly quarrelsome.

A long conversation followed, which became embittered at the first hint from them that he should not come to the village. The millwright drew a quart bottle from his pocket, and chal-

lenged them to drink if they meant friendly and called themselves men. Neither of the two had touched alcohol for years,
but for once they thought it best to accept, so as not to need-
lessly provoke him.

'What's in it?' said Joshua.

'A drop of weak gin-and-water. It won't hurt 'ee. Drink
from the bottle.' Joshua did so, and his father pushed up the
bottom of the vessel so as to make him swallow a good deal in
spite of himself. It went down into his stomach like molten
lead.

'Ha, ha, that's right!' said old Halborough. 'But 'twas raw
spirit – ha, ha!'

'Why should you take me in so!' said Joshua, losing his self-
command, try as he would to keep calm.

'Because you took me in, my lad, in banishing me to that
cursed country under pretence that it was for my good. You
were a pair of hypocrites to say so. It was done to get rid of me
– no more nor less. But, by Jerry, I'm a match for ye now! I'll
spoil your souls for preaching. My daughter is going to be
married to the squire here. I've heard the news – I saw it in a
paper!'

'It is premature –'

'I know it is true; and I'm her father, and I shall give her
away, or there'll be a hell of a row, I can assure 'ee! Is that
where the gennleman lives?'

Joshua Halborough writhed in impotent despair. Fellmer had
not yet positively declared himself, his mother was hardly won
round; a scene with their father in the parish would demolish
as fair a palace of hopes as was ever builded. The millwright
rose. 'If that's where the squire lives I'm going to call. Just
arrived from Canady with her fortune – ha, ha! I wish no harm
to the gennleman, and the gennleman will wish no harm to me.
But I like to take my place in the family, and stand upon my
rights, and lower people's pride!'

'You've succeeded already! Where's that woman you took
with you –'

'Woman! She was my wife as lawful as the Constitution – a

sight more lawful than your mother was till some time after you were born!'

Joshua had for many years before heard whispers that his father had cajoled his mother in their early acquaintance, and had made somewhat tardy amends; but never from his father's lips till now. It was the last stroke, and he could not bear it. He sank back against the hedge. 'It is over!' he said. 'He ruins us all!'

The millwright moved on, waving his stick triumphantly, and the two brothers stood still. They could see his drab figure stalking along the path, and over his head the lights from the conservatory of Narrobourne House, inside which Albert Fellmer might possibly be sitting with Rosa at that moment, holding her hand, and asking her to share his home with him.

The staggering whitey-brown form, advancing to put a blot on all this, had been diminishing in the shade; and now suddenly disappeared beside a weir. There was the noise of a flounce in the water.

'He has fallen in!' said Cornelius, starting forward to run for the place at which his father had vanished.

Joshua, awaking from the stupefied reverie into which he had sunk, rushed to the other's side before he had taken ten steps. 'Stop, stop, what are you thinking of?' he whispered hoarsely, grasping Cornelius's arm.

'Pulling him out!'

'Yes, yes – so am I. But – wait a moment –'

'But, Joshua!'

'Her life and happiness, you know – Cornelius – and your reputation and mine – and our chance of rising together, all three –'

He clutched his brother's arm to the bone; and as they stood breathless the splashing and floundering in the weir continued; over it they saw the hopeful lights from the manor-house conservatory winking through the trees as their bare branches waved to and fro. In their pause there had been time to save him twice over.

The floundering and splashing grew weaker, and they could hear gurgling words: 'Help – I'm drownded! Rosie – Rosie!'

'We'll go – we *must* save him. O Joshua!'

'Yes, yes! we must!'

Still they did not move, but waited, holding each other, each thinking the same thought. Weights of lead seemed to be affixed to their feet, which would no longer obey their wills. The mead became silent. Over it they fancied they could see figures moving in the conservatory. The air up there seemed to emit gentle kisses.

Cornelius started forward at last, and Joshua almost simultaneously. Two or three minutes brought them to the brink of the stream. At first they could see nothing in the water, though it was not so deep nor the night so dark but that their father's light kerseymere[21] coat would have been visible if he had lain at the bottom. Joshua looked this way and that.

'He has drifted into the culvert,' he said.

Below the foot-bridge of the weir the stream suddenly narrowed to half its width, to pass under a barrel arch or culvert constructed for waggons to cross into the middle of the mead in haymaking time. It being at present the season of high water the arch was full to the crown, against which the ripples clucked every now and then. At this point he had just caught sight of a pale object slipping under. In a moment it was gone.

They went to the lower end, but nothing emerged. For a long time they tried at both ends to effect some communication with the interior, but to no purpose.

'We ought to have come sooner!' said the conscience-stricken Cornelius, when they were quite exhausted, and dripping wet.

'I suppose we ought,' replied Joshua heavily. He perceived his father's walking-stick on the bank; hastily picking it up he stuck it into the mud among the sedge. Then they went on.

'Shall we – say anything about this accident?' whispered Cornelius as they approached the door of Joshua's house.

'What's the use? It can do no good. We must wait until he is found.'

They went indoors and changed their clothes; after which

they started for the manor-house, reaching it about ten o'clock. Besides their sister there were only three guests; an adjoining landowner and his wife, and the infirm old rector.

Rosa, although she had parted from them so recently, grasped their hands in an ecstatic, brimming, joyful manner, as if she had not seen them for years. 'You look pale,' she said.

The brothers answered that they had had a long walk, and were somewhat tired. Everybody in the room seemed charged full with some sort of interesting knowledge: the squire's neighbour and neighbour's wife looked wisely around; and Fellmer himself played the part of host with a preoccupied bearing which approached fervour. They left at eleven, not accepting the carriage offered, the distance being so short and the roads dry. The squire came rather further into the dark with them than he need have done, and wished Rosa good-night in a mysterious manner, slightly apart from the rest.

When they were walking along Joshua said, with a desperate attempt at joviality, 'Rosa, what's going on?'

'O, I –' she began between a gasp and a bound. 'He –'

'Never mind – if it disturbs you.'

She was so excited that she could not speak connectedly at first, the practised air which she had brought home with her having disappeared. Calming herself she added, 'I am not disturbed, and nothing has happened. Only he said he wanted to ask me *something*, some day; and I said never mind that now. He hasn't asked yet, and is coming to speak to you about it. He would have done so to-night, only I asked him not to be in a hurry. But he will come to-morrow, I am sure!'

v

It was summer-time, six months later, and mowers and haymakers were at work in the meads. The manor-house, being opposite them, frequently formed a peg for conversation during these operations; and the doings of the squire, and the squire's young wife, the curate's sister – who was at present the admired of most of them, and the interest of all – met with their due amount of criticism.

Rosa was happy, if ever woman could be said to be so. She had not learnt the fate of her father, and sometimes wondered – perhaps with a sense of relief – why he did not write to her from his supposed home in Canada. Her brother Joshua had been presented to a living in a small town, shortly after her marriage, and Cornelius had thereupon succeeded to the vacant curacy of Narrobourne.

These two had awaited in deep suspense the discovery of their father's body; and yet the discovery had not been made. Every day they expected a man or a boy to run up from the meads with the intelligence; but he had never come. Days had accumulated to weeks and months; the wedding had come and gone: Joshua had tolled and read himself in at his new parish; and never a shout of amazement over the millwright's remains.

But now, in June, when they were mowing the meads, the hatches had to be drawn [22] and the water let out of its channels for the convenience of the mowers. It was thus that the discovery was made. A man, stooping low with his scythe, caught a view of the culvert lengthwise, and saw something entangled in the recently bared weeds of its bed. A day or two after there was an inquest: but the body was unrecognizable. Fish and flood had been busy with the millwright; he had no watch or marked article which could be identified; and a verdict of the accidental drowning of a person unknown settled the matter.

As the body was found in Narrobourne parish, there it had to be buried. Cornelius wrote to Joshua, begging him to come and read the service, or to send some one; he himself could not do it. Rather than let in a stranger Joshua came, and silently scanned the coroner's order handed him by the undertaker:

'I, Henry Giles, Coroner for the Mid-Division of Outer Wessex, do hereby order the Burial of the Body now shown to the Inquest Jury as the Body of an Adult Male Person Unknown . . .,' etc.

Joshua Halborough got through the service in some way, and rejoined his brother Cornelius at his house. Neither accepted an invitation to lunch at their sister's; they wished to discuss parish matters together. In the afternoon she came down, though they had already called on her, and had not expected to see her again. Her bright eyes, brown hair, flowery bonnet, lemon-coloured gloves, and flush beauty, were like an irradiation into the apartment, which they in their gloom could hardly bear.

'I forgot to tell you,' she said, 'of a curious thing which happened to me a month or two before my marriage – something which I have thought may have had a connection with the accident to the poor man you have buried to-day. It was on that evening I was at the manor-house waiting for you to fetch me; I was in the winter-garden with Albert, and we were sitting silent together, when we fancied we heard a cry in the distant meadow. We opened the door, and while Albert ran to fetch his hat, leaving me standing there, the cry was repeated, and my excited senses made me think I heard my own name. When Albert came back all was silent, and we decided that it was only a drunken shout, and not a cry for help. We both forgot the incident, and it never has occurred to me till since the funeral to-day that it might have been this stranger's cry. The name of course was only fancy, or he might have had a wife or child with a name something like mine, poor man!'

When she was gone the brothers were silent till Cornelius said, 'Now mark this, Joshua. Sooner or later she'll know.'

'How?'

'From one of us. Do you think human hearts are iron-cased safes, that you suppose we can keep this secret for ever?'

'Yes, I think they are, sometimes,' said Joshua.

'No. It will out. We shall tell.'

'What, and ruin her – kill her? Disgrace her children, and pull down the whole auspicious house of Fellmer about our ears? No! May I – drown where he was drowned before I do it! Never, never. Surely you can say the same, Cornelius!'

Cornelius seemed fortified, and no more was said. For a

long time after that day he did not see Joshua, and before the next year was out a son and heir was born to the Fellmers. The villagers rang the three bells every evening for a week and more, and were made merry by Mr Fellmer's ale; and when the christening came on Joshua paid Narrobourne another visit.

Among all the people who assembled on that day the brother clergymen were the least interested. Their minds were haunted by a spirit in kerseymere. In the evening they walked together in the fields.

'She's all right,' said Joshua. 'But here are you doing journey-work, Cornelius, and likely to continue at it till the end of the day, as far as I can see. I, too, with my petty living – what am I after all? ... To tell the truth, the Church is a poor forlorn hope for people without influence, particularly when their enthusiasm begins to flag. A social regenerator has a better chance outside, where he is unhampered by dogma and tradition. As for me, I would rather have gone on mending mills, with my crust of bread and liberty.'

Almost automatically they had bent their steps along the margin of the river; they now paused. They were standing on the brink of the well-known weir. There were the hatches, there was the culvert; they could see the pebbly bed of the stream through the pellucid water. The notes of the church-bells were audible, still jangled by the enthusiastic villagers.

'Why see – it was there I hid his walking-stick!' said Joshua, looking towards the sedge. The next moment, during a passing breeze, something flashed white on the spot to which the attention of Cornelius was drawn.

From the sedge rose a straight little silver-poplar, and it was the leaves of this sapling which caused the flicker of whiteness.

'His walking-stick has grown!' Joshua added. 'It was a rough one – cut from the hedge, I remember.'

At every puff of wind the tree turned white, till they could not bear to look at it; and they walked away.

'I see him every night.' Cornelius murmured... 'Ah, we read our *Hebrews* to little account, Jos! ʽΥπέμεινε σταυρὸν, αἰσχύνης καταφρονήσας.²³ To have *endured* the cross, *despising* the shame – there lay greatness! But now I often feel that I should like to put an end to trouble here in this self-same spot.'

'I have thought of it myself,' said Joshua.

'Perhaps we shall, some day,' murmured his brother.

'Perhaps,' said Joshua moodily.

With that contingency to consider in the silence of their nights and days they bent their steps homewards.

THE MELANCHOLY HUSSAR OF THE
GERMAN LEGION

HERE stretch the downs; high and breezy and green, absolutely unchanged since those eventful days. A plough has never disturbed the turf, and the sod that was uppermost then is uppermost now. Here stood the camp; here are distinct traces of the banks thrown up for the horses of the cavalry, and spots where the midden-heaps lay are still to be observed. At night, when I walk across the lonely place, it is impossible to avoid hearing, amid the scourings of the wind over the grass-bents and thistles, the old trumpet and bugle calls, the rattle of the halters; to help seeing rows of spectral tents and the *impedimenta*[1] of the soldiery. From within the canvases come guttural syllables of foreign tongues, and broken songs of the fatherland; for they were mainly regiments of the King's German Legion[2] that slept round the tent-poles hereabout at that time.

It was nearly ninety years ago. The British uniform of the period, with its immense epaulettes,[3] queer cocked-hat, breeches, gaiters, ponderous cartridge-box,[4] buckled shoes, and what not, would look strange and barbarous now. Ideas have changed; invention has followed invention. Soldiers were monumental objects then. A divinity still hedged kings here and there; and war was considered a glorious thing.

Secluded old manor-houses and hamlets lie in the ravines and hollows among these hills, where a stranger had hardly ever been seen till the King chose to take the baths[5] yearly at the sea-side watering-place a few miles to the south; as a consequence of which battalions descended in a cloud upon the open country around. Is it necessary to add that the echoes of many characteristic tales, dating from that picturesque time, still linger about here in more or less fragmentary form, to be caught by the attentive ear? Some of them I have repeated; most of them I have forgotten; one I have never repeated, and assuredly can never forget.

Phyllis told me the story with her own lips. She was then an old lady of seventy-five, and her auditor a lad of fifteen. She enjoined silence as to her share of the incident, till she should be 'dead, buried, and forgotten'. Her life was prolonged twelve years after the day of her narration, and she has now been dead nearly twenty. The oblivion which in her modesty and humility she courted for herself has only partially fallen on her, with the unfortunate result of inflicting an injustice upon her memory; since such fragments of her story as got abroad at the time, and have been kept alive ever since, are precisely those which are most unfavourable to her character.

It all began with the arrival of the York Hussars;[6] one of the foreign regiments above alluded to. Before that day scarcely a soul had been seen near her father's house for weeks. When a noise like the brushing skirt of a visitor was heard on the door-step, it proved to be a scudding leaf; when a carriage seemed to be nearing the door, it was her father grinding his sickle on the stone in the garden for his favourite relaxation of trimming the box-tree borders to the plots. A sound like luggage thrown down from the coach was a gun far away at sea; and what looked like a tall man by the gate at dusk was a yew bush cut into a quaint and attenuated shape. There is no such solitude in country places now as there was in those old days.

Yet all the while King George and his court were at his favourite sea-side resort, not more than five miles off.

The daughter's seclusion was great, but beyond the seclusion of the girl lay the seclusion of the father. If her social condition was twilight, his was darkness. Yet he enjoyed his darkness, while her twilight oppressed her. Dr Grove had been a professional man whose taste for lonely meditation over metaphysical questions had diminished his practice till it no longer paid him to keep it going; after which he had relinquished it and hired at a nominal rent the small, dilapidated, half farm half manor-house of this obscure inland nook, to make a sufficiency of an income which in a town would have been inadequate for their maintenance. He stayed in his garden the greater part of the day, growing more and more irritable with the lapse of time, and the increasing perception that he had wasted his life in the pursuit of illusions. He saw his friends less and less frequently. Phyllis became so shy that if she met a stranger anywhere in her short rambles she felt ashamed at his gaze, walked awkwardly, and blushed to her shoulders.

Yet Phyllis was discovered even here by an admirer, and her hand most unexpectedly asked in marriage.

The King, as aforesaid, was at the neighbouring town, where he had taken up his abode at Gloucester Lodge;[7] and his presence in the town naturally brought many county people thither. Among these idlers – many of whom professed to have connections and interests with the Court – was one Humphrey Gould, a bachelor; a personage neither young nor old; neither good-looking nor positively plain. Too steady-going to be 'a buck' (as fast and unmarried men were then called), he was an approximately fashionable man of a mild type. This bachelor of thirty found his way to the village on the down: beheld Phyllis; made her father's acquaintance in order to make hers; and by some means or other she sufficiently inflamed his heart to lead him in that direction almost daily; till he became engaged to marry her.

As he was of an old local family, some of whose members were held in respect in the county, Phyllis, in bringing him to her feet, had accomplished what was considered a brilliant move for one in her constrained position. How she had done it was not quite known to Phyllis herself. In those days unequal marriages[8] were regarded rather as a violation of the laws of nature than as a mere infringement of convention, the more modern view, and hence when Phyllis, of the watering-place *bourgeoisie*,[9] was chosen by such a gentlemanly[10] fellow, it was as if she were going to be taken to heaven, though perhaps the uninformed would have seen no great difference in the respective positions of the pair, the said Gould being as poor as a crow.

This pecuniary condition was his excuse – probably a true

one – for postponing their union, and as the winter drew nearer, and the King departed for the season, Mr Humphrey Gould set out for Bath, promising to return to Phyllis in a few weeks. The winter arrived, the date of his promise passed, yet Gould postponed his coming, on the ground that he could not very easily leave his father in the city of their sojourn, the elder having no other relative near him. Phyllis, though lonely in the extreme, was content. The man who had asked her in marriage was a desirable husband for her in many ways; her father highly approved of his suit; but this neglect of her was awkward, if not painful, for Phyllis. Love him in the true sense of the word she assured me she never did, but she had a genuine regard for him; admired a certain methodical and dogged way in which he sometimes took his pleasure; valued his knowledge of what the Court was doing, had done, or was about to do; and she was not without a feeling of pride that he had chosen her when he might have exercised a more ambitious choice.

But he did not come; and the spring developed. His letters were regular though formal; and it is not to be wondered that the uncertainty of her position, linked with the fact that there was not much passion in her thoughts of Humphrey, bred an indescribable dreariness in the heart of Phyllis Grove. The spring was soon summer, and the summer brought the King; but still no Humphrey Gould. All this while the engagement by letter was maintained intact.

At this point of time a golden radiance flashed in upon the lives of people here, and charged all youthful thought with emotional interest. This radiance was the aforesaid York Hussars.

II

The present generation has probably but a very dim notion of the celebrated York Hussars of ninety years ago. They were one of the regiments of the King's German Legion, and (though they somewhat degenerated later on) their brilliant uniform, their splendid horses, and above all, their foreign air and mustachios (rare appendages then), drew crowds of admirers of both sexes wherever they went. These with other regiments had come to encamp on the downs and pastures, because of the presence of the King in the neighbouring town.

The spot was high and airy, and the view extensive, commanding Portland – the Isle of Slingers – in front, and reaching to St Aldhelm's Head eastward, and almost to the Start on the west.

Phyllis, though not precisely a girl of the village, was as interested as any of them in this military investment. Her father's home stood somewhat apart, and on the highest point of ground to which the lane ascended, so that it was almost level with the top of the church tower in the lower part of the parish. Immediately from the outside of the garden-wall the grass spread away to a great distance, and it was crossed by a path which came close to the wall. Ever since her childhood it had been Phyllis's pleasure to clamber up this fence and sit on the top – a feat not so difficult as it may seem, the walls in this district being built of rubble, without mortar, so that there were plenty of crevices for small toes.

She was sitting up here one day, listlessly surveying the pasture without, when her attention was arrested by a solitary figure walking along the path. It was one of the renowned German Hussars, and he moved onward with his eyes on the ground, and with the manner of one who wished to escape company. His head would probably have been bent like his eyes but for his stiff neck-gear. On nearer view she perceived that his face was marked with deep sadness. Without observing her, he advanced by the footpath till it brought him almost immediately under the wall.

Phyllis was much surprised to see a fine, tall soldier in such a mood as this. Her theory of the military, and of the York Hussars in particular (derived entirely from hearsay, for she had never talked to a soldier in her life), was that their hearts were as gay as their accoutrements.[11]

At this moment the Hussar lifted his eyes and noticed her on her perch, the white muslin neckerchief which covered her shoulders and neck where left bare by her low gown, and her white raiment in general, showing conspicuously in the bright sunlight of this summer day. He blushed a little at the suddenness of the encounter, and without halting a moment from his pace passed on.

All that day the foreigner's face haunted Phyllis; its aspect was so striking, so handsome, and his eyes were so blue, and sad, and abstracted. It was perhaps only natural that on some following day at the same hour she should look over that wall again, and wait till he had passed a second time. On this occasion he was reading a letter, and at the sight of her his manner was that of one who had half expected or hoped to discover her. He almost stopped, smiled, and made a courteous salute. The end of the meeting was that they exchanged a few words. She asked him what he was reading, and he readily informed her that he was re-perusing letters from his mother in Germany; he did not get them often, he said, and was forced to read the old ones a great many times. This was all that passed at the present interview, but others of the same kind followed.

Phyllis used to say that his English, though not good, was quite intelligible to her, so that their acquaintance was never hindered by difficulties of speech. Whenever the subject became too delicate, subtle, or tender, for such words of English as were at his command, the eyes no doubt helped out the tongue, and – though this was later on – the lips helped out the eyes. In short this acquaintance, unguardedly made, and rash enough on her part, developed and ripened. Like Desdemona, she pitied him, and learnt his history.[12]

His name was Matthäus Tina, and Saarbrück[13] his native town, where his mother was still living. His age was twenty-two, and he had already risen to the grade of corporal, though he had not long been in the army. Phyllis used to assert that no such refined or well-educated young man could have been found in the ranks of the purely English regiments, some of these foreign soldiers having rather the graceful manner and presence of our native officers than of our rank and file.

She by degrees learnt from her foreign friend a circumstance about himself and his comrades which Phyllis would least have expected of the York Hussars. So far from being as gay as its uniform, the regiment was pervaded by a dreadful melancholy, a chronic home-sickness, which depressed many of the men to such an extent that they could hardly attend to their drill. The worst sufferers were the younger soldiers who had not been over here long. They hated England and English life; they took no interest whatever in King George and his island kingdom, and they only wished to be out of it and never to see it any more. Their bodies were here, but their hearts and minds were always far away in their dear fatherland, of which — brave men and stoical as they were in many ways — they would speak with tears in their eyes. One of the worst of the sufferers from this home-woe, as he called it in his own tongue, was Matthäus Tina, whose dreamy musing nature felt the gloom of exile still more intensely from the fact that he had left a lonely mother at home with nobody to cheer her.

Though Phyllis, touched by all this, and interested in his history, did not disdain her soldier's acquaintance, she declined (according to her own account, at least) to permit the young man to overstep the line of mere friendship for a long while — as long, indeed, as she considered herself likely to become the possession of another; though it is probable that she had lost her heart to Matthäus before she was herself aware. The stone wall of necessity made anything like intimacy difficult; and he had never ventured to come, or to ask to come, inside the garden, so that all their conversation had been overtly conducted across this boundary.

III

But news reached the village from a friend of Phyllis's father concerning Mr Humphrey Gould, her remarkably cool and patient betrothed. This gentleman had been heard to say in Bath that he considered his overtures to Miss Phyllis Grove to have reached only the stage of a half-understanding; and in view of his enforced absence on his father's account, who was too great an invalid now to attend to his affairs, he thought it best that there should be no definite promise as yet on either side. He was not sure, indeed, that he might not cast his eyes elsewhere.

This account – though only a piece of hearsay, and as such entitled to no absolute credit – tallied so well with the infrequency of his letters and their lack of warmth, that Phyllis did not doubt its truth for one moment; and from that hour she felt herself free to bestow her heart as she should choose. Not so her father; he declared the whole story to be a fabrication. He had known Mr Gould's family from his boyhood; and if there was one proverb which expressed the matrimonial aspect of that family well, it was 'Love me little, love me long.' Humphrey was an honourable man, who would not think of treating his engagement so lightly. 'Do you wait in patience,' he said; 'all will be right in time.'

From these words Phyllis at first imagined that her father was in correspondence with Mr Gould; and her heart sank within her; for in spite of her original intentions she had been relieved to hear that her engagement had come to nothing. But she presently learnt that her father had heard no more of Humphrey Gould than she herself had done; while he would not write and address her affianced directly on the subject, lest it should be deemed an imputation on that bachelor's honour.

'You want an excuse for encouraging one or other of those foreign fellows to flatter you with his unmeaning attentions,' her father exclaimed, his mood having of late been a very unkind one towards her. 'I see more than I say. Don't you ever set foot outside that garden-fence without my permission. If you want to see that camp I'll take you myself some Sunday afternoon.'

Phyllis had not the smallest intention of disobeying him in her actions, but she assumed herself to be independent with respect to her feelings. She no longer checked her fancy for the Hussar, though she was far from regarding him as her lover in the serious sense in which an Englishman might have been regarded as such. The young foreign soldier was almost an ideal being to her, with none of the appurtenances of an ordinary house-dweller; one who had descended she knew not

whence, and would disappear she knew not whither; the subject of a fascinating dream – no more.

They met continually now – mostly at dusk – during the
brief interval between the going down of the sun and the
minute at which the last trumpet-call summoned him to his
tent. Perhaps her manner had become less restrained latterly;
at any rate that of the Hussar was so; he had grown more
tender every day, and at parting after these hurried interviews
she reached down her hand from the top of the wall that he
might press it. One evening he held it such a while that she
exclaimed, 'The wall is white, and somebody in the field may
see your shape against it!'

He lingered so long that night that it was with the greatest
difficulty that he could run across the intervening stretch of
ground and enter the camp in time. On the next occasion of his
awaiting her she did not appear in her usual place at the usual
hour. His disappointment was unspeakably keen; he remained
staring blankly at the spot, like a man in a trance. The trumpets and tattoo [14] sounded, and still he did not go.

She had been delayed purely by an accident. When she arrived she was anxious because of the lateness of the hour,
having heard as well as he the sounds denoting the closing of
the camp. She implored him to leave immediately.

'No,' he said gloomily. 'I shall not go in yet – the moment
you come – I have thought of your coming all day.'

'But you may be disgraced at being after time?'

'I don't mind that. I should have disappeared from the world
some time ago if it had not been for two persons – my beloved,
here, and my mother in Saarbrück. I hate the army. I care more
for a minute of your company than for all the promotion in the
world.'

Thus he stayed and talked to her, and told her interesting
details of his native place, and incidents of his childhood, till
she was in a simmer of distress at his recklessness in remaining.
It was only because she insisted on bidding him good-night and
leaving the wall that he returned to his quarters.

The next time that she saw him he was without the stripes
that had adorned his sleeve. He had been broken to the level

of private for his lateness that night; and as Phyllis considered herself to be the cause of his disgrace her sorrow was great. But the position was now reversed; it was his turn to cheer her.

'Don't grieve, meine Liebliche!'[15] he said. 'I have got a remedy for whatever comes. First, even supposing I regain my stripes, would your father allow you to marry a non-commissioned officer in the York Hussars?'

She flushed. This practical step had not been in her mind in relation to such an unrealistic person as he was; and a moment's reflection was enough for it. 'My father would not — certainly would not,' she answered unflinchingly. 'It cannot be thought of! My dear friend, please do forget me: I fear I am ruining you and your prospects!'

'Not at all!' said he. 'You are giving this country of yours just sufficient interest to me to make me care to keep alive in it. If my dear land were here also, and my old parent, with you, I could be happy as I am, and would do my best as a soldier. But it is not so. And now listen. This is my plan. That you go with me to my own country, and be my wife there, and live there, with my mother and me. I am not a Hanoverian,[16] as you know, though I entered the army as such; my country is by the Saar, and is at peace with France, and if I were once in it I should be free.'

'But how get there?' she asked. Phyllis had been rather amazed than shocked at his proposition. Her position in her father's house was growing irksome and painful in the extreme; his parental affection seemed to be quite dried up. She was not a native of the village, like all the joyous girls around her; and in some way Matthäus Tina had infected her with his own passionate longing for his country, and mother, and home.

'But how?' she repeated, finding that he did not answer. 'Will you buy your discharge?'

'Ah, no,' he said. 'That's impossible in these times. No; I came here against my will; why should I not escape? Now is the time, as we shall soon be striking camp, and I might see you no more. This is my scheme. I will ask you to meet me on the highway two miles off, on some calm night next week that may be appointed. There will be nothing unbecoming in it, or to cause you shame; you will not fly alone with me, for I will bring with me my devoted young friend Christoph, an Alsatian,[17] who has lately joined the regiment, and who has agreed to assist in this enterprise. We shall have come from yonder harbour, where we shall have examined the boats, and found one suited to our purpose. Christoph has already a chart of the Channel, and we will then go to the harbour, and at midnight cut the boat from her moorings, and row away round the point out of sight; and by the next morning we are on the coast of France, near Cherbourg. The rest is easy, for I have saved money for the land journey, and can get a change of clothes. I will write to my mother, who will meet us on the way.'

He added details in reply to her inquiries, which left no doubt in Phyllis's mind of the feasibility of the undertaking. But its magnitude almost appalled her; and it is questionable if she would ever have gone further in the wild adventure if, on entering the house that night, her father had not accosted her in the most significant terms.

'How about the York Hussars?' he said.

'They are still at the camp; but they are soon going away, I believe.'

'It is useless for you to attempt to cloak your actions in that way. You have been meeting one of those fellows; you have been seen walking with him – foreign barbarians, not much better than the French themselves! I have made up my mind – don't speak a word till I have done, please! – I have made up my mind that you shall stay here no longer while they are on the spot. You shall go to your aunt's.'

It was useless for her to protest that she had never taken a walk with any soldier or man under the sun except himself. Her protestations were feeble, too, for though he was not literally correct in his assertion, he was virtually only half in error.

The house of her father's sister was a prison to Phyllis. She had quite recently undergone experience of its gloom; and when her father went on to direct her to pack what would be necessary for her to take, her heart died within her. In after years she never attempted to excuse her conduct during this week of agitation; but the result of her self-communing was that she decided to join in the scheme of her lover and his friend, and fly to the country which he had coloured with such lovely hues in her imagination. She always said that the one feature in his proposal which overcame her hesitation was the obvious purity and straightforwardness of his intentions. He showed himself to be so virtuous and kind; he treated her with a respect to which she had never before been accustomed; and she was braced to the obvious risks of the voyage by her confidence in him.

IV

It was on a soft, dark evening of the following week that they engaged in the adventure. Tina was to meet her at a point in the highway at which the lane to the village branched off. Christoph was to go ahead of them to the harbour where the boat lay, row it round the Nothe[18] – or Look-out as it was called in those days – and pick them up on the other side of the promontory, which they were to reach by crossing the harbour-bridge on foot, and climbing over the Look-out hill.

As soon as her father had ascended to his room she left the house, and, bundle in hand, proceeded at a trot along the lane. At such an hour not a soul was afoot anywhere in the village, and she reached the junction of the lane with the highway unobserved. Here she took up her position in the obscurity formed by the angle of a fence, whence she could discern every one who approached along the turnpike-road,[19] without being herself seen.

She had not remained thus waiting for her lover longer than a minute – though from the tension of her nerves the lapse of even that short time was trying – when, instead of the expected footsteps, the stage-coach could be heard descending the hill. She knew that Tina would not show himself till the road was clear, and waited impatiently for the coach to pass. Nearing the corner where she was it slackened speed, and, instead of going by as usual, drew up within a few yards of her. A passenger alighted, and she heard his voice. It was Humphrey Gould's.

He had brought a friend with him, and luggage. The luggage was deposited on the grass, and the coach went on its route to the royal watering-place.

'I wonder where that young man is with the horse and trap?' said her former admirer to his companion. 'I hope we shan't have to wait here long. I told him half-past nine o'clock precisely.'

'Have you got her present safe?'

'Phyllis's? O, yes. It is in this trunk. I hope it will please her.'

'Of course it will. What woman would not be pleased with such a handsome peace-offering?'

'Well – she deserves it. I've treated her rather badly. But she has been in my mind these last two days much more than I should care to confess to everybody. Ah, well; I'll say no more about that. It cannot be that she is so bad as they make out. I am quite sure that a girl of her good wit would know better than to get entangled with any of those Hanoverian soldiers. I won't believe it of her, and there's an end on't.'

More words in the same strain were casually dropped as the two men waited; words which revealed to her, as by a sudden illumination, the enormity of her conduct. The conversation was at length cut off by the arrival of the man with the vehicle. The luggage was placed in it, and they mounted, and were driven on in the direction from which she had just come.

Phyllis was so conscious-stricken that she was at first inclined to follow them; but a moment's reflection led her to feel that it would only be bare justice to Matthäus to wait till he arrived, and explain candidly that she had changed her mind – difficult as the struggle would be when she stood face to face with him. She bitterly reproached herself for having believed reports which represented Humphrey Gould as false to his engagement, when, from what she now heard from his own lips, she gathered that he had been living full of trust in her. But she knew well enough who had won her love. Without him her life seemed a dreary prospect, yet the more she looked at his proposal the more she feared to accept it – so wild as it was, so vague, so venturesome. She had promised Humphrey Gould, and it was only his assumed faithlessness which had led her to treat that promise as nought. His solicitude in bringing her these gifts touched her; her promise must be kept, and esteem must take the place of love. She would preserve her self-respect. She would stay at home, and marry him, and suffer.

Phyllis had thus braced herself to an exceptional fortitude when, a few minutes later, the outline of Matthäus Tina appeared behind a field-gate, over which he lightly leapt as she stepped forward. There was no evading it, he pressed her to his breast.

'It is the first and last time!' she wildly thought as she stood encircled by his arms.

How Phyllis got through the terrible ordeal of that night she could never clearly recollect. She always attributed her success in carrying out her resolve to her lover's honour, for as soon as she declared to him in feeble words that she had changed her mind, and felt that she could not, dared not, fly with him, he forbore to urge her, grieved as he was at her decision. Unscrupulous pressure on his part, seeing how romantically she had become attached to him, would no doubt have turned the balance in his favour. But he did nothing to tempt her unduly or unfairly.

On her side, fearing for his safety, she begged him to remain. This, he declared, could not be. 'I cannot break faith with my friend,' said he. Had he stood alone he would have abandoned his plan. But Christoph, with the boat and compass and chart, was waiting on the shore; the tide would soon turn; his mother had been warned of his coming; go he must.

Many precious minutes were lost while he tarried, unable to tear himself away. Phyllis held to her resolve, though it cost her many a bitter pang. At last they parted, and he went down the hill. Before his footsteps had quite died away she felt a desire to behold at least his outline once more, and running noiselessly after him regained view of his diminishing figure. For one moment she was sufficiently excited to be on the point of rushing forward and linking her fate with his. But she could not. The courage which at the critical instant failed Cleopatra of Egypt[20] could scarcely be expected of Phyllis Grove.

A dark shape, similar to his own, joined him in the highway. It was Christoph, his friend. She could see no more; they had hastened on in the direction of the town and harbour, four miles ahead. With a feeling akin to despair she turned and slowly pursued her way homeward.

Tattoo sounded in the camp; but there was no camp for her now. It was as dead as the camp of the Assyrians after the passage of the Destroying Angel.[21]

She noiselessly entered the house, seeing nobody, and went to bed. Grief, which kept her awake at first, ultimately wrapped her in a heavy sleep. The next morning her father met her at the foot of the stairs.

'Mr Gould is come!' he said triumphantly.

Humphrey was staying at the inn, and had already called to inquire for her. He had brought her a present of a very handsome looking-glass in a frame of *repoussé*[22] silverwork, which her father held in his hand. He had promised to call again in the course of an hour, to ask Phyllis to walk with him.

Pretty mirrors were rarer in country-houses at that day than they are now, and the one before her won Phyllis's admiration. She looked into it, saw how heavy her eyes were, and endeavoured to brighten them. She was in that wretched state of mind which leads a woman to move mechanically onward in what she conceives to be her allotted path. Mr Humphrey had, in his undemonstrative way, been adhering all along to the old understanding; it was for her to do the same, and to say not a word of her own lapse. She put on her bonnet and tippet,[23] and when he arrived at the hour named she was at the door awaiting him.

v

Phyllis thanked him for his beautiful gift; but the talking was soon entirely on Humphrey's side as they walked along. He told her of the latest movements of the world of fashion – a sub-

ject which she willingly discussed to the exclusion of anything
more personal – and his measured language helped to still her
disquieted heart and brain. Had not her own sadness been what
it was she must have observed his embarrassment. At last he
abruptly changed the subject.

'I am glad you are pleased with my little present,' he said.
'The truth is that I brought it to propitiate 'ee, and to get you
to help me out of a mighty difficulty.'

It was inconceivable to Phyllis that this independent
bachelor – whom she admired in some respects – could have a
difficulty.

'Phyllis – I'll tell you my secret at once; for I have a monstrous secret to confide before I can ask your counsel. The
case is, then, that I am married: yes, I have privately married
a dear young belle; and if you knew her, and I hope you will,
you would say everything in her praise. But she is not quite the
one that my father would have chose for me – you know the
paternal idea as well as I – and I have kept it secret. There
will be a terrible noise, no doubt; but I think that with your
help I may get over it. If you would only do me this good turn
– when I have told my father, I mean – say that you never
could have married me, you know, or something of that sort –
'pon my life it will help to smooth the way vastly. I am so
anxious to win him round to my point of view, and not to cause
any estrangement.'

What Phyllis replied she scarcely knew, or how she coun-
selled him as to his unexpected situation. Yet the relief that
his announcement brought her was perceptible. To have con-
fided her trouble in return was what her aching heart longed
to do; and had Humphrey been a woman she would instantly
have poured out her tale. But to him she feared to confess;
and there was a real reason for silence, till a sufficient time
had elapsed to allow her lover and his comrade to get out of
harm's way.

As soon as she reached home again she sought a solitary
place, and spent the time in half regretting that she had not
gone away, and in dreaming over the meetings with Matthäus
Tina from their beginning to their end. In his own country,

amongst his own countrywomen, he would possibly soon forget her, even to her very name.

Her listlessness was such that she did not go out of the house for several days. There came a morning which broke in fog and mist, behind which the dawn could be discerned in greenish grey; and the outlines of the tents, and the rows of horses at the ropes. The smoke from the canteen fires drooped heavily.

The spot at the bottom of the garden where she had been accustomed to climb the wall to meet Matthäus, was the only inch of English ground in which she took any interest; and in spite of the disagreeable haze prevailing she walked out there till she reached the well-known corner. Every blade of grass was weighted with little liquid globes, and slugs and snails had crept out upon the plots. She could hear the usual faint noises from the camp, and in the other direction the trot of farmers on the road to the town, for it was market-day. She observed that her frequent visits to this corner had quite trodden down the grass in the angle of the wall, and left marks of garden soil on the stepping-stones by which she had mounted to look over the top. Seldom having gone there till dusk, she had not considered that her traces might be visible by day. Perhaps it was these which had revealed her trysts to her father.

While she paused in melancholy regard, she fancied that the customary sounds from the tents were changing their character. Indifferent as Phyllis was to camp doings now, she mounted by the steps to the old place. What she beheld at first awed and perplexed her; then she stood rigid, her fingers hooked to the wall, her eyes staring out of her head, and her face as if hardened to stone.

On the open green stretching before her all the regiments in the camp were drawn up in line, in the mid-front of which two empty coffins lay on the ground. The unwonted sounds which she had noticed came from an advancing procession. It consisted of the band of the York Hussars playing a dead march;[24] next two soldiers of that regiment in a mourning coach,[25] guarded on each side, and accompanied by two priests. Behind came a crowd of rustics who had been attracted by the event.

The melancholy procession marched along the front of the line, returned to the centre, and halted beside the coffins, where the two condemned men were blind-folded, and each placed kneeling on his coffin; a few minutes' pause was now given, while they prayed.

A firing-party of twenty-four men stood ready with levelled carbines.[26] The commanding officer, who had his sword drawn, waved it through some cuts of the sword-exercise till he reached the downward stroke, whereat the firing party discharged their volley. The two victims fell, one upon his face across his coffin, the other backwards.

As the volley resounded there arose a shriek from the wall of Dr Grove's garden, and some one fell down inside; but nobody among the spectators without noticed it at the time. The two executed Hussars were Matthäus Tina and his friend Christoph. The soldiers on guard placed the bodies in the coffins almost instantly; but the colonel of the regiment, an Englishman, rode up and exclaimed in a stern voice: 'Turn them out – as an example to the men!'

The coffins were lifted endwise, and the dead Germans flung out upon their faces on the grass. Then all the regiments wheeled in sections, and marched past the spot in slow time. When the survey was over the corpses were again coffined, and borne away.

Meanwhile Dr Grove, attracted by the noise of the volley, had rushed out into his garden, where he saw his wretched daughter lying motionless against the wall. She was taken indoors, but it was long before she recovered consciousness; and for weeks they despaired of her reason.

It transpired that the luckless deserters from the York Hussars had cut the boat from her moorings in the adjacent harbour, according to their plan, and, with two other comrades who were smarting under ill-treatment from their colonel, had sailed in safety across the Channel. But mistaking their bearings they steered into Jersey, thinking that island the French coast. Here they were perceived to be deserters, and delivered up to the authorities. Matthäus and Christoph interceded for the other two at the court-martial, saying that it was entirely by the former's representations that these were induced to go. Their sentence was accordingly commuted to flogging, the death punishment being reserved for their leaders.

The visitor to the well-known old Georgian watering-place, who may care to ramble to the neighbouring village under the hills, and examine the register of burials, will there find two entries in these words:

Matth: Tina (Corpl.) in His Majesty's Regmt. of York Hussars, and Shot for Desertion, was Buried June 30th, 1801, aged 22 years. Born in the town of Sarrbruk, Germany.

Christoph Bless, belonging to His Majesty's Regmt. of York Hussars, who was Shot for Desertion, was Buried June 30th, 1801, aged 22 years. Born at Lothaargen, Alsatia.

Their graves were dug at the back of the little church, near the wall. There is no memorial to mark the spot, but Phyllis pointed it out to me. While she lived she used to keep their mounds neat; but now they are overgrown with nettles, and sunk nearly flat. The older villagers, however, who know of the episode from their parents, still recollect the place where the soldiers lie. Phyllis lies near.

IT WAS apparently an idea, rather than a passion, that inspired Lord Uplandtowers' resolve to win her. Nobody ever knew when he formed it, or whence he got his assurance of success in the face of her manifest dislike of him. Possibly not until after that first important act of her life which I shall presently mention. His matured and cynical doggedness at the age of nineteen, when impulse mostly rules calculation, was remarkable, and might have owed its existence as much to his succession to the earldom and its accompanying local honours in childhood, as to the family character; an elevation which jerked him into maturity, so to speak, without his having known adolescence. He had only reached his twelfth year when his father, the fourth Earl, died, after a course of the Bath waters.

Nevertheless, the family character had a great deal to do with it. Determination was hereditary in the bearers of that escutcheon,[1] sometimes for good, sometimes for evil.

The seats of the two families were about ten miles apart, the way between them lying along the now old, then new, turnpike-road connecting Havenpool and Warborne with the city of Melchester; a road which, though only a branch from what was known as the Great Western Highway, is probably, even at present, as it has been for the last hundred years, one of the finest examples of a macadamized turnpike-track[2] that can be found in England.

The mansion of the Earl, as well as that of his neighbour, Barbara's father, stood back about a mile from the highway, with which each was connected by an ordinary drive and lodge. It was along this particular highway that the young Earl drove on a certain evening at Christmastide some twenty years before the end of the last century, to attend a ball at Chene Manor, the home of Barbara and her parents Sir John and Lady Grebe. Sir John's was a baronetcy created a few years before the break-

ing out of the Civil War, and his lands were even more extensive
than those of Lord Uplandtowers himself, comprising this
Manor of Chene, another on the coast near, half the Hundred
of Cockdene, and well-enclosed lands in several other parishes,
notably Warborne and those contiguous. At this time Barbara
was barely seventeen, and the ball is the first occasion on which
we have any tradition of Lord Uplandtowers attempting tender
relations with her; it was early enough, God knows.

An intimate friend — one of the Drenkhards — is said to have
dined with him that day, and Lord Uplandtowers had, for a
wonder, communicated to his guest the secret design of his
heart.

'You'll never get her — sure; you'll never get her!' this friend
had said at parting. 'She's not drawn to your lordship by love:
and as for thought of a good match, why, there's no more calculation in her than in a bird.'

'We'll see,' said Lord Uplandtowers impassively.

He no doubt thought of his friend's forecast as he travelled
along the highway in his chariot; but the sculptural repose of
his profile against the vanishing daylight on his right hand
would have shown his friend that the Earl's equanimity was
undisturbed. He reached the solitary wayside tavern called
Lornton Inn — the rendezvous of many a daring poacher for
operations in the adjoining forest; and he might have observed,
if he had taken the trouble, a strange post-chaise[3] standing in
the halting-space before the inn. He duly sped past it, and half-
an-hour after through the little town of Warborne. Onward, a
mile further, was the house of his entertainer.

At this date it was an imposing edifice — or, rather, congeries[4] of edifices — as extensive as the residence of the Earl
himself, though far less regular. One wing showed extreme
antiquity, having huge chimneys, whose substructures projected from the external walls like towers; and a kitchen of
vast dimensions, in which (it was said) breakfasts had been
cooked for John of Gaunt.[5] Whilst he was yet in the forecourt
he could hear the rhythm of French horns and clarionets, the
favourite instruments of those days at such entertainments.

Entering the long parlour, in which the dance had just been

opened by Lady Grebe with a minuet – it being now seven
o'clock, according to the tradition – he was received with a
welcome befitting his rank, and looked round for Barbara. She
was not dancing, and seemed to be preoccupied – almost, indeed, as though she had been waiting for him. Barbara at this
time was a good and pretty girl, who never spoke ill of any
one, and hated other pretty women the very least possible. She
did not refuse him for the country-dance which followed, and
soon after was his partner in a second.

The evening wore on, and the horns and clarionets tootled
merrily. Barbara evinced towards her lover neither distinct preference nor aversion; but old eyes would have seen that she
pondered something. However, after supper she pleaded a
headache, and disappeared. To pass the time of her absence,
Lord Uplandtowers went into a little room adjoining the long
gallery, where some elderly ones were sitting by the fire – for
he had a phlegmatic[6] dislike of dancing for its own sake, –
and, lifting the window-curtains, he looked out of the window
into the park and wood, dark now as a cavern. Some of the
guests appeared to be leaving even so soon as this, two lights
showing themselves as turning away from the door and sinking to nothing in the distance.

His hostess put her head into the room to look for partners
for the ladies, and Lord Uplandtowers came out. Lady Grebe
informed him that Barbara had not returned to the ball-room:
she had gone to bed in sheer necessity.

'She has been so excited over the ball all day,' her mother
continued, 'that I feared she would be worn out early ... But
sure, Lord Uplandtowers, you won't be leaving yet?'

He said that it was near twelve o'clock, and that some had
already left.

'I protest nobody has gone yet,' said Lady Grebe.

To humour her he stayed till midnight, and then set out. He
had made no progress in his suit; but he had assured himself
that Barbara gave no other guest the preference, and nearly
everybody in the neighbourhood was there.

' 'Tis only a matter of time,' said the calm young philosopher.

The next morning he lay till near ten o'clock, and he had only just come out upon the head of the staircase when he heard hoofs upon the gravel without; in a few moments the door had been opened, and Sir John Grebe met him in the hall, as he set foot on the lowest stair.

'My lord – where's Barbara – my daughter?'

Even the Earl of Uplandtowers could not repress amazement. 'What's the matter, my dear Sir John,' says he.

The news was startling, indeed. From the Baronet's disjointed explanation Lord Uplandtowers gathered that after his own and the other guests' departure Sir John and Lady Grebe had gone to rest without seeing any more of Barbara; it being understood by them that she had retired to bed when she sent word to say that she could not join the dancers again. Before then she had told her maid that she would dispense with her services for this night; and there was evidence to show that the young lady had never lain down at all, the bed remaining unpressed. Circumstances seemed to prove that the deceitful girl had feigned indisposition to get an excuse for leaving the ball-room, and that she had left the house within ten minutes, presumably during the first dance after supper.

'I saw her go,' said Lord Uplandtowers.

'The devil you did!' says Sir John.

'Yes.' And he mentioned the retreating carriage-lights, and how he was assured by Lady Grebe that no guest had departed.

'Surely that was it!' said the father. 'But she's not gone alone, d'ye know!'

'Ah – who is the young man?'

'I can on'y guess. My worst fear is my most likely guess. I'll say no more. I thought – yet I would not believe – it possible that you was the sinner. Would that you had been! But 'tis t'other, 'tis t'other, by Heaven! I must e'en up and after 'em!'

'Whom do you suspect?'

Sir John would not give a name, and, stultified rather than agitated, Lord Uplandtowers accompanied him back to Chene. He again asked upon whom were the Baronet's suspicions directed; and the impulsive Sir John was no match for the insistence of Uplandtowers.

He said at length, 'I fear 'tis Edmond Willowes.'

'Who's he?'

'A young fellow of Shottsford-Forum – a widow-woman's son,' the other told him, and explained that Willowes's father, or grandfather, was the last of the old glass-painters[7] in that place, where (as you may know) the art lingered on when it had died out in every other part of England.

'By God that's bad – mighty bad!' said Lord Uplandtowers, throwing himself back in the chaise in frigid despair.

They despatched emissaries in all directions; one by the Melchester Road, another by Shottsford-Forum, another coastwards.

But the lovers had a ten-hours' start; and it was apparent that sound judgement had been exercised in choosing as their time of flight the particular night when the movements of a strange carriage would not be noticed, either in the park or on the neighbouring highway, owing to the general press of vehicles. The chaise which had been seen waiting at Lornton Inn was, no doubt, the one they had escaped in; and the pair of heads which had planned so cleverly thus far had probably contrived marriage ere now.

The fears of her parents were realized. A letter sent by special messenger from Barbara, on the evening of that day, briefly informed them that her lover and herself were on the way to London, and before this communication reached her home they would be united as husband and wife. She had taken this extreme step because she loved her dear Edmond as she could love no other man, and because she had seen closing round her the doom of marriage with Lord Uplandtowers, unless she put that threatened fate out of possibility by doing as she had done. She had well considered the step beforehand, and was prepared to live like any other country-townsman's wife if her father repudiated her for her action.

'Damn her!' said Lord Uplandtowers, as he drove homeward that night. 'Damn her for a fool!' – which shows the kind of love he bore her.

Well; Sir John had already started in pursuit of them as a matter of duty, driving like a wild man to Melchester, and thence by the direct highway to the capital. But he soon saw that he was acting to no purpose; and by and by, discovering that the marriage had actually taken place, he forebore all attempts to unearth them in the City, and returned and sat down with his lady to digest the event as best they could.

To proceed against this Willowes for the abduction of our heiress was, possibly, in their power; yet, when they considered the now unalterable facts, they refrained from violent retribution. Some six weeks passed, during which time Barbara's parents, though they keenly felt her loss, held no communication with the truant, either for reproach or condonation. They continued to think of the disgrace she had brought upon herself; for, though the young man was an honest fellow, and the son of an honest father, the latter had died so early, and his widow had had such struggles to maintain herself, that the son was very imperfectly educated. Moreover, his blood was, as far as they knew, of no distinction whatever, whilst hers, through her mother, was compounded of the best juices of ancient baronial distillation, containing tinctures of Maundeville, and Mohun, and Syward, and Peverell, and Culliford, and Talbot, and Plantagenet, and York, and Lancaster,[8] and God knows what besides, which it was a thousand pities to throw away.

The father and mother sat by the fireplace that was spanned by the four-centred arch bearing the family shields on its haunches,[9] and groaned aloud – the lady more than Sir John.

'To think this should have come upon us in our old age!' said he.

'Speak for yourself!' she snapped through her sobs, 'I am only one-and-forty! ... Why didn't ye ride faster and overtake 'em!'

In the meantime the young married lovers, caring no more about their blood than about ditch-water, were intensely happy – happy, that is, in the descending scale which, as we all know, Heaven in its wisdom has ordained for such rash cases; that is to say, the first week they were in the seventh heaven, the second in the sixth, the third week temperate, the fourth reflective, and so on; a lover's heart after possession being comparable to the earth in its geologic stages, as described to us sometimes by our worthy President; first a hot coal, then a warm one, then a cooling cinder, then chilly – the simile shall be pursued no further. The long and the short of it was that one day a letter, sealed with their daughter's own little seal, came into Sir John and Lady Grebe's hands; and, on opening it, they found it to contain an appeal from the young couple to Sir John to forgive them for what they had done, and they would fall on their naked knees and be most dutiful children for evermore.

Then Sir John and his lady sat down again by the fireplace with the four-centred arch, and consulted, and re-read the letter. Sir John Grebe, if the truth must be told, loved his daughter's happiness far more, poor man, than he loved his name and lineage; he recalled to his mind all her little ways, gave vent to a sigh; and, by this time acclimatized to the idea of the marriage, said that what was done could not be undone, and that he supposed they must not be too harsh with her. Perhaps Barbara and her husband were in actual need; and how could they let their only child starve?

A slight consolation had come to them in an unexpected manner. They had been credibly informed that an ancestor of plebeian Willowes was once honoured with intermarriage with a scion of the aristocracy who had gone to the dogs. In short, such is the foolishness of distinguished parents, and sometimes of others also, that they wrote that very day to the address Barbara had given them, informing her that she might return home and bring her husband with her; they would not object to see him, would not reproach her, and would endeavour to welcome both, and to discuss with them what could best be arranged for their future.

In three or four days a rather shabby post-chaise drew up at the door of Chene Manor-house, at sound of which the tender-hearted baronet and his wife ran out as if to welcome a prince and princess of the blood. They were overjoyed to see their spoilt child return safe and sound – though she was only Mrs Willowes, wife of Edmond Willowes of nowhere. Barbara burst into penitential tears, and both husband and wife were contrite enough, as well they might be, considering that they had not a guinea to call their own.

When the four had calmed themselves, and not a word of chiding had been uttered to the pair, they discussed the position soberly, young Willowes sitting in the background with great modesty till invited forward by Lady Grebe in no frigid tone.

'How handsome he is!' she said to herself. 'I don't wonder at Barbara's craze for him.'

He was, indeed, one of the handsomest men who ever set his lips on a maid's. A blue coat, murrey[10] waistcoat, and breeches of drab[11] set off a figure that could scarcely be surpassed. He had large dark eyes, anxious now, as they glanced from Barbara to her parents and tenderly back again to her; observing whom, even now in her trepidation, one could see why the *sang froid*[12] of Lord Uplandtowers had been raised to more than lukewarmness. Her fair young face (according to the tale handed down by old women) looked out from under a grey conical hat, trimmed with white ostrich-feathers, and her little toes peeped from a buff petticoat worn under a puce gown. Her features were not regular: they were almost infantine, as you may see from miniatures in possession of the family, her mouth showing much sensitiveness, and one could be sure that her faults would not lie on the side of bad temper unless for urgent reasons.

Well, they discussed their state as became them, and the desire of the young couple to gain the goodwill of those upon whom they were literally dependent for everything induced them to agree to any temporizing measure that was not too irksome. Therefore, having been nearly two months united, they did not oppose Sir John's proposal that he should furnish Edmond Willowes with funds sufficient for him to travel a year on the Continent in the company of a tutor, the young man undertaking to lend himself with the utmost diligence to the tutor's instructions, till he became polished outwardly and inwardly to the degree required in the husband of such a lady as Barbara. He was to apply himself to the study of languages, manners, history, society, ruins, and everything else that came under his eyes, till he should return to take his place without blushing by Barbara's side.

'And by that time,' said worthy Sir John, 'I'll get my little place out at Yewsholt ready for you and Barbara to occupy on your return. The house is small and out of the way; but it will do for a young couple for a while.'

'If 'twere no bigger than a summer-house it would do!' says Barbara.

'If 'twere no bigger than a sedan-chair!'[13] says Willowes. 'And the more lonely the better.'

'We can put up with the loneliness,' said Barbara, with less zest. 'Some friends will come, no doubt.'

All this being laid down, a travelled tutor was called in – a man of many gifts and great experience, – and on a fine morning away tutor and pupil went. A great reason urged against Barbara accompanying her youthful husband was that his attentions to her would naturally be such as to prevent his zealously applying every hour of his time to learning and seeing – an argument of wise prescience, and unanswerable. Regular days for letter-writing were fixed, Barbara and her Edmond exchanged their last kisses at the door, and the chaise swept under the archway into the drive.

He wrote to her from Le Havre, as soon as he reached that port, which was not for seven days, on account of adverse winds; he wrote from Rouen, and from Paris; described to her his sight of the King and Court at Versailles, and the wonderful marblework and mirrors in that palace; wrote next from Lyons; then, after a comparatively long interval, from Turin, narrating his fearful adventures in crossing Mont Cenis on mules, and how he was overtaken with a terrific snowstorm, which had well-nigh been the end of him, and his tutor, and his guides. Then he wrote glowingly of Italy; and Barbara could see the development of her husband's mind reflected in his letters month by month; and she much admired the forethought of her father in suggesting this education for Edmond. Yet she sighed sometimes – her husband being no longer in evidence to fortify her in her choice of him – and timidly dreaded what mortifications might be in store for her by reason of this *mésalliance*.[14] She went out very little; for on the one or two occasions on which she had shown herself to former friends she noticed a distinct difference in their manner, as though they should say, 'Ah, my happy swain's wife; you're caught!'

Edmond's letters were as affectionate as ever; even more affectionate, after a while, than hers were to him. Barbara observed this growing coolness in herself; and like a good and honest lady was horrified and grieved, since her only wish was to act faithfully and uprightly. It troubled her so much that she prayed for a warmer heart, and at last wrote to her husband to beg him, now that he was in the land of Art, to send her his portrait, ever so small, that she might look at it all day and every day, and never for a moment forget his features.

Willowes was nothing loth, and replied that he would do more than she wished: he had made friends with a sculptor in Pisa, who was much interested in him and his history; and he had commissioned this artist to make a bust of himself in marble, which when finished he would send her. What Barbara had wanted was something immediate; but she expressed no objection to the delay; and in his next communication Edmond told her that the sculptor, of his own choice, had decided to extend the bust to a full-length statue, so anxious was he to get a specimen of his skill introduced to the notice of the English aristocracy. It was progressing well, and rapidly.

Meanwhile, Barbara's attention began to be occupied at home with Yewsholt Lodge, the house that her kind-hearted father was preparing for her residence when her husband returned. It was a small place on the plan of a large one – a cottage built in the form of a mansion, having a central hall with a wooden gallery running round it, and rooms no bigger than closets to support this introduction. It stood on a slope so solitary, and surrounded by trees so dense, that the birds who inhabited the boughs sang at strange hours, as if they hardly could distinguish night from day.

During the progress of repairs at this bower Barbara frequently visited it. Though so secluded by the dense growth, it was near the high road, and one day while looking over the fence she saw Lord Uplandtowers riding past. He saluted her courteously, yet with mechanical stiffness, and did not halt. Barbara went home, and continued to pray that she might never cease to love her husband. After that she sickened, and did not come out of doors again for a long time.

The year of education had extended to fourteen months, and the house was in order for Edmond's return to take up his abode there with Barbara, when, instead of the accustomed letter for her, came one to Sir John Grebe in the handwriting of the said tutor, informing him of a terrible catastrophe that had occurred to them at Venice. Mr Willowes and himself had attended the theatre one night during the Carnival of the preceding week, to witness the Italian comedy, when, owing to the carelessness of one of the candle-snuffers,[15] the theatre had caught fire, and been burnt to the ground. Few persons had lost their lives, owing to the superhuman exertions of some of the audience in getting out the senseless sufferers; and, among them all, he who had risked his own life the most heroically was Mr Willowes. In re-entering for the fifth time to save his fellow-creatures some fiery beams had fallen upon him, and he had been given up for lost. He was, however, by the blessing of Providence, recovered, with the life still in him, though he was fearfully burnt; and by almost a miracle he seemed likely to survive, his constitution being wondrously sound. He was, of course, unable to write, but he was receiving the attention of several skilful surgeons. Further report would be made by the next mail or by private hand.

The tutor said nothing in detail of poor Willowes's sufferings, but as soon as the news was broken to Barbara she realized how intense they must have been, and her immediate instinct was to rush to his side, though, on consideration, the journey seemed impossible to her. Her health was by no means what it had been, and to post across Europe at that season of the year, or to traverse the Bay of Biscay in a sailing-craft, was an undertaking that would hardly be justified by the result. But she was anxious to go till, on reading to the end of the letter, her husband's tutor was found to hint very strongly against such a step if it should be contemplated, this being also the opinion of the surgeons. And though Willowes's comrade refrained from giving his reasons, they disclosed themselves plainly enough in the sequel.

The truth was that the worst of the wounds resulting from the fire had occurred to his head and face – that handsome face which had won her heart from her, – and both the tutor and the surgeons knew that for a sensitive young woman to see him before his wounds had healed would cause more misery to her by the shock than happiness to him by her ministrations.

Lady Grebe blurted out what Sir John and Barbara had thought, but had had too much delicacy to express.

'Sure, 'tis mighty hard for you, poor Barbara, that the one little gift he had to justify your rash choice of him – his wonderful good looks – should be taken away like this, to leave 'ee no excuse at all for your conduct in the world's eyes ... Well, I wish you'd married t'other – that do I!' And the lady sighed.

'He'll soon get right again,' said her father soothingly.

Such remarks as the above were not often made; but they were frequent enough to cause Barbara an uneasy sense of self-stultification. She determined to hear them no longer; and the house at Yewsholt being ready and furnished, she withdrew thither with her maids, where for the first time she could feel mistress of a home that would be hers and her husband's exclusively, when he came.

After long weeks Willowes had recovered sufficiently to be able to write himself, and slowly and tenderly he enlightened her upon the full extent of his injuries. It was a mercy, he said, that he had not lost his sight entirely; but he was thankful to say that he still retained full vision in one eye, though the other was dark for ever. The sparing manner in which he meted out particulars of his condition told Barbara how appalling had been his experience. He was grateful for her assurance that nothing could change her; but feared she did not fully realize that he was so sadly disfigured as to make it doubtful if she would recognize him. However, in spite of all, his heart was as true to her as it ever had been.

Barbara saw from his anxiety how much lay behind. She replied that she submitted to the decrees of Fate, and would welcome him in any shape as soon as he could come. She told him of the pretty retreat in which she had taken up her abode, pending their joint occupation of it, and did not reveal how much she had sighed over the information that all his good looks were gone. Still less did she say that she felt a certain strangeness in awaiting him, the weeks they had lived together having been so short by comparison with the length of his absence.

Slowly drew on the time when Willowes found himself well enough to come home. He landed at Southampton, and posted thence towards Yewsholt. Barbara arranged to go out to meet him as far as Lornton Inn – the spot between the Forest and the Chase at which he had waited for night on the evening of their elopement. Thither she drove at the appointed hour in a little pony-chaise, presented her by her father on her birthday for her especial use in her new house; which vehicle she sent back on arriving at the inn, the plan agreed upon being that she should perform the return journey with her husband in his hired coach.

There was not much accommodation for a lady at this way-side tavern; but, as it was a fine evening in early summer, she did not mind – walking about outside, and straining her eyes along the highway for the expected one. But each cloud of dust that enlarged in the distance and drew near was found to disclose a conveyance other than his post-chaise. Barbara remained till the appointment was two hours passed, and then began to fear that owing to some adverse wind in the Channel he was not coming that night.

While waiting she was conscious of a curious trepidation that was not entirely solicitude, and did not amount to dread; her tense state of incertitude bordered both on disappointment and on relief. She had lived six or seven weeks with an imperfectly educated yet handsome husband whom now she had not seen for seventeen months, and who was so changed physically by an accident that she was assured she would hardly know him. Can we wonder at her compound state of mind?

But her immediate difficulty was to get away from Lornton Inn, for her situation was becoming embarrassing. Like too many of Barbara's actions, this drive had been undertaken without much reflection. Expecting to wait no more than a few minutes for her husband in his post-chaise, and to enter it with him, she had not hesitated to isolate herself by sending back her own little vehicle. She now found that, being so well known in this neighbourhood, her excursion to meet her long-absent husband was exciting great interest. She was conscious that more eyes were watching her from the inn-windows than met her own gaze. Barbara had decided to get home by hiring whatever kind of conveyance the tavern afforded, when, straining her eyes for the last time over the now darkening highway, she perceived yet another dust-cloud drawing near. She paused; a chariot ascended to the inn, and would have passed had not its occupant caught sight of her standing expectantly. The horses were checked on the instant.

'You here – and alone, my dear Mrs Willowes?' said Lord Uplandtowers, whose carriage it was.

She explained what had brought her into this lonely situation; and, as he was going in the direction of her own home, she accepted his offer of a seat beside him. Their conversation was embarrassed and fragmentary at first; but when they had driven a mile or two she was surprised to find herself talking earnestly and warmly to him: her impulsiveness was in truth but the natural consequence of her late existence – a somewhat desolate one by reason of the strange marriage she had made; and there is no more indiscreet mood than that of a woman surprised into talk who has long been imposing upon herself a policy of reserve. Therefore her ingenuous heart rose with a bound into her throat when, in response to his leading questions, or rather hints, she allowed her troubles to leak out of her. Lord Uplandtowers took her quite to her own door, although he had driven three miles out of his way to do so; and in handing her down she heard from him a whisper of stern reproach: 'It need not have been thus if you had listened to me!'

She made no reply, and went indoors. There, as the evening wore away, she regretted more and more that she had been so friendly with Lord Uplandtowers. But he had launched himself upon her so unexpectedly: if she had only foreseen the meeting with him, what a careful line of conduct she would have marked out! Barbara broke into a perspiration of disquiet when she thought of her unreserve, and, in self-chastisement, resolved to sit up till midnight on the bare chance of Edmond's return; directing that supper should be laid for him, improbable as his arrival till the morrow was.

The hours went past, and there was dead silence in and round about Yewsholt Lodge, except for the soughing of the trees; till, when it was near upon midnight, she heard the noise of hoofs and wheels approaching the door. Knowing that it could only be her husband, Barbara instantly went into the hall to meet him. Yet she stood there not without a sensation of faintness, so many were the changes since their parting! And, owing to her casual encounter with Lord Uplandtowers, his voice and image still remained with her, excluding Edmond, her husband, from the inner circle of her impressions.

But she went to the door, and the next moment a figure stepped inside, of which she knew the outline, but little besides. Her husband was attired ·in a flapping black cloak and slouched hat, appearing altogether as a foreigner, and not as the young English burgess[16] who had left her side. When he came forward into the light of the lamp, she perceived with surprise, and almost with fright, that he wore a mask. At first she had not noticed this – there being nothing in its colour which would lead a casual observer to think he was looking on anything but a real countenance.

He must have seen her start of dismay at the unexpectedness of his appearance, for he said hastily: 'I did not mean to come in to you like this – I thought you would have been in bed. How good you are, dear Barbara!' He put his arm round her, but he did not attempt to kiss her.

'O Edmond – it *is* you? – it must be?' she said, with clasped hands, for though his figure and movement were almost enough to prove it, and the tones were not unlike the old tones, the enunciation was so altered as to seem that of a stranger.

'I am covered like this to hide myself from the curious eyes of the inn-servants and others,' he said, in a low voice. 'I will send back the carriage and join you in a moment.'

'You are quite alone?'

'Quite. My companion stopped at Southampton.'

The wheels of the post-chaise rolled away as she entered the dining-room, where the supper was spread; and presently he rejoined her there. He had removed his cloak and hat, but the mask was still retained; and she could now see that it was of special make, of some flexible material like silk, coloured so as to represent flesh; it joined naturally to the front hair, and was otherwise cleverly executed.

'Barbara – you look ill,' he said, removing his glove, and taking her hand.

'Yes – I have been ill,' said she.

'Is this pretty little house ours?'

'O – yes.' She was hardly conscious of her words, for the hand he had ungloved in order to take hers was contorted, and had one or two of its fingers missing; while through the mask she discerned the twinkle of one eye only.

'I would give anything to kiss you, dearest, now at this moment!' he continued, with mournful passionateness. 'But I cannot – in this guise. The servants are abed, I suppose?'

'Yes,' said she. 'But I can call them? You will have some supper?'

He said he would have some, but that it was not necessary to call anybody at that hour. Thereupon they approached the table, and sat down, facing each other.

Despite Barbara's scared state of mind, it was forced upon her notice that her husband trembled, as if he feared the impression he was producing, or was about to produce, as much as, or more than, she. He drew nearer, and took her hand again.

'I had this mask made at Venice,' he began, in evident embarrassment. 'My darling Barbara – my dearest wife – do you think you – will mind when I take it off? You will not dislike me – will you?'

'O Edmond, of course I shall not mind,' said she. 'What has happened to you is our misfortune; but I am prepared for it.'

'Are you sure you are prepared?'

'O yes! You are my husband.'

'You really feel quite confident that nothing external can

affect you?' he said again, in a voice rendered uncertain by his agitation.

'I think I am – quite,' she answered faintly.

He bent his head. 'I hope, I hope you are,' he whispered.

In the pause which followed, the ticking of the clock in the hall seemed to grow loud; and he turned a little aside to remove the mask. She breathlessly awaited the operation, which was one of some tediousness, watching him one moment, averting her face the next; and when it was done she shut her eyes at the dreadful spectacle that was revealed. A quick spasm of horror had passed through her; but though she quailed she forced herself to regard him anew, repressing the cry that would naturally have escaped from her ashy lips. Unable to look at him longer, Barbara sank down on the floor beside her chair, covering her eyes.

'You cannot look at me!' he groaned in a hopeless way. 'I am too terrible an object even for you to bear! I knew it; yet I hoped against it. O, this is a bitter fate – curse the skill of those Venetian surgeons who saved me alive! ... Look up, Barbara,' he continued beseechingly; 'view me completely; say you loathe me, if you do loathe me, and settle the case between us for ever!'

His unhappy wife pulled herself together for a desperate strain. He was her Edmond; he had done her no wrong; he had suffered. A momentary devotion to him helped her, and lifting her eyes as bidden she regarded this human remnant, this *écorché*,[17] a second time. But the sight was too much. She again involuntarily looked aside and shuddered.

'Do you think you can get used to this?' he said. 'Yes or no! Can you bear such a thing of the charnel-house[18] near you? Judge for yourself, Barbara. Your Adonis,[19] your matchless man, has come to this!'

The poor lady stood beside him motionless, save for the restlessness of her eyes. All her natural sentiments of affection and pity were driven clean out of her by a sort of panic; she had just the same sense of dismay and fearfulness that she would have had in the presence of an apparition. She could nohow fancy this to be her chosen one – the man she had loved; he was metamorphosed[20] to a specimen of another species. 'I do not loathe you,' she said with trembling. 'But I am so horrified – so overcome! Let me recover myself. Will you sup now? And while you do so may I go to my room to – regain my old feeling for you? I will try, if I may leave you awhile? Yes, I will try!'

Without waiting for an answer from him, and keeping her gaze carefully averted, the frightened woman crept to the door and out of the room. She heard him sit down to the table, as if to begin supper; though, Heaven knows, his appetite was slight enough after a reception which had confirmed his worst surmises. When Barbara had ascended the stairs and arrived in her chamber she sank down, and buried her face in the coverlet of the bed.

Thus she remained for some time. The bedchamber was over the dining-room, and presently as she knelt Barbara heard Willowes thrust back his chair, and rise to go into the hall. In five minutes that figure would probably come up the stairs and confront her again; it, – this new and terrible form, that was not her husband's. In the loneliness of this night, with neither maid nor friend beside her, she lost all self-control, and at the first sound of his footstep on the stairs, without so much as flinging a cloak round her, she flew from the room, ran along the gallery to the back staircase, which she descended, and, unlocking the back door, let herself out. She scarcely was aware what she had done till she found herself in the green-house, crouching on a flower-stand.

Here she remained, her great timid eyes strained through the glass upon the garden without, and her skirts gathered up, in fear of the field-mice which sometimes came there. Every moment she dreaded to hear footsteps which she ought by law to have longed for, and a voice that should have been as music to her soul. But Edmond Willowes came not that way. The nights were getting short at this season, and soon the dawn appeared, and the first rays of the sun. By daylight she had less fear than in the dark. She thought she could meet him, and accustom herself to the spectacle.

So the much-tried young woman unfastened the door of the

hot-house, and went back by the way she had emerged a few hours ago. Her poor husband was probably in bed and asleep, his journey having been long; and she made as little noise as possible in her entry. The house was just as she had left it, and she looked about in the hall for his cloak and hat, but she could not see them; nor did she perceive the small trunk which had been all that he brought with him, his heavier baggage having been left at Southampton for the road-waggon. She summoned courage to mount the stairs; the bedroom-door was open as she had left it. She fearfully peeped round; the bed had not been pressed. Perhaps he had lain down on the dining-room sofa. She descended and entered; he was not there. On the table beside his unsoiled plate lay a note, hastily written on the leaf of a pocket-book. It was something like this:

MY EVER-BELOVED WIFE. – The effect that my forbidding appearance has produced upon you was one which I foresaw as quite possible. I hoped against it, but foolishly so. I was aware that no *human* love could survive such a catastrophe. I confess I thought yours *divine*; but, after so long an absence, there could not be left sufficient warmth to overcome the too natural first aversion. It was an experiment, and it has failed. I do not blame you; perhaps, even, it is better so. Good-bye. I leave England for one year. You will see me again at the expiration of that time, if I live. Then I will ascertain your true feeling; and, if it be against me, go away for ever.

E.W.

On recovering from her surprise, Barbara's remorse was such that she felt herself absolutely unforgiveable. She should have regarded him as an afflicted being, and not have been this slave to mere eyesight, like a child. To follow him and entreat him to return was her first thought. But on making inquiries she found that nobody had seen him: he had silently disappeared.

More than this, to undo the scene of last night was impossible. Her terror had been too plain, and he was a man unlikely to be coaxed back by her efforts to do her duty. She went and confessed to her parents all that had occurred; which, indeed, soon became known to more persons than those of her own family.

The year passed, and he did not return; and it was doubted if he were alive. Barbara's contrition for her unconquerable repugnance was now such that she longed to build a church-aisle, or erect a monument, and devote herself to deeds of charity for the remainder of her days. To that end she made inquiry of the excellent parson under whom she sat on Sundays, at a vertical distance of a dozen feet. But he could only adjust his wig and tap his snuff-box; for such was the lukewarm state of religion in those days, that not an aisle, steeple, porch, east window, Ten-Commandment board,[21] lion-and-unicorn,[22] or brass candlestick, was required anywhere at all in the neighbourhood as a votive offering from a distracted soul – the last century contrasting greatly in this respect with the happy times in which we live, when urgent appeals for contributions to such objects pour in by every morning's post, and nearly all churches have been made to look like new pennies. As the poor lady could not ease her conscience this way, she determined at least to be charitable, and soon had the satisfaction of finding her porch thronged every morning by the raggedest, idlest, most drunken, hypocritical, and worthless tramps in Christendom.

But human hearts are as prone to change as the leaves of the creeper on the wall, and in the course of time, hearing nothing of her husband, Barbara could sit unmoved whilst her mother and friends said in her hearing, 'Well, what has happened is for the best.' She began to think so herself, for even now she could not summon up that lopped and mutilated form without a shiver, though whenever her mind flew back to her early wedded days, and the man who had stood beside her then, a thrill of tenderness moved her, which if quickened by his living presence might have become strong. She was young and inexperienced, and had hardly on his late return grown out of the capricious fancies of girlhood.

But he did not come again, and when she thought of his word that he would return once more, if living, and how unlikely he was to break his word, she gave him up for dead. So did her parents; so also did another person – that man of silence, of irresistible incisiveness, of still countenance, who was as awake as seven sentinels when he seemed to be as sound asleep as the figures on his family monument. Lord Uplandtowers, though not yet thirty, had chuckled like a caustic fogey of threescore when he heard of Barbara's terror and flight at her husband's return, and of the latter's prompt departure. He felt pretty sure, however, that Willowes, despite his hurt feelings, would have reappeared to claim his bright-eyed property if he had been alive at the end of the twelve months.

As there was no husband to live with her, Barbara had relinquished the house prepared for them by her father, and taken up her abode anew at Chene Manor, as in the days of her girlhood. By degrees the episode with Edmond Willowes seemed but a fevered dream, and as the months grew to years Lord Uplandtowers' friendship with the people at Chene — which had somewhat cooled after Barbara's elopement — revived considerably, and he again became a frequent visitor there. He could not make the most trivial alteration or improvement at Knollingwood Hall, where he lived, without riding off to consult with his friend Sir John at Chene; and thus putting himself frequently under her eyes, Barbara grew accustomed to him, and talked to him as freely as to a brother. She even began to look up to him as a person of authority, judgement, and prudence; and though his severity on the bench towards poachers, smugglers, and turnip-stealers was matter of common notoriety, she trusted that much of what was said might be misrepresentation.

Thus they lived on till her husband's absence had stretched to years, and there could be no longer any doubt of his death. A passionless manner of renewing his addresses seemed no longer out of place in Lord Uplandtowers. Barbara did not love him, but hers was essentially one of those sweet-pea or with-wind[23] natures which require a twig of stouter fibre than its own to hang upon and bloom. Now, too, she was older, and admitted to herself that a man whose ancestor had run scores of Saracens through and through in fighting for the site of the Holy Sepulchre[24] was a more desirable husband, socially considered, than one who could only claim with certainty to know that his father and grandfather were respectable burgesses.

Sir John took occasion to inform her that she might legally consider herself a widow; and, in brief, Lord Uplandtowers carried his point with her, and she married him, though he could never get her to own that she loved him as she had loved Willowes. In my childhood I knew an old lady whose mother saw the wedding, and she said that when Lord and Lady Uplandtowers drove away from her father's house in the evening it was in a coach-and-four, and that my lady was dressed in green and silver, and wore the gayest hat and feather that ever were seen; though whether it was that the green did not suit her complexion, or otherwise, the Countess looked pale, and the reverse of blooming. After their marriage her husband took her to London, and she saw the gaieties of a season there; then they returned to Knollingwood Hall, and thus a year passed away.

Before their marriage her husband had seemed to care but little about her inability to love him passionately. 'Only let me win you,' he had said, 'and I will submit to all that.' But now her lack of warmth seemed to irritate him, and he conducted himself towards her with a resentfulness which led to her passing many hours with him in painful silence. The heir-presumptive to the title was a remote relative, whom Lord Uplandtowers did not exclude from the dislike he entertained towards many persons and things besides, and he had set his mind upon a lineal successor. He blamed her much that there was no promise of this, and asked her what she was good for.

On a particular day in her gloomy life a letter, addressed to her as Mrs Willowes, reached Lady Uplandtowers from an unexpected quarter. A sculptor in Pisa, knowing nothing of her second marriage, informed her that the long-delayed life-size statue of Mr Willowes, which, when her husband left that city, he had been directed to retain till it was sent for, was still in his studio. As his commission had not wholly been paid, and the statue was taking up room he could ill spare, he should be glad to have the debt cleared off, and directions where to forward the figure. Arriving at a time when the Countess was beginning to have little secrets (of a harmless kind, it is true) from her husband, by reason of their growing estrangement,

she replied to this letter without saying a word to Lord Uplandtowers, sending off the balance that was owing to the
sculptor, and telling him to despatch the statue to her without
delay.

It was some weeks before it arrived at Knollingwood Hall,
and, by a singular coincidence, during the interval she received
the first absolutely conclusive tidings of her Edmond's death.
It had taken place years before, in a foreign land, about six
months after their parting, and had been induced by the sufferings he had already undergone, coupled with much depression of spirit, which had caused him to succumb to a slight
ailment. The news was sent her in a brief and formal letter from
some relative of Willowes's in another part of England.

Her grief took the form of passionate pity for his misfortunes, and of reproach to herself for never having been able
to conquer her aversion to his latter image by recollection of
what Nature had originally made him. The sad spectacle that
had gone from earth had never been her Edmond at all to her.
O that she could have met him as he was at first! Thus Barbara thought. It was only a few days later that a waggon with
two horses, containing an immense packing-case, was seen at
breakfast-time both by Barbara and her husband to drive round
to the back of the house, and by-and-by they were informed
that a case labelled 'Sculpture' had arrived for her ladyship.

'What can that be?' said Lord Uplandtowers.

'It is the statue of poor Edmond, which belongs to me, but
has never been sent till now,' she answered.

'Where are you going to put it?' asked he.

'I have not decided,' said the Countess. 'Anywhere, so that
it will not annoy you.'

'Oh, it won't annoy me,' says he.

When it had been unpacked in a back room of the house,
they went to examine it. The statue was a full-length figure, in
the purest Carrara marble, representing Edmond Willowes in
all his original beauty, as he had stood at parting from her
when about to set out on his travels; a specimen of manhood
almost perfect in every line and contour. The work had been
carried out with absolute fidelity.

'Phoebus-Apollo,[25] sure,' said the Earl of Uplandtowers, who had never seen Willowes, real or represented, till now.

Barbara did not hear him. She was standing in a sort of trance before the first husband, as if she had no consciousness of the other husband at her side. The mutilated features of Willowes had disappeared from her mind's eye; this perfect being was really the man she had loved, and not that later pitiable figure; in whom tenderness and truth should have seen this image always, but had not done so.

It was not till Lord Uplandtowers said roughly, 'Are you going to stay here all the morning worshipping him?' that she roused herself.

Her husband had not till now the least suspicion that Edmond Willowes originally looked thus, and he thought how deep would have been his jealousy years ago if Willowes had been known to him. Returning to the Hall in the afternoon he found his wife in the gallery, whither the statue had been brought.

She was lost in reverie before it, just as in the morning.

'What are you doing?' he asked.

She started and turned. 'I am looking at my husb— my statue, to see if it is well done,' she stammered. 'Why should I not?'

'There's no reason why,' he said. 'What are you going to do with the monstrous thing? It can't stand here for ever.'

'I don't wish it,' she said. 'I'll find a place.'

In her boudoir there was a deep recess, and while the Earl was absent from home for a few days in the following week, she hired joiners from the village, who under her directions enclosed the recess with a panelled door. Into the tabernacle thus formed she had the statue placed, fastening the door with a lock, the key of which she kept in her pocket.

When her husband returned he missed the statue from the gallery, and, concluding that it had been put away out of deference to his feelings, made no remark. Yet at moments he noticed something on his lady's face which he had never noticed there before. He could not construe it; it was a sort of silent ecstasy, a reserved beatification.[26] What had become of the statue he could not divine, and growing more and more curious, looked about here and there for it till, thinking of her private room, he went towards that spot. After knocking he heard the shutting of a door, and the click of a key; but when he entered his wife was sitting at work, on what was in those days called knotting.[27] Lord Uplandtowers' eye fell upon the newly-painted door where the recess had formerly been.

'You have been carpentering in my absence then, Barbara,' he said carelessly.

'Yes, Uplandtowers.'

'Why did you go putting up such a tasteless enclosure as that — spoiling the handsome arch of the alcove?'

'I wanted more closet-room; and I thought that as this was my own apartment —'

'Of course,' he returned. Lord Uplandtowers knew now where the statue of young Willowes was.

One night, or rather in the smallest hours of the morning, he missed the Countess from his side. Not being a man of nervous imaginings he fell asleep again before he had much considered the matter, and the next morning had forgotten the incident. But a few nights later the same circumstances occurred. This time he fully roused himself; but before he had moved to search for her she returned to the chamber in her dressing-gown, carrying a candle, which she extinguished as she approached, deeming him asleep. He could discover from her breathing that she was strangely moved; but not on this occasion either did he reveal that he had seen her. Presently, when she had lain down, affecting to wake, he asked her some trivial questions. 'Yes, *Edmond*,' she replied absently.

Lord Uplandtowers became convinced that she was in the habit of leaving the chamber in this queer way more frequently than he had observed, and he determined to watch. The next midnight he feigned deep sleep, and shortly after perceived her stealthily rise and let herself out of the room in the dark. He slipped on some clothing and followed. At the further end of the corridor, where the clash of flint and steel[28] would be out of the hearing of one in the bedchamber, she struck a light. He stepped aside into an empty room till she had lit a taper and had passed on to her boudoir. In a minute or two he followed. Arrived at the door of the boudoir, he beheld the door of the private recess open, and Barbara within it, standing with her arms clasped tightly round the neck of her Edmond, and her mouth on his. The shawl which she had thrown round her nightclothes had slipped from her shoulders, and her long white robe and pale face lent her the blanched appearance of a second statue embracing the first. Between her kisses, she apostrophized it in a low murmur of infantine tenderness:

'My only love – how could I be so cruel to you, my perfect one – so good and true – I am ever faithful to you, despite my seeming infidelity! I always think of you – dream of you – during the long hours of the day, and in the night-watches! O Edmond, I am always yours!' Such words as these, intermingled with sobs, and streaming tears, and dishevelled hair, testified to an intensity of feeling in his wife which Lord Uplandtowers had not dreamed of her possessing.

'Ha, ha!' says he to himself. 'This is where we evaporate – this is where my hopes of a successor in the title dissolve – ha! ha! This must be seen to, verily!'

Lord Uplandtowers was a subtle man when once he set himself to strategy; though in the present instance he never thought of the simple stratagem of constant tenderness. Nor did he enter the room and surprise his wife as a blunderer would have done, but went back to his chamber as silently as he had left it. When the Countess returned thither, shaken by spent sobs and sighs, he appeared to be soundly sleeping as usual. The next day he began his countermoves by making inquiries as to the whereabouts of the tutor who had travelled with his wife's first husband; this gentleman, he found, was now master of a grammar-school at no great distance from Knollingwood. At the first convenient moment Lord Uplandtowers went thither and obtained an interview with the said gentleman. The schoolmaster was much gratified by a visit from such an influential neighbour, and was ready to communicate anything that his lordship desired to know.

After some general conversation on the school and its progress, the visitor observed that he believed the schoolmaster had once travelled a good deal with the unfortunate Mr Willowes, and had been with him on the occasion of his accident. He, Lord Uplandtowers, was interested in knowing what had really happened at that time, and had often thought of inquiring. And then the Earl not only heard by word of mouth as much as he wished to know, but, their chat becoming more intimate, the schoolmaster drew upon paper a sketch of the disfigured head, explaining with bated breath various details in the representation.

'It was very strange and terrible!' said Lord Uplandtowers, taking the sketch in his hand. 'Neither nose nor ears, nor lips scarcely!'

A poor man in the town nearest to Knollingwood Hall, who combined the art of sign-painting with ingenious mechanical occupations, was sent for by Lord Uplandtowers to come to the Hall on a day in that week when the Countess had gone on a short visit to her parents. His employer made the man understand that the business in which his assistance was demanded was to be considered private, and money insured the observance of this request. The lock of the cupboard was picked, and the ingenious mechanic and painter, assisted by the schoolmaster's sketch, which Lord Uplandtowers had put in his pocket, set to work upon the god-like countenance of the statue under my lord's direction. What the fire had maimed in the original the chisel maimed in the copy. It was a fiendish disfigurement, ruthlessly carried out, and was rendered still more shocking by being tinted to the hues of life, as life had been after the wreck.

Six hours after, when the workman was gone, Lord Uplandtowers looked upon the result, and smiled grimly, and said:

'A statue should represent a man as he appeared in life, and that's as he appeared. Ha! ha! But 'tis done to good purpose, and not idly.'

He locked the door of the closet with a skeleton key, and went his way to fetch the Countess home.

That night she slept, but he kept awake. According to the tale, she murmured soft words in her dream; and he knew that the tender converse of her imaginings was held with one whom he had supplanted but in name. At the end of her dream the

Countess of Uplandtowers awoke and arose, and then the enactment of former nights was repeated. Her husband remained still and listened. Two strokes sounded from the clock in the pediment without, when, leaving the chamber-door ajar, she passed along the corridor to the other end, where, as usual, she obtained a light. So deep was the silence that he could even from his bed hear her softly blowing the tinder to a glow after striking the steel. She moved on into the boudoir, and he heard, or fancied he heard, the turning of the key in the closet-door. The next moment there came from that direction a loud and prolonged shriek, which resounded to the furthest corners of the house. It was repeated, and there was the noise of a heavy fall.

Lord Uplandtowers sprang out of bed. He hastened along the dark corridor to the door of the boudoir, which stood ajar, and, by the light of the candle within, saw his poor young Countess lying in a heap in her nightdress on the floor of the closet. When he reached her side he found that she had fainted, much to the relief of his fears that matters were worse. He quickly shut up and locked in the hated image which had done the mischief, and lifted his wife in his arms, where in a few instants she opened her eyes. Pressing her face to his without saying a word, he carried her back to her room, endeavouring as he went to disperse her terrors by a laugh in her ear, oddly compounded of causticity, predilection, and brutality.

'Ho – ho – ho!' says he: 'Frightened, dear one, hey? What a baby 'tis! Only a joke, sure, Barbara – a splendid joke! But a baby should not go to closets at midnight to look for the ghost of the dear departed! If it do it must expect to be terrified at his aspect – ho – ho – ho!'

When she was in her bed-chamber, and had quite come to herself, though her nerves were still much shaken, he spoke to her more sternly. 'Now, my lady, answer me: do you love him – eh?'

'No – no!' she faltered, shuddering, with her expanded eyes fixed on her husband. 'He is too terrible – no, no!'

'You are sure?'

'Quite sure!' replied the poor broken-spirited Countess.

But her natural elasticity asserted itself. Next morning he again inquired of her: 'Do you love him now?' She quailed under his gaze, but did not reply.

'That means that you do still, by God!' he continued.

'It means that I will not tell an untruth, and do not wish to incense my lord,' she answered, with dignity.

'Then suppose we go and have another look at him?' As he spoke, he suddenly took her by the wrist, and turned as if to lead her towards the ghastly closet.

'No – no! O – no!' she cried, and her desperate wriggle out of his hand revealed that the fright of the night had left more impression upon her delicate soul than superficially appeared.

'Another dose or two, and she will be cured,' he said to himself.

It was now so generally known that the Earl and Countess were not in accord, that he took no great trouble to disguise his deeds in relation to this matter. During the day he ordered four men with ropes and rollers to attend him in the boudoir. When they arrived, the closet was open, and the upper part of the statue tied up in canvas. He had it taken to the sleeping-chamber. What followed is more or less matter of conjecture. The story, as told to me, goes on to say that, when Lady Up-landtowers retired with him that night, she saw facing the foot of the heavy oak four-poster, a tall dark wardrobe, which had not stood there before; but she did not ask what its presence meant.

'I have had a little whim,' he explained when they were in the dark.

'Have you?' says she.

'To erect a little shrine, as it may be called.'

'A little shrine?'

'Yes; to one whom we both equally adore – eh? I'll show you what it contains.'

He pulled a cord which hung covered by the bedcurtains, and the doors of the wardrobe slowly opened, disclosing that the shelves within had been removed throughout, and the interior adapted to receive the ghastly figure, which stood there as it had stood in the boudoir, but with a wax candle burning on each side of it to throw the cropped and distorted features into relief. She clutched him, uttered a low scream, and buried her head in the bedclothes. 'O, take it away – please take it away!' she implored.

'All in good time; namely, when you love me best,' he returned calmly. 'You don't quite yet – eh?'

'I don't know – I think – O Uplandtowers, have mercy – I cannot bear it – O, in pity, take it away!'

'Nonsense; one gets accustomed to anything. Take another gaze.'

In short, he allowed the doors to remain unclosed at the foot of the bed, and the wax-tapers burning; and such was the strange fascination of the grisly exhibition that a morbid curiosity took possession of the Countess as she lay, and, at his repeated request, she did again look out from the coverlet, shuddered, hid her eyes, and looked again, all the while begging him to take it away, or it would drive her out of her senses. But he would not do so yet, and the wardrobe was not locked till dawn.

The scene was repeated the next night. Firm in enforcing his ferocious correctives, he continued the treatment till the nerves of the poor lady were quivering in agony under the virtuous tortures inflicted by her lord, to bring her truant heart back to faithfulness.

The third night, when the scene had opened as usual, and she lay staring with immense wild eyes at the horrid fascination, on a sudden she gave an unnatural laugh; she laughed more and more, staring at the image, till she literally shrieked with laughter: then there was silence, and he found her to have become insensible. He thought she had fainted, but soon saw that the event was worse: she was in an epileptic fit. He started up, dismayed by the sense that, like many other subtle personages, he had been too exacting for his own interests. Such love as he was capable of, though rather a selfish gloating than a cherishing solicitude, was fanned into life on the instant. He closed the wardrobe with the pulley, clasped her in his arms, took her gently to the window, and did all he could to restore her.

It was a long time before the Countess came to herself, and

when she did so, a considerable change seemed to have taken place in her emotions. She flung her arms around him, and with gasps of fear abjectly kissed him many times, at last bursting into tears. She had never wept in this scene before.

'You'll take it away, dearest – you will!' she begged plaintively.

'If you love me.'

'I do – oh, I do!'

'And hate him, and his memory?'

'Yes – yes!'

'Thoroughly?'

'I cannot endure recollection of him!' cried the poor Countess slavishly. 'It fills me with shame – how could I ever be so depraved! I'll never behave badly again, Uplandtowers; and you will never put the hated statue again before my eyes?'

He felt that he could promise with perfect safety. 'Never,' said he.

'And then I'll love you,' she returned eagerly, as if dreading lest the scourge should be applied anew. 'And I'll never, never dream of thinking a single thought that seems like faithlessness to my marriage vow.'

The strange thing now was that this fictitious love wrung from her by terror took on, through mere habit of enactment, a certain quality of reality. A servile mood of attachment to the Earl became distinctly visible in her contemporaneously with an actual dislike for her late husband's memory. The mood of attachment grew and continued when the statue was removed. A permanent revulsion was operant in her, which intensified as time wore on. How fright could have effected such a change of idiosyncrasy learned physicians alone can say; but I believe such cases of reactionary instinct are not unknown.

The upshot was that the cure became so permanent as to be itself a new disease. She clung to him so tightly that she would not willingly be out of his sight for a moment. She would have no sitting-room apart from his, though she could not help starting when he entered suddenly to her. Her eyes were well-nigh always fixed upon him. If he drove out, she wished to go with him; his slightest civilities to other women made her frantically jealous; till at length her very fidelity became a burden to him, absorbing his time, and curtailing his liberty, and causing him to curse and swear. If he ever spoke sharply to her now, she did not revenge herself by flying off to a mental world of her own; all that affection for another, which had provided her with a resource, was now a cold black cinder.

From that time the life of this scared and enervated lady – whose existence might have been developed to so much higher purpose but for the ignoble ambition of her parents and the conventions of the time – was one of obsequious amativeness [29] towards a perverse and cruel man. Little personal events came to her in quick succession – half a dozen, eight, nine, ten such events, – in brief, she bore him no less than eleven children in the nine following years, but half of them came prematurely into the world, or died a few days old; only one, a girl, attained to maturity; she in after years became the wife of the Honourable Mr Beltonleigh, who was created Lord d'Almaine, as may be remembered.

There was no living son and heir. At length, completely worn out in mind and body, Lady Uplandtowers was taken abroad by her husband, to try the effect of a more genial climate upon her wasted frame. But nothing availed to strengthen her, and she died at Florence, a few months after her arrival in Italy.

Contrary to expectation, the Earl of Uplandtowers did not marry again. Such affection as existed in him – strange, hard, brutal as it was – seemed untransferable, and the title, as is known, passed at his death to his nephew. Perhaps it may not be so generally known that, during the enlargement of the Hall for the sixth Earl, while digging in the grounds for the new foundations, the broken fragments of a marble statue were unearthed. They were submitted to various antiquaries, who said that, so far as the damaged pieces would allow them to form an opinion, the statue seemed to be that of a mutilated Roman satyr; or, if not, an allegorical figure of Death. Only one or two old inhabitants guessed whose statue those fragments had composed.

I should have added that, shortly after the death of the

Countess, an excellent sermon was preached by the Dean of Melchester, the subject of which, though names were not mentioned, was unquestionably suggested by the aforesaid events. He dwelt upon the folly of indulgence in sensuous love for a handsome form merely; and showed that the only rational and virtuous growths of that affection were those based upon intrinsic worth. In the case of the tender but somewhat shallow lady whose life I have related, there is no doubt that an infatuation for the person of young Willowes was the chief feeling that induced her to marry him; which was the more deplorable in that his beauty, by all tradition, was the least of his recommendations, every report bearing out the inference that he must have been a man of steadfast nature, bright intelligence, and promising life.

ON THE WESTERN CIRCUIT[1]

THE man who played the disturbing part in the two quiet feminine lives hereunder depicted – no great man, in any sense, by the way – first had knowledge of them on an October evening, in the city of Melchester. He had been standing in the Close, vainly endeavouring to gain amid the darkness a glimpse of the most homogeneous pile of mediaeval architecture in England, which towered and tapered from the damp and level sward[2] in front of him. While he stood the presence of the Cathedral walls was revealed rather by the ear than by the eyes; he could not see them, but they reflected sharply a roar of sound which entered the Close by a street leading from the city square, and, falling upon the building, was flung back upon him.

He postponed till the morrow his attempt to examine the deserted edifice, and turned his attention to the noise. It was compounded of steam barrel-organs,[3] the clanging of gongs, the ringing of handbells, the clack of rattles, and the undistinguishable shouts of men. A lurid light hung in the air in the direction of the tumult. Thitherward he went, passing under the arched gateway, along a straight street, and into the square.

He might have searched Europe over for a greater contrast between juxtaposed scenes. The spectacle was that of the eighth chasm of the Inferno[4] as to colour and flame, and, as to mirth, a development of the Homeric heaven.[5] A smoky glare, of the complexion of brass-filings, ascended from the fiery tongues of innumerable naphtha lamps[6] affixed to booths, stalls, and other temporary erections which crowded the spacious market-square. In front of this irradiation scores of human figures, more or less in profile, were darting athwart and across, up, down, and around, like gnats against a sunset.

Their motions were so rhythmical that they seemed to be moved by machinery. And it presently appeared that they were moved by machinery indeed; the figures being those of the patrons of swings, see-saws, flying-leaps, above all of the three steam roundabouts which occupied the centre of the position. It was from the latter that the din of steam-organs came.

Throbbing humanity in full light was, on second thoughts, better than architecture in the dark. The young man, lighting a short pipe, and putting his hat on one side and one hand in his pocket, to throw himself into harmony with his new environment, drew near to the largest and most patronized of the steam circuses, as the roundabouts were called by their owners. This was one of brilliant finish, and it was now in full revolution. The musical instrument around which and to whose tones the riders revolved, directed its trumpet-mouths of brass upon the young man, and the long plate-glass mirrors set at angles, which revolved with the machine, flashed the gyrating personages and hobby-horses kaleidoscopically into his eyes.

It could now be seen that he was unlike the majority of the crowd. A gentlemanly young fellow, one of the species found in large towns only, and London particularly, built on delicate lines, well, though not fashionably dressed, he appeared to belong to the professional class; he had nothing square or practical about his look, much that was curvilinear and sensuous. Indeed, some would have called him a man not altogether typical of the middle-class male of a century wherein sordid ambition is the master-passion that seems to be taking the time-honoured place of love.

The revolving figures passed before his eyes with an unexpected and quiet grace in a throng whose natural movements did not suggest gracefulness or quietude as a rule. By some contrivance there was imparted to each of the hobby-horses a motion which was really the triumph and perfection of roundabout inventiveness – a galloping rise and fall, so timed that, of each pair of steeds, one was on the spring[7] while the other was on the pitch.[8] The riders were quite fascinated by these equine undulations in this most delightful holiday-game of our times. There were riders as young as six, and as old as sixty years, with every age between. At first it was difficult to catch a personality, but by and by the observer's eyes centred on the prettiest girl out of the several pretty ones revolving.

It was not that one with the light frock and light hat whom he had been at first attracted by; no, it was the one with the black cape, grey skirt, light gloves and – no, not even she, but the one behind her; she with the crimson skirt, dark jacket, brown hat and brown gloves. Unmistakably that was the prettiest girl.

Having finally selected her, this idle spectator studied her as well as he was able during each of her brief transits across his visual field. She was absolutely unconscious of everything save the act of riding: her features were rapt in an ecstatic dreaminess: for the moment she did not know her age or her history or her lineaments, much less her troubles. He himself was full of vague latter-day glooms and popular melancholies, and it was a refreshing sensation to behold this young thing then and there, absolutely as happy as if she were in a Paradise.

Dreading the moment when the inexorable stoker,[9] grimily lurking behind the glittering rococo-work,[10] should decide that this set of riders had had their pennyworth, and bring the whole concern of steam-engine, horses, mirrors, trumpets, drums, cymbals, and such-like to pause and silence, he waited for her every reappearance, glancing indifferently over the intervening forms, including the two plainer girls, the old woman and child, the two youngsters, the newly-married couple, the old man with a clay pipe, the sparkish[11] youth with a ring, the young ladies in the chariot, the pair of journeyman[12]-carpenters, and others, till his select country beauty followed on again in her place. He had never seen a fairer product of nature, and at each round she made a deeper mark in his sentiments. The stoppage then came, and the sighs of the riders were audible.

He moved round to the place at which he reckoned she would alight; but she retained her seat. The empty saddles began to refill, and she plainly was deciding to have another turn. The young man drew up to the side of her steed, and pleasantly asked her if she had enjoyed her ride.

'O yes!' she said, with dancing eyes. 'It has been quite unlike anything I have ever felt in my life before!'

It was not difficult to fall into conversation with her. Unreserved – too unreserved – by nature, she was not experienced enough to be reserved by art, and after a little coaxing she answered his remarks readily. She had come to live in Melchester from a village on the Great Plain, and this was the first time that she had ever seen a steam-circus; she could not understand how such wonderful machines were made. She had come to the city on the invitation of Mrs Harnham, who had taken her into her household to train her as a servant, if she showed any aptitude. Mrs Harnham was a young lady who before she married had been Miss Edith White, living in the country near the speaker's cottage; she was now very kind to her through knowing her in childhood so well. She was even taking the trouble to educate her. Mrs Harnham was the only friend she had in the world, and being without children had wished to have her near her in preference to anybody else, though she had only lately come; allowed her to do almost as she liked, and to have a holiday whenever she asked for it. The husband of this kind young lady was a rich wine-merchant of the town, but Mrs Harnham did not care much about him. In the daytime you could see the house from where they were talking. She, the speaker, liked Melchester better than the lonely country, and she was going to have a new hat for next Sunday that was to cost fifteen and ninepence.

Then she inquired of her acquaintance where he lived, and he told her in London, that ancient and smoky city, where everybody lived who lived at all, and died because they could not live there. He came into Wessex two or three times a year for professional reasons; he had arrived from Wintoncester yesterday, and was going on into the next county in a day or two. For one thing he did like the country better than the town, and it was because it contained such girls as herself.

Then the pleasure-machine started again, and, to the light-hearted girl, the figure of the handsome young man, the market-square with its lights and crowd, the houses beyond, and the world at large, began moving round as before, counter-moving in the revolving mirrors on her right hand, she being as it were the fixed point in an undulating, dazzling, lurid universe, in which loomed forward most prominently of all the form of her late interlocutor. Each time that she approached the half of her orbit that lay nearest him they gazed at each other with smiles, and with that unmistakable expression which means so little at the moment, yet so often leads up to passion, heart-ache, union, disunion, devotion, overpopulation, drudgery, content, resignation, despair.

When the horses slowed anew he stepped to her side and proposed another heat. 'Hang the expense for once,' he said. 'I'll pay!'

She laughed till the tears came.

'Why do you laugh, dear?' said he.

'Because — you are so genteel that you must have plenty of money, and only say that for fun!' she returned.

'Ha-ha!' laughed the young man in unison, and gallantly producing his money she was enabled to whirl on again.

As he stood smiling there in the motley crowd, with his pipe in his hand, and clad in the rough pea-jacket [13] and wideawake [14] that he had put on for his stroll, who would have supposed him to be Charles Bradford Raye, Esquire, stuff-gownsman, [15] educated at Wintoncester, called to the Bar at Lincoln's-Inn, now going the Western Circuit, merely detained in Melchester by a small arbitration after his brethren had moved on to the next county-town?

II

The square was overlooked from its remoter corner by the house of which the young girl had spoken, a dignified residence of considerable size, having several windows on each floor. Inside one of these, on the first floor, the apartment being a large drawing-room, sat a lady, in appearance from twenty-eight to thirty years of age. The blinds were still undrawn, and the lady was absently surveying the weird scene without, her cheek resting on her hand. The room was unlit from within, but enough of the glare from the market-place entered it to reveal the lady's face. She was what is called an interesting creature rather than a handsome woman; dark-eyed, thoughtful, and with sensitive lips.

A man sauntered into the room from behind and came forward.

'O, Edith, I didn't see you,' he said. 'Why are you sitting here in the dark?'

'I am looking at the fair,' replied the lady in a languid voice.

'Oh? Horrid nuisance every year! I wish it could be put a stop to.'

'I like it.'

'H'm. There's no accounting for taste.'

For a moment he gazed from the window with her, for politeness sake, and then went out again.

In a few minutes she rang.

'Hasn't Anna come in?' asked Mrs Harnham.

'No m'm.'

'She ought to be in by this time. I meant her to go for ten minutes only.'

'Shall I go and look for her, m'm?' said the housemaid alertly.

'No. It is not necessary: she is a good girl and will come soon.'

However, when the servant had gone Mrs Harnham arose, went up to her room, cloaked and bonneted herself, and proceeded downstairs, where she found her husband.

'I want to see the fair,' she said; 'and I am going to look for Anna. I have made myself responsible for her, and must see she comes to no harm. She ought to be indoors. Will you come with me?'

'Oh, she's all right. I saw her on one of those whirligig things, talking to her young man as I came in. But I'll go if you wish, though I'd rather go a hundred miles the other way.'

'Then please do so. I shall come to no harm alone.'

She left the house and entered the crowd which thronged the market-place, where she soon discovered Anna, seated on the revolving horse. As soon as it stopped Mrs Harnham advanced and said severely, 'Anna, how can you be such a wild girl? You were only to be out for ten minutes.'

Anna looked blank, and the young man, who had dropped into the background, came to help her alight.

'Please don't blame her,' he said politely. 'It is my fault that she has stayed. She looked so graceful on the horse that I induced her to go round again. I assure you that she has been quite safe.'

'In that case I'll leave her in your hands,' said Mrs Harnham, turning to retrace her steps.

But this for the moment it was not so easy to do. Something had attracted the crowd to a spot in their rear, and the wine-merchant's wife, caught by its sway, found herself pressed against Anna's acquaintance without power to move away. Their faces were within a few inches of each other, his breath fanned her cheek as well as Anna's. They could do no other than smile at the accident; but neither spoke, and each waited passively. Mrs Harnham then felt a man's hand clasping her fingers, and from the look of consciousness on the young fellow's face she knew the hand to be his: she also knew that from the position of the girl he had no other thought than that the imprisoned hand was Anna's. What prompted her to refrain from undeceiving him she could hardly tell. Not content with holding the hand, he playfully slipped two of his fingers inside her glove, against her palm. Thus matters continued till the pressure lessened; but several minutes passed before the crowd thinned sufficiently to allow Mrs Harnham to withdraw.

'How did they get to know each other, I wonder?' she mused as she retreated. 'Anna is really very forward – and he very wicked and nice.'

She was so gently stirred with the stranger's manner and voice, with the tenderness of his idle touch, that instead of re-entering the house she turned back again and observed the pair from a screened nook. Really she argued (being little less impulsive than Anna herself) it was very excusable in Anna to encourage him, however she might have contrived to make his acquaintance; he was so gentlemanly, so fascinating, had such beautiful eyes. The thought that he was several years her junior produced a reasonless sigh.

At length the couple turned from the roundabout towards the door of Mrs Harnham's house, and the young man could be heard saying that he would accompany her home. Anna, then, had found a lover, apparently a very devoted one. Mrs Harnham was quite interested in him. When they drew near the door of the wine-merchant's house, a comparatively deserted spot by this time, they stood invisible for a little while in the shadow of a wall, where they separated, Anna going on to the entrance, and her acquaintance returning across the square.

'Anna,' said Mrs Harnham, coming up. 'I've been looking at you! That young man kissed you at parting, I am almost sure.'

'Well,' stammered Anna; 'he said, if I didn't mind – it would do me no harm, and, and, him a great deal of good!'

'Ah, I thought so! And he was a stranger till to-night?'

'Yes ma'am.'

'Yet I warrant you told him your name and everything about yourself?'

'He asked me.'

'But he didn't tell you his?'

'Yes ma'am, he did!' cried Anna victoriously. 'It is Charles Bradford, of London.'

'Well, if he's respectable, of course I've nothing to say against your knowing him,' remarked her mistress, prepossessed, in spite of general principles, in the young man's favour. 'But I must reconsider all that, if he attempts to renew your acquaintance. A country-bred girl like you, who has never lived in Melchester till this month, who had hardly ever seen a black-coated man [16] till you came here, to be so sharp as to capture a young Londoner like him!'

'I didn't capture him. I didn't do anything,' said Anna, in confusion.

When she was indoors and alone Mrs Harnham thought what a well-bred and chivalrous young man Anna's companion had seemed. There had been a magic in his wooing touch of her hand; and she wondered how he had come to be attracted by the girl.

The next morning the emotional Edith Harnham went to the usual week-day service in Melchester cathedral. In crossing the Close through the fog she again perceived him who had interested her the previous evening, gazing up thoughtfully at the high-piled architecture of the nave: and as soon as she had taken her seat he entered and sat down in a stall opposite hers.

He did not particularly heed her; but Mrs Harnham was continually occupying her eyes with him, and wondered more than ever what had attracted him in her unfledged maid-servant. The mistress was almost as unaccustomed as the maiden herself to the end-of-the-age young man, or she might have wondered less. Raye, having looked about him awhile, left abruptly, without regard to the service that was proceeding; and Mrs Harnham – lonely, impressionable creature that she was – took no further interest in praising the Lord. She wished she had married a London man who knew the subtleties of love-making as they were evidently known to him who had mistakenly caressed her hand.

III

The calendar [17] at Melchester had been light, occupying the court only a few hours; and the assizes at Casterbridge, the next county-town on the Western Circuit, having no business for Raye, he had not gone thither. At the next town after that they did not open till the following Monday, trials to begin on Tuesday morning. In the natural order of things Raye would have arrived at the latter place on Monday afternoon; but it was not till the middle of Wednesday that his gown and grey wig, curled in tiers, in the best fashion of Assyrian bas-reliefs, [18] were seen blowing and bobbing behind him as he hastily walked up the High Street from his lodgings. But though he entered the assize building there was nothing for him to do, and sitting at the blue baize table in the well of the court, he mended pens with a mind far away from the case in progress. Thoughts of unpremeditated conduct, of which a week earlier he would not have believed himself capable, threw him into a mood of dissatisfied depression.

He had contrived to see again the pretty rural maiden Anna, the day after the fair, had walked out of the city with her to the earthworks of Old Melchester, and feeling a violent fancy for her, had remained in Melchester all Sunday, Monday, and Tuesday; by persuasion obtaining walks and meetings with the girl six or seven times during the interval; had in brief won her, body and soul.

He supposed it must have been owing to the seclusion in which he had lived of late in town that he had given way so unrestrainedly to a passion for an artless creature whose inexperience had, from the first, led her to place herself unreservedly in his hands. Much he deplored trifling with her feelings for the sake of a passing desire; and he could only hope that she might not live to suffer on his account.

She had begged him to come to her again; entreated him; wept. He had promised that he would do so, and he meant to carry out that promise. He could not desert her now. Awkward as such unintentional connections were, the interspace of a hundred miles – which to a girl of her limited capabilities was like a thousand – would effectually hinder this summer fancy from greatly encumbering his life; while thought of her simple love might do him the negative good of keeping him from idle pleasures in town when he wished to work hard. His circuit journeys would take him to Melchester three or four times a year; and then he could always see her.

The pseudonym, or rather partial name, that he had given her as his before knowing how far the acquaintance was going to carry him, had been spoken on the spur of the moment, without any ulterior intention whatever. He had not afterwards disturbed Anna's error, but on leaving her he had felt bound to give her an address at a stationer's not far from his chambers, at which she might write to him under the initials 'C. B.'

In due time Raye returned to his London abode, having called at Melchester on his way and spent a few additional hours with his fascinating child of nature. In town he lived monotonously every day. Often he and his rooms were enclosed by a tawny fog from all the world besides, and when he lighted the gas to read or write by, his situation seemed so unnatural that he would look into the fire and think of that trusting girl at Melchester again and again. Often, oppressed by absurd fondness for her, he would enter the dim religious nave of the Law Courts by the north door, elbow other juniors habited like himself, and like him unretained;[19] edge himself into this or that crowded court where a sensational case was going on, just as if he were in it, though the police officers at the door knew as well as he knew himself that he had no more concern with the business in hand than the patient idlers at the gallery-door outside, who had waited to enter since eight in the morning because, like him, they belonged to the classes that live on expectation. But he would do these things to no purpose, and think how greatly the characters in such scenes contrasted with the pink and breezy Anna.

An unexpected feature in that peasant maiden's conduct was that she had not as yet written to him, though he had told her she might do so if she wished. Surely a young creature had never before been so reticent in such circumstances. At length he sent her a brief line, positively requesting her to write. There was no answer by the return post, but the day after a letter in a neat feminine hand, and bearing the Melchester post-mark, was handed to him by the stationer.

The fact alone of its arrival was sufficient to satisfy his imaginative sentiment. He was not anxious to open the epistle, and in truth did not begin to read it for nearly half-an-hour, anticipating readily its terms of passionate retrospect and tender adjuration. When at last he turned his feet to the fireplace and unfolded the sheet, he was surprised and pleased to find that neither extravagance nor vulgarity was there. It was the most charming little missive he had ever received from woman. To be sure the language was simple and the ideas were slight; but it was so self-possessed; so purely that of a young girl who felt her womanhood to be enough for her dignity that he read it through twice. Four sides were filled, and a few lines written across, after the fashion of former days; the paper, too, was common, and not of the latest shade and surface. But what of those things? He had received letters from women who were fairly called ladies, but never so sensible, so human a letter as this. He could not single out any one sentence and say it was at all remarkable or clever; the *ensemble*[20] of the letter it was which won him; and beyond the one request that he would write or come to her again soon there was nothing to show her sense of a claim upon him.

To write again and develop a correspondence was the last thing Raye would have preconceived as his conduct in such a situation; yet he did send a short, encouraging line or two, signed with his pseudonym, in which he asked for another letter, and cheeringly promised that he would try to see her again on some near day, and would never forget how much they had been to each other during their short acquaintance.

IV

To return now to the moment at which Anna, at Melchester, had received Raye's letter.

It had been put into her own hand by the postman on his morning rounds. She flushed down to her neck on receipt of it, and turned it over and over. 'It is mine?' she said.

'Why, yes, can't you see it is?' said the postman, smiling as he guessed the nature of the document and the cause of the confusion.

'O yes, of course!' replied Anna, looking at the letter, forcedly tittering, and blushing still more.

Her look of embarrassment did not leave her with the postman's departure. She opened the envelope, kissed its contents, put away the letter in her pocket, and remained musing till her eyes filled with tears.

A few minutes later she carried up a cup of tea to Mrs Harnham in her bed-chamber. Anna's mistress looked at her, and said: 'How dismal you seem this morning, Anna. What's the matter?'

'I'm not dismal, I'm glad; only I –' She stopped to stifle a sob.
'Well?'

'I've got a letter – and what good is it to me, if I can't read a word in it!'

'Why, I'll read it, child, if necessary.'

'But this is from somebody – I don't want anybody to read it but myself!' Anna murmured.

'I shall not tell anybody. Is it from that young man?'

'I think so.' Anna slowly produced the letter, saying: 'Then will you read it to me, ma'am?'

This was the secret of Anna's embarrassment and flutterings. She could neither read nor write. She had grown up under the care of an aunt by marriage, at one of the lonely hamlets on the Great Mid-Wessex Plain where, even in days of national education, there had been no school within a distance of two miles. Her aunt was an ignorant woman; there had been nobody to investigate Anna's circumstances, nobody to care about her learning the rudiments; though, as often in such cases, she had been well fed and clothed and not unkindly treated. Since she had come to live at Melchester with Mrs Harnham, the latter, who took a kindly interest in the girl, had taught her to speak correctly, in which accomplishment Anna showed considerable readiness, as is not unusual with the illiterate; and soon became quite fluent in the use of her mistress's phraseology. Mrs Harnham also insisted upon her getting a spelling and copy book, and beginning to practise in these. Anna was slower in this branch of her education, and meanwhile here was the letter.

Edith Harnham's large dark eyes expressed some interest in the contents, though, in her character of mere interpreter, she threw into her tone as much as she could of mechanical passiveness. She read the short epistle on to its concluding sentence, which idly requested Anna to send him a tender answer.

'Now – you'll do it for me, won't you, dear mistress?' said Anna eagerly. 'And you'll do it as well as ever you can, please? Because I couldn't bear him to think I am not able to do it myself. I should sink into the earth with shame if he knew that!'

From some words in the letter Mrs Harnham was led to ask questions, and the answers she received confirmed her suspicions. Deep concern filled Edith's heart at perceiving how the girl had committed her happiness to the issue of this new-sprung attachment. She blamed herself for not interfering in a flirtation which had resulted so seriously for the poor little creature in her charge; though at the time of seeing the pair together she had a feeling that it was hardly within her province to nip young affection in the bud. However, what was done could not be undone, and it behoved her now, as Anna's only protector, to help her as much as she could. To Anna's eager request that she, Mrs Harnham, should compose and write the answer to this young London man's letter, she felt bound to accede, to keep alive his attachment to the girl if possible; though in other circumstances she might have suggested the cook as an amanuensis.

A tender reply was thereupon concocted, and set down in Edith Harnham's hand. This letter it had been which Raye had received and delighted in. Written in the presence of Anna it certainly was, and on Anna's humble note-paper, and in a measure indited by the young girl; but the life, the spirit, the individuality, were Edith Harnham's.

'Won't you at least put your name yourself?' she said. 'You can manage to write that by this time?'

'No, no,' said Anna, shrinking back. 'I should do it so bad. He'd be ashamed of me, and never see me again!'

The note, so prettily requesting another from him, had, as we have seen, power enough in its pages to bring one. He declared it to be such a pleasure to hear from her that she must write every week. The same process of manufacture was accordingly repeated by Anna and her mistress, and continued for several weeks in succession; each letter being penned and suggested by Edith, the girl standing by; the answer read and commented on by Edith, Anna standing by and listening again.

Late on a winter evening, after the dispatch of the sixth letter, Mrs Harnham was sitting alone by the remains of her fire. Her husband had retired to bed, and she had fallen into that fixity of musing which takes no count of hour or temperature. The state of mind had been brought about in Edith by a strange thing which she had done that day. For the first time since Raye's visit Anna had gone to stay over a night or two with her cottage friends on the Plain, and in her absence had arrived, out of its time, a letter from Raye. To this Edith had replied on her own responsibility, from the depths of her own heart, without waiting for her maid's collaboration. The luxury of writing to him what would be known to no consciousness but his was great, and she had indulged herself therein.

Why was it a luxury?

Edith Harnham led a lonely life. Influenced by the belief of the British parent that a bad marriage with its aversions is better than free womanhood with its interests, dignity, and leisure, she had consented to marry the elderly wine-merchant as a *pis aller*,[21] at the age of seven-and-twenty – some three years before this date – to find afterwards that she had made a mistake. That contract had left her still a woman whose deeper nature had never been stirred.

She was now clearly realizing that she had become possessed to the bottom of her soul with the image of a man to whom she was hardly so much as a name. From the first he had attracted her by his looks and voice; by his tender touch; and, with these as generators, the writing of letter after letter and the reading of their soft answers had insensibly developed on her side an emotion which fanned his; till there had resulted a magnetic reciprocity between the correspondents, notwithstanding that one of them wrote in a character not her own. That he had been able to seduce another woman in two days was his crowning though unrecognized fascination for her as the she-animal.

They were her own impassioned and pent-up ideas – lowered to monosyllabic phraseology in order to keep up the disguise – that Edith put into letters signed with another name, much to the shallow Anna's delight, who, unassisted, could not for the world have conceived such pretty fancies for winning him, even had she been able to write them. Edith found that it was these, her own foisted-in sentiments, to which the young barrister mainly responded. The few sentences occasionally added from Anna's own lips made apparently no impression upon him.

The letter-writing in her absence Anna never discovered; but on her return the next morning she declared she wished to see her lover about something at once, and begged Mrs Harnham to ask him to come.

There was a strange anxiety in her manner which did not escape Mrs Harnham, and ultimately resolved itself into a flood of tears. Sinking down at Edith's knees, she made confession that the result of her relations with her lover it would soon become necessary to disclose.

Edith Harnham was generous enough to be very far from inclined to cast Anna adrift at this conjuncture. No true woman ever is so inclined from her own personal point of view, however prompt she may be in taking such steps to safeguard those dear to her. Although she had written to Raye so short a time previously, she instantly penned another Anna-note hinting clearly though delicately the state of affairs.

Raye replied by a hasty line to say how much he was concerned at her news: he felt that he must run down to see her almost immediately.

But a week later the girl came to her mistress's room with another note, which on being read informed her that after all he could not find time for the journey. Anna was broken with grief; but by Mrs Harnham's counsel strictly refrained from hurling at him the reproaches and bitterness customary from young women so situated. One thing was imperative: to keep the young man's romantic interest in her alive. Rather therefore did Edith, in the name of her *protégée*,[22] request him on no account to be distressed about the looming event, and not to inconvenience himself to hasten down. She desired above everything to be no weight upon him in his career, no clog upon his high activities. She had wished him to know what had befallen: he was to dismiss it again from his mind. Only he must write tenderly as ever, and when he should come again on the spring circuit it would be soon enough to discuss what had better be done.

It may well be supposed that Anna's own feelings had not

been quite in accord with these generous expressions; but the mistress's judgement had ruled, and Anna had acquiesced. 'All I want is that *niceness* you can so well put into your letters, my dear, dear mistress, and that I can't for the life o' me make up out of my own head; though I mean the same thing and feel it exactly when you've written it down!'

When the letter had been sent off, and Edith Harnham was left alone, she bowed herself on the back of her chair and wept.

'I wish his child was mine — I wish it was!' she murmured. 'Yet how can I say such a wicked thing!'

v

The letter moved Raye considerably when it reached him. The intelligence itself had affected him less than her unexpected manner of treating him in relation to it. The absence of any word of reproach, the devotion to his interests, the self-sacrifice apparent in every line, all made up a nobility of character that he had never dreamt of finding in womankind.

'God forgive me!' he said tremulously. 'I have been a wicked wretch. I did not know she was such a treasure as this!'

He reassured her instantly; declaring that he would not of course desert her, that he would provide a home for her somewhere. Meanwhile she was to stay where she was as long as her mistress would allow her.

But a misfortune supervened in this direction. Whether an inkling of Anna's circumstances reached the knowledge of Mrs Harnham's husband or not cannot be said, but the girl was compelled, in spite of Edith's entreaties, to leave the house. By her own choice she decided to go back for a while to the cottage on the Plain. This arrangement led to a consultation as to how the correspondence should be carried on; and in the girl's inability to continue personally what had been begun in her name, and in the difficulty of their acting in concert as heretofore, she requested Mrs Harnham — the only well-to-do friend she had in the world — to receive the letters and reply to them off-hand, sending them on afterwards to herself on the Plain, where she might at least get some neighbour to read them to her, if a trustworthy one could be met with. Anna and her box then departed for the Plain.

Thus it befell that Edith Harnham found herself in the strange position of having to correspond, under no supervision by the real woman, with a man not her husband, in terms which were virtually those of a wife, concerning a corporeal condition that was not Edith's at all; the man being one for whom, mainly through the sympathies involved in playing this part, she secretly cherished a predilection, subtle and imaginative truly, but strong and absorbing. She opened each letter, read it as if intended for herself, and replied from the promptings of her own heart and no other.

Throughout this correspondence, carried on in the girl's absence, the high-strung Edith Harnham lived in the ecstasy of fancy; the vicarious intimacy engendered such a flow of passionateness as was never exceeded. For conscience's sake Edith at first sent on each of his letters to Anna, and even rough copies of her replies; but later on these so-called copies were much abridged, and many letters on both sides were not sent on at all.

Though sensuous, and, superficially at least, infested with the self-indulgent vices of artificial society, there was a substratum of honesty and fairness in Raye's character. He had really a tender regard for the country girl, and it grew more tender than ever when he found her apparently capable of expressing the deepest sensibilities in the simplest words. He meditated, he wavered; and finally resolved to consult his sister, a maiden lady much older than himself, of lively sympathies and good intent. In making this confidence he showed her some of the letters.

'She seems fairly educated,' Miss Raye observed. 'And bright in ideas. She expresses herself with a taste that must be innate.'

'Yes. She writes very prettily, doesn't she, thanks to these elementary schools?'

'One is drawn out towards her, in spite of one's self, poor thing.'

The upshot of the discussion was that though he had not been directly advised to do it, Raye wrote, in his real name, what he would never have decided to write on his own responsibility; namely that he could not live without her, and would come down in the spring and shelve her looming difficulty by marrying her.

This bold acceptance of the situation was made known to Anna by Mrs Harnham driving out immediately to the cottage on the Plain. Anna jumped for joy like a little child. And poor, crude directions for answering appropriately were given to Edith Harnham, who on her return to the city carried them out with warm intensifications.

'O!' she groaned, as she threw down the pen. 'Anna – poor good little fool – hasn't intelligence enough to appreciate him! How should she? While I – don't bear his child!'

It was now February. The correspondence had continued altogether for four months; and the next letter from Raye contained incidentally a statement of his position and prospects. He said that in offering to wed her he had, at first, contemplated the step of retiring from a profession which hitherto had brought him very slight emolument, and which, to speak plainly, he had thought might be difficult of practice after his union with her. But the unexpected mines of brightness and warmth that her letters had disclosed to be lurking in her sweet nature had led him to abandon that somewhat sad prospect. He felt sure that, with her powers of development, after a little private training in the social forms of London under his supervision, and a little help from a governess if necessary, she would make as good a professional man's wife as could be desired, even if he should rise to the woolsack. Many a Lord Chancellor's wife had been less intuitively a lady than she had shown herself to be in her lines to him.

'O – poor fellow, poor fellow!' mourned Edith Harnham.

Her distress now raged as high as her infatuation. It was she who had wrought him to this pitch – to a marriage which meant his ruin; yet she could not, in mercy to her maid, do anything to hinder his plan. Anna was coming to Melchester that week, but she could hardly show the girl this last reply from the young man; it told too much of the second individuality that had usurped the place of the first.

Anna came, and her mistress took her into her own room for privacy. Anna began by saying with some anxiety that she was glad the wedding was so near.

'O Anna!' replied Mrs Harnham. 'I think we must tell him all – that I have been doing your writing for you? – lest he should not know it till after you become his wife, and it might lead to dissension and recriminations –'

'O mis'ess, dear mis'ess – please don't tell him now!' cried Anna in distress. 'If you were to do it, perhaps he would not marry me; and what should I do then? It would be terrible what would come to me! And I am getting on with my writing, too. I have brought with me the copybook you were so good as to give me, and I practise every day, and though it is so, so hard, I shall do it well at last, I believe, if I keep on trying.'

Edith looked at the copybook. The copies had been set by herself, and such progress as the girl had made was in the way of grotesque facsimile of her mistress's hand. But even if Edith's flowing calligraphy were reproduced the inspiration would be another thing.

'You do it so beautifully,' continued Anna, 'and say all that I want to say so much better than I could say it, that I do hope you won't leave me in the lurch just now!'

'Very well,' replied the other. 'But I – but I thought I ought not to go on!'

'Why?'

Her strong desire to confide her sentiments led Edith to answer truly:

'Because of its effect upon me.'

'But it *can't* have any!'

'Why, child?'

'Because you are married already!' said Anna with lucid simplicity.

'Of course it can't,' said her mistress hastily; yet glad, despite her conscience, that two or three outpourings still remained to her. 'But you must concentrate your attention on writing your name as I write it here.'

VI

Soon Raye wrote about the wedding. Having decided to make the best of what he feared was a piece of romantic folly, he had acquired more zest for the grand experiment. He wished the ceremony to be in London, for greater privacy. Edith Harnham would have preferred it at Melchester; Anna was passive. His reasoning prevailed, and Mrs Harnham threw herself with mournful zeal into the preparations for Anna's departure. In a last desperate feeling that she must at every hazard be in at the death of her dream, and see once again the man who by a species of telepathy had exercised such an influence on her, she offered to go up with Anna and be with her through the ceremony – 'to see the end of her,' as her mistress put it with forced gaiety; an offer which the girl gratefully accepted; for she had no other friend capable of playing the part of companion and witness, in the presence of a gentlemanly bridegroom, in such a way as not to hasten an opinion that he had made an irremediable social blunder.

It was a muddy morning in March when Raye alighted from a four-wheel cab at the door of a registry-office in the S.W. district of London, and carefully handed down Anna and her companion Mrs Harnham. Anna looked attractive in the somewhat fashionable clothes which Mrs Harnham had helped her to buy, though not quite so attractive as, an innocent child, she had appeared in her country gown on the back of the wooden horse at Melchester Fair.

Mrs Harnham had come up this morning by an early train, and a young man – a friend of Raye's – having met them at the door, all four entered the registry-office together. Till an hour before this time Raye had never known the wine-merchant's wife, except at that first casual encounter, and in the flutter of the performance before them he had little opportunity for more than a brief acquaintance. The contract of marriage at a registry is soon got through; but somehow, during its progress, Raye discovered a strange and secret gravitation between himself and Anna's friend.

The formalities of the wedding – or rather ratification of a previous union – being concluded, the four went in one cab to Raye's lodgings, newly taken in a new suburb in preference to a house, the rent of which he could ill afford just then. Here Anna cut the little cake which Raye had bought at a pastry-cook's on his way home from Lincoln's Inn the night before. But she did not do much besides. Raye's friend was obliged to depart almost immediately, and when he had left the only ones virtually present were Edith and Raye, who exchanged ideas with much animation. The conversation was indeed theirs only, Anna being as a domestic animal who humbly heard but understood not. Raye seemed startled in awakening to this fact, and began to feel dissatisfied with her inadequacy.

At last, more disappointed than he cared to own, he said, 'Mrs Harnham, my darling is so flurried that she doesn't know what she is doing or saying. I see that after this event a little quietude will be necessary before she gives tongue to that tender philosophy which she used to treat me to in her letters.'

They had planned to start early that afternoon for Knollsea, to spend the few opening days of their married life there, and as the hour for departure was drawing near Raye asked his wife if she would go to the writing-desk in the next room and scribble a little note to his sister, who had been unable to attend through indisposition, informing her that the ceremony was over, thanking her for her little present, and hoping to know her well now that she was the writer's sister as well as Charles's.

'Say it in the pretty poetical way you know so well how to adopt,' he added, 'for I want you particularly to win her, and both of you to be dear friends.'

Anna looked uneasy, but departed to her task, Raye remaining to talk to their guest. Anna was a long while absent, and her husband suddenly rose and went to her.

He found her still bending over the writing-table, with tears brimming up in her eyes; and he looked down upon the sheet of note-paper with some interest, to discover with what tact she had expressed her goodwill in the delicate circumstances. To his surprise she had progressed but a few lines, in the characters and spelling of a child of eight, and with the ideas of a goose.

'Anna,' he said, staring; 'what's this?'

'It only means – that I can't do it any better!' she answered, through her tears.

'Eh? Nonsense!'

'I can't!' she insisted, with miserable, sobbing hardihood. 'I – I – didn't write those letters, Charles! I only told *her* what to write! And not always that! But I am learning, O so fast, my dear, dear husband! And you'll forgive me, won't you, for not telling you before?' She slid to her knees, abjectly clasped his waist and laid her face against him.

He stood a few moments, raised her, abruptly turned, and shut the door upon her, rejoining Edith in the drawing-room. She saw that something untoward had been discovered, and their eyes remained fixed on each other.

'Do I guess rightly?' he asked, with wan quietude. '*You* were her scribe through all this?'

'It was necessary,' said Edith.

'Did she dictate every word you ever wrote to me?'

'Not every word.'

'In fact, very little?'

'Very little.'

'You wrote a great part of those pages every week from your own conceptions, though in her name!'

'Yes.'

'Perhaps you wrote many of the letters when you were alone, without communication with her?'

'I did.'

He turned to the bookcase, and leant with his hand over his face; and Edith, seeing his distress, became white as a sheet.

'You have deceived me – ruined me!' he murmured.

'O, don't say it!' she cried in her anguish, jumping up and putting her hand on his shoulder. 'I can't bear that!'

'Delighting me deceptively! Why did you do it – *why* did you!'

'I began doing it in kindness to her! How could I do otherwise than try to save such a simple girl from misery? But I admit that I continued it for pleasure to myself.'

Raye looked up. 'Why did it give you pleasure?' he asked.

'I must not tell,' said she.

He continued to regard her, and saw that her lips suddenly began to quiver under his scrutiny, and her eyes to fill and droop. She started aside, and said that she must go to the station to catch the return train: could a cab be called immediately?

But Raye went up to her, and took her unresisting hand. 'Well, to think of such a thing as this!' he said. 'Why, you and I are friends – lovers – devoted lovers – by correspondence!'

'Yes; I suppose.'

'More.'

'More?'

'Plainly more. It is no use blinking that. Legally I have married her – God help us both! – in soul and spirit I have married you, and no other woman in the world!'

'Hush!'

'But I will not hush! Why should you try to disguise the full truth, when you have already owned half of it? Yes, it is between you and me that the bond is – not between me and her! Now I'll say no more. But, O my cruel one, I think I have one claim upon you!'

She did not say what, and he drew her towards him, and bent over her. 'If it was all pure invention in those letters,' he said emphatically, 'give me your cheek only. If you meant what you said, let it be lips. It is for the first and last time, remember!'

She put up her mouth, and he kissed her long. 'You forgive me?' she said, crying.

'Yes.'

'But you are ruined!'

'What matter!' he said, shrugging his shoulders. 'It serves me right!'

She withdrew, wiped her eyes, entered and bade good-bye to Anna, who had not expected her to go so soon, and was still wrestling with the letter. Raye followed Edith downstairs, and in three minutes she was in a hansom driving to the Waterloo station.

He went back to his wife. 'Never mind the letter, Anna, to-day,' he said gently. 'Put on your things. We, too, must be off shortly.'

The simple girl, upheld by the sense that she was indeed married, showed her delight at finding that he was as kind as ever after the disclosure. She did not know that before his eyes he beheld as it were a galley, in which he, the fastidious urban, was chained to work for the remainder of his life, with her, the unlettered peasant, chained to his side.

Edith travelled back to Melchester that day with a face that showed the very stupor of grief, her lips still tingling from the desperate pressure of his kiss. The end of her impassioned dream had come. When at dusk she reached the Melchester station her husband was there to meet her, but in his perfunc-toriness and her preoccupation they did not see each other, and she went out of the station alone.

She walked mechanically homewards without calling a fly. Entering, she could not bear the silence of the house, and went up in the dark to where Anna had slept, where she remained thinking awhile. She then returned to the drawing-room, and not knowing what she did, crouched down upon the floor.

'I have ruined him!' she kept repeating. 'I have ruined him; because I would not deal treacherously towards her!'

In the course of half an hour a figure opened the door of the apartment.

'Ah – who's that?' she said, starting up, for it was dark.

'Your husband – who should it be?' said the worthy mer-chant.

'Ah – my husband! – I forgot I had a husband!' she whisp-ered to herself.

'I missed you at the station,' he continued. 'Did you see Anna safely tied up? I hope so, for 'twas time.'

'Yes – Anna is married.'

Simultaneously with Edith's journey home Anna and her husband were sitting at the opposite windows of a second-class carriage which sped along to Knollsea. In his hand was a pocket-book full of creased sheets closely written over. Unfolding them one after another he read them in silence, and sighed.

'What are you doing, dear Charles?' she said timidly from the other window, and drew nearer to him as if he were a god.

'Reading over all those sweet letters to me signed "Anna," ' he replied with dreary resignation.

I

To the eyes of a man viewing it from behind, the nut-brown hair was a wonder and a mystery. Under the black beaver hat surmounted by its tuft of black feathers, the long locks, braided and twisted and coiled like the rushes of a basket, composed a rare, if somewhat barbaric, example of ingenious art. One could understand such weavings and coilings being wrought to last intact for a year, or even a calendar month; but that they should be all demolished regularly at bedtime, after a single day of permanence, seemed a reckless waste of successful fabrication.

And she had done it all herself, poor thing. She had no maid, and it was almost the only accomplishment she could boast of. Hence the unstinted pains.

She was a young invalid lady – not so very much of an invalid – sitting in a wheeled chair, which had been pulled up in the front part of a green enclosure, close to a bandstand where a concert was going on, during a warm June afternoon. It had place in one of the minor parks or private gardens that are to be found in the suburbs of London, and was the effort of a local association to raise money for some charity. There are worlds within worlds in the great city, and though nobody outside the immediate district had ever heard of the charity, or the band, or the garden, the enclosure was filled with an interested audience sufficiently informed on all these.

As the strains proceeded many of the listeners observed the chaired lady, whose back hair, by reason of her prominent position, so challenged inspection. Her face was not easily discernible, but the aforesaid cunning tress-weavings, the white ear and poll,[1] and the curve of a cheek which was neither flaccid nor sallow, were signals that led to the expectation of good beauty in front. Such expectations are not infrequently disappointed as soon as the disclosure comes; and in the present case, when the lady, by a turn of the head, at length revealed herself, she was not so handsome as the people behind her had supposed, and even hoped – they did not know why.

For one thing (alas! the commonness of this complaint), she was less young than they had fancied her to be. Yet attractive her face unquestionably was, and not at all sickly. The revelation of its details came each time she turned to talk to a boy of twelve or thirteen who stood beside her, and the shape of whose hat and jacket implied that he belonged to a well-known public school. The immediate bystanders could hear that he called her 'Mother'.

When the end of the recital was reached, and the audience withdrew, many chose to find their way out by passing at her elbow. Almost all turned their heads to take a full and near look at the interesting woman, who remained stationary in the chair till the way should be clear enough for her to be wheeled out without obstruction. As if she expected their glances, and did not mind gratifying their curiosity, she met the eyes of several of her observers by lifting her own, showing these to be soft, brown, and affectionate orbs, a little plaintive in their regard.

She was conducted out of the gardens, and passed along the pavement till she disappeared from view, the schoolboy walking beside her. To inquiries made by some persons who watched her away, the answer came that she was the second wife of the incumbent of a neighbouring parish, and that she was lame. She was generally believed to be a woman with a story – an innocent one, but a story of some sort or other.

In conversing with her on their way home the boy who walked at her elbow said that he hoped his father had not missed them.

'He have been so comfortable these last few hours that I am sure he cannot have missed us,' she replied.

'*Has*, dear mother – not *have!*' exclaimed the public-school boy, with an impatient fastidiousness that was almost harsh. 'Surely you know that by this time!'

His mother hastily adopted the correction, and did not

resent his making it, or retaliate, as she might well have done, by bidding him to wipe that crumby mouth of his, whose condition had been caused by surreptitious attempts to eat a piece of cake without taking it out of the pocket wherein it lay concealed. After this the pretty woman and the boy went onward in silence.

That question of grammar bore upon her history, and she fell into reverie, of a somewhat sad kind to all appearance. It might have been assumed that she was wondering if she had done wisely in shaping her life as she had shaped it, to bring out such a result as this.

In a remote nook in North Wessex, forty miles from London, near the thriving county-town of Aldbrickham, there stood a pretty village with its church and parsonage, which she knew well enough, but her son had never seen. It was her native village, Gaymead, and the first event bearing upon her present situation had occurred at that place when she was only a girl of nineteen.

How well she remembered it, that first act in her little tragicomedy, the death of her reverend husband's first wife. It happened on a spring evening, and she who now and for many years had filled that first wife's place was then parlour-maid in the parson's house.

When everything had been done that could be done, and the death was announced, she had gone out in the dusk to visit her parents, who were living in the same village, to tell them the sad news. As she opened the white swing-gate and looked towards the trees which rose westward, shutting out the pale light of the evening sky, she discerned, without much surprise, the figure of a man standing in the hedge, though she roguishly exclaimed as a matter of form, 'O, Sam, how you frightened me!'

He was a young gardener of her acquaintance. She told him the particulars of the late event, and they stood silent, these two young people, in that elevated, calmly philosophic mind which is engendered when a tragedy has happened close at hand, and has not happened to the philosophers themselves. But it had its bearing upon their relations.

'And will you stay on now at the Vicarage, just the same?' asked he.

She had hardly thought of that. 'O yes — I suppose!' she said. 'Everything will be just as usual, I imagine?'

He walked beside her towards her mother's. Presently his arm stole round her waist. She gently removed it; but he placed it there again, and she yielded the point. 'You see, dear Sophy, you don't know that you'll stay on; you may want a home; and I shall be ready to offer one some day, though I may not be ready just yet.'

'Why, Sam, how can you be so fast! I've never even said I liked 'ee; and it is all your own doing, coming after me!'

'Still, it is nonsense to say I am not to have a try at you like the rest.' He stooped to kiss her a farewell, for they had reached her mother's door.

'No, Sam; you sha'n't!' she cried, putting her hand over his mouth. 'You ought to be more serious on such a night as this.' And she bade him adieu without allowing him to kiss her or to come indoors.

The vicar just left a widower was at this time a man about forty years of age, of good family, and childless. He had led a secluded existence in this college living, partly because there were no resident landowners; and his loss now intensified his habit of withdrawal from outward observation. He was seen still less than heretofore, kept himself still less in time with the rhythm and racket of the movements called progress in the world without. For many months after his wife's decease the economy of his household remained as before; the cook, the housemaid, the parlour-maid, and the man out-of-doors performed their duties or left them undone, just as Nature prompted them — the vicar knew not which. It was then represented to him that his servants seemed to have nothing to do in his small family of one. He was struck with the truth of this representation, and decided to cut down his establishment. But he was forestalled by Sophy, the parlour-maid, who said one evening that she wished to leave him.

'And why?' said the parson.

'Sam Hobson has asked me to marry him, sir.'

'Well – do you want to marry?'

'Not much. But it would be a home for me. And we have heard that one of us will have to leave.'

A day or two after she said: 'I don't want to leave just yet, sir, if you don't wish it. Sam and I have quarrelled.'

He looked up at her. He had hardly ever observed her before, though he had been frequently conscious of her soft presence in the room. What a kitten-like, flexuous, tender creature she was! She was the only one of the servants with whom he came into immediate and continuous relation. What should he do if Sophy were gone?

Sophy did not go, but one of the others did, and things went on quietly again.

When Mr Twycott, the vicar, was ill, Sophy brought up his meals to him, and she had no sooner left the room one day than he heard a noise on the stairs. She had slipped down with the tray, and so twisted her foot that she could not stand. The village surgeon was called in; the vicar got better, but Sophy was incapacitated for a long time; and she was informed that she must never again walk much or engage in any occupation which required her to stand long on her feet. As soon as she was comparatively well she spoke to him alone. Since she was forbidden to walk and bustle about, and, indeed, could not do so, it became her duty to leave. She could very well work at something sitting down, and she had an aunt a seamstress.

The parson had been very greatly moved by what she had suffered on his account, and he exclaimed, 'No, Sophy; lame or not lame, I cannot let you go. You must never leave me again!'

He came close to her, and, though she could never exactly tell how it happened, she became conscious of his lips upon her cheek. He then asked her to marry him. Sophy did not exactly love him, but she had a respect for him which almost amounted to veneration. Even if she had wished to get away from him she hardly dared refuse a personage so reverend and august in her eyes, and she assented forthwith to be his wife.

Thus it happened that one fine morning, when the doors of the church were naturally open for ventilation, and the singing birds fluttered in and alighted on the tie-beams[2] of the roof, there was a marriage-service at the communion-rails, which hardly a soul knew of. The parson and a neighbouring curate had entered at one door, and Sophy at another, followed by two necessary persons, whereupon in a short time there emerged a newly-made husband and wife.

Mr Twycott knew perfectly well that he had committed social suicide by this step, despite Sophy's spotless character, and he had taken his measures accordingly. An exchange of livings had been arranged with an acquaintance who was incumbent of a church in the south of London, and as soon as possible the couple removed thither, abandoning their pretty home, with trees and shrubs and glebe,[3] for a narrow, dusty house in a long, straight street, and their fine peal of bells for the wretchedest one-tongued clangour that ever tortured mortal ears. It was all on her account. They were, however, away from every one who had known her former position; and also under less observation from without than they would have had to put up with in any country parish.

Sophy the woman was as charming a partner as a man could possess, though Sophy the lady had her deficiencies. She showed a natural aptitude for little domestic refinements, so far as related to things and manners; but in what is called culture she was less intuitive. She had now been married more than fourteen years, and her husband had taken much trouble with her education; but she still held confused ideas on the use of 'was' and 'were', which did not beget a respect for her among the few acquaintances she made. Her great grief in this relation was that her only child, on whose education no expense had been and would be spared, was now old enough to perceive these deficiencies in his mother, and not only to see them but to feel irritated at their existence.

Thus she lived on in the city, and wasted hours in braiding her beautiful hair, till her once apple cheeks waned to pink of the very faintest. Her foot had never regained its natural strength after the accident, and she was mostly obliged to avoid walking altogether. Her husband had grown to like London for its freedom and its domestic privacy; but he was twenty years his Sophy's senior, and had latterly been seized with a serious illness. On this day, however, he had seemed to be well enough to justify her accompanying her son Randolph to the concert.

II

The next time we get a glimpse of her is when she appears in the mournful attire of a widow.

Mr Twycott had never rallied, and now lay in a well-packed cemetery to the south of the great city, where, if all the dead it contained had stood erect and alive, not one would have known him or recognized his name. The boy had dutifully followed him to the grave, and was now again at school.

Throughout these changes Sophy had been treated like the child she was in nature though not in years. She was left with no control over anything that had been her husband's beyond her modest personal income. In his anxiety lest her inexperience should be over-reached he had safeguarded with trustees all he possibly could. The completion of the boy's course at the public school, to be followed in due time by Oxford and ordination, had been all previsioned and arranged, and she really had nothing to occupy her in the world but to eat and drink, and make a business of indolence, and go on weaving and coiling the nut-brown hair, merely keeping a home open for the son whenever he came to her during vacations.

Foreseeing his probable decease long years before her, her husband in his lifetime had purchased for her use a semi-detached villa in the same long, straight road whereon the church and parsonage faced, which was to be hers as long as she chose to live in it. Here she now resided, looking out upon the fragment of lawn in front, and through the railings at the ever-flowing traffic; or, bending forward over the window-sill on the first floor, stretching her eyes far up and down the vista of sooty trees, hazy air, and drab house-façades, along which echoed the noises common to a suburban main thoroughfare.

Somehow, her boy, with his aristocratic school-knowledge, his grammars, and his aversions, was losing those wide infan-

tine sympathies, extending as far as to the sun and moon
themselves, with which he, like other children, had been born,
and which his mother, a child of nature herself, had loved in
him; he was reducing their compass to a population of a few
thousand wealthy and titled people, the mere veneer of a
thousand million or so of others who did not interest him at all.
He drifted further and further away from her. Sophy's *milieu*[4]
being a suburb of minor tradesmen and under-clerks, and her
almost only companions the two servants of her own house, it
was not surprising that after her husband's death she soon lost
the little artificial tastes she had acquired from him, and became – in her son's eyes – a mother whose mistakes and origin
it was his painful lot as a gentleman to blush for. As yet he was
far from being man enough – if he ever would be – to rate these
sins of hers at their true infinitesimal value beside the yearn-
ing fondness that welled up and remained penned in her heart
till it should be more fully accepted by him, or by some other
person or thing. If he had lived at home with her he would have
had all of it; but he seemed to require so very little in present
circumstances, and it remained stored.

Her life became insupportably dreary; she could not take
walks, and had no interest in going for drives, or, indeed, in
travelling anywhere. Nearly two years passed without an event,
and still she looked on that suburban road, thinking of the village in which she had been born, and whither she would have
gone back – O how gladly! – even to work in the fields.

Taking no exercise she often could not sleep, and would rise
in the night or early morning to look out upon the then vacant
thoroughfare, where the lamps stood like sentinels waiting for
some procession to go by. An approximation to such a procession was indeed made early every morning about one o'clock,
when the country vehicles passed up with loads of vegetables
for Covent Garden market. She often saw them creeping along
at this silent and dusky hour – waggon after waggon, bearing
green bastions of cabbages nodding to their fall, yet never falling, walls of baskets enclosing masses of beans and peas,
pyramids of snow-white turnips, swaying howdahs[5] of mixed
produce – creeping along behind aged nighthorses, who seemed

ever patiently wondering between their hollow coughs why they had always to work at that still hour when all other sentient creatures were privileged to rest. Wrapped in a cloak, it was soothing to watch and sympathize with them when depression and nervousness hindered sleep, and to see how the fresh green-stuff brightened to life as it came opposite the lamp, and how the sweating animals steamed and shone with their miles of travel.

They had an interest, almost a charm, for Sophy, these semirural people and vehicles moving in an urban atmosphere, leading a life quite distinct from that of the daytime toilers on the same road. One morning a man who accompanied a waggon-load of potatoes gazed rather hard at the house-fronts as he passed, and with a curious emotion she thought his form was familiar to her. She looked out for him again. His being an old-fashioned conveyance, with a yellow front, it was easily recognizable, and on the third night after she saw it a second time. The man alongside was, as she had fancied, Sam Hob-son, formerly gardener at Gaymead, who would at one time have married her.

She had occasionally thought of him, and wondered if life in a cottage with him would not have been a happier lot than the life she had accepted. She had not thought of him passionately, but her now dismal situation lent an interest to his resurrection – a tender interest which it is impossible to exaggerate. She went back to bed, and began thinking. When did these market-gardeners, who travelled up to town so regularly at one or two in the morning, come back? She dimly recollected seeing their empty waggons, hardly noticeable amid the ordinary day-traffic, passing down at some hour before noon.

It was only April, but that morning, after breakfast, she had the window opened, and sat looking out, the feeble sun shining full upon her. She affected to sew, but her eyes never left the street. Between ten and eleven the desired waggon, now un-laden, reappeared on its return journey. But Sam was not look-ing round him then, and drove on in a reverie.

'Sam!' cried she.

Turning with a start, his face lighted up. He called to him a little boy to hold the horse, alighted, and came and stood under the window.

'I can't come down easily, Sam, or I would!' she said. 'Did you know I lived here?'

'Well, Mrs Twycott, I knew you lived along here somewhere. I have often looked out for 'ee.'

He briefly explained his own presence on the scene. He had long since given up his gardening in the village near Aldbrickham, and was now manager at a market-gardener's on the south side of London, it being part of his duty to go up to Covent Garden with waggon-loads of produce two or three times a week. In answer to her curious inquiry, he admitted that he had come to this particular district because he had seen in the Aldbrickham paper, a year or two before, the announcement of the death in South London of the aforetime vicar of Gaymead, which had revived an interest in her dwelling-place that he could not extinguish, leading him to hover about the locality till his present post had been secured.

They spoke of their native village in dear old North Wessex, the spots in which they had played together as children. She tried to feel that she was a dignified personage now, that she must not be too confidential with Sam. But she could not keep it up, and the tears hanging in her eyes were indicated in her voice.

'You are not happy, Mrs Twycott, I'm afraid?' he said.

'O, of course not! I lost my husband only the year before last.'

'Ah! I meant in another way. You'd like to be home again?'

'This is my home – for life. The house belongs to me. But I understand' – She let it out then. 'Yes, Sam. I long for home – *our* home! I *should* like to be there, and never leave it, and die there.' But she remembered herself. 'That's only a momentary feeling. I have a son, you know, a dear boy. He's at school now.'

'Somewhere handy, I suppose? I see there's lots on 'em along this road.'

'O no! Not in one of these wretched holes! At a public school – one of the most distinguished in England.'

'Chok' it all! of course! I forget, ma'am, that you've been a lady for so many years.'

'No, I am not a lady,' she said sadly. 'I never shall be. But he's a gentleman, and that – makes it – O how difficult for me!'

III

The acquaintance thus oddly reopened proceeded apace. She often looked out to get a few words with him, by night or by day. Her sorrow was that she could not accompany her one old friend on foot a little way, and talk more freely than she could do while he paused before the house. One night, at the beginning of June, when she was again on the watch after an absence of some days from the window, he entered the gate and said softly, 'Now, wouldn't some air do you good? I've only half a load this morning. Why not ride up to Covent Garden with me? There's a nice seat on the cabbages, where I've spread a sack. You can be home again in a cab before anybody is up.'

She refused at first, and then, trembling with excitement, hastily finished her dressing, and wrapped herself up in cloak and veil, afterwards sidling downstairs by the aid of the hand-rail, in a way she could adopt on an emergency. When she had opened the door she found Sam on the step, and he lifted her bodily on his strong arm across the little forecourt into his vehicle. Not a soul was visible or audible in the infinite length of the straight, flat highway, with its ever-waiting lamps converging to points in each direction. The air was fresh as country air at this hour, and the stars shone, except to the north-eastward, where there was a whitish light – the dawn. Sam carefully placed her in the seat, and drove on.

They talked as they had talked in old days, Sam pulling himself up now and then, when he thought himself too familiar. More than once she said with misgiving that she wondered if she ought to have indulged in the freak. 'But I am so lonely in my house,' she added, 'and this makes me so happy!'

'You must come again, dear Mrs Twycott. There is no time o' day for taking the air like this.'

It grew lighter and lighter. The sparrows became busy in the

streets, and the city waxed denser around them. When they
approached the river it was day, and on the bridge they beheld
the full blaze of morning sunlight in the direction of St Paul's,
the river glistening towards it, and not a craft stirring.

Near Covent Garden he put her into a cab, and they parted,
looking into each other's faces like the very old friends they
were. She reached home without adventure, limped to the door,
and let herself in with her latch-key unseen.

The air and Sam's presence had revived her: her cheeks were
quite pink – almost beautiful. She had something to live for in
addition to her son. A woman of pure instincts, she knew there
had been nothing really wrong in the journey, but supposed it
conventionally to be very wrong indeed.

Soon, however, she gave way to the temptation of going
with him again, and on this occasion their conversation was
distinctly tender, and Sam said he never should forget her,
notwithstanding that she had served him rather badly at one
time. After much hesitation he told her of a plan it was in his
power to carry out, and one he should like to take in hand,
since he did not care for London work: it was to set up as a
master greengrocer down at Aldbrickham, the county-town of
their native place. He knew of an opening – a shop kept by
aged people who wished to retire.

'And why don't you do it, then, Sam?' she asked with a
slight heartsinking.

'Because I'm not sure if – you'd join me. I know you wouldn't
– couldn't! Such a lady as ye've been so long, you couldn't be
a wife to a man like me.'

'I hardly suppose I could!' she assented, also frightened at
the idea.

'If you could,' he said eagerly, 'you'd on'y have to sit in the
back parlour and look through the glass partition when I was
away sometimes – just to keep an eye on things. The lameness
wouldn't hinder that . . . I'd keep you as genteel as ever I could,
dear Sophy – if I might think of it!' he pleaded.

'Sam, I'll be frank,' she said, putting her hand on his. 'If it
were only myself I would do it, and gladly, though everything
I possess would be lost to me by marrying again.'

'I don't mind that! It's more independent.'

'That's good of you, dear, dear Sam. But there's something else. I have a son ... I almost fancy when I am miserable sometimes that he is not really mine, but one I hold in trust for my late husband. He seems to belong so little to me personally, so entirely to his dead father. He is so much educated and I so little that I do not feel dignified enough to be his mother ... Well, he would have to be told.'

'Yes. Unquestionably.' Sam saw her thought and her fear. 'Still, you can do as you like, Sophy – Mrs Twycott,' he added. 'It is not you who are the child, but he.'

'Ah, you don't know! Sam, if I could, I would marry you, some day. But you must wait a while, and let me think.'

It was enough for him, and he was blithe at their parting. Not so she. To tell Randolph seemed impossible. She could wait till he had gone up to Oxford, when what she did would affect his life but little. But would he ever tolerate the idea? And if not, could she defy him?

She had not told him a word when the yearly cricket-match came on at Lord's between the public schools, though Sam had already gone back to Aldbrickham. Mrs Twycott felt stronger than usual: she went to the match with Randolph, and was able to leave her chair and walk about occasionally. The bright idea occurred to her that she could casually broach the subject while moving round among the spectators, when the boy's spirits were high with interest in the game, and he would weigh domestic matters as feathers in the scale beside the day's victory. They promenaded under the lurid July sun, this pair, so wide apart, yet so near, and Sophy saw the large proportion of boys like her own, in their broad white collars and dwarf hats, and all around the rows of great coaches under which was jumbled the *débris* of luxurious luncheons; bones, pie-crusts, champagne-bottles, glasses, plates, napkins, and the family silver; while on the coaches sat the proud fathers and mothers; but never a poor mother like her. If Randolph had not appertained to these, had not centred all his interests in them, had not cared exclusively for the class they belonged to, how happy would things have been! A great huzza at some small performance with the bat burst from the multitude of relatives, and Randolph jumped wildly into the air to see what had happened. Sophy fetched up the sentence that had been already shaped; but she could not get it out. The occasion was, perhaps, an inopportune one. The contrast between her story and the display of fashion to which Randolph had grown to regard himself as akin would be fatal. She awaited a better time.

It was on an evening when they were alone in their plain suburban residence, where life was not blue but brown, that she ultimately broke silence, qualifying her announcement of a probable second marriage by assuring him that it would not take place for a long time to come, when he would be living quite independently of her.

The boy thought the idea a very reasonable one, and asked if she had chosen anybody? She hesitated; and he seemed to have a misgiving. He hoped his stepfather would be a gentleman? he said.

'Not what you call a gentleman,' she answered timidly. 'He'll be much as I was before I knew your father'; and by degrees she acquainted him with the whole. The youth's face remained fixed for a moment; then he flushed, leant on the table, and burst into passionate tears.

His mother went up to him, kissed all of his face that she could get at, and patted his back as if he were still the baby he once had been, crying herself the while. When he had somewhat recovered from his paroxysm he went hastily to his own room and fastened the door.

Parleyings were attempted through the keyhole, outside which she waited and listened. It was long before he would reply, and when he did it was to say sternly at her from within: 'I am ashamed of you! It will ruin me! A miserable boor! a churl! a clown! It will degrade me in the eyes of all the gentlemen of England!'

'Say no more — perhaps I am wrong! I will struggle against it!' she cried miserably.

Before Randolph left her that summer a letter arrived from Sam to inform her that he had been unexpectedly fortunate in obtaining the shop. He was in possession; it was the largest in the town, combining fruit with vegetables, and he thought it would form a home worthy even of her some day. Might he not run up to town to see her?

She met him by stealth, and said he must still wait for her final answer. The autumn dragged on, and when Randolph was home at Christmas for the holidays she broached the matter again. But the young gentleman was inexorable.

It was dropped for months; renewed again; abandoned under his repugnance; again attempted; and thus the gentle creature reasoned and pleaded till four or five long years had passed. Then the faithful Sam revived his suit with some peremptoriness. Sophy's son, now an undergraduate, was down from Oxford one Easter, when she again opened the subject. As soon as he was ordained, she argued, he would have a home of his own, wherein she, with her bad grammar and her ignorance, would be an encumbrance to him. Better obliterate her as much as possible.

He showed a more manly anger now, but would not agree. She on her side was more persistent, and he had doubts whether she could be trusted in his absence. But by indignation and contempt for her taste he completely maintained his ascendancy; and finally taking her before a little cross and altar that he had erected in his bedroom for his private devotions, there bade her kneel, and swear that she would not wed Samuel Hobson without his consent. 'I owe this to my father!' he said.

The poor woman swore, thinking he would soften as soon as he was ordained and in full swing of clerical work. But he did not. His education had by this time sufficiently ousted his humanity to keep him quite firm; though his mother might have led an idyllic life with her faithful fruiterer and greengrocer, and nobody have been anything the worse in the world.

Her lameness became more confirmed as time went on, and she seldom or never left the house in the long southern thoroughfare, where she seemed to be pining her heart away. 'Why mayn't I say to Sam that I'll marry him? Why mayn't I?' she would murmur plaintively to herself when nobody was near.

Some four years after this date a middle-aged man was standing at the door of the largest fruiterer's shop in Aldbrickham. He was the proprietor, but to-day, instead of his usual business attire, he wore a neat suit of black; and his window was partly shuttered. From the railway-station a funeral procession was seen approaching: it passed his door and went out of the town towards the village of Gaymead. The man, whose eyes were wet, held his hat in his hand as the vehicle moved by; while from the mourning coach a young smooth-shaven priest in a high waistcoat looked black as a cloud at the shop-keeper standing there.

'TALKING of Exhibitions, World's Fairs, and what not,' said the old gentleman, 'I would not go round the corner to see a dozen of them nowadays. The only exhibition that ever made, or ever will make, any impression upon my imagination was the first of the series, the parent of them all, and now a thing of old times – the Great Exhibition of 1851, in Hyde Park, London. None of the younger generation can realize the sense of novelty it produced in us who were then in our prime. A noun substantive went so far as to become an adjective in honour of the occasion. It was "exhibition" hat, "exhibition" razor-strop, "exhibition" watch; nay, even "exhibition" weather, "exhibition" spirits, sweethearts, babies, wives – for the time.

'For South Wessex, the year formed in many ways an extraordinary chronological frontier or transit-line, at which there occurred what one might call a precipice in Time. As in a geological "fault",[1] we had presented to us a sudden bringing of ancient and modern into absolute contact, such as probably in no other single year since the Conquest was ever witnessed in this part of the country.'

These observations led us onward to talk of the different personages, gentle and simple, who lived and moved within our narrow and peaceful horizon at that time; and of three people in particular, whose queer little history was oddly touched at points by the Exhibition, more concerned with it than that of anybody else who dwelt in those outlying shades of the world, Stickleford, Mellstock, and Egdon. First in prominence among these three came Wat Ollamoor – if that were his real name – whom the seniors in our party had known well.

He was a woman's man, they said, – supremely so – externally little else. To men he was not attractive; perhaps a little repulsive at times. Musician, dandy, and company-man in practice; veterinary surgeon in theory, he lodged awhile in Mellstock village, coming from nobody knew where; though some said his first appearance in this neighbourhood had been as fiddle-player in a show at Greenhill Fair.

Many a worthy villager envied him his power over un-sophisticated maidenhood – a power which seemed sometimes to have a touch of the weird and wizardly in it. Personally he was not ill-favoured, though rather un-English, his complexion being a rich olive, his rank hair dark and rather clammy – made still clammier by secret ointments, which, when he came fresh to a party, caused him to smell like 'boys'-love' (southern-wood)[2] steeped in lamp-oil. On occasion he wore curls – a double row – running almost horizontally around his head. But as these were sometimes noticeably absent, it was concluded that they were not altogether of Nature's making. By girls whose love for him had turned to hatred he had been nick-named 'Mop', from this abundance of hair, which was long enough to rest upon his shoulders; as time passed the name more and more prevailed.

His fiddling possibly had the most to do with the fascination he exercised, for, to speak fairly, it could claim for itself a most peculiar and personal quality, like that in a moving preacher. There were tones in it which bred the immediate conviction that indolence and averseness to systematic application were all that lay between 'Mop' and the career of a second Paganini.[3]

While playing he invariably closed his eyes; using no notes, and, as it were, allowing the violin to wander on at will into the most plaintive passages ever heard by rustic man. There was a certain lingual character[4] in the supplicatory expressions he produced, which would well-nigh have drawn an ache from the heart of a gate-post. He could make any child in the parish, who was at all sensitive to music, burst into tears in a few minutes by simply fiddling one of the old dance-tunes he almost entirely affected – country jigs, reels, and 'Favourite Quick Steps' of the last century – some mutilated remains of which even now reappear as nameless phantoms in new quadrilles and gallops, where they are recognized only by the curious, or by such old-fashioned and far-between people as have been thrown with men like Wat Ollamoor in their early life.

His date was a little later than that of the old Mellstock quire-band[5] which comprised the Dewys, Mail, and the rest — in fact, he did not rise above the horizon thereabout till those well-known musicians were disbanded as ecclesiastical functionaries. In their honest love of thoroughness they despised the new man's style. Theophilus Dewy (Reuben the tranter's[6] younger brother) used to say there was no 'plumness' in it – no bowing, no solidity – it was all fantastical. And probably this was true. Anyhow, Mop had, very obviously, never bowed a note of church-music from his birth; he never once sat in the gallery of Mellstock church where the others had tuned their venerable psalmody so many hundreds of times; had never, in all likelihood, entered a church at all. All were devil's tunes in his repertory. 'He could no more play the Wold Hundredth[7] to his true time than he could play the brazen serpent,'[8] the tranter would say. (The brazen serpent was supposed in Mellstock to be a musical instrument particularly hard to blow.)

Occasionally Mop could produce the aforesaid moving effect upon the souls of grown-up persons, especially young women of fragile and responsive organization. Such an one was Car'line Aspent. Though she was already engaged to be married before she met him, Car'line, of them all, was the most influenced by Mop Ollamoor's heart-stealing melodies, to her discomfort, nay, positive pain and ultimate injury. She was a pretty, invocating, weak-mouthed girl, whose chief defect as a companion with her sex was a tendency to peevishness now and then. At this time she was not a resident in Mellstock parish where Mop lodged, but lived some miles off at Stickleford, further down the river.

How and where she first made acquaintance with him and his fiddling is not truly known, but the story was that it either began or was developed on one spring evening, when, in passing through Lower Mellstock, she chanced to pause on the bridge near his house to rest herself, and languidly leaned over the parapet. Mop was standing on his door-step, as was his custom, spinning the insidious thread of semi- and demi-semiquavers from the E string of his fiddle for the benefit of passers-by, and laughing as the tears rolled down the cheeks of the little children hanging around him. Car'line pretended to be engrossed with the rippling of the stream under the arches, but in reality she was listening, as he knew. Presently the aching of the heart seized her simultaneously with a wild desire to glide airily in the mazes of an infinite dance. To shake off the fascination she resolved to go on, although it would be necessary to pass him as he played. On stealthily glancing ahead at the performer, she found to her relief that his eyes were closed in abandonment to instrumentation, and she strode on boldly. But when closer her step grew timid, her tread convulsed itself more and more accordantly with the time of the melody, till she very nearly danced along. Gaining another glance at him when immediately opposite, she saw that *one* of his eyes was open, quizzing her as he smiled at her emotional state. Her gait could not divest itself of its compelled capers till she had gone a long way past the house; and Car'line was unable to shake off the strange infatuation for hours.

After that day, whenever there was to be in the neighbour-hood a dance to which she could get an invitation, and where Mop Ollamoor was to be the musician, Car'line contrived to be present, though it sometimes involved a walk of several miles; for he did not play so often in Stickleford as elsewhere.

The next evidences of his influence over her were singular enough, and it would require a neurologist to fully explain them. She would be sitting quietly, any evening after dark, in the house of her father, the parish clerk, which stood in the middle of Stickleford village street, this being the highroad between Lower Mellstock and Moreford, five miles eastward. Here, without a moment's warning, and in the midst of a general conversation between her father, sister, and the young man before alluded to, who devotedly wooed her in ignorance of her infatuation, she would start from her seat in the chimney-corner as if she had received a galvanic[9] shock, and spring convulsively towards the ceiling; then she would burst into tears, and it was not till some half-hour had passed that she grew calm as usual. Her father, knowing her hysterical tendencies, was always excessively anxious about this trait in his youngest girl, and feared the attack to be a species of epileptic fit. Not so her sister Julia. Julia had found out what was the cause. At the moment before the jumping, only an exceptionally sensitive ear situated in the chimney-nook could have caught from down the flue the beat of a man's footstep along the highway without. But it was in that footfall, for which she had been waiting, that the origin of Car'line's involuntary springing lay. The pedestrian was Mop Ollamoor, as the girl well knew; but his business that way was not to visit her; he sought another woman whom he spoke of as his Intended, and who lived at Moreford, two miles further on. On one, and only one, occasion did it happen that Car'line could not control her utterance; it was when her sister alone chanced to be present. 'O – O – O –!' she cried. 'He's going to *her*, and not coming to *me!*'

To do the fiddler justice he had not at first thought greatly of, or spoken much to, this girl of impressionable mould. But he had soon found out her secret, and could not resist a little by-play with her too easily hurt heart, as an interlude between his more serious lovemakings at Moreford. The two became well acquainted, though only by stealth, hardly a soul in Stickleford except her sister, and her lover Ned Hipcroft, being aware of the attachment. Her father disapproved of her coldness to Ned; her sister, too, hoped she might get over this nervous passion for a man of whom so little was known. The ultimate result was that Car'line's manly and simple wooer Edward found his suit becoming practically hopeless. He was a respectable mechanic, in a far sounder position than Mop the nominal horse-doctor; but when, before leaving her, Ned put his flat and final question, would she marry him, then and there, now or never, it was with little expectation of obtaining more than the negative she gave him. Though her father supported him and her sister supported him, he could not play the fiddle so as to draw your soul out of your body like a spider's thread, as Mop did, till you felt as limp as withywind[10] and yearned for something to cling to. Indeed, Hipcroft had not the slightest ear for music; could not sing two notes in tune, much less play them.

The No he had expected and got from her, in spite of a preliminary encouragement, gave Ned a new start in life. It had been uttered in such a tone of sad entreaty that he resolved to persecute her no more; she should not even be distressed by a sight of his form in the distant perspective of the street and lane. He left the place, and his natural course was to London.

The railway to South Wessex was in process of construction, but it was not as yet opened for traffic; and Hipcroft reached the capital by a six days' trudge on foot, as many a better man had done before him. He was one of the last of the artisan class who used that now extinct method of travel to the great centres of labour, so customary then from time immemorial.

In London he lived and worked regularly at his trade. More fortunate than many, his disinterested willingness recommended him from the first. During the ensuing four years he was never out of employment. He neither advanced nor receded in the modern sense; he improved as a workman, but he did not shift one jot in social position. About his love for Car'line he maintained a rigid silence. No doubt he often thought of her; but being always occupied, and having no relations at Stickleford, he held no communication with that part of the country, and showed no desire to return. In his quiet lodging in Lambeth he moved about after working-hours with the facility of a woman, doing his own cooking, attending to his stocking-heels, and shaping himself by degrees to a life-long bachelorhood. For this conduct one is bound to advance the canonical reason that time could not efface from his heart the image of little Car'line Aspent – and it may be in part true; but there was also the inference that his was a nature not greatly dependent upon the ministrations of the other sex for its comforts.

The fourth year of his residence as a mechanic in London was the year of the Hyde-Park Exhibition already mentioned, and at the construction of this huge glass-house, then unexampled in the world's history, he worked daily. It was an era of great hope and activity among the nations and industries. Though Hipcroft was, in his small way, a central man in the movement, he plodded on with his usual outward placidity. Yet for him, too, the year was destined to have its surprises, for when the bustle of getting the building ready for the opening day was past, the ceremonies had been witnessed, and people were flocking thither from all parts of the globe, he received a letter from Car'line. Till that day the silence of four years between himself and Stickleford had never been broken.

She informed her old lover, in an uncertain penmanship which suggested a trembling hand, of the trouble she had been put to in ascertaining his address, and then broached the subject which had prompted her to write. Four years ago, she said with the greatest delicacy of which she was capable, she had been so foolish as to refuse him. Her wilful wrong-headedness had since been a grief to her many times, and of late particularly. As for Mr Ollamoor, he had been absent almost as long as Ned – she did not know where. She would gladly marry Ned now if he were to ask her again, and be a tender little wife to him till her life's end.

A tide of warm feeling must have surged through Ned Hipcroft's frame on receipt of this news, if we may judge by the issue. Unquestionably he loved her still, even if not to the exclusion of every other happiness. This from his Car'line, she who had been dead to him these many years, alive to him again as of old, was in itself a pleasant, gratifying thing. Ned had grown so resigned to, or satisfied with, his lonely lot, that he probably would not have shown much jubilation at anything. Still, a certain ardour of preoccupation, after his first surprise, revealed how deeply her confession of faith in him had stirred him. Measured and methodical in his ways, he did not answer the letter that day, nor the next, nor the next. He was having 'a good think'. When he did answer it, there was a great deal of sound reasoning mixed in with the unmistakable tenderness of his reply; but the tenderness itself was sufficient to reveal that he was pleased with her straightforward frankness; that the anchorage she had once obtained in his heart was renewable, if it had not been continuously firm.

He told her – and as he wrote his lips twitched humorously over the few gentle words of raillery he indited among the rest of his sentences – that it was all very well for her to come round at this time of day. Why wouldn't she have him when he wanted her? She had no doubt learned that he was not married, but suppose his affections had since been fixed on another? She ought to beg his pardon. Still, he was not the man to forget her. But considering how he had been used, and what he had suffered, she could not quite expect him to go down to Stickleford and fetch her. But if she would come to him, and say she was sorry, as was only fair; why, yes, he would marry her, knowing what a good little woman she was at the core. He added that the request for her to come to him was a less one to make than it would have been when he first left Stickleford, or even a few months ago; for the new railway into South Wessex was now open, and there had just begun to be run wonderfully contrived special trains, called excursion-trains, on account of the Great Exhibition; so that she could come up easily alone.

She said in her reply how good it was of him to treat her so generously, after her hot and cold treatment of him; that though she felt frightened at the magnitude of the journey, and was never as yet in a railway-train, having only seen one pass at a distance, she embraced his offer with all her heart; and would, indeed, own to him how sorry she was, and beg his pardon, and try to be a good wife always, and make up for lost time.

The remaining details of when and where were soon settled, Car'line informing him, for her ready identification in the crowd, that she would be wearing 'my new sprigged-laylock[11] cotton gown', and Ned gaily responding that, having married her the morning after her arrival, he would make a day of it by taking her to the Exhibition. One early summer afternoon, accordingly, he came from his place of work, and hastened towards Waterloo Station to meet her. It was as wet and chilly as an English June day can occasionally be, but as he waited on the platform in the drizzle he glowed inwardly, and seemed to have something to live for again.

The 'excursion-train' – an absolutely new departure in the history of travel – was still a novelty on the Wessex line, and probably everywhere. Crowds of people had flocked to all the stations on the way up to witness the unwonted sight of so long a train's passage, even where they did not take advantage of the opportunity it offered. The seats for the humbler class of travellers in these early experiments in steam-locomotion, were open trucks, without any protection whatever from the wind and rain; and damp weather having set in with the afternoon, the unfortunate occupants of these vehicles were, on the train drawing up at the London terminus, found to be in a pitiable condition from their long journey; blue-faced, stiff-necked, sneezing, rain-beaten, chilled to the marrow, many of the men being hatless; in fact, they resembled people who had been out all night in an open boat on a rough sea, rather than inland excursionists for pleasure. The women had in some degree protected themselves by turning up the skirts of their gowns over their heads, but as by this arrangement they were additionally exposed about the hips, they were all more or less in a sorry plight.

In the bustle and crush of alighting forms of both sexes which followed the entry of the huge concatenation into the station, Ned Hipcroft soon discerned the slim little figure his eye was in search of, in the sprigged lilac, as described. She came up to him with a frightened smile – still pretty, though so damp, weather-beaten, and shivering from long exposure to the wind.

'O Ned!' she sputtered, 'I – I –' He clasped her in his arms and kissed her, whereupon she burst into a flood of tears.

'You are wet, my poor dear! I hope you'll not get cold,' he said. And surveying her and her multifarious surrounding packages, he noticed that by the hand she led a toddling child – a little girl of three or so – whose hood was as clammy and tender face as blue as those of the other travellers.

'Who is this – somebody you know?' asked Ned curiously.

'Yes, Ned. She's mine.'

'Yours?'

'Yes – my own.'

'Your own child?'

'Yes!'

'But who's the father?'

'The young man I had after you courted me.'

'Well – as God's in –'

'Ned, I didn't name it in my letter, because, you see, it would have been so hard to explain! I thought that when we met I could tell you how she happened to be born, so much better than in writing! I hope you'll excuse it this once, dear Ned, and not scold me, now I've come so many, many miles!'

'This means Mr Mop Ollamoor, I reckon!' said Hipcroft, gazing palely at them from the distance of the yard or two to which he had withdrawn with a start.

Car'line gasped. 'But he's been gone away for years!' she supplicated. 'And I never had a young man before! And I was so onlucky to be catched the first time he took advantage o' me, though some of the girls down there go on like anything!'

Ned remained in silence, pondering.

'You'll forgive me, dear Ned?' she added, beginning to sob outright. 'I haven't taken 'ee in after all, because – because you can pack us back again, if you want to; though 'tis hundreds o' miles, and so wet, and night a-coming on, and I with no money!'

'What the devil can I do!' Hipcroft groaned.

A more pitiable picture than the pair of helpless creatures presented was never seen on a rainy day, as they stood on the great, gaunt, puddled platform, a whiff of drizzle blowing under the roof upon them now and then; the pretty attire in which they had started from Stickleford in the early morning bemuddled and sodden, weariness on their faces, and fear of him in their eyes; for the child began to look as if she thought she too had done some wrong, remaining in an appalled silence till the tears rolled down her chubby cheeks.

'What's the matter, my little maid?' said Ned mechanically.

'I do want to go home!' she let out, in tones that told of a bursting heart. 'And my totties[12] be cold, an' I shan't have no bread an' butter no more!'

'I don't know what to say to it all!' declared Ned, his own

eye moist as he turned and walked a few steps with his head down; then regarded them again point-blank. From the child escaped troubled breaths and silently welling tears.

'Want some bread and butter, do 'ee?' he said, with factitious hardness.

'Ye – e – s!'

'Well, I dare say I can get 'ee a bit! Naturally, you must want some. And you, too, for that matter, Car'line.'

'I do feel a little hungered. But I can keep it off,' she murmured.

'Folk shouldn't do that,' he said gruffly ... 'There, come along!' He caught up the child, as he added, 'You must bide here to-night, anyhow, I s'pose! What can you do otherwise? I'll get 'ee some tea and victuals; and as for this job, I'm sure I don't know what to say! This is the way out.'

They pursued their way, without speaking, to Ned's lodgings, which were not far off. There he dried them and made them comfortable, and prepared tea; they thankfully sat down. The ready-made household of which he suddenly found himself the head imparted a cosy aspect to his room, and a paternal one to himself. Presently he turned to the child and kissed her now blooming cheeks; and, looking wistfully at Car'line, kissed her also.

'I don't see how I can send you back all them miles,' he growled, 'now you've come all the way o' purpose to join me. But you must trust me, Car'line, and show you've real faith in me. Well, do you feel better now, my little woman?'

The child nodded beamingly, her mouth being otherwise occupied.

'I did trust you, Ned, in coming; and I shall always!'

Thus, without any definite agreement to forgive her, he tacitly acquiesced in the fate that Heaven had sent him; and on the day of their marriage (which was not quite so soon as he had expected it could be, on account of the time necessary for banns) he took her to the Exhibition when they came back from church, as he had promised. While standing near a large mirror in one of the courts devoted to furniture, Car'line started, for in the glass appeared the reflection of a form exactly resembling Mop Ollamoor's – so exactly, that it seemed impossible to believe anybody but that artist in person to be the original. On passing round the objects which hemmed in Ned, her, and the child from a direct view, no Mop was to be seen. Whether he were really in London or not at that time was never known; and Car'line always stoutly denied that her readiness to go and meet Ned in town arose from any rumour that Mop had also gone thither; which denial there was no reasonable ground for doubting.

And then the year glided away, and the Exhibition folded itself up and became a thing of the past. The park trees that had been enclosed for six months were again exposed to the winds and storms, and the sod grew green anew. Ned found that Car'line resolved herself into a very good wife and companion, though she had made herself what is called cheap to him; but in that she was like another domestic article, a cheap tea-pot, which often brews better tea than a dear one. One autumn Hipcroft found himself with but little work to do, and a prospect of less for the winter. Both being country born and bred, they fancied they would like to live again in their natural atmosphere. It was accordingly decided between them that they should leave the pent-up London lodging, and that Ned should seek out employment near his native place, his wife and her daughter staying with Car'line's father during the search for occupation and an abode of their own.

Tinglings of pride pervaded Car'line's spasmodic little frame as she journeyed down with Ned to the place she had left two or three years before, in silence and under a cloud. To return to where she had once been despised, a smiling London wife with a distinct London accent, was a triumph which the world did not witness every day.

The train did not stop at the petty roadside station that lay nearest to Stickleford, and the trio went on to Casterbridge. Ned thought it a good opportunity to make a few preliminary inquiries for employment at workshops in the borough where he had been known; and feeling cold from her journey, and it being dry underfoot and only dusk as yet, with a moon on the point of rising, Car'line and her little girl walked on towards

Stickleford, leaving Ned to follow at a quicker pace, and pick her up at a certain half-way house, widely known as an inn.

The woman and child pursued the well-remembered way comfortably enough, though they were both becoming wearied. In the course of three miles they had passed Heedless-William's Pond, the familiar landmark by Bloom's End, and were drawing near the Quiet Woman, a lone roadside hostel on the lower verge of the Egdon Heath, since and for many years abolished. In stepping up towards it Car'line heard more voices within than had formerly been customary at such an hour, and she learned that an auction of fat stock had been held near the spot that afternoon. The child would be the better for a rest as well as herself, she thought, and she entered.

The guests and customers overflowed into the passage, and Car'line had no sooner crossed the threshold than a man whom she remembered by sight came forward with a glass and mug in his hands towards a friend leaning against the wall; but, seeing her, very gallantly offered her a drink of the liquor, which was gin-and-beer hot, pouring her out a tumblerful and saying, in a moment or two: 'Surely, 'tis little Car'line Aspent that was – down at Stickleford?'

She assented, and, though she did not exactly want this beverage, she drank it since it was offered, and her entertainer begged her to come in further and sit down. Once within the room she found that all the persons present were seated close against the walls, and there being a chair vacant she did the same. An explanation of their position occurred the next moment. In the opposite corner stood Mop, rosining his bow and looking just the same as ever. The company had cleared the middle of the room for dancing, and they were about to dance again. As she wore a veil to keep off the wind she did not think he had recognized her, or could possibly guess the identity of the child; and to her satisfied surprise she found that she could confront him quite calmly – mistress of herself in the dignity her London life had given her. Before she had quite emptied her glass the dance was called, the dancers formed in two lines, the music sounded, and the figure began.

Then matters changed for Car'line. A tremor quickened

itself to life in her, and her hand so shook that she could hardly set down her glass. It was not the dance nor the dancers, but the notes of that old violin which thrilled the London wife, these having still all the witchery that she had so well known of yore, and under which she had used to lose her power of independent will. How it all came back! There was the fiddling figure against the wall; the large, oily, mop-like head of him, and beneath the mop the face with closed eyes.

After the first moments of paralyzed reverie the familiar tune in the familiar rendering made her laugh and shed tears simultaneously. Then a man at the bottom of the dance, whose partner had dropped away, stretched out his hand and beckoned to her to take the place. She did not want to dance; she entreated by signs to be left where she was, but she was entreating of the tune and its player rather than of the dancing man. The saltatory[13] tendency which the fiddler and his cunning instrument had ever been able to start in her was seizing Car'line just as it had done in earlier years, possibly assisted by the gin-and-beer hot. Tired as she was she grasped her little girl by the hand, and plunging in at the bottom of the figure, whirled about with the rest. She found that her companions were mostly people of the neighbouring hamlets and farms – Bloom's End, Mellstock, Lewgate, and elsewhere; and by degrees she was recognized as she convulsively danced on, wishing that Mop would cease and let her heart rest from the aching he caused, and her feet also.

After long and many minutes the dance ended, when she was urged to fortify herself with more gin-and-beer; which she did, feeling very weak and overpowered with hysteric emotion. She refrained from unveiling, to keep Mop in ignorance of her presence, if possible. Several of the guests having left, Car'line hastily wiped her lips and also turned to go; but, according to the account of some who remained, at that very moment a five-handed reel was proposed, in which two or three begged her to join.

She declined on the plea of being tired and having to walk to Stickleford, when Mop began aggressively tweedling 'My Fancy-Lad', in D major, as the air to which the reel was to be footed. He must have recognized her, though she did not know it, for it was the strain of all seductive strains which she was least able to resist – the one he had played when she was lean-ing over the bridge at the date of their first acquaintance. Car'line stepped despairingly into the middle of the room with the other four.

Reels were resorted to hereabouts at this time by the more robust spirits, for the reduction of superfluous energy which the ordinary figure-dances were not powerful enough to exhaust. As everybody knows, or does not know, the five reelers stood in the form of a cross, the reel being performed by each line of three alternately, the persons who successively came to the middle place dancing in both directions. Car'line soon found herself in this place, the axis of the whole performance, and could not get out of it, the tune turning into the first part without giving her opportunity. And now she began to suspect that Mop did know her, and was doing this on purpose, though whenever she stole a glance at him his closed eyes betokened obliviousness to everything outside his own brain. She con-tinued to wend her way through the figure of 8 that was formed by her course, the fiddler introducing into his notes the wild and agonizing sweetness of a living voice in one too highly wrought; its pathos running high and running low in endless variation, projecting through her nerves excruciating spasms, a sort of blissful torture. The room swam, the tune was endless; and in about a quarter of an hour the only other woman in the figure dropped out exhausted, and sank panting on a bench.

The reel instantly resolved itself into a four-handed one. Car'line would have given anything to leave off; but she had, or fancied she had, no power, while Mop played such tunes; and thus another ten minutes slipped by, a haze of dust now cloud-ing the candles, the floor being of stone, sanded. Then another dancer fell out – one of the men – and went into the passage in a frantic search for liquor. To turn the figure into a three-handed reel was the work of a second, Mop modulating at the same time into 'The Fairy Dance', as better suited to the con-tracted movement, and no less one of those foods of love which, as manufactured by his bow, had always intoxicated her.

In a reel for three there was no rest whatever, and four or five minutes were enough to make her remaining two partners, now thoroughly blown, stamp their last bar, and, like their predecessors, limp off into the next room to get something to drink. Car'line, half stifled inside her veil, was left dancing alone, the apartment now being empty of everybody save herself, Mop, and their little girl.

She flung up the veil, and cast her eyes upon him, as if imploring him to withdraw himself and his acoustic magnetism from the atmosphere. Mop opened one of his own orbs, as though for the first time, fixed it peeringly upon her, and smiling dreamily, threw into his strains the reserve of expression which he could not afford to waste on a big and noisy dance. Crowds of little chromatic subtleties, capable of drawing tears from a statue, proceeded straightway from the ancient fiddle, as if it were dying of the emotion which had been pent up within it ever since its banishment from some Italian or German city where it first took shape and sound. There was that in the look of Mop's one dark eye which said: 'You cannot leave off, dear, whether you would or no!' and it bred in her a paroxysm of desperation that defied him to tire her down.

She thus continued to dance alone, defiantly as she thought, but in truth slavishly and abjectly, subject to every wave of the melody, and probed by the gimlet-like gaze of her fascinator's open eye; keeping up at the same time a feeble smile in his face, as a feint to signify it was still her own pleasure which led her on. A terrified embarrassment as to what she could say to him if she were to leave off, had its unrecognized share in keeping her going. The child, who was beginning to be distressed by the strange situation, came up and whimpered: 'Stop, mother, stop, and let's go home!' as she seized Car'line's hand.

Suddenly Car'line sank staggering to the floor; and rolling over on her face, prone she remained. Mop's fiddle thereupon emitted an elfin shriek of finality; stepping quickly down from the nine-gallon beer-cask which had formed his rostrum, he went to the little girl, who disconsolately bent over her mother.

The guests who had gone into the back-room for liquor and

change of air, hearing something unusual, trooped back hither-ward, where they endeavoured to revive poor, weak Car'line by blowing her with the bellows and opening the window. Ned, her husband, who had been detained in Casterbridge, as afore-said, came along the road at this juncture, and hearing excited voices through the open casement, and to his great surprise, the mention of his wife's name, he entered amid the rest upon the scene. Car'line was now in convulsions, weeping violently, and for a long time nothing could be done with her. While he was sending for a cart to take her onward to Stickleford Hip-croft anxiously inquired how it had all happened; and then the assembly explained that a fiddler formerly known in the locality had lately visited his old haunts, and had taken upon himself without invitation to play that evening at the inn and raise a dance.

Ned demanded the fiddler's name, and they said Ollamoor.

'Ah!' exclaimed Ned, looking round him. 'Where is he, and where – where's my little girl?'

Ollamoor had disappeared, and so had the child. Hipcroft was in ordinary a quiet and tractable fellow, but a determina-tion which was to be feared settled in his face now. 'Blast him!' he cried. 'I'll beat his skull in for'n, if I swing for it to-morrow!'

He had rushed to the poker which lay on the hearth, and hastened down the passage, the people following. Outside the house, on the other side of the highway, a mass of dark heath-land rose sullenly upward to its not easily accessible interior, a ravined plateau, whereon jutted into the sky, at the distance of a couple of miles, the fir-woods of Mistover backed by the Yalbury coppices – a place of Dantesque[14] gloom at this hour, which would have afforded secure hiding for a battery of artillery, much less a man and a child.

Some other men plunged thitherward with him, and more went along the road. They were gone about twenty minutes altogether, returning without result to the inn. Ned sat down in the settle, and clasped his forehead with his hands.

'Well – what a fool the man is, and hev been all these years, if he thinks the child his, as a' do seem to!' they whispered. 'And everybody else knowing otherwise!'

'No, I don't think 'tis mine!' cried Ned hoarsely, as he looked up from his hands. 'But she *is* mine, all the same! Ha'n't I nussed her? Ha'n't I fed her and teached her? Ha'n't I played wi' her? O, little Carry – gone with that rogue – gone!'

'You ha'n't lost your mis'ess, anyhow,' they said to console him. 'She's throwed up the sperrits,[15] and she is feeling better, and she's more to 'ee than a child that isn't yours.'

'She isn't! She's not so particular much to me, especially now she's lost the little maid! But Carry's the whole world to me!'

'Well, ver' like you'll find her to-morrow.'

'Ah – but shall I? Yet he *can't* hurt her – surely he can't! Well – how's Car'line now? I am ready. Is the cart here?'

She was lifted into the vehicle, and they sadly lumbered on towards Stickleford. Next day she was calmer; but the fits were still upon her; and her will seemed shattered. For the child she appeared to show singularly little anxiety, though Ned was nearly distracted by his passionate paternal love for a child not his own. It was nevertheless quite expected that the impish Mop would restore the lost one after a freak of a day or two; but time went on, and neither he nor she could be heard of, and Hipcroft murmured that perhaps he was exercising upon her some unholy musical charm, as he had done upon Car'line herself. Weeks passed, and still they could obtain no clue either to the fiddler's whereabouts or to the girl's; and how he could have induced her to go with him remained a mystery.

Then Ned, who had obtained only temporary employment in the neighbourhood, took a sudden hatred towards his native district, and a rumour reaching his ears through the police that a somewhat similar man and child had been seen at a fair near London, he playing a violin, she dancing on stilts, a new interest in the capital took possession of Hipcroft with an intensity which would scarcely allow him time to pack before returning thither. He did not, however, find the lost one, though he made it the entire business of his over-hours to stand about in by-streets in the hope of discovering her, and would start up in the night, saying, 'That rascal's torturing her to maintain him!' To which his wife would answer peevishly,

'Don't 'ee raft [16] yourself so, Ned! You prevent my getting a bit o' rest! He won't hurt her!' and fall asleep again.

That Carry and her father had emigrated to America was the general opinion; Mop, no doubt, finding the girl a highly desirable companion when he had trained her to keep him by her earnings as a dancer. There, for that matter, they may be performing in some capacity now, though he must be an old scamp verging on three-score-and-ten, and she a woman of four-and-forty.

WHEN William Marchmill had finished his inquiries for lodgings at the well-known watering-place of Solentsea in Upper
Wessex, he returned to the hotel to find his wife. She, with
the children, had rambled along the shore, and Marchmill followed in the direction indicated by the military-looking hall-
porter.

'By Jove, how far you've gone! I am quite out of breath,'
Marchmill said, rather impatiently, when he came up with his
wife, who was reading as she walked, the three children being
considerably further ahead with the nurse.

Mrs Marchmill started out of the reverie into which the book
had thrown her. 'Yes,' she said, 'you've been such a long time.
I was tired of staying in that dreary hotel. But I am sorry if you
have wanted me, Will?'

'Well, I have had trouble to suit myself. When you see the
airy and comfortable rooms heard of, you find they are stuffy
and uncomfortable. Will you come and see if what I've fixed on
will do? There is not much room, I am afraid; but I can light on
nothing better. The town is rather full.'

The pair left the children and nurse to continue their ramble,
and went back together.

In age well-balanced, in personal appearance fairly matched,
and in domestic requirements conformable, in temper this
couple differed, though even here they did not often clash, he
being equable, if not lymphatic,[1] and she decidedly nervous
and sanguine.[2] It was to their tastes and fancies, those smallest,
greatest particulars, that no common denominator could be
applied. Marchmill considered his wife's likes and inclinations
somewhat silly; she considered his sordid and material. The
husband's business was that of a gunmaker in a thriving city
northwards, and his soul was in that business always; the lady
was best characterized by that superannuated phrase of ele-

gance 'a votary of the muse'.[3] An impressionable, palpitating
creature was Ella, shrinking humanely from detailed knowledge
of her husband's trade whenever she reflected that everything
he manufactured had for its purpose the destruction of life.
She could only recover her equanimity by assuring herself that
some, at least, of his weapons were sooner or later used for
the extermination of horrid vermin and animals almost as
cruel to their inferiors in species as human beings were to
theirs.

She had never antecedently regarded this occupation of his
as any objection to having him for a husband. Indeed, the
necessity of getting life-leased at all cost, a cardinal virtue
which all good mothers teach, kept her from thinking of it at
all till she had closed with William, had passed the honeymoon,
and reached the reflecting stage. Then, like a person who has
stumbled upon some object in the dark, she wondered what
she had got; mentally walked round it, estimated it; whether
it were rare or common; contained gold, silver, or lead; were a
clog or a pedestal, everything to her or nothing.

She came to some vague conclusions, and since then had
kept her heart alive by pitying her proprietor's obtuseness and
want of refinement, pitying herself, and letting off her delicate
and ethereal emotions in imaginative occupations, day-dreams,
and night-sighs, which perhaps would not much have disturbed
William if he had known of them.

Her figure was small, elegant, and slight in build, tripping,
or rather bounding, in movement. She was dark-eyed, and had
that marvellously bright and liquid sparkle in each pupil which
characterizes persons of Ella's cast of soul, and is too often a
cause of heartache to the possessor's male friends, ultimately
sometimes to herself. Her husband was a tall, long-featured
man, with a brown beard; he had a pondering regard; and was,
it must be added, usually kind and tolerant to her. He spoke
in squarely shaped sentences, and was supremely satisfied with
a condition of sublunary[4] things which made weapons a
necessity.

Husband and wife walked till they had reached the house
they were in search of, which stood in a terrace facing the sea,

and was fronted by a small garden of wind-proof and salt-proof evergreens, stone steps leading up to the porch. It had its number in the row, but, being rather larger than the rest, was in addition sedulously distinguished as Coburg House by its landlady, though everybody else called it 'Thirteen, New Parade'. The spot was bright and lively now; but in winter it became necessary to place sandbags against the door, and to stuff up the keyhole against the wind and rain, which had worn the paint so thin that the priming and knotting showed through.

The householder, who had been watching for the gentleman's return, met them in the passage, and showed the rooms. She informed them that she was a professional man's widow, left in needy circumstances by the rather sudden death of her husband, and she spoke anxiously of the conveniences of the establishment.

Mrs Marchmill said that she liked the situation and the house; but, it being small, there would not be accommodation enough, unless she could have all the rooms.

The landlady mused with an air of disappointment. She wanted the visitors to be her tenants very badly, she said, with obvious honesty. But unfortunately two of the rooms were occupied permanently by a bachelor gentleman. He did not pay season prices, it was true; but as he kept on his apartments all the year round, and was an extremely nice and interesting young man, who gave no trouble, she did not like to turn him out for a month's 'let', even at a high figure. 'Perhaps, however,' she added, 'he might offer to go for a time.'

They would not hear of this, and went back to the hotel, intending to proceed to the agent's to inquire further. Hardly had they sat down to tea when the landlady called. Her gentleman, she said, had been so obliging as to offer to give up his rooms for three or four weeks rather than drive the new-comers away.

'It is very kind, but we won't inconvenience him in that way,' said the Marchmills.

'O, it won't inconvenience him, I assure you!' said the landlady eloquently. 'You see, he's a different sort of young man from most – dreamy, solitary, rather melancholy – and he cares more to be here when the south-westerly gales are beating against the door, and the sea washes over the Parade, and there's not a soul in the place, than he does now in the season. He'd just as soon be where, in fact, he's going temporarily, to a little cottage on the Island opposite, for a change.' She hoped therefore that they would come.

The Marchmill family accordingly took possession of the house next day, and it seemed to suit them very well. After luncheon Mr Marchmill strolled out towards the pier, and Mrs Marchmill, having despatched the children to their outdoor amusements on the sands, settled herself in more completely, examining this and that article, and testing the reflecting powers of the mirror in the wardrobe door.

In the small back sitting-room, which had been the young bachelor's, she found furniture of a more personal nature than in the rest. Shabby books, of correct rather than rare editions, were piled up in a queerly reserved manner in corners, as if the previous occupant had not conceived the possibility that any incoming person of the season's bringing could care to look inside them. The landlady hovered on the threshold to rectify anything that Mrs Marchmill might not find to her satisfaction.

'I'll make this my own little room,' said the latter, 'because the books are here. By the way, the person who has left seems to have a good many. He won't mind my reading some of them, Mrs Hooper, I hope?'

'O dear no, ma'am. Yes, he has a good many. You see, he is in the literary line himself somewhat. He is a poet – yes, really a poet – and he has a little income of his own, which is enough to write verses on, but not enough for cutting a figure, even if he cared to.'

'A poet! O, I did not know that.'

Mrs Marchmill opened one of the books, and saw the owner's name written on the title-page. 'Dear me!' she continued; 'I know his name very well – Robert Trewe – of course I do; and his writings! And it is *his* rooms we have taken, and *him* we have turned out of his home?'

Ella Marchmill, sitting down alone a few minutes later, thought with interested surprise of Robert Trewe. Her own latter history will best explain that interest. Herself the only daughter of a struggling man of letters, she had during the last year or two taken to writing poems, in an endeavour to find a congenial channel in which to let flow her painfully embayed[5] emotions, whose former limpidity and sparkle seemed departing in the stagnation caused by the routine of a practical household and the gloom of bearing children to a commonplace father. These poems, subscribed with a masculine pseudonym, had appeared in various obscure magazines, and in two cases in rather prominent ones. In the second of the latter the page which bore her effusion at the bottom, in smallish print, bore at the top, in large print, a few verses on the same subject by this very man, Robert Trewe. Both of them had, in fact, been struck by a tragic incident reported in the daily papers, and had used it simultaneously as an inspiration, the editor remarking in a note upon the coincidence, and that the excellence of both poems .prompted him to give them together.

After that event Ella, otherwise 'John Ivy', had watched with much attention the appearance anywhere in print of verse bearing the signature of Robert Trewe, who, with a man's unsusceptibility on the question of sex, had never once thought of passing himself off as a woman. To be sure, Mrs Marchmill had satisfied herself with a sort of reason for doing the contrary in her case; since nobody might believe in her inspiration if they found that the sentiments came from a pushing tradesman's wife, from the mother of three children by a matter-of-fact small-arms manufacturer.

Trewe's verse contrasted with that of the rank and file of recent minor poets in being impassioned rather than ingenious, luxuriant rather than finished. Neither *symboliste* nor *décadent*,[6] he was a pessimist in so far as that character applies to a man who looks at the worst contingencies as well as the best in the human condition. Being little attracted by excellences of form and rhythm apart from content, he sometimes, when feeling outran his artistic speed, perpetrated sonnets in the loosely rhymed Elizabethan fashion, which every right-minded reviewer said he ought not to have done.

With sad and hopeless envy Ella Marchmill had often and often scanned the rival poet's work, so much stronger as it always was than her own feeble lines. She had imitated him, and her inability to touch his level would send her into fits of despondency. Months passed away thus, till she observed from the publishers' list that Trewe had collected his fugitive pieces into a volume, which was duly issued, and was much or little praised according to chance, and had a sale quite sufficient to pay for the printing.

This step onward had suggested to John Ivy the idea of collecting her pieces also, or at any rate of making up a book of her rhymes by adding many in manuscript to the few that had seen the light, for she had been able to get no great number into print. A ruinous charge was made for costs of publication; a few reviews noticed her poor little volume; but nobody talked of it, nobody bought it, and it fell dead in a fortnight – if it had ever been alive.

The author's thoughts were diverted to another groove just then by the discovery that she was going to have a third child, and the collapse of her poetical venture had perhaps less effect upon her mind than it might have done if she had been domestically unoccupied. Her husband had paid the publisher's bill with the doctor's, and there it all had ended for the time. But, though less than a poet of her century, Ella was more than a mere multiplier of her kind, and latterly she had begun to feel the old afflatus[7] once more. And now by an odd conjunction she found herself in the rooms of Robert Trewe.

She thoughtfully rose from her chair and searched the apartment with the interest of a fellow-tradesman. Yes, the volume of his own verse was among the rest. Though quite familiar with its contents, she read it here as if it spoke aloud to her, then called up Mrs Hooper, the landlady, for some trivial service, and inquired again about the young man.

'Well, I'm sure you'd be interested in him, ma'am, if you could see him, only he's so shy that I don't suppose you will.' Mrs

Hooper seemed nothing loth to minister to her tenant's curiosity about her predecessor. 'Lived here long? Yes, nearly two years. He keeps on his rooms even when he's not here: the soft air of this place suits his chest, and he likes to be able to come back at any time. He is mostly writing or reading, and doesn't see many people, though, for the matter of that, he is such a good, kind young fellow that folks would only be too glad to be friendly with him if they knew him. You don't meet kind-hearted people every day.'

'Ah, he's kind-hearted . . . and good.'

'Yes; he'll oblige me in anything if I ask him. "Mr Trewe," I say to him sometimes, "you are rather out of spirits." "Well, I am, Mrs Hooper," he'll say, "though I don't know how you should find it out." "Why not take a little change?" I ask. Then in a day or two he'll say that he will take a trip to Paris, or Norway, or somewhere; and I assure you he comes back all the better for it.'

'Ah, indeed! His is a sensitive nature, no doubt.'

'Yes. Still he's odd in some things. Once when he had finished a poem of his composition late at night he walked up and down the room rehearsing it; and the floors being so thin – jerry-built houses, you know, though I say it myself – he kept me awake up above him till I wished him further . . . But we get on very well.'

This was but the beginning of a series of conversations about the rising poet as the days went on. On one of these occasions Mrs Hooper drew Ella's attention to what she had not noticed before: minute scribblings in pencil on the wall-paper behind the curtains at the head of the bed.

'O! let me look,' said Mrs Marchmill, unable to conceal a rush of tender curiosity as she bent her pretty face close to the wall.

'These,' said Mrs Hooper, with the manner of a woman who knew things, 'are the very beginnings and first thoughts of his verses. He has tried to rub most of them out, but you can read them still. My belief is that he wakes up in the night, you know, with some rhyme in his head, and jots it down there on the wall lest he should forget it by the morning. Some of these very lines you see here I have seen afterwards in print in the magazines. Some are newer; indeed, I have not seen that one before. It must have been done only a few days ago.'

'O yes! ...'

Ella Marchmill flushed without knowing why, and suddenly wished her companion would go away, now that the information was imparted. An indescribable consciousness of personal interest rather than literary made her anxious to read the inscription alone; and she accordingly waited till she could do so, with a sense that a great store of emotion would be enjoyed in the act.

Perhaps because the sea was choppy outside the Island, Ella's husband found it much pleasanter to go sailing and steaming about without his wife, who was a bad sailor, than with her. He did not disdain to go thus alone on board the steamboats of the cheap-trippers, where there was dancing by moonlight, and where the couples would come suddenly down with a lurch into each other's arms; for, as he blandly told her, the company was too mixed for him to take her amid such scenes. Thus, while this thriving manufacturer got a great deal of change and sea-air out of his sojourn here, the life, external at least, of Ella was monotonous enough, and mainly consisted in passing a certain number of hours each day in bathing and walking up and down a stretch of shore. But the poetic impulse having again waxed strong, she was possessed by an inner flame which left her hardly conscious of what was proceeding around her.

She had read till she knew by heart Trewe's last little volume of verses, and spent a great deal of time in vainly attempting to rival some of them, till, in her failure, she burst into tears. The personal element in the magnetic attraction exercised by this circumambient, unapproachable master of hers was so much stronger than the intellectual and abstract that she could not understand it. To be sure, she was surrounded noon and night by his customary environment, which literally whispered of him to her at every moment; but he was a man she had never seen, and that all that moved her was the instinct to specialize a waiting emotion on the first fit thing that came to hand did not, of course, suggest itself to Ella.

In the natural way of passion under the too practical conditions which civilization has devised for its fruition, her husband's love for her had not survived, except in the form of fitful friendship, any more than, or even so much as, her own for him; and, being a woman of very living ardours, that required sustenance of some sort, they were beginning to feed on this chancing material, which was, indeed, of a quality far better than chance usually offers.

One day the children had been playing hide-and-seek in a closet, whence, in their excitement, they pulled out some clothing. Mrs Hooper explained that it belonged to Mr Trewe, and hung it up in the closet again. Possessed of her fantasy, Ella went later in the afternoon, when nobody was in that part of the house, opened the closet, unhitched one of the articles, a mackintosh, and put it on, with the waterproof cap belonging to it.

'The mantle of Elijah!'[8] she said. 'Would it might inspire me to rival him, glorious genius that he is!'

Her eyes always grew wet when she thought like that, and she turned to look at herself in the glass. *His* heart had beat inside that coat, and *his* brain had worked under that hat at levels of thought she would never reach. The consciousness of her weakness beside him made her feel quite sick. Before she had got the things off her the door opened, and her husband entered the room.

'What the devil —'

She blushed, and removed them.

'I found them in the closet here,' she said, 'and put them on in a freak. What have I else to do? You are always away!'

'Always away? Well ...'

That evening she had a further talk with the landlady, who might herself have nourished a half-tender regard for the poet, so ready was she to discourse ardently about him.

'You are interested in Mr Trewe, I know, ma'am,' she said; 'and he has just sent to say that he is going to call to-morrow afternoon to look up some books of his that he wants, if I'll be in, and he may select them from your room?'

'O yes!'

'You could very well meet Mr Trewe then, if you'd like to be in the way!'

She promised with secret delight, and went to bed musing of him.

Next morning her husband observed: 'I've been thinking of what you said, Ell: that I have gone about a good deal and left you without much to amuse you. Perhaps it's true. To-day, as there's not much sea, I'll take you with me on board the yacht.'

For the first time in her experience of such an offer Ella was not glad. But she accepted it for the moment. The time for setting out drew near, and she went to get ready. She stood reflecting. The longing to see the poet she was now distinctly in love with overpowered all other considerations.

'I don't want to go,' she said to herself. 'I can't bear to be away! And I won't go.'

She told her husband that she had changed her mind about wishing to sail. He was indifferent, and went his way.

For the rest of the day the house was quiet, the children having gone out upon the sands. The blinds waved in the sunshine to the soft, steady stroke of the sea beyond the wall; and the notes of the Green Silesian band, a troop of foreign gentlemen hired for the season, had drawn almost all the residents and promenaders away from the vicinity of Coburg House. A knock was audible at the door.

Mrs Marchmill did not hear any servant go to answer it, and she became impatient. The books were in the room where she sat; but nobody came up. She rang the bell.

'There is some person waiting at the door,' she said.

'O no, ma'am! He's gone long ago. I answered it,' the servant replied, and Mrs Hooper came in herself.

'So disappointing!' she said. 'Mr Trewe not coming after all!'

'But I heard him knock, I fancy!'

'No; that was somebody inquiring for lodgings who came to the wrong house. I forgot to tell you that Mr Trewe sent a note just before lunch to say I needn't get any tea for him, as he should not require the books, and wouldn't come to select them.'

Ella was miserable, and for a long time could not even re-read his mournful ballad on 'Severed Lives', so aching was her erratic little heart, and so tearful her eyes. When the children came in with wet stockings, and ran up to her to tell her of their adventures, she could not feel that she cared about them half as much as usual.

'Mrs Hooper, have you a photograph of – the gentleman who lived here?' She was getting to be curiously shy in mentioning his name.

'Why, yes. It's in the ornamental frame on the mantelpiece in your own bedroom, ma'am.'

'No; the Royal Duke and Duchess are in that.'

'Yes, so they are; but he's behind them. He belongs rightly to that frame, which I bought on purpose; but as he went away he said: "Cover me up from those strangers that are coming, for God's sake. I don't want them staring at me, and I am sure they won't want me staring at them." So I slipped in the Duke and Duchess temporarily in front of him, as they had no frame, and Royalties are more suitable for letting furnished than a private young man. If you take 'em out you'll see him under. Lord, ma'am, he wouldn't mind if he knew it! He didn't think the next tenant would be such an attractive lady as you, or he wouldn't have thought of hiding himself, perhaps.'

'Is he handsome?' she asked timidly.

'*I* call him so. Some, perhaps, wouldn't.'

'Should I?' she asked, with eagerness.

'I think you would, though some would say he's more strik-ing than handsome; a large-eyed thoughtful fellow, you know, with a very electric flash in his eye when he looks round quickly, such as you'd expect a poet to be who doesn't get his living by it.'

'How old is he?'

'Several years older than yourself, ma'am; about thirty-one or two, I think.'

Ella was, as a matter of fact, a few months over thirty herself; but she did not look nearly so much. Though so immature in nature, she was entering on that tract of life in which emotional women begin to suspect that last love may be stronger than first love; and she would soon, alas, enter on the still more melancholy tract when at least the vainer ones of her sex shrink from receiving a male visitor otherwise than with their backs to the window or the blinds half down. She reflected on Mrs Hooper's remark, and said no more about age.

Just then a telegram was brought up. It came from her husband, who had gone down the Channel as far as Budmouth with his friends in the yacht, and would not be able to get back till next day.

After her light dinner Ella idled about the shore with the children till dusk, thinking of the yet uncovered photograph in her room, with a serene sense of something ecstatic to come. For, with the subtle luxuriousness of fancy in which this young woman was an adept, on learning that her husband was to be absent that night she had refrained from incontinently rushing upstairs and opening the picture-frame, preferring to reserve the inspection till she could be alone, and a more romantic tinge be imparted to the occasion by silence, candles, solemn sea and stars outside, than was afforded by the garish afternoon sunlight.

The children had been sent to bed, and Ella soon followed, though it was not yet ten o'clock. To gratify her passionate curiosity she now made her preparations, first getting rid of superfluous garments and putting on her dressing-gown, then arranging a chair in front of the table and reading several pages of Trewe's tenderest utterances. Next she fetched the portrait-frame to the light, opened the back, took out the likeness, and set it up before her.

It was a striking countenance to look upon. The poet wore a luxuriant black moustache and imperial,[9] and a slouched hat which shaded the forehead. The large dark eyes described by the landlady showed an unlimited capacity for misery; they looked out from beneath well-shaped brows as if they were reading the universe in the microcosm of the confronter's face, and were not altogether overjoyed at what the spectacle portended.

Ella murmured in her lowest, richest, tenderest tone: 'And it's *you* who've so cruelly eclipsed me these many times!'

As she gazed long at the portrait she fell into thought, till her eyes filled with tears, and she touched the cardboard with her lips. Then she laughed with a nervous lightness, and wiped her eyes.

She thought how wicked she was, a woman having a husband and three children, to let her mind stray to a stranger in this unconscionable manner. No, he was not a stranger! She knew his thoughts and feelings as well as she knew her own; they were, in fact, the self-same thoughts and feelings as hers, which her husband distinctly lacked; perhaps luckily for himself, considering that he had to provide for family expenses.

'He's nearer my real self, he's more intimate with the real me than Will is, after all, even though I've never seen him,' she said.

She laid his book and picture on the table at the bedside, and when she was reclining on the pillow she re-read those of Robert Trewe's verses which she had marked from time to time as most touching and true. Putting these aside she set up the photograph on its edge upon the coverlet, and contemplated it as she lay. Then she scanned again by the light of the candle the half-obliterated pencillings on the wallpaper beside her head. There they were – phrases, couplets, *bouts-rimés*,[10] beginnings and middles of lines, ideas in the rough, like Shelley's scraps,[11] and the least of them so intense, so sweet, so palpitating, that it seemed as if his very breath, warm and loving, fanned her cheeks from those walls, walls that had surrounded his head times and times as they surrounded her own now. He must often have put up his hand so – with the pencil in it. Yes, the writing was sideways, as it would be if executed by one who extended his arm thus.

These inscribed shapes of the poet's world,

> Forms more real than living man,
> Nurslings of immortality,[12]

were, no doubt, the thoughts and spirit-strivings which had come to him in the dead of night, when he could let himself go and have no fear of the frost of criticism. No doubt they had often been written up hastily by the light of the moon, the rays of the lamp, in the blue-grey dawn, in full daylight perhaps never. And now her hair was dragging where his arm had lain when he secured the fugitive fancies; she was sleeping on a poet's lips,[13] immersed in the very essence of him, permeated by his spirit as by an ether.[14]

While she was dreaming the minutes away thus, a footstep came upon the stairs, and in a moment she heard her husband's heavy step on the landing immediately without.

'Ell, where are you?'

What possessed her she could not have described, but, with an instinctive objection to let her husband know what she had been doing, she slipped the photograph under the pillow just as he flung open the door with the air of a man who had dined not badly.

'O, I beg pardon,' said William Marchmill. 'Have you a head-ache? I am afraid I have disturbed you.'

'No, I've not got a headache,' said she. 'How is it you've come?'

'Well, we found we could get back in very good time after all, and I didn't want to make another day of it, because of going somewhere else to-morrow.'

'Shall I come down again?'

'O no. I'm as tired as a dog. I've had a good feed, and I shall turn in straight off. I want to get out at six o'clock to-morrow if I can ... I shan't disturb you by my getting up; it will be long before you are awake.' And he came forward into the room.

While her eyes followed his movements, Ella softly pushed the photograph further out of sight.

'Sure you're not ill?' he asked, bending over her.

'No, only wicked!'

'Never mind that.' And he stooped and kissed her. 'I wanted to be with you to-night.'

Next morning Marchmill was called at six o'clock; and in

waking and yawning she heard him muttering to himself: 'What the deuce is this that's been crackling under me so?' Imagining her asleep he searched round him and withdrew something. Through her half-opened eyes she perceived it to be Mr Trewe.

'Well, I'm damned!' her husband exclaimed.

'What, dear?' said she.

'O, you are awake? Ha! ha!'

'What *do* you mean?'

'Some bloke's photograph – a friend of our landlady's, I suppose. I wonder how it came here; whisked off the mantel-piece by accident perhaps when they were making the bed.'

'I was looking at it yesterday, and it must have dropped in then.'

'O, he's a friend of yours? Bless his picturesque heart!'

Ella's loyalty to the object of her admiration could not endure to hear him ridiculed. 'He's a clever man!' she said, with a tremor in her gentle voice which she herself felt to be absurdly uncalled for. 'He is a rising poet – the gentleman who occupied two of these rooms before we came, though I've never seen him.'

'How do you know, if you've never seen him?'

'Mrs Hooper told me when she showed me the photograph.'

'O, well, I must up and be off. I shall be home rather early. Sorry I can't take you to-day, dear. Mind the children don't go getting drowned.'

That day Mrs Marchmill inquired if Mr Trewe were likely to call at any other time.

'Yes,' said Mrs Hooper. 'He's coming this day week to stay with a friend near here till you leave. He'll be sure to call.'

Marchmill did return quite early in the afternoon; and, opening some letters which had arrived in his absence, declared suddenly that he and his family would have to leave a week earlier than they had expected to do – in short, in three days.

'Surely we can stay a week longer?' she pleaded. 'I like it here.'

'I don't. It is getting rather slow.'

'Then you might leave me and the children!'

'How perverse you are, Ell! What's the use? And have to
come to fetch you! No: we'll all return together; and we'll
make out our time in North Wales or Brighton a little later on.
Besides, you've three days longer yet.'

It seemed to be her doom not to meet the man for whose
rival talent she had a despairing admiration, and to whose
person she was now absolutely attached. Yet she determined
to make a last effort; and having gathered from her landlady
that Trewe was living in a lonely spot not far from the fashionable town on the Island opposite, she crossed over in the
packet from the neighbouring pier the following afternoon.

What a useless journey it was! Ella knew but vaguely where
the house stood, and when she fancied she had found it, and
ventured to inquire of a pedestrian if he lived there, the answer
returned by the man was that he did not know. And if he did
live there, how could she call upon him? Some women might
have the assurance to do it, but she had not. How crazy he
would think her. She might have asked him to call upon her,
perhaps; but she had not the courage for that, either. She
lingered mournfully about the picturesque seaside eminence
till it was time to return to the town and enter the steamer for
recrossing, reaching home for dinner without having been
greatly missed.

At the last moment, unexpectedly enough, her husband said
that he should have no objection to letting her and the children
stay on till the end of the week, since she wished to do so, if
she felt herself able to get home without him. She concealed
the pleasure this extension of time gave her; and Marchmill
went off the next morning alone.

But the week passed, and Trewe did not call.

On Saturday morning the remaining members of the
Marchmill family departed from the place which had been
productive of so much fervour in her. The dreary, dreary train;
the sun shining in moted beams upon the hot cushions; the
dusty permanent way;[15] the mean rows of wire – these things
were her accompaniment: while out of the window the deep
blue sea-levels disappeared from her gaze, and with them her

poet's home. Heavy-hearted, she tried to read, and wept instead.

Mr Marchmill was in a thriving way of business, and he and his family lived in a large new house, which stood in rather extensive grounds a few miles outside the midland city wherein he carried on his trade. Ella's life was lonely here, as the sub-urban life is apt to be, particularly at certain seasons; and she had ample time to indulge her taste for lyric and elegiac com-position. She had hardly got back when she encountered a piece by Robert Trewe in the new number of her favourite magazine, which must have been written almost immediately before her visit to Solentsea, for it contained the very couplet she had seen pencilled on the wall-paper by the bed, and Mrs Hooper had declared to be recent. Ella could resist no longer, but seizing a pen impulsively, wrote to him as a brother-poet, using the name of John Ivy, congratulating him in her letter on his triumphant executions in metre and rhythm of thoughts that moved his soul, as compared with her own brow-beaten efforts in the same pathetic trade.

To this address there came a response in a few days, little as she had dared to hope for it – a civil and brief note, in which the young poet stated that, though he was not well acquainted with Mr Ivy's verse, he recalled the name as being one he had seen attached to some very promising pieces; that he was glad to gain Mr Ivy's acquaintance by letter, and should certainly look with much interest for his productions in the future.

There must have been something juvenile or timid in her own epistle, as one ostensibly coming from a man, she declared to herself; for Trewe quite adopted the tone of an elder and superior in this reply. But what did it matter? He had replied; he had written to her with his own hand from that very room she knew so well, for he was now back again in his quarters.

The correspondence thus begun was continued for two months or more, Ella Marchmill sending him from time to time some that she considered to be the best of her pieces, which he very kindly accepted, though he did not say he sedulously read them, nor did he send her any of his own in return. Ella would have been more hurt at this than she was if she had not known that Trewe laboured under the impression that she was one of his own sex.

Yet the situation was unsatisfactory. A flattering little voice told her that, were he only to see her, matters would be otherwise. No doubt she would have helped on this by making a frank confession of womanhood, to begin with, if something had not happened, to her delight, to render it unnecessary. A friend of her husband's, the editor of the most important newspaper in their city and county, who was dining with them one day, observed during their conversation about the poet that his (the editor's) brother the landscape-painter was a friend of Mr Trewe's, and that the two men were at that very moment in Wales together.

Ella was slightly acquainted with the editor's brother. The next morning down she sat and wrote, inviting him to stay at her house for a short time on his way back, and requesting him to bring with him, if practicable, his companion Mr Trewe, whose acquaintance she was anxious to make. The answer arrived after some few days. Her correspondent and his friend Trewe would have much satisfaction in accepting her invitation on their way southward, which would be on such and such a day in the following week.

Ella was blithe and buoyant. Her scheme had succeeded; her beloved though as yet unseen one was coming. 'Behold, he standeth behind our wall; he looked forth at the windows, showing himself through the lattice,' she thought ecstatically. 'And, lo, the winter is past, the rain is over and gone, the flowers appear on the earth, the time of the singing of birds is come, and the voice of the turtle is heard in our land.'[16]

But it was necessary to consider the details of lodging and feeding him. This she did most solicitously, and awaited the pregnant day and hour.

It was about five in the afternoon when she heard a ring at the door and the editor's brother's voice in the hall. Poetess as she was, or as she thought herself, she had not been too sublime that day to dress with infinite trouble in a fashionable robe of rich material, having a faint resemblance to the *chiton* [17] of the Greeks, a style just then in vogue among ladies of an artistic and romantic turn, which had been obtained by Ella of her Bond Street dressmaker when she was last in London. Her visitor entered the drawing-room. She looked towards his rear; nobody else came through the door. Where, in the name of the God of Love, was Robert Trewe?

'O, I'm sorry,' said the painter, after their introductory words had been spoken. 'Trewe is a curious fellow, you know, Mrs Marchmill. He said he'd come; then he said he couldn't. He's rather dusty. We've been doing a few miles with knapsacks, you know; and he wanted to get on home.'

'He – he's not coming?'

'He's not; and he asked me to make his apologies.'

'When did you p-p-part from him?' she asked, her nether lip starting off quivering so much that it was like a *tremolo-stop*[18] opened in her speech. She longed to run away from this dreadful bore and cry her eyes out.

'Just now, in the turnpike road yonder there.'

'What! he has actually gone past my gates?'

'Yes. When we got to them – handsome gates they are, too, the finest bit of modern wrought-iron work I have seen – when we came to them we stopped, talking there a little while, and then he wished me good-bye and went on. The truth is, he's a little bit depressed just now, and doesn't want to see anybody. He's a very good fellow, and a warm friend, but a little uncertain and gloomy sometimes; he thinks too much of things. His poetry is rather too erotic and passionate, you know, for some tastes; and he has just come in for a terrible slating from the — *Review* that was published yesterday; he saw a copy of it at the station by accident. Perhaps you've read it?'

'No.'

'So much the better. O, it is not worth thinking of; just one of those articles written to order, to please the narrow-minded set of subscribers upon whom the circulation depends. But he's upset by it. He says it is the misrepresentation that hurts him so; that, though he can stand a fair attack, he can't stand lies that he's powerless to refute and stop from spreading. That's just Trewe's weak point. He lives so much by himself that these things affect him much more than they would if he were in the bustle of fashionable or commercial life. So he wouldn't come here, making the excuse that it all looked so new and monied – if you'll pardon –'

'But – he must have known – there was sympathy here! Has he never said anything about getting letters from this address?'

'Yes, yes, he has, from John Ivy – perhaps a relative of yours, he thought, visiting here at the time?'

'Did he – like Ivy, did he say?'

'Well, I don't know that he took any great interest in Ivy.'

'Or in his poems?'

'Or in his poems – so far as I know, that is.'

Robert Trewe took no interest in her house, in her poems, or in their writer. As soon as she could get away she went into the nursery and tried to let off her emotion by unnecessarily kissing the children, till she had a sudden sense of disgust at being reminded how plain-looking they were, like their father.

The obtuse and single-minded landscape-painter never once perceived from her conversation that it was only Trewe she wanted, and not himself. He made the best of his visit, seeming to enjoy the society of Ella's husband, who also took a great fancy to him, and showed him everywhere about the neighbourhood, neither of them noticing Ella's mood.

The painter had been gone only a day or two when, while sitting upstairs alone one morning, she glanced over the London paper just arrived, and read the following paragraph:

SUICIDE OF A POET

Mr Robert Trewe, who has been favourably known for some years as one of our rising lyrists, committed suicide at his lodgings at Solentsea on Saturday evening last by shooting himself in the right temple with a revolver. Readers hardly need to be reminded that Mr Trewe has recently attracted the attention of a much wider public than had hitherto known him, by his new volume of verse, mostly of an impassioned kind, entitled 'Lyrics to a Woman Unknown', which has been already favourably noticed in these pages for the extraordinary gamut of feeling it traverses, and which has been made the subject of a severe, if not ferocious, criticism in the — *Review*. It is supposed, though not certainly known, that the article may have partially conduced to the sad act, as a copy of the review in question was found on his writing-table; and he has been observed to be in a somewhat depressed state of mind since the critique appeared.

Then came the report of the inquest, at which the following letter was read, it having been addressed to a friend at a distance:

DEAR —, – Before these lines reach your hands I shall be delivered from the inconveniences of seeing, hearing, and knowing more of the things around me. I will not trouble you by giving my reasons for the step I have taken, though I can assure you they were sound and logical. Perhaps had I been blessed with a mother, or a sister, or a female friend of another sort tenderly devoted to me, I might have thought it worth while to continue my present existence. I have long dreamt of such an unattainable creature, as you know; and she, this undiscoverable, elusive one, inspired my last volume; the imaginary woman alone, for, in spite of what has been said in some quarters, there is no real woman behind the title. She has continued to the last unrevealed, unmet, unwon. I think it desirable to mention this in order that no blame may attach to any real woman as having been the cause of my decease by cruel or cavalier treatment of me. Tell my landlady that I am sorry to have caused her this unpleasantness; but my occupancy of the rooms will soon be forgotten. There are ample funds in my name at the bank to pay all expenses.

R. TREWE

Ella sat for a while as if stunned, then rushed into the adjoining chamber and flung herself upon her face on the bed.

Her grief and distraction shook her to pieces; and she lay in this frenzy of sorrow for more than an hour. Broken words came every now and then from her quivering lips: 'O, if he had only known of me – known of me – me! ... O, if I had only once met him – only once; and put my hand upon his hot forehead – kissed him – let him know how I loved him – that I would have suffered shame and scorn, would have lived and died, for him! Perhaps it would have saved his dear life! ... But no – it was not allowed! God is a jealous God; and that happiness was not for him and me!'

All possibilities were over; the meeting was stultified. Yet it

was almost visible to her in her fantasy even now, though it
could never be substantiated –

> The hour which might have been, yet might not be,
> Which man's and woman's heart conceived and bore,
> Yet whereof life was barren.[19]

She wrote to the landlady at Solentsea in the third person,
in as subdued a style as she could command, enclosing a postal
order for a sovereign, and informing Mrs Hooper that Mrs
Marchmill had seen in the papers the sad account of the poet's
death, and having been, as Mrs Hooper was aware, much interested in Mr Trewe during her stay at Coburg House, she
would be obliged if Mrs Hooper could obtain a small portion of
his hair before his coffin was closed down, and send it her as a
memorial of him, as also the photograph that was in the frame.

By the return-post a letter arrived containing what had been
requested. Ella wept over the portrait and secured it in her
private drawer; the lock of hair she tied with white ribbon and
put in her bosom, whence she drew it and kissed it every now
and then in some unobserved nook.

'What's the matter?' said her husband, looking up from his
newspaper on one of these occasions. 'Crying over something?
A lock of hair? Whose is it?'

'He's dead!' she murmured.

'Who?'

'I don't want to tell you, Will, just now, unless you insist!'
she said, a sob hanging heavy in her voice.

'O, all right.'

'Do you mind my refusing? I will tell you some day.'

'It doesn't matter in the least, of course.'

He walked away whistling a few bars of no tune in particular; and when he had got down to his factory in the city the
subject came into Marchmill's head again.

He, too, was aware that a suicide had taken place recently
at the house they had occupied at Solentsea. Having seen the
volume of poems in his wife's hand of late, and heard fragments of the landlady's conversation about Trewe when they
were her tenants, he all at once said to himself, 'Why of course

it's he! ... How the devil did she get to know him? What sly animals women are!'

Then he placidly dismissed the matter, and went on with his daily affairs. By this time Ella at home had come to a determination. Mrs Hooper, in sending the hair and photograph, had informed her of the day of the funeral; and as the morning and noon wore on an overpowering wish to know where they were laying him took possession of the sympathetic woman. Caring very little now what her husband or any one else might think of her eccentricities, she wrote Marchmill a brief note, stating that she was called away for the afternoon and evening, but would return on the following morning. This she left on his desk, and having given the same information to the servants, went out of the house on foot.

When Mr Marchmill reached home early in the afternoon the servants looked anxious. The nurse took him privately aside, and hinted that her mistress's sadness during the past few days had been such that she feared she had gone out to drown herself. Marchmill reflected. Upon the whole he thought that she had not done that. Without saying whither he was bound he also started off, telling them not to sit up for him. He drove to the railway-station, and took a ticket for Solentsea.

It was dark when he reached the place, though he had come by a fast train, and he knew that if his wife had preceded him thither it could only have been by a slower train, arriving not a great while before his own. The season at Solentsea was now past: the parade was gloomy, and the flys were few and cheap. He asked the way to the Cemetery, and soon reached it. The gate was locked, but the keeper let him in, declaring, however, that there was nobody within the precincts. Although it was not late, the autumnal darkness had now become intense; and he found some difficulty in keeping to the serpentine path which led to the quarter where, as the man had told him, the one or two interments for the day had taken place. He stepped upon the grass, and, stumbling over some pegs, stooped now and then to discern if possible a figure against the sky. He could see none; but lighting on a spot where the soil was trodden, beheld a crouching object beside a newly made grave. She heard him, and sprang up.

'Ell, how silly this is!' he said indignantly. 'Running away from home — I never heard such a thing! Of course I am not jealous of this unfortunate man; but it is too ridiculous that you, a married woman with three children and a fourth coming, should go losing your head like this over a dead lover! . . . Do you know you were locked in? You might not have been able to get out all night.'

She did not answer.

'I hope it didn't go far between you and him, for your own sake.'

'Don't insult me, Will.'

'Mind, I won't have any more of this sort of thing; do you hear?'

'Very well,' she said.

He drew her arm within his own, and conducted her out of the Cemetery. It was impossible to get back that night; and not wishing to be recognized in their present sorry condition he took her to a miserable little coffee-house close to the station, whence they departed early in the morning, travelling almost without speaking, under the sense that it was one of those dreary situations occurring in married life which words could not mend, and reaching their own door at noon.

The months passed, and neither of the twain ever ventured to start a conversation upon this episode. Ella seemed to be only too frequently in a sad and listless mood, which might almost have been called pining. The time was approaching when she would have to undergo the stress of childbirth for a fourth time, and that apparently did not tend to raise her spirits.

'I don't think I shall get over it this time!' she said one day.

'Pooh! what childish foreboding! Why shouldn't it be as well now as ever?'

She shook her head. 'I feel almost sure I am going to die; and I should be glad, if it were not for Nelly, and Frank, and Tiny.'

'And me!'

'You'll soon find somebody to fill my place,' she murmured,

with a sad smile. 'And you'll have a perfect right to; I assure you of that.'

'Ell, you are not thinking still about that – poetical friend of yours?'

She neither admitted nor denied the charge. 'I am not going to get over my illness this time,' she reiterated. 'Something tells me I shan't.'

This view of things was rather a bad beginning, as it usually is; and, in fact, six weeks later, in the month of May, she was lying in her room, pulseless and bloodless, with hardly strength enough left to follow up one feeble breath with another, the infant for whose unnecessary life she was slowly parting with her own being fat and well. Just before her death she spoke to Marchmill softly:

'Will, I want to confess to you the entire circumstances of that – about you know what – that time we visited Solentsea. I can't tell what possessed me – how I could forget you so, my husband! But I had got into a morbid state: I thought you had been unkind; that you had neglected me; that you weren't up to my intellectual level, while he was, and far above it. I wanted a fuller appreciator, perhaps, rather than another lover –'

She could get no further then for very exhaustion; and she went off in sudden collapse a few hours later, without having said anything more to her husband on the subject of her love for the poet. William Marchmill, in truth, like most husbands of several years' standing, was little disturbed by retrospective jealousies, and had not shown the least anxiety to press her for confessions concerning a man dead and gone beyond any power of inconveniencing him more.

But when she had been buried a couple of years it chanced one day that, in turning over some forgotten papers that he wished to destroy before his second wife entered the house, he lighted on a lock of hair in an envelope, with the photograph of the deceased poet, a date being written on the back in his late wife's hand. It was that of the time they spent at Solentsea.

Marchmill looked long and musingly at the hair and portrait, for something struck him. Fetching the little boy who had been the death of his mother, now a noisy toddler, he took him on his knee, held the lock of hair against the child's head, and set up the photograph on the table behind, so that he could closely compare the features each countenance presented. By a known but inexplicable trick of Nature there were undoubtedly strong traces of resemblance to the man Ella had never seen; the dreamy and peculiar expression of the poet's face sat, as the transmitted idea, upon the child's, and the hair was of the same hue.

'I'm damned if I didn't think so!' murmured Marchmill. 'Then she *did* play me false with that fellow at the lodgings! Let me see: the dates – the second week in August ... the third week in May ... Yes ... yes ... Get away, you poor little brat! You are nothing to me!'

I NEVER pass through Chalk-Newton without turning to regard
the neighbouring upland, at a point where a lane crosses the
lone straight highway dividing this from the next parish; a
sight which does not fail to recall the event that once happened there; and, though it may seem superfluous, at this date,
to disinter more memories of village history, the whispers of
that spot may claim to be preserved.

It was on a dark, yet mild and exceptionally dry evening
at Christmas-time (according to the testimony of William
Dewy of Mellstock, Michael Mail, and others), that the choir of
Chalk-Newton – a large parish situate about half-way between
the towns of Ivel and Casterbridge, and now a railway station
– left their homes just before midnight to repeat their annual
harmonies under the windows of the local population. The
band of instrumentalists and singers was one of the largest in
the county; and, unlike the smaller and finer Mellstock string-
band, which eschewed all but the catgut, it included brass and
reed performers at full Sunday services, and reached all across
the west gallery.

On this night there were two or three violins, two 'cellos, a
tenor viol, double bass, hautboy,[1] clarionets, serpent,[2] and
seven singers. It was, however, not the choir's labours, but
what its members chanced to witness, that particularly marked
the occasion.

They had pursued their rounds for many years without meeting with any incident of an unusual kind, but to-night, according to the assertions of several, there prevailed, to begin with,
an exceptionally solemn and thoughtful mood among two or
three of the oldest in the band, as if they were thinking they
might be joined by the phantoms of dead friends who had been
of their number in earlier years, and now were mute in the
churchyard under flattening mounds – friends who had shown

greater zest for melody in their time than was shown in this; or that some past voice of a semi-transparent figure might quaver from some bedroom-window its acknowledgment of their nocturnal greeting, instead of a familiar living neighbour. Whether this were fact or fancy, the younger members of the choir met together with their customary thoughtlessness and buoyancy. When they had gathered by the stone stump of the cross in the middle of the village, near the White Horse Inn, which they made their starting point, some one observed that they were full early, that it was not yet twelve o'clock. The local waits[3] of those days mostly refrained from sounding a note before Christmas morning had astronomically arrived, and not caring to return to their beer, they decided to begin with some outlying cottages in Sidlinch Lane, where the people had no clocks, and would not know whether it were night or morning. In that direction they accordingly went; and as they ascended to higher ground their attention was attracted by a light beyond the houses, quite at the top of the lane.

The road from Chalk-Newton to Broad Sidlinch is about two miles long and in the middle of its course, where it passes over the ridge dividing the two villages, it crosses at right angles, as has been stated, the lonely monotonous old highway known as Long Ash Lane, which runs, straight as a surveyor's line, many miles north and south of this spot, on the foundation of a Roman road, and has often been mentioned in these narratives. Though now quite deserted and grass-grown, at the beginning of the century it was well kept and frequented by traffic. The glimmering light appeared to come from the precise point where the roads intersected.

'I think I know what that mid[4] mean!' one of the group remarked.

They stood a few moments, discussing the probability of the light having origin in an event of which rumours had reached them, and resolved to go up the hill.

Approaching the high land their conjectures were strengthened. Long Ash Lane cut athwart them, right and left; and they saw that at the junction of the four ways, under the hand-post, a grave was dug, into which, as the choir drew nigh, a corpse had just been thrown by the four Sidlinch men employed for the purpose. The cart and horse which had brought the body thither stood silently by.

The singers and musicians from Chalk-Newton halted, and looked on while the gravediggers shovelled in and trod down the earth, till, the hole being filled, the latter threw their spades into the cart, and prepared to depart.

'Who mid ye be a-burying there?' asked Lot Swanhills in a raised voice. 'Not the sergeant?'

The Sidlinch men had been so deeply engrossed in their task that they had not noticed the lanterns of the Chalk-Newton choir till now.

'What — be you the Newton carol-singers?' returned the representatives of Sidlinch.

'Ay, sure. Can it be that it is old Sergeant Holway you've a-buried there?'

' 'Tis so. You've heard about it, then?'

The choir knew no particulars — only that he had shot himself in his apple-closet[5] on the previous Sunday. 'Nobody seem'th to know what 'a did it for, 'a b'lieve? Leastwise, we don't know at Chalk-Newton,' continued Lot.

'O yes. It all came out at the inquest.'

The singers drew close, and the Sidlinch men, pausing to rest after their labours, told the story. 'It was all owing to that son of his, poor old man. It broke his heart.'

'But the son is a soldier, surely; now with his regiment in the East Indies?'

'Ay. And it have been rough with the army over there lately. 'Twas a pity his father persuaded him to go. But Luke shouldn't have twyted[6] the sergeant o't, since 'a did it for the best.'

The circumstances, in brief, were these: The sergeant who had come to this lamentable end, father of the young soldier who had gone with his regiment to the East, had been singularly comfortable in his military experiences, these having ended long before the outbreak of the great war with France.[7] On his discharge, after duly serving his time, he had returned to his native village, and married, and taken kindly to domestic life. But the war in which England next involved herself had cost him many frettings that age and infirmity prevented him from being ever again an active unit of the army. When his only son grew to young manhood, and the question arose of his going out in life, the lad expressed his wish to be a mechanic. But his father advised enthusiastically for the army.

'Trade is coming to nothing in these days,' he said. 'And if the war with the French lasts, as it will, trade will be still worse. The army, Luke – that's the thing for 'ee. 'Twas the making of me, and 'twill be the making of you. I hadn't half such a chance as you'll have in these splendid hotter times.'

Luke demurred, for he was a home-keeping, peace-loving youth. But, putting respectful trust in his father's judgement, he at length gave way, and enlisted in the ––d Foot. In the course of a few weeks he was sent out to India to his regiment, which had distinguished itself in the East under General Wellesley.

But Luke was unlucky. News came home indirectly that he lay sick out there; and then on one recent day when his father was out walking, the old man had received tidings that a letter awaited him at Casterbridge. The sergeant sent a special messenger the whole nine miles, and the letter was paid for and brought home; but though, as he had guessed, it came from Luke, its contents were of an unexpected tenor.

The letter had been written during a time of deep depression. Luke said that his life was a burden and a slavery, and bitterly reproached his father for advising him to embark on a career for which he felt unsuited. He found himself suffering fatigues and illnesses without gaining glory, and engaged in a cause which he did not understand or appreciate. If it had not been for his father's bad advice he, Luke, would now have been working comfortably at a trade in the village that he had never wished to leave.

After reading the letter the sergeant advanced a few steps till he was quite out of sight of everybody, and then sat down on the bank by the wayside.

When he arose half-an-hour later he looked withered and broken, and from that day his natural spirits left him. Wounded to the quick by his son's sarcastic stings, he indulged in liquor more and more frequently. His wife had died some years before this date, and the sergeant lived alone in the house which had been hers. One morning in the December under notice the report of a gun had been heard on his premises, and on entering the neighbours found him in a dying state. He had shot himself with an old firelock that he used for scaring birds; and from what he had said the day before, and the arrangements he had made for his decease, there was no doubt that his end had been deliberately planned, as a consequence of the despondency into which he had been thrown by his son's letter. The coroner's jury returned a verdict of *felo de se*.[8]

'Here's his son's letter,' said one of the Sidlinch men. ' 'Twas found in his father's pocket. You can see by the state o't how many times he read it over. Howsomever, the Lord's will be done, since it must, whether or no.'

The grave was filled up and levelled, no mound being shaped over it. The Sidlinch men then bade the Chalk-Newton choir good-night, and departed with the cart in which they had brought the sergeant's body to the hill. When their tread had died away from the ear, and the wind swept over the isolated grave with its customary siffle of indifference, Lot Swanhills turned and spoke to old Richard Toller, the hautboy player.

' 'Tis hard upon a man, and he a wold sojer,[9] to serve en so, Richard. Not that the sergeant was ever in a battle bigger than would go into a half-acre paddock, that's true. Still, his soul ought to hae as good a chance as another man's, all the same, hey?'

Richard replied that he was quite of the same opinion. 'What d'ye say to lifting up a carrel[10] over his grave, as 'tis Christmas, and no hurry to begin down in parish, and 'twouldn't take up ten minutes, and not a soul up here to say us nay, or know anything about it?'

Lot nodded assent. 'The man ought to hae his chances,' he repeated.

'Ye may as well spet[11] upon his grave, for all the good we shall do en by what we lift up, now he's got so far,' said Notton, the clarionet man and professed sceptic of the choir. 'But I'm agreed if the rest be.'

They thereupon placed themselves in a semicircle by the newly stirred earth, and roused the dull air with the well-known Number Sixteen of their collection, which Lot gave out as being the one he thought best suited to the occasion and the mood:

> He comes' the pri'-soners to' re-lease',
> In Sa'-tan's bon'-dage held'.

'Jown [12] it – we've never played to a dead man afore,' said Ezra Cattstock, when, having concluded the last verse, they stood reflecting for a breath or two. 'But it do seem more merciful than to go away and leave en, as they t'other fellers have done.'

'Now backalong to Newton, and by the time we get over-right [13] the pa'son's 'twill be half after twelve,' said the leader.

They had not, however, done more than gather up their instruments when the wind brought to their notice the noise of a vehicle rapidly driven up the same lane from Sidlinch which the gravediggers had lately retracted. To avoid being run over when moving on, they waited till the benighted traveller, whoever he might be, should pass them where they stood in the wider area of the Cross.

In half a minute the light of the lanterns fell upon a hired fly, [14] drawn by a steaming and jaded horse. It reached the handpost, when a voice from the inside cried, 'Stop here!' The driver pulled rein. The carriage door was opened from within, and there leapt out a private soldier in the uniform of some line [15] regiment. He looked around, and was apparently surprised to see the musicians standing there.

'Have you buried a man here?' he asked.

'No. We bain't Sidlinch folk, thank God; we be Newton choir. Though a man is just buried here, that's true; and we've raised a carrel over the poor mortal's natomy. [16] What – do my eyes see before me young Luke Holway, that went wi' his regiment to the East Indies, or do I see his spirit straight from the battlefield? Be you the son that wrote the letter –'

'Don't – don't ask me. The funeral is over, then?'

336

'There wer no funeral, in a Christen manner of speaking. But's buried, sure enough. You must have met the men going back in the empty cart.'

'Like a dog in a ditch, and all through me!'

He remained silent, looking at the grave, and they could not help pitying him. 'My friends,' he said, 'I understand better now. You have, I suppose, in neighbourly charity, sung peace to his soul? I thank you, from my heart, for your kind pity. Yes; I am Sergeant Holway's miserable son – I'm the son who has brought about his father's death, as truly as if I had done it with my own hand!'

'No, no. Don't ye take on so, young man. He'd been naturally low for a good while, off and on, so we hear.'

'We were out in the East when I wrote to him. Everything had seemed to go wrong with me. Just after my letter had gone we were ordered home. That's how it is you see me here. As soon as we got into barracks at Casterbridge I heard o' this – ... Damn me! I'll dare to follow my father, and make away with myself, too. It is the only thing left to do!'

'Don't ye be rash, Luke Holway, I say again; but try to make amends by your future life. And maybe your father will smile a smile down from heaven upon 'ee for 't.'

He shook his head. 'I don't know about that!' he answered bitterly.

'Try and be worthy of your father at his best. 'Tis not too late.'

'D' ye think not? I fancy it is! ... Well, I'll turn it over. Thank you for your good counsel. I'll live for one thing, at any rate. I'll move father's body to a decent Christian churchyard, if I do it with my own hands. I can't save his life, but I can give him an honourable grave. He shan't lie in this accursed place!'

'Ay, as our pa'son says, 'tis a barbarous custom they keep up at Sidlinch, and ought to be done away wi'. The man a' old soldier, too. You see, our pa'son is not like yours at Sidlinch.'

'He says it is barbarous, does he? So it is!' cried the soldier. 'Now hearken, my friends.' Then he proceeded to inquire if they would increase his indebtedness to them by undertaking the removal, privately, of the body of the suicide to the churchyard, not of Sidlinch, a parish he now hated, but of Chalk-Newton. He would give them all he possessed to do it.

Lot asked Ezra Cattstock what he thought of it.

Cattstock, the 'cello player, who was also the sexton,[17] demurred, and advised the young soldier to sound the rector about it first. 'Mid be he would object, and yet 'a midn't. The pa'son o' Sidlinch is a hard man, I own[18] ye, and 'a said if folk will kill theirselves in hot blood they must take the consequences. But ours don't think like that at all, and might allow it.'

'What's his name?'

'The honourable and reverent Mr Oldham, brother to Lord Wessex. But you needn't be afeard o' en on that account. He'll talk to 'ee like a common man, if so be you haven't had enough drink to gie 'ee bad breath.'

'O, the same as formerly. I'll ask him. Thank you. And that duty done –'

'What then?'

'There's war in Spain. I hear our next move is there. I'll try to show myself to be what my father wished me. I don't suppose I shall – but I'll try in my feeble way. That much I swear – here over his body. So help me God.'

Luke smacked his palm against the white handpost with such force that it shook. 'Yes, there's war in Spain; and another chance for me to be worthy of father.'

So the matter ended that night. That the private acted in one thing as he had vowed to do soon became apparent, for during the Christmas week the rector came into the churchyard when Cattstock was there, and asked him to find a spot that would be suitable for the purpose of such an interment, adding that he had slightly known the late sergeant, and was not aware of any law which forbade him to assent to the removal, the letter of the rule having been observed. But as he did not wish to seem moved by opposition to his neighbour at Sidlinch, he had stipulated that the act of charity should be carried out at night, and as privately as possible, and that the grave should be in an obscure part of the enclosure. 'You had better see the young man about it at once,' added the rector.

But before Ezra had done anything Luke came down to his house. His furlough[19] had been cut short, owing to new developments of the war in the Peninsula, and being obliged to go back to his regiment immediately, he was compelled to leave the exhumation and reinterment to his friends. Everything was paid for, and he implored them all to see it carried out forthwith.

With this the soldier left. The next day Ezra, on thinking the matter over, again went across to the rectory, struck with sudden misgiving. He had remembered that the sergeant had been buried without a coffin, and he was not sure that a stake had not been driven through him. The business would be more troublesome than they had at first supposed.

'Yes, indeed!' murmured the rector. 'I am afraid it is not feasible after all.'

The next event was the arrival of a headstone by carrier from the nearest town; to be left at Mr Ezra Cattstock's; all expenses paid. The sexton and the carrier deposited the stone in the former's outhouse; and Ezra, left alone, put on his spectacles and read the brief and simple inscription:

HERE LYETH THE BODY OF SAMUEL HOLWAY, LATE SERGEANT IN HIS MAJESTY'S —D REGIMENT OF FOOT, WHO DEPARTED THIS LIFE DECEMBER THE 20TH, 180–. ERECTED BY L. H.

'I AM NOT WORTHY TO BE CALLED THY SON.'[20]

Ezra again called at the riverside rectory. 'The stone is come, sir. But I'm afeard we can't do it nohow.'

'I should like to oblige him,' said the gentlemanly old incumbent. 'And I would forego all fees willingly. Still, if you and the others don't think you can carry it out, I am in doubt what to say.'

'Well, sir; I've made inquiry of a Sidlinch woman as to his burial, and what I thought seems true. They buried en wi' a new six-foot hurdle-saul[21] drough's[22] body, from the sheep-pen up in North Ewelease, though they won't own to it now. And the question is, Is the moving worth while, considering the awkwardness?'

'Have you heard anything more of the young man?'

Ezra had only heard that he had embarked that week for Spain with the rest of the regiment. 'And if he's as desperate as 'a seemed, we shall never see him here in England again.'

'It is an awkward case,' said the rector.

Ezra talked it over with the choir; one of whom suggested that the stone might be erected at the crossroads. This was regarded as impracticable. Another said that it might be set up in the churchyard without removing the body; but this was seen to be dishonest. So nothing was done.

The headstone remained in Ezra's outhouse till, growing tired of seeing it there, he put it away among the bushes at the bottom of his garden. The subject was sometimes revived among them, but it always ended with: 'Considering how 'a was buried, we can hardly make a job o't.'

There was always the consciousness that Luke would never come back, an impression strengthened by the disasters which were rumoured to have befallen the army in Spain. This tended to make their inertness permanent. The headstone grew green as it lay on its back under Ezra's bushes; then a tree by the river was blown down, and, falling across the stone, cracked it in three pieces. Ultimately the pieces became buried in the leaves and mould.

Luke had not been born a Chalk-Newton man, and he had no relations left in Sidlinch, so that no tidings of him reached either village throughout the war. But after Waterloo and the fall of Napoleon there arrived at Sidlinch one day an English sergeant-major covered with stripes and, as it turned out, rich in glory. Foreign service had so totally changed Luke Holway that it was not until he told his name that the inhabitants recognized him as the sergeant's only son.

He had served with unswerving effectiveness through the Peninsular campaigns under Wellington; had fought at Busaco, Fuentes d'Onore, Ciudad Rodrigo, Badajoz, Salamanca, Vittoria, Quatre Bras, and Waterloo; and had now returned to enjoy a more than earned pension and repose in his native district.

He hardly stayed in Sidlinch longer than to take a meal on his arrival. The same evening he started on foot over the hill to Chalk-Newton, passing the handpost, and saying as he glanced at the spot, 'Thank God: he's not there!' Nightfall was approaching when he reached the latter village; but he made straight for the churchyard. On his entering it there remained light enough to discern the headstones by, and these he narrowly scanned. But though he searched the front part by the road, and the back part by the river, what he sought he could not find – the grave of Sergeant Holway, and a memorial bearing the inscription: 'I AM NOT WORTHY TO BE CALLED THY SON.'

He left the churchyard and made inquiries. The honourable and reverend old rector was dead, and so were many of the choir; but by degrees the sergeant-major learnt that his father still lay at the cross-roads in Long Ash Lane.

Luke pursued his way moodily homewards, to do which, in the natural course, he would be compelled to repass the spot, there being no other road between the two villages. But he could not now go by that place, vociferous with reproaches in his father's tones; and he got over the hedge and wandered deviously through the ploughed fields to avoid the scene. Through many a fight and fatigue Luke had been sustained by the thought that he was restoring the family honour and making noble amends. Yet his father lay still in degradation. It was rather a sentiment than a fact that his father's body had been made to suffer for his own misdeeds; but to his super-sensitiveness it seemed that his efforts to retrieve his character and to propitiate the shade of the insulted one had ended in failure.

He endeavoured, however, to shake off his lethargy, and, not liking the associations of Sidlinch, hired a small cottage at Chalk-Newton which had long been empty. Here he lived alone, becoming quite a hermit, and allowing no woman to enter the house.

The Christmas after taking up his abode herein he was sitting in the chimney corner by himself, when he heard faint notes in the distance, and soon a melody burst forth immediately outside his own window. It came from the carol-singers, as usual; and though many of the old hands, Ezra and Lot included, had gone to their rest, the same old carols were still played out of the same old books. There resounded through the sergeant-major's window-shutters the familiar lines that the deceased choir had rendered over his father's grave:

> He comes' the pri'-soners to' re-lease',
> In Sa'-tan's bon'-dage held'.

When they had finished they went on to another house, leaving him to silence and loneliness as before.

The candle wanted snuffing, but he did not snuff it, and he sat on till it had burnt down into the socket and made waves of shadow on the ceiling.

The Christmas cheerfulness of next morning was broken at breakfast-time by tragic intelligence which went down the village like wind. Sergeant-Major Holway had been found shot through the head by his own hand at the cross-roads in Long Ash Lane where his father lay buried.

On the table in the cottage he had left a piece of paper, on which he had written his wish that he might be buried at the Cross beside his father. But the paper was accidentally swept to the floor, and overlooked till after his funeral, which took place in the ordinary way in the churchyard.

GENERAL PREFACE TO THE
WESSEX EDITION OF 1912

In accepting a proposal for a definite edition of these productions in prose and verse I have found an opportunity of classifying the novels under heads that show approximately the author's aim, if not his achievement, in each book of the series at the date of its composition. Sometimes the aim was lower than at other times; sometimes, where the intention was primarily high, force of circumstances (among which the chief were the necessities of magazine publication) compelled a modification, great or slight, of the original plan. Of a few, however, of the longer novels, and of many of the shorter tales, it may be assumed that they stand today much as they would have stood if no accidents had obstructed the channel between the writer and the public. That many of them, if any, stand as they would stand if written *now* is not to be supposed.

In the classification of these fictitious chronicles – for which the name of 'The Wessex Novels' was adopted, and is still retained – the first group is called 'Novels of Character and Environment', and contains those which approach most nearly to uninfluenced works; also one or two which, whatever their quality in some few of their episodes, may claim a verisimilitude in general treatment and detail.

The second group is distinguished as 'Romances and Fantasies,' a sufficiently descriptive definition. The third class – 'Novels of Ingenuity' – show a not infrequent disregard of the probable in the chain of events, and depend for their interest mainly on the incidents themselves. They might also be characterized as 'Experiments', and were written for the nonce simply; though despite the artificiality of their fable some of their scenes are not without fidelity to life.

It will not be supposed that these differences are distinctly perceptible in every page of every volume. It was inevitable that blendings and alternations should occur in all. Moreover, as it was not thought desirable in every instance to change the arrangement of the shorter stories to which readers have grown accustomed, certain of these may be found under headings to which an acute judgement might deny appropriateness.

It has sometimes been conceived of novels that evolve their action on a circumscribed scene – as do many (though not all) of these – that they cannot be so inclusive in their exhibition of human nature as novels wherein the scenes cover large extents of country, in which events figure amid towns and cities, even wander over the four quarters of the globe. I am not concerned to argue this point further than to suggest that the conception is an untrue one in respect of the elementary passions. But I would state that the geographical limits of the stage here trodden were not absolutely forced upon the writer by circumstances; he forced them upon himself from judgement. I considered that our magnificent heritage from the Greeks in dramatic literature found sufficient room for a large proportion of its action in an extent of their country not much larger than the half-dozen counties here reunited under the old name of Wessex, that the domestic emotions have throbbed in Wessex nooks with as much intensity as in the palaces of Europe, and that, anyhow, there was quite enough human nature in Wessex for one man's literary purpose. So far was I possessed by this idea that I kept within the frontiers when it would have been easier to overlap them and give more cosmopolitan features to the narrative.

Thus, though the people in most of the novels (and in much of the shorter verse) are dwellers in a province bounded on the north by the Thames, on the south by the English Channel, on the east by a line running from Hayling Island to Windsor Forest, and on the west by the Cornish coast, they were meant to be typically and essentially those of any and every place where

Thought's the slave of life, and life time's fool

– beings in whose hearts and minds that which is apparently local should be really universal.

But whatever the success of this intention, and the value of these novels as delineations of humanity, they have at least a humble supplementary quality of which I may be justified in reminding the reader, though it is one that was quite unintentional and unforeseen. At the dates represented in the various narrations things were like that in Wessex: the inhabitants lived in certain ways, engaged in certain occupations, kept alive certain customs, just as they are shown doing in these pages. And in particularizing such I have often been reminded of Boswell's remarks on the trouble to which he was put and the pilgrimages he was obliged to make to authenticate some detail, though the labour was one which would bring him no praise. Unlike his achievement, however, on which an error would as he says have brought discredit, if these country customs and vocations, obsolete and obsolescent, had been detailed wrongly, nobody would have discovered such errors to the end of Time. Yet I have instituted inquiries to correct tricks of memory, and striven against temptations to exaggerate, in order to preserve for my own satisfaction a fairly true record of a vanishing life.

It is advisable also to state here, in response to inquiries from readers interested in landscape, prehistoric antiquities, and especially old English architecture, that the description of these backgrounds has been done from the real – that is to say, has something real for its basis, however illusively treated. Many features of the first two kinds have been given under their existing names; for instance, the Vale of Blackmoor or Blakemore, Hambledon Hill, Bulbarrow, Nettlecombe Tout, Dogbury Hill, High-Stoy, Bubb-Down Hill, The Devil's Kitchen, Cross-in-Hand, Long-Ash Lane, Benvill Lane, Giant's Hill, Crimmercrock Lane, and Stonehenge. The rivers Froom, or Frome, and Stour, are, of course, well known as such. And the further idea was that large towns and points tending to mark the outline of Wessex – such as Bath, Plymouth, The Start, Portland Bill, Southampton, etc. – should be named clearly. The scheme was not greatly elaborated, but, whatever its value, the names remain still.

In respect of places described under fictitious or ancient names in the novels – for reasons that seemed good at the time of writing them – and kept up in the poems – discerning people have affirmed in print that they clearly recognize the originals: such as Shaftesbury in 'Shaston', Sturminster Newton in 'Stourcastle', Dorchester in 'Casterbridge', Salisbury Plain in 'The Great Plain', Cranborne Chase in 'The Chase', Beaminster in 'Emminster', Bere Regis in 'Kingsbere', Woodbury Hill in 'Greenhill', Wool Bridge in 'Wellbridge', Harfoot or Harput Lane in 'Stagfoot Lane', Hazlebury in 'Nuttlebury', Bridport in 'Port Bredy', Maiden Newton in 'Chalk Newton', a farm near Nettlecombe Tout in 'Flintcomb Ash', Sherborne in 'Sherton Abbas', Milton Abbey in 'Middleton Abbey', Cerne Abbas in 'Abbot's Cernel', Evershot in 'Evershed', Taunton in 'Toneborough', Bournemouth in 'Sandbourne', Winchester in 'Wintoncester', Oxford in 'Christminster', Reading in 'Aldbrickham', Newbury in 'Kennetbridge', Wantage in 'Alfredston', Basingstoke in 'Stoke Barehills', and so on. Subject to the qualifications above given, that no detail is guaranteed – that the portraiture of fictitiously named towns and villages was only suggested by certain real places, and wantonly wanders from inventorial descriptions of them – I do not contradict these keen hunters for the real; I am satisfied with their statements as at least an indication of their interest in the scenes.

Thus much for the novels. Turning now to the verse – to myself the more individual part of my literary fruitage – I would say that, unlike some of the fiction, nothing interfered with the writer's freedom in respect of its form or content. Several of the poems – indeed many – were produced before novel-writing had been thought of as a pursuit; but few saw the light till all the novels had been published. The limited stage to which the majority of the latter confine their exhibitions has not been adhered to here in the same proportion, the dramatic part especially having a very broad theatre of action. It may thus relieve the circumscribed areas treated in the prose, if such relief be needed. To be sure, one might argue that by surveying Europe from a celestial point of vision – as in *The Dynasts* – that continent becomes virtually a province – a Wessex, an Attica, even a mere garden – and hence is made to conform to the principle of the novels, however far it out-measures their region. But that may be as it will.

The few volumes filled by the verse cover a producing period of some eighteen years first and last, while the seventeen or more volumes of novels represent correspondingly about four-and-twenty years. One is reminded by this disproportion in time and result how much more concise and quintessential expression becomes when given in rhythmic form than when shaped in the language of prose.

One word on what has been called the present writer's philosophy of life, as exhibited more particularly in this metrical section of his compositions. Positive views on the Whence and the Wherefore of things have never been advanced by this pen as a consistent philosophy. Nor is it likely, indeed, that imaginative writings extended over more than forty years would exhibit a coherent scientific theory of the universe even if it had been attempted – of that universe concerning which Spencer owns to the 'paralysing thought' that possibly there exists no comprehension of it anywhere. But such objectless consistency never has been attempted, and the sentiments in the following pages have been stated truly to be mere impressions of the moment, and not convictions or arguments.

That these impressions have been condemned as 'pessimistic' – as if that were a very wicked adjective – shows a curious muddle-mindedness. It must be obvious that there is a higher characteristic of philosophy than pessimism, or than meliorism, or even than the optimism of these critics – which is truth. Existence is either ordered in a certain way, or it is not so ordered, and conjectures which harmonize best with experience are removed above all comparison with other conjectures which do not so harmonize. So that to say one view is worse than other views without proving it erroneous implies the possibility of a false view being better or more expedient than a true view; and no pragmatic proppings can make that *idolum specus* stand on its feet, for it postulates a prescience denied to humanity.

And there is another consideration. Differing natures find their tongue in the presence of differing spectacles. Some natures become vocal at tragedy, some are made vocal by comedy, and it seems to me that to whichever of these aspects of life a writer's instinct for expression the more readily responds, to that he should allow it to respond. That before a contrasting side of things he remains undemonstrative need not be assumed to mean that he remains unperceiving.

It was my hope to add to these volumes of verse as many more as would make a fairly comprehensive cycle of the whole. I had wished that those in dramatic, ballad, and narrative form should include most of the cardinal situations which occur in social and public life, and those in lyric form a round of emotional experiences of some completeness. But

The petty done, the undone vast!

The more written the more seems to remain to be written; and the night cometh. I realize that these hopes and plans, except possibly to the extent of a volume or two, must remain unfulfilled.

October 1911   T.H.

BIBLIOGRAPHICAL NOTE

I AM indebted to the following books, which are indispensable to the serious student of Hardy and most useful and interesting for the general reader.

R. L. Purdy, *Thomas Hardy: a bibliographical study*. Revised edition. Oxford University Press, 1978.

F. B. Pinion, *A Hardy Companion*. Macmillan, 1968.

Florence Emily Hardy, *The Life of Thomas Hardy*. One-volume edition. Macmillan, 1962.

Robert Gittings, *Young Thomas Hardy*. Heinemann, 1975.

Robert Gittings, *The Older Hardy*. Heinemann, 1978.

NOTE ON THE TEXT

THE text of the stories in this selection is that of the definitive Wessex Edition, revised and authorized by Thomas Hardy and published by Macmillan & Co. as follows:

1912. *Wessex Tales, A Group of Noble Dames* and *Life's Little Ironies.*
1914. *A Changed Man.*

The individual stories were first published as follows:

The Distracted Preacher (as *The Distracted Young Preacher*), *New Quarterly Magazine*, April 1879.
A Mere Interlude, Bolton Weekly Journal, October 1885.
The Withered Arm, Blackwood's Edinburgh Magazine, January 1888.
A Tragedy of Two Ambitions, University Review, December 1888.
The Melancholy Hussar of the German Legion, Bristol Times and Mirror, January 1890.
Barbara of the House of Grebe, Graphic (a bowdlerized version), December 1890. *Harper's Weekly* (in America; printed as written, and as it appeared in book form), December 1890.
On the Western Circuit, English Illustrated Magazine, December 1891.
The Son's Veto, Illustrated London News, December 1891.
The Fiddler of the Reels, Scribner's Magazine (New York), May 1893.
An Imaginative Woman, Pall Mall Magazine, April 1894.
The Grave by the Handpost, St James's Budget, November 1897.

EXPLANATORY NOTES

In his Preface to the 1912 edition of *Wessex Tales*, Hardy gives the following background information to this story:

'Among the many devices for concealing smuggled goods in caves and pits of the earth, that of planting an apple-tree in a tray or box which was placed over the mouth of the pit is, I believe, unique, and it is detailed in *The Distracted Preacher* precisely as described by an old carrier of "tubs" – a man who was afterwards in my father's employ for over thirty years. I never gathered from his reminiscences what means were adopted for lifting the tree, which, with its roots, earth, and receptacle, must have been of considerable weight. There is no doubt, however, that the thing was done through many years. My informant often spoke, too, of the horribly suffocating sensation produced by the pair of spirit-tubs slung upon the chest and back, after stumbling with the burden of them for several miles inland over a rough country and in darkness. He said that though years of his youth and young manhood were spent in this irregular business, his profits from the same, taken all together, did not average the wages he might have earned in a steady employment, whilst the fatigues and risks were excessive.

'I may add that the action of this story is founded on certain smuggling exploits that occurred between 1825 and 1830, and were brought to a close in the latter year by the trial of the chief actors at the Assizes before Baron Bolland for their desperate armed resistance to the Customhouse officers during the landing of a cargo of spirits. This happened only a little time after the doings recorded in the narrative, in which some incidents that came out at the trial are also embodied.

'In the culminating affray the character called Owlett was badly wounded, and several of the Preventive-men would have lost their lives through being overpowered by the far more numerous body of smugglers, but for the forbearance and manly conduct of the latter. This served them in good stead at their trial, in which the younger Erskine prosecuted, their defence being entrusted to Erle. Baron Bolland's summing up was strongly in their favour; they were merely ordered to enter into their own recognizances for good behaviour and discharged.'

1. (p. 40) *Episcopalians*. Members of the Church of England.
2. (p. 40) *Dissenters*. Non-conformists.

3. (p. 41) *trimmers.* Those who incline to each of two opposed sides, as interest dictates.

4. (p. 41) *gover'ment folks.* Local government officers. Customs men.

5. (p. 45) *singing-gallery stairs.* Stairs leading to an upper balcony in the church which was reserved for the choir and instrumental musicians.

6. (p. 45) *nave.* Hub of a wheel.

7. (p. 46) *'nation.* Darnation.

8. (p. 51) *tutelary saints.* Saints who protect and watch over one.

9. (p. 51) *posset.* Hot milk with wine or spirits, sugar and spices.

10. (p. 58) *Seven Sleepers.* Seven Christian youths of Ephesus, said to have hidden in a cave during the Diocletian Persecution (303 A.D.) and slept there for several hundred years.

11. (p. 58) *skimmers.* Shallow perforated pans for separating milk from cream.

12. (p. 62) *tinder-box.* This early form of torch worked as follows: lighted rags were put in the bottom of the tinder-box and covered with a metal damper. The steel was a piece of metal bent round, held in the left hand and struck with a flint until a spark dropped on to the tinder. This spark was blown up, and the match – a splinter dipped in brimstone, lighted from the glow.

13. (p. 64) *I go ... off.* i.e. to light a fire on the cliff-top to warn the sailing vessel, bringing smuggled liquor from France, away from that section of the coast under observation by customs men.

14. (p. 67) *preventive-men.* Customs men concerned with prevention of smuggling.

15. (p. 68) *stray-line.* Line attached to anything which is let down into the sea.

16. (p. 68) *tribute-money.* See Matthew xxii, 21.

17. (p. 70) *bleachy.* (dial.) Salty, brackish.

18. (p. 72) *earthwork.* A bank or mound of earth used as a rampart or fortification.

19. (p. 73) *chine hoops.* Iron hoops on either side of the projecting rim at the bottom of a liquor cask.

20. (p. 74) *mixen.* (dial.) Dung, or rubbish-heap.

21. (p. 75) *riding-officer.* Mounted revenue officer.

22. (p. 77) *tole.* (dial.) Lure, decoy.

23. (p. 78) *drawn the hatch.* Opened the flood-gate to let in the water which drove the mill-wheel.

24. (p. 79) *chimmers.* (dial.) Rooms.

25. (p. 79) *myrmidons.* Henchmen. Assistants. The original Myrmidons were a tribe of warriors who accompanied Achilles to Troy.

26. (p. 79) *potato-graves.* Shallow pits covered with straw and earth in which potatoes were stored in winter.

27. (p. 79) *faggot-ricks.* Storage stacks of twigs used for kindling.

28. (p. 80) *knee-naps.* Protective leather knee-pads worn by gardeners.

29. (p. 81) *jineral.* (dial.) General.

30. (p. 82) *consecrated bells.* Bells dedicated by a bishop.

31. (p. 83) *as lief*. Rather.

32. (p. 83) *mid*. (dial.) Might.

33. (p. 83) *be dazed*. (dial.) Be damned.

34. (p. 86) *stoor*. (dial.) Commotion.

35. (p. 87) *strakes*. Sections of the iron rim of a cartwheel.

36. (p. 91) *fain*. (dial.) Gladly, willingly.

37. (p. 92) *clitches* (dial.) Crooks.

38. (p. 97) *blood-money*. Money paid to a witness who gives evidence leading to conviction on a capital charge.

A MERE INTERLUDE

1. (p. 100) *Committee of Council*. Committee of the Privy Council, responsible for state education.

2. (p. 100) *Code*. The Revised Code for Elementary Education, introduced in 1862, which established syllabuses.

3. (p. 101) *packet*. Ferry boat plying regularly between two ports.

4. (p. 104) *Phoenicians*. Inhabitants of Phoenicia, a country on the coast of Syria, important pioneers of trade and navigation.

5. (p. 105) *saponaceous matter*. Soap.

6. (p. 111) *flexuous*. Moving in wide waves.

7. (p. 111) *vermiculated*. Broken into narrow wavy lines.

8. (p. 115) *Western Duchy*. West Country areas governed by the Duke of Cornwall.

9. (p. 119) *tay*. Tea.

10. (p. 121) *nostrums*. Patent medicines.

11. (p. 123) *bandbox*. Hat box.

12. (p. 124) *wisht*. (dial.) Sickly.

13. (p. 127) *privileged*. Granted rights of residence in the area by the landlord, the Duke of Cornwall.

14. (p. 131) *Pan pipes*. A row of pipes of graduated length – an early wind instrument.

15. (p. 132) *Troglodytean*. Hidden away (literally, cave-dwelling).

THE WITHERED ARM

1. (p. 134) *'in full pail'*. In full milk.

2. (p. 134) *tisty-tosty*. Round like a ball. A tisty-tosty was a ball made of cowslips or primroses.

3. (p. 134) *barton*. Farmyard.

4. (p. 134) *laved*. Baled or drew water.

5. (p. 135) *what the Turk*. What the devil.

6. (p. 135) *milchers*. Cows kept for milking.

7. (p. 135) *the evening is pinking in.* The sun is beginning to set (a favourite country expression of Hardy's).

8. (p. 136) *gig.* Two-wheeled, one-horse carriage.

9. (p. 139) *The hare you wired.* i.e. caught in a wire snare.

10. (p. 139) *gownd.* (dial.) Gown, dress.

11. (p. 140) *incubus.* Evil spirit, supposed to descend upon people in their sleep.

12. (p. 141) *chimmer.* (dial.) Room, chamber.

13. (p. 142) *meads.* Meadow lands.

14. (p. 144) *fatality.* A predestined liability to disaster (O.E.D.), a fatal influence.

15. (p. 146) *Conjuror.* One believed to possess magical powers of healing, spell-casting, etc. A Conjuror Trendle is mentioned in *Tess of the D'Urbervilles*, Chapter 21.

16. (p. 148) *the Wessex King Ina.* The story of Ina, King of the West Saxons, is told by William Camden in *Britannica* (1586), and is similar to that of Shakespeare's play, *King Lear*.

17. (p. 148) *furze.* Spiny evergreen shrub with yellow flowers, used for fuel when dried.

18. (p. 148) *sharp sand.* (dial.) Clean, gritty sand, used in building.

19. (p. 149) *He brought a tumbler ... assumed.* Oomancy, or divination of the future by eggs, was a widespread superstitious practice, stemming from many primitive cultures.

20. (p. 149) *garniture.* Vegetation.

21. (p. 150) *overlooked.* Bewitched.

22. (p. 153) *white wizard.* (i.e. Conjuror Trendle) One who practised his magic for positive, curative ends.

23. (p. 155) *turnpike-road.* Main road, with a toll for its upkeep, levied on vehicles and cattle, and collected at turnpike barriers.

24. (p. 156) *Enclosure Acts.* During the eighteenth century much land formerly held in common was enclosed by Act of Parliament, making each farmer independent of his neighbour. Between 1750 and 1810, nearly 3,000 Enclosure Acts gradually changed the face of the English countryside.

25. (p. 156) *turbary privileges.* The right to cut turf, for fuel, on common land.

26. (p. 158) *cunning-man.* Diviner (i.e. Conjuror Trendle).

27. (p. 159) *gentle nor simple.* Neither high nor low-born (i.e. for nobody).

28. (p. 160) *all a-scram.* (dial.) Withered, roughened.

29. (p. 160) *glum.* (dial.) Gloom, darkness.

30. (p. 161) *cot.* Cottage.

31. (p. 161) *ashlar.* Square hewn stone (O.E.D.).

32. (p. 162) *fustian.* Thick cotton cloth, usually of a dark colour.

33. (p. 162) *galvanism.* Name of the phenomenon by which an electric current passed through a lifeless body can create an upholding force.

A TRAGEDY OF TWO AMBITIONS

1. (p. 165) *Homeric blows and knocks*. Misfortunes and setbacks of the kind chronicled by the Greek poet Homer, in the epics *The Iliad* and *The Odyssey*.

2. (p. 165) *Argonautic voyaging*. The story of the voyage of Jason and the Argonauts, sailors of the ship Argo, in quest of the golden fleece, was told in *The Argonautica* by the Greek poet Apollonius.

3. (p. 165) *Theban family woe*. Greek legends about the royal house of Thebes are much concerned with family incest, murder and tragic downfall.

4. (p. 165) *Dog-day*. Traditionally, days of great heat, between 3–11 July.

5. (p. 166) *float-boards*. Boards of a mill-wheel, driven by water passing below them.

6. (p. 166) *Donnegan's Lexicon*. *New Greek and English Lexicon*, by James Donnegan (1826).

7. (p. 166) *national schoolmasters*. Masters at schools set up by the National Society for Promoting the Education of the Poor on the Principles of the Established Church. The largest single provider of elementary schools in early Victorian Britain.

8. (p. 166) *licentiates*. Those holding a licence to preach but no regular church appointment.

9. (p. 167) *without a hood*. Not in possession of a university degree.

10. (p. 169) *construing*. Translating.

11. (p. 169) *a title*. Guarantee of financial support, required by a bishop before a candidate could be ordained.

12. (p. 170) *Paley's Evidences*. *Evidences of Christianity* by William Paley (1794). A standard work of Christian apologetics.

13. (p. 171) *Pusey's Library of the Fathers*. E. B. Pusey (1800–1882) in fact edited only Vol. 1 of a *Collected Lives of the Fathers*, but the Preface to this became a classic of English theological writing.

14. (p. 171) *Archbishop Tillotson*. 1630–94. Archbishop of Canterbury, 1691. Famous as a preacher. His selected sermons were reprinted in 1886, two years before this story was probably written.

15. (p. 171) *alma mater*. (Latin) The university we attended.

16. (p. 173) *house-of-correction*. Prison.

17. (p. 174) *'O Lord, be thou my helper!'*. Psalms xxx, 10.

18. (p. 177) *désinvolture*. (Fr.) Unselfconsciousness or flippancy of manner.

19. (p. 177) *Dorcas, or Martha, or Rhoda*. i.e. a plain, industrious, homely girl.

20. (p. 179) *the cloud ... hand*. 1 Kings xviii, 44. Forerunner of a great storm.

21. (p. 186) *kerseymere*. Fine, ribbed woollen cloth.

22. (p. 188) *hatches ... drawn*. Flood-gates opened.

23. (p. 190) Ὑπέμεινε σταυρόν, αἰσχύνης καταφρονήσας. (Gr.) Hebrews xii, 2. 'Jesus ... who for the joy that was set before him endured the cross, despising the shame.'

THE MELANCHOLY HUSSAR OF THE GERMAN LEGION

The action of the story takes place at the very beginning of the nineteenth century, when the war between Britain and Revolutionary France, which started in 1792, was approaching deadlock. Britain's erstwhile allies in the anti-French coalition had all dropped out of the war and Britain faced France alone. Napoleon Bonaparte, ruler of France since 1799, was victorious on all fronts, needed a breathing space, and both countries were weary of war. Hardy's story ends in June 1801 – the preliminaries of peace between Britain and France were signed in the following October.

1. (p. 192) *impedimenta.* Equipment, baggage.

2. (p. 192) *the King's German Legion.* King George III of England was also King of the North German state of Hanover, where he recruited Germans to fight in his armies against France.

3. (p. 192) *epaulettes.* Shoulder ornament on military uniform.

4. (p. 192) *cartridge-box.* Large pouch in which cartridges, containing the powder to discharge firearms, were kept.

5. (p. 192) *chose to take the baths.* Sea-bathing became fashionable in the eighteenth century and certain towns developed as the seaside equivalent of the inland spas, where fashionable people drank the waters for their health. The resort referred to here is Weymouth, a favourite of George III, and featured prominently in Hardy's novel, *The Trumpet Major.*

6. (p. 193) *York Hussars.* A light cavalry regiment.

7. (p. 194) *Gloucester Lodge.* King George III's residence at Weymouth, now the Gloucester Hotel.

8. (p. 194) *unequal marriages.* i.e. between those from different social classes.

9. (p. 194) *bourgeoisie* (Fr.) Middle class.

10. (p. 194) *gentlemanly.* Upper-class.

11. (p. 196) *accoutrements.* Military dress and equipment.

12. (p. 197) *Like Desdemona ... history.* See Shakespeare's play *Othello,* Act 1, Scene 3, in which Othello recounts how he told the story of his adventures, which greatly interested Desdemona.

> My story being done,
> She gave me for my pains a world of sighs.
> She swore, i'faith, 'twas strange, 'twas passing strange;
> 'Twas pitiful, 'twas wondrous pitiful.

13. (p. 197) *Saarbrück.* German town on the border with France.

14. (p. 200) *tattoo*. Drum or bugle signal recalling soldiers to their quarters.

15. (p. 201) *meine Liebliche* (Ger.) My love.

16. (p. 201) *Hanoverian*. A subject of King George's German kingdom of Hanover.

17. (p. 202) *Alsatian*. Inhabitant of Alsace, the borderland between France and Germany.

18. (p. 203) *the Nothe*. To the east of Weymouth, the Nothe (or nose) projects into the sea between Weymouth Bay and Portland Harbour.

19. (p. 203) *turnpike-road*. Main road, with a toll for its upkeep, levied on vehicles and collected at turnpike barriers.

20. (p. 206) *the courage which ... Cleopatra of Egypt*. See Shakespeare's play *Antony and Cleopatra*, Act III, Scene 10, when Cleopatra and her army fled from the sea-battle against Caesar.

21. (p. 206) *It was as dead ... Destroying Angel*. See 1 Kings, xix.

22. (p. 206) *repoussé*. (Fr.) Ornamented in relief, by hammering on the reverse side.

23. (p. 206) *tippet*. Garment like a shawl, covering neck and shoulders.

24. (p. 208) *dead march*. Funeral march.

25. (p. 208) *mourning coach*. Black, horse-drawn coach used at funerals.

26. (p. 209) *carbines*. Firearms carried by horse-soldiers, usually attached to the saddle.

BARBARA OF THE HOUSE OF GREBE

1. (p. 211) *escutcheon*. Shield depicting a family coat-of-arms.

2. (p. 211) *turnpike-track*. Road with a toll for its upkeep, levied on vehicles and cattle, collected at turnpike barriers.

3. (p. 212) *post-chaise*. Small horse-drawn carriage.

4. (p. 212) *congeries*. Haphazard collection.

5. (p. 212) *John of Gaunt*. 1340–99. Duke of Lancaster and fourth son of Edward III.

6. (p. 213) *phlegmatic*. Of dull or cold character, not easily excited.

7. (p. 215) *glass-painters*. Stained-glass window artists, for churches, etc.

8. (p. 216) *Maundeville ... Lancaster*. Names of ancient aristocratic British families.

9. (p. 216) *haunches*. Sides of an arch, between the crown and the pillars.

10. (p. 218) *murrey*. Mulberry-coloured cloth.

11. (p. 218) *drab*. Dull, lightish-brown cloth.

12. (p. 218) *sang froid*. (Fr.) Coolness.

13. (p. 219) *sedan-chair*. Closed seat for one, carried by poles on the shoulders of two bearers.

14. (p. 220) *mésalliance*. (Fr.) Marriage to a social inferior.

15. (p. 221) *candle-snuffers*. Men employed to extinguish the candles used to light theatres in the eighteenth century.

16. (p. 225) *burgess*. Middle-class citizen.

17. (p. 227) *écorché*. (Fr.) Body skinned by burning.

18. (p. 227) *charnel-house*. Vault for the bones of the dead.

19. (p. 227) *Adonis*. A beautiful youth of Greek mythology.

20. (p. 228) *metamorphosed*. Transformed in shape.

21. (p. 230) *Ten-Commandment board*. A hanging board displaying the Ten Commandments was a feature of many churches in the eighteenth century.

22. (p. 230) *lion-and-unicorn*. Plaque depicting the Royal coat-of-arms, formerly hung in Anglican churches.

23. (p. 231) *with-wind*. (dial.) Bindweed, or other climbing plant.

24. (p. 231) *Saracens ... Sepulchre*. i.e took part in the Crusades, the wars of the Christians against Mohammedan conquerors of the Holy Land in the late middle ages.

25. (p. 234) *Phoebus-Apollo*. Greek and Roman god of the sun, figure of great beauty.

26. (p. 234) *beatification*. Heavenly happiness.

27. (p. 235) *knotting*. Knitting.

28. (p. 235) *clash of flint and steel*. See note **12** to *The Distracted Preacher*.

29. (p. 242) *amativeness*. Loving behaviour.

ON THE WESTERN CIRCUIT

1. (p. 244) *Western Circuit*. The journey of judges and other lawyers through various towns and cities of the west of England in succession, for the purpose of holding courts.

2. (p. 244) *sward*. Grassy area.

3. (p. 244) *steam barrel-organs*. Large mechanical organs whose drums, which turned to play tunes, were driven by steam-engines.

4. (p. 244) *eighth ... Inferno*. 'The Inferno' in Dante's fourteenth-century Italian epic poem of that title was an enormous pit, divided into descending stages called chasms. The eighth was a hell of burning, where it snowed flakes of fire.

5. (p. 244) *Homeric heaven*. In *The Iliad*, Homer several times refers to the mirth of the gods.

6. (p. 244) *naphtha lamps*. Lamps lit by naphtha oil, a liquid distilled from coal-tar, wood, etc.

7. (p. 245) *spring*. Rise.

8. (p. 246) *pitch*. Fall.

9. (p. 246) *stoker*. Man who fuelled the steam-engine which drove the roundabout.

10. (p. 246) *rococo-work*. Ornate carving and decoration, in garish

imitation of an eighteenth-century European style, adorning churches, etc.

11. (p. 246) *sparkish*. Sprightly.

12. (p. 246) *journeyman*. Workman hired by the day.

13. (p. 248) *pea-jacket*. Short overcoat of heavy wool.

14. (p. 248) *wideawake*. Soft felt hat with broad brim and low crown (O.E.D.).

15. (p. 248) *stuff-gownsman*. Junior barrister, who wore a gown made of cloth.

16. (p. 251) *black-coated man*. One of the professional classes.

17. (p. 252) *calendar*. List of prisoners for trial at an Assize Court.

18. (p. 252) *Assyrian bas-reliefs*. Sculptures carved so as to stand away from the flat stone background.

19. (p. 254) *unretained*. Not engaged in a case at law.

20. (p. 255) *ensemble*. (Fr.) Effect as a whole.

21. (p. 258) *pis aller*. (Fr.) Last resort.

22. (p. 259) *protégée*. (Fr.) Ward.

THE SON'S VETO

1. (p. 270) *poll*. Nape of the neck.

2. (p. 274) *tie-beams*. Horizontal wooden beams joining two parts of a roof.

3. (p. 275) *glebe*. Portion of land, once assigned to a clergyman as part of his living.

4. (p. 277) *milieu*. (Fr.) Social circle.

5. (p. 277) *howdahs*. Seat for carrying people on an elephant. Here used for crates of produce on swaying horse-waggons.

THE FIDDLER OF THE REELS

1. (p. 286) *geological 'fault'*. A break in the continuity of rock layers.

2. (p. 287) *'boys'-love'/southernwood*. Hardy plant with sweet-smelling leaves.

3. (p. 287) *Paganini*. (1782–1840). Famous Italian violinist whose playing produced such a spellbinding effect on his hearers that he was said to have demonic powers.

4. (p. 287) *lingual character*. As expressive as speech.

5. (p. 288) *quire-band*. Band of musicians who played in church on an assortment of instruments.

6. (p. 288) *tranter*. Self-employed carrier.

7. (p. 288) *Wold Hundredth*. 'Old Hundredth', a famous musical setting of Psalm 100 ('All people that on earth do dwell'), dating from the mid-sixteenth century.

8. (p. 288) *brazen serpent.* Bass wind instrument, about 8 feet long, with three U-shaped turns in its body, made of brass.

9. (p. 289) *galvanic.* Electric.

10. (p. 290) *withywind.* Bindweed.

11. (p. 293) *sprigged-laylock.* Flower-embroidered, lilac-coloured.

12. (p. 295) *totties.* Toes.

13. (p. 299) *saltatory.* Leaping, dancing.

14. (p. 302) *Dantesque.* See note 4 to *On the Western Circuit.*

15. (p. 303) *sperrits.* Spirits.

16. (p. 304) *raft.* (dial.) Upset.

AN IMAGINATIVE WOMAN

1. (p. 305) *lymphatic.* Sluggish.

2. (p. 305) *sanguine.* Ardent, hopeful.

3. (p. 306) *'a votary of the muse'.* Devout poetry-lover. The Nine Muses were inspirers of the arts, especially poetry, in Greek mythology.

4. (p. 306) *sublunary.* Earthly.

5. (p. 309) *embayed.* Dammed-up.

6. (p. 309) *symboliste ... décadent.* (Fr.) Both words were applied to a group of French writers who revolted against Naturalism, towards the end of the nineteenth century, and aimed to suggest rather than depict or transcribe.

7. (p. 310) *afflatus.* Inspiration.

8. (p. 313) *The mantle of Elijah.* See 1 Kings xix. The prophet Elijah cast his mantle upon Elisha to show that he was his chosen successor.

9. (p. 316) *imperial.* Small tuft of hair growing beneath the lower lip (so called because the Emperor Napoleon III of France wore one).

10. (p. 317) *bouts-rimés.* (Fr.) Sets of rhyming words, for the end of lines in poetry.

11. (p. 317) *Shelley's scraps.* At his death, Shelley left a large number of notebooks containing fragments of projected, uncompleted poems.

12. (p. 317) *'Forms ... immortality'.* Shelley, *Prometheus Unbound* I, 747.

13. (p. 318) *'On a poet's lips I slept/Dreaming like a love-adept.'* Shelley, *Prometheus Unbound* I, 737.

14. (p. 318) *ether.* Invisible substance, believed to permeate all space.

15. (p. 320) *permanent way.* Finished road of a railway.

16. (p. 322) *Behold ... our land.* See *Song of Solomon*, ii, 8, 9 and 11, 12.

17. (p. 322) *chiton.* Flowing tunic, usually white.

18. (p. 323) *tremolo-stop.* Device on an organ for producing a tremulous, vibrato effect on a note.

19. (p. 326) *'The hour ... barren'.* See D. G. Rossetti, Sonnet XXVIII, *Stillborn Love.*

THE GRAVE BY THE HANDPOST

1. (p. 331) *hautboy*. Oboe.
2. (p. 331) *serpent*. Large, twisted, bass wind-instrument of leather-covered wood or brass.
3. (p. 332) *waits*. Carol singers and players.
4. (p. 332) *mid*. Might.
5. (p. 333) *apple-closet*. Small room used for storing apples.
6. (p. 333) *twyted*. (dial.) Reproached.
7. (p. 333) *outbreak ... France*. 1792.
8. (p. 335) *felo de se*. (Latin) Suicide.
9. (p. 335) *a wold sojer*. (dial.) An old soldier.
10. (p. 335) *carrel*. Carol.
11. (p. 335) *spet*. (dial.) Spit.
12. (p. 336) *jown*. (dial.) Damn.
13. (p. 336) *overright*. (dial.) Directly opposite.
14. (p. 336) *fly*. Small carriage.
15. (p. 336) *line*. Regular army.
16. (p. 336) *natomy*. Anatomy. Body.
17. (p. 338) *sexton*. Church assistant who rang the bell, dug graves, etc.
18. (p. 338) *own*. Grant, admit.
19. (p. 339) *furlough*. Leave.
20. (p. 339) *'I am ... son'*. See Luke xv, 18, 19.
21. (p. 339) *hurdle-saul*. Stake for fixing a sheep hurdle.
22. (p. 339) *drough's*. (dial.) Through his.

READ MORE IN PENGUIN

In every corner of the world, on every subject under the sun, Penguin represents quality and variety – the very best in publishing today.

For complete information about books available from Penguin – including Puffins, Penguin Classics and Arkana – and how to order them, write to us at the appropriate address below. Please note that for copyright reasons the selection of books varies from country to country.

In the United Kingdom: Please write to *Dept. EP, Penguin Books Ltd, Bath Road, Harmondsworth, West Drayton, Middlesex UB7 ODA*

In the United States: Please write to *Consumer Sales, Penguin Putnam Inc., P.O. Box 12289 Dept. B, Newark, New Jersey 07101-5289.* VISA and MasterCard holders call 1-800-788-6262 to order Penguin titles

In Canada: Please write to *Penguin Books Canada Ltd, 10 Alcorn Avenue, Suite 300, Toronto, Ontario M4V 3B2*

In Australia: Please write to *Penguin Books Australia Ltd, P.O. Box 257, Ringwood, Victoria 3134*

In New Zealand: Please write to *Penguin Books (NZ) Ltd, Private Bag 102902, North Shore Mail Centre, Auckland 10*

In India: Please write to *Penguin Books India Pvt Ltd, 11 Community Centre, Panchsheel Park, New Delhi 110017*

In the Netherlands: Please write to *Penguin Books Netherlands bv, Postbus 3507, NL-1001 AH Amsterdam*

In Germany: Please write to *Penguin Books Deutschland GmbH, Metzlerstrasse 26, 60594 Frankfurt am Main*

In Spain: Please write to *Penguin Books S. A., Bravo Murillo 19, 1° B, 28015 Madrid*

In Italy: Please write to *Penguin Italia s.r.l., Via Benedetto Croce 2, 20094 Corsico, Milano*

In France: Please write to *Penguin France, Le Carré Wilson, 62 rue Benjamin Baillaud, 31500 Toulouse*

In Japan: Please write to *Penguin Books Japan Ltd, Kaneko Building, 2-3-25 Koraku, Bunkyo-Ku, Tokyo 112*

In South Africa: Please write to *Penguin Books South Africa (Pty) Ltd, Private Bag X14, Parkview, 2122 Johannesburg*

READ MORE IN PENGUIN

A CHOICE OF CLASSICS

Matthew Arnold	**Selected Prose**
Jane Austen	**Emma**
	Lady Susan/The Watsons/Sanditon
	Mansfield Park
	Northanger Abbey
	Persuasion
	Pride and Prejudice
	Sense and Sensibility
William Barnes	**Selected Poems**
Mary Braddon	**Lady Audley's Secret**
Anne Brontë	**Agnes Grey**
	The Tenant of Wildfell Hall
Charlotte Brontë	**Jane Eyre**
	Juvenilia: 1829–35
	The Professor
	Shirley
	Villette
Emily Brontë	**Complete Poems**
	Wuthering Heights
Samuel Butler	**Erewhon**
	The Way of All Flesh
Lord Byron	**Don Juan**
	Selected Poems
Lewis Carroll	**Alice's Adventures in Wonderland**
	The Hunting of the Snark
Thomas Carlyle	**Selected Writings**
Arthur Hugh Clough	**Selected Poems**
Wilkie Collins	**Armadale**
	The Law and the Lady
	The Moonstone
	No Name
	The Woman in White
Charles Darwin	**The Origin of Species**
	Voyage of the Beagle
Benjamin Disraeli	**Coningsby**
	Sybil

READ MORE IN PENGUIN

A CHOICE OF CLASSICS

Walter Scott	**The Antiquary**
	Heart of Mid-Lothian
	Ivanhoe
	Kenilworth
	The Tale of Old Mortality
	Rob Roy
	Waverley
Robert Louis Stevenson	**Kidnapped**
	Dr Jekyll and Mr Hyde and Other Stories
	In the South Seas
	The Master of Ballantrae
	Selected Poems
	Weir of Hermiston
William Makepeace Thackeray	**The History of Henry Esmond**
	The History of Pendennis
	The Newcomes
	Vanity Fair
Anthony Trollope	**Barchester Towers**
	Can You Forgive Her?
	Doctor Thorne
	The Eustace Diamonds
	Framley Parsonage
	He Knew He Was Right
	The Last Chronicle of Barset
	Phineas Finn
	The Prime Minister
	The Small House at Allington
	The Warden
	The Way We Live Now
Oscar Wilde	**Complete Short Fiction**
Mary Wollstonecraft	**A Vindication of the Rights of Woman**
	Mary and **Maria** (includes Mary Shelley's **Matilda**)
Dorothy and William Wordsworth	**Home at Grasmere**

READ MORE IN PENGUIN

THOMAS HARDY

'Hardy is one of the relatively few writers who produced, by common consent, both major fiction and major poetry' – Martin Seymour-Smith

Tess of the D'Urbervilles
'An extraordinarily beautiful book ... Perhaps this is another way of saying that *Tess* is a poetic novel' – A. Alvarez

Far From the Madding Crowd
'The novel which announced Hardy's arrival as a great writer' – Ronald Blythe

Jude the Obscure
'The characters ... are built up not merely against the background of the huge and now changing Wessex, but out of it. It is this which makes the novel the completion of an oeuvre' – C. H. Sisson

The Woodlanders
'In no other novel does Hardy seem more confidently in control of what he has to say, more assured of the tone in which to say it' – Ian Gregor

The Return of the Native
'It came to embody more faithfully than any other book the quintessence of all that Wessex already represented in Hardy's mind' – George Woodcock

The Mayor of Casterbridge
In depicting a man who overreaches the limits, Hardy once again demonstrates his uncanny psychological grasp and his deeply rooted knowledge of mid-nineteenth-century Dorset.

and

The Trumpet-Major
A Pair of Blue Eyes
Under the Greenwood Tree
The Hand of Ethelberta
The Well-Beloved
Two on a Tower

**The Distracted Preacher
   and Other Tales**
Selected Poetry
A Laodicean
Desperate Remedies